Where Are You From?

FICTION

Where Are You From?

FICTION

LOLA AKANDE

TUNMIKE PAGES

Published by

TUNMIKE PAGES

20, St. Finbarr's College Road

Akoka, Yaba

Lagos, Nigeria

E-mail: tunmike.pages@gmail.com

© Lola Akande

First published by Kraft Books 2016

This impression 2018

ISBN 978-978-965-748-3

Cover design & Formating by Kayode Odukoya

DEDICATION

for my parents

AKNOWLEDGEMENTS

I am most grateful to the Almighty God for all. I am profoundly indebted to my late father, Alhaji Salaudeen Akande, for directing my path and for his exemplary forthrightness. I am grateful to my mother, Alhaja Sadia Oyelowo Akande, for her prayers and encouragement. Ma'ami, thanks for believing in me even when I say little in order to shield you from my challenges. I am extremely grateful to my eldest brother, Mr. Kola Akande, who funded my education from primary to bachelor's level. B'oda, I thank you for giving me a good start in life. I thank my children for co-writing with mum. Can you guys recall our numerous arguments and fierce debates over this book? I trust your dad is still feeling thoroughly entertained by our 'drama' where he is. May his kind soul continue to rest in peace. I am grateful to Taiwo Obe whose selflessness is inspiring. You read the draft and your contribution made the difference. I thank my editor, Adewale Maja-Pearce for his 'brutality'. I extend my gratitude to Toyin Ibrahim, Bunmi Ishola, Khadijat Ayansola Raji, Remi Anifowose, Segun Adegbiji, Wale Omotajo, Lateef Yusuff, Teju Olakiigbe, Patrick Emoukhare, Thomas Abel, Akinloye Isioye, Bode Ogunmola, and John Ayere. I thank you all for your love, support and encouragement.

I am homeless in my own house

I remain homeless in my own house
strutting outside time no mat is mine
no space avails in my footloose search
for a handle to unravel the hours

I am the last to hear my own wailing
when the moment comes to mourn
the hours I have lost floundering
in search of space in my own house

– **Odia Ofeimun** – *I will ask questions with stones if they take my voice*

AUTHOR'S NOTE

This is a work of fiction. Events in this novel are the result of my own imagination rather than actual incidents. Any resemblance to real persons, living or dead is coincidental

PART ONE

JULY 1985 – AUGUST 1986

CHAPTER 1

Optimism was my friend. I thought exultantly as I undressed slowly and allowed my clothes to fall in a heap on the floor. I lay gently on my bed, stretched, covered myself and closed my eyes, thinking about how it had dominated my psyche from childhood. My thoughts were interrupted by a sharp rap on the door. I sat up and quickly got back into my dress. I had hardly made it to the door when I heard another bold knock. It must be my mother, I thought. She bustled in as soon as I opened the door, looking tall and regal.

"You didn't finish your food?" she asked in a surprised sounding voice, her eyes twinkling warmly.

"I didn't have any appetite, Mother. I felt bloated and giddy with joy," I confessed. Her laugh could be heard across the street. My mother was obviously filled with euphoria, too.

"Everyone is overjoyed, Anjola," she said breathlessly. "There are issues we need to discuss," she added quickly, "but I want to go to the market now. I want to make fresh fish pepper soup for us."

"I trust you, Mother!" I exclaimed dramatically. She burst into another round of laughter and hurried off, her laughter trailing behind her. How could I ever repay my mother, Wuraola Adeniyi, for all she had done for me? She was exceedingly loving, caring and dutiful. She was a paragon of virtue. I smiled at her retreating back and lay on my stomach as I tried to make sense of my thoughts.

My excitement reached its zenith. A new military government had just jackbooted its way into power after ousting the previous one. The country was groaning under incessant military dictatorships but I didn't think it should be a source of worry to me. I had just finished my finals at the University of Ilorin and was happily awaiting the National Youth Service Corps call-up letter for the one-year programme. I was enthusiastic, eager to prove myself. I would possess the world! I resolved silently. I had numerous expectations; I never ceased to tell myself that life had great things in store for me. It would begin with an exciting career which I was convinced lay ahead of me. In my mind's eye, I saw myself becoming an accomplished civil servant, just like my father, Makinde Adeniyi, who had been at the Federal Ministry of Works. Unlike him, however, my appointment would be with the Ministry of Foreign Affairs, where I would quickly rise to the post of ambassador. I would serve in countries like the United States, Germany, Spain, France, Canada, Japan and the Netherlands. In the process, I would become proficient in French, German and Spanish, which would enable me to improve bilateral and multilateral relations between Nigeria and other countries of the world.

My other expectation was marriage to one of the famous television newscasters, Bolaji Badejo. We would have three absolutely adorable children. I had fallen in love with him one night when I was watching the nine o'clock Network News and I had fallen in love with him even before he announced his name. He fitted perfectly my mental picture of an ideal life-partner. He looked adorable, resplendent in his white agbada and wine-coloured cap. But it was more than his handsomeness or dexterity that fascinated me. I was mesmerised by what I saw as his quiet arrogance. He exuded uncommon confidence and self-assuredness which thrilled me no end. Thereafter, I would position myself at a vantage point in the students' common room and watch him in sheer ecstasy. Just seeing his image on the screen made my blood rush. One night in particular, he looked especially handsome and

I gushed: BB mi! The guy standing next to me shot me a pitying look, as if I was manifesting early stages of insanity, but I didn't mind. Why deny it? I loved Bolaji and I would always love him. He was my king, my prince, my only love.

As I watched him night after night, unable to take in what he was reading, I would fantasise about us being joined together in holy wedlock, each taking turns to say "I do" to the officiating priest. I would then picture us making love. Ours would be a marriage made in heaven and we would live happily ever after. It was the only logical thing that could happen to someone like me. I was young, beautiful, vivacious and full of incredible energy. I was also brilliant. All my mates attested to my academic prowess. Young men and even a few women had told me how beautiful I was. Many said they had never seen anyone more captivating. I was tall at 5ft, 9inches; I was also endowed with perfect dentition. I had long, dark hair which I usually wore in a ponytail although I occasionally had it rolled into shiny waves. I was often told that I had what it took to attract and retain a man, any man no matter how handsome or sophisticated and I believed them. In short, I was flushed with satisfaction and now, I was a university graduate, which greatly increased my self-esteem.

The only dark cloud on my horizon was that many of the things they were telling me also puzzled me while some even confused me. I snapped back into the real world and sighed as I turned over on my back and clasped my hands behind my head. My apprehension was borne out of the realisation that when people told you about an impending difficulty, there was always an edge of betrayal to it, masked but imperfectly hidden jubilation in their voices. This was what worried me. Consider, for example, what my project supervisor told me shortly before I left the campus. He had invited me to his office under the pretext that he had something important to say, adding darkly, "Anjola, you are now going into the world." Indeed, everyone was saying this to me and the more they did so the more curious I became about this mysterious world I was supposed to be entering. I couldn't wait to discover the world but my anxiety was always heightened by the different expressions on their faces whenever they said it. Yet, what was confusing was that some said it with a smile, some with a frown and some with a look of sobriety. Others laughed out loud or said it with a subdued, protective tone. Even my mother had just told me we needed to discuss issues. What issues? I forced a smile and my mind drifted to my project supervisor. Teachers had a way of bringing their profession into everything they did. I remembered how some of my schoolmates, whose parents were lecturers, had complained to me about this and how they couldn't tell their parents to their face so as not to be branded as naughty and disrespectful. I used to laugh at them and they would be angry with me for being unsympathetic but now, as I prepared to honour my supervisor's invitation, I prayed he would explain in detail all I needed to know about my new world. I was happy about his invitation since it would offer me the opportunity to get to the root of the mysterious world everyone was telling me about without giving me any details. This was one occasion when talking too much promised to be a virtue and I went to see him, determined to be attentive.

I wore a blue blouse which clung tightly to my body and a black skirt so restricting that when I walked, I had to take short steps. My shoes were slip-ons and my hair was bound up behind my back. My supervisor was a round-headed, cheerful-looking man in his late forties or early fifties. His face was square. He had a heavy, greying moustache which made him look older than he really was. There was concentrated passion in all his actions and statements. I knocked deferentially on his door and waited.

"Yes, come in," he said. I drew a deep breath to steady myself, turned the knob and entered. He motioned for me to take a seat but I remained standing. There was something about his demeanour that I couldn't fathom.

"Do have a seat," he repeated in a voice scarcely above a whisper. I did so. He pursed his lips, folded his arms and stared at me. I averted my eyes but he remained silent as he continued fixing me with an impassive look that nearly unnerved me. What was wrong with him? He leaned back in his chair and tucked one leg under the other. I waited and wondered what all the fuss was about. Was this the prelude to our previous teacher-student relationship of argument and counter-argument that was over now? Well, I was no longer a student. I was a graduate about to go into the world even if I didn't know what it meant.

"It seems to me you are an honest person, Anjola," he said, breaking into my thoughts. I chuckled and nodded, abashed. Feeling relaxed, I placed my elbows on the table and fixed him with a gaze.

"Thanks for your kind words, sir," I said, beaming. It was in tune with all the accolades and words of encouragement that were fast becoming synonymous with my personality. I was in a new and happier world already. It was evident and I could feel it.

"You contributed a great deal to making me what I have become, sir," I said, and meant it, but if I was expecting him to smile in appreciation, I was wrong. He looked as if he was about to protest but said nothing. Rather, he kept a straight face as he stared fixedly at me. I was perplexed. I shifted uncomfortably in my seat, my face twitching nervously.

"No, Anjola, I don't think it's something you need to thank me for or be happy about. That's why I have invited you so we could talk," he continued in a practical tone. I felt sweat start out of my armpits as raw fear began to crop up inside of me. What was he getting at? I shot him a searching, exasperated look. He smiled benignly and went on.

"The world does not like honesty and I find your tendencies comparable to that of a man who catches a snake and decides to keep it as a friend. He feeds it faithfully, nurtures and cherishes it but the snake is no friend to anyone; so, one day, the snake bites the man as he feeds it. I do not have a crystal ball but it shouldn't be too hard for me to figure out that you will be having lots of problems as you go into the world. I feel I should warn you about a few of them," he said without flinching.

I dug my nails into my palms to stop from trembling. I could feel beads of perspiration beginning to trickle down from my forehead to my nose. I looked at the air conditioner. It appeared to be working at full capacity. He followed my eyes, saw that my mood had changed and probably understood the way I was feeling but he remained calm. There was an eerie silence for some moments. Then he leaned back in his chair and placed his fingers together, still showing no reaction. Well, I would have to say something. I opened my mouth but he stopped me with a wave of his hand. He leaned forward and opened one of the files on his table but he didn't read or take anything from it. He continued talking.

"Don't be afraid, Anjola. You see, I no longer see myself solely as your lecturer and project supervisor. I believe I have become more than that to you, especially as you are no longer a student. I see myself more as your friend now and as a friend who is not only much older, but who is also a lot more experienced about life. I consider it my responsibility to guide you because, properly speaking, you are just going into the world and I can assure you that you do not know it yet."

He paused and placed the tips of his fingers together again. I sat upright, my fingers gripping the arms of my chair. I looked at him in confusion. I didn't understand him at all but I was determined to demonstrate courage and fearlessness.

"I appreciate your interest in my life and concern for my well-being, sir. I'm willing to draw as much as I can from your wealth of experience," I managed to blurt out but I must have looked worried. The truth was that I couldn't make much sense from what he had told me but I reasoned it would be discourteous of me to say so. This was the first time the man would be confusing me in this manner. He had always made himself very clear in all our previous discussions. Now, he seemed to me to be going around in circles without actually saying anything. I again shifted uncomfortably in my chair. He must have sensed my discomfort and impatience. He went on.

"The world celebrates hypocrisy and falsehood. It is a

dishonest and pretentious world you are going into, which means you have to be on your guard at all times. It is also a cruel world. No one sympathises with the weak, the vulnerable and the foolish," he concluded.

"What must I do or not do in this mysterious new world I'm going into, sir?" I asked with an air of innocence.

"You must be very careful, my dear friend," he said severely.

I frowned. My heart was beating at twice its normal rate.

"Would you be more specific sir?" I ventured but he ignored me and continued.

"As you go into the world, always show kindness, compassion, respect and humility to people you meet. Be humane and fair to all those you relate and interact with but you must strive never to be foolish, weak or vulnerable because the world will only take advantage of you."

He lowered his head and took some time to recover. I could now hear my heart thumping away. How was I to respond? I didn't even know how to feel. I allowed some moments to pass, during which I tried to summon all my courage

"I will remember your wise counsel at all times, sir," I finally said and paused to regard him. An uncertain look flickered in his eyes. He seemed doubtful, unconvinced and it was clear he wasn't yet done with me. I let out an audible sigh. He resumed.

"I must also warn you to be slow at advising people. Advice is good only when it works and the advisee finds justification to blame the advisor when it fails. I'm very slow and extremely careful at advising my friends. Anjola, people will blame you whenever the advice you give them fails to yield the desired result, irrespective of the nobility of your intention. Don't be in a hurry to advise your friends." There was a brief silence. "Most importantly," he continued, "you must bear in mind at all times that it's a truism that the world is not a bed of roses; it is full of thorns and challenges. Most of the challenges will be unexpected, daunting and with the capacity to destabilise and derail your journey through life."

He stared at me with wide eyes. My heart began to thud

alarmingly. I toyed uncomfortably with the handkerchief in my hand while thinking of what to say.

"You scare me sir," I said sourly.

"Don't be scared. As you go into the world, I have no doubt that you will find value in some of the things I have told you. Let me emphasise that your greatest problem with the world may border on your honesty which, as I have already told you, the world abhors. The world does not like honest people but I am not advising you to embrace dishonesty. The task before you, I urge you, is to be careful at all times with the way you handle the truth. This may prove to be your greatest challenge but I wish you well indeed," he concluded with ominous cheerfulness.

He rose from his chair, placed the palms of his hands on his table and stared down at me. His eyes bore into mine but I couldn't hold his gaze for long. I bit down on my lower lip and shifted my eyes. Numbly, I shook my head and rose in savage dejection. It wasn't until then that I realised tears were streaming down my cheeks and hurried off so that he wouldn't see them. Once outside, I rubbed my cheeks with my palms. My supervisor was the nicest person I had come to know throughout my stay in the university. He was a father, brother and friend all rolled into one.

C HAPTER 2

As soon as I stepped outside Dr Agbebi's office, however, I snapped out of my melancholia and repossessed the world. Streets, houses, traffic and, most important of all, people came back to my consciousness in their familiar shapes. They were communicative and trusting; they didn't seem to me to abhor honesty as Dr Agbebi had postulated. I waved his concern aside and allowed my world to resume its natural importance. I embraced my vivacious, boisterous self and was ready to breathe again. I told myself that there were two reasons why I must not permit pessimism to be my anchor. No one I knew ever had sad tales to share about their experience during the one-year youth corps programme, which was to be my first step into my new world. Females, especially, talked about their NYSC experience with nostalgia. They recounted their escapades as if they wished they could turn back the clock so they could go through it over again. I recalled the reaction of past female students of the University of Ilorin who came to the campus to collect their call-up letters while I was still a student. Those who were posted to the northern states congratulated themselves and celebrated their good fortune with hugs and warm embraces. Initially, I couldn't make sense of their excitement. What was the big deal about their posting? I wondered aloud. Receiving no response, I moved closer to a fellow student to ask why some prospective corps members were flushed with satisfaction while others looked confused.

"The ones who are happy have been posted to the northern part of the country," she said in a conspiratorial tone, adding quickly; "those who are wearing long faces are not so lucky; they will be spending their service year in places other than the north." The corners of her mouth drooped sadly, as if commiserating with the unlucky girls.

"The lucky girls have been posted to the north to do their NYSC?" I asked, my face clouding in confusion. I didn't know what it meant to be posted to the north but I didn't want to show my ignorance. I waited, hoping she would come to my rescue but she didn't. I summoned up my nerve.

"What makes the girls posted to the north luckier than those posted to the other parts of the country?" I asked.

"What's the matter with you? Don't tell me you are so daft and mumucious," she said, clasping her hands together and pressing them to her bosom.

I gazed at her as if she were a noxious worm. What gave her the audacity to insult me so pointedly? Was it a crime to ask to be educated about something one didn't know?

"Are you this rude?" I asked, giving her a deprecating smile. Her face softened and she let out a loud, rattling laugh.

"Now, tell me, why are girls posted to the north celebrating while others posted elsewhere are grieving? I demanded.

"The average man in the north is the best boyfriend any young girl could ever have," she said, as if revealing the most banal of truths; and added: "Look, northerners are not only kind but their men are also mostly rich." She put her mouth to my ear and whispered, "Any girl who goes to the north to serve comes back wealthy." I opened my mouth in sudden comprehension as we clasped our hands in comradeship.

"Tell me more about it, ol' girl. At least, it will get to our turn someday soon. It's good to know about these things so as to pray for our own good fortune," I said.

"If you are fortunate to be posted to the north, ehn, you will come back with a huge bank account, loads of wrappers, boxes of jewellery and lots of other precious gifts. Maybe even a Honda car. Above all, you can choose where you want to work," she said in a slightly out of breath voice.

"Is that so?" I asked in a disbelieving voice; and quickly added: "I can't wait to be posted to the north."

Suddenly, the tenor of the moment changed from playful to serious. I picked up the change immediately. She shuffled nervously from one foot to the other, obviously seized by apprehension about where she herself might be posted. There was an uncomfortable silence. I let out an audible sigh of relief when a tall, thin, anonymous-looking girl who had been jumping in celebration came close to us. We shifted our attention to her immediately even though her target was a white-shirted girl standing nearby, staring into space. She trotted happily to the white-shirted girl's side.

"I can't believe my luck," she told her happily. We watched silently. "I can't just believe it's true," she said again but the girl ignored her. I tried not to smile. Whoever said sadness could take care of itself but that happiness must be shared had a point. The happy girl was undeterred. Realising she wasn't likely to get the white-shirted girl's attention with mere words; she poked her in the stomach, saying, "Look at me, I have strained my ankle from jubilation." That did it for her. The troubled girl's eyes flicked warily toward her friend's ankle and asked reluctantly: "Which state have you been posted to?"

"Kano, can you believe it? I don't know how to celebrate it," she said with bated breath and, as if she suddenly realised it was selfish of her to be celebrating her good luck alone, she asked the other: "What about you? Where have they posted you?"

"Anambra," the girl said, swallowing nervously. For the first time, a worried look crossed over the hitherto happy face.

"Arrgh! Eiya, poor you, sorry o. Those people? They are too stingy. They don't know how to take care of their girlfriends. It is always 'my wife, my wife'. They know they have their wife yet they want to have girlfriends they can't spend money on. Abeg, I no like those people sam-sam," she concluded with a long, contemptuous hiss. There was anger in her eyes as she walked away.

I had watched the entire scenario with amusement and not without a tinge of envy for the lucky ones. I also felt a momentary flash of pity for the unlucky girls and dreamt that I would be among those celebrating when my own time came. And now it was here. I had finished my final exams and was anxiously waiting for my NYSC call-up letter. It was only sensible that I not allow doubt or fear to becloud the mental picture I had conjured up of an enjoyable experience.

The other reason why I was excited was that I wanted to enjoy sex and I had concluded that there could not be a better time than the NYSC period. It wasn't as if I had never had sex or even that what I once told my supervisor about being a virgin was an absolute truth; although, it wasn't a complete lie either. The truth was that I had attempted to have sex way back in my 100-level but the experience hadn't turned out as I had been told it would. I was more-or-less goaded into it at a time when I was psychologically unprepared. I had hardly settled down on campus when a 300-level male student began to show interest in me. He told me a lot of things I had not been told before. He said that as an undergraduate student my status had changed and that I had now become a 'big girl.' I needed to begin to do the things 'big girls' were doing, adding that having sex was foremost among them.

When I squealed to one of my roommates what the boy said about sex, she smiled enigmatically and said he was right. She said it was normal for old boys on campus to chase newly admitted females. It was known as 'Octo-rush' in university parlance. She went on to encourage me to have fun, corroborating the things the boy said. I believed her and went ahead to encourage him. He soon invited me on a date outside the campus and I agreed, as my roommate had advised. I looked forward to the date thinking he would take me to see interesting places in town but it turned out that he had his mind fixed only on one thing.

That was how I had my sexual 'baptism.' In retrospect, I regretted the incaution as it turned out to be no fun at all. It was accompanied with so much pain that I moved about languidly for days, unable to hide the discomfort. Apart from the physical pain, my roommate hadn't prepared me for the psychological trauma that followed. I felt dehumanised and abused. Each time I saw the boy I felt fear and hatred. It pained me to realise how I had allowed myself to be used despite his assurances that there was no need for me to feel that way. He insisted that I had only just become a 'big girl' and that my feeling of revulsion was normal since it was my first time. Subsequent experiences would make me feel good, he assured, but I knew it was over between us. The worst part for me was that my mum came visiting just two days after the incident, urging me to face my studies and avoid the company of students who could be a bad influence. I escorted her to the university gate where we again stood for minutes on end with her repeating everything she had told me over and over again.

"Remember the child of whom you are, Anjola," she said for the billionth time, to which I replied: "Yes Ma," again and again.

"Face your studies," she said finally, putting her hand on my shoulder and turning me around.

"Yes Ma." I mumbled.

"Be decent."

"Yes Ma."

"This is not the time for you to start thinking of having a boyfriend or anything of the sort," she counselled. As her warning sank in, my chest began heaving as if I had just run a gruelling marathon. "There will be plenty of time for that when you graduate," she added tenderly.

"Yes, plenty of time," I agreed, although my lips scarcely moved.

She went on to tell me with admiring smiles how proud of me she and my dad were and how they were determined to ensure that I lacked nothing. The major task before me was to face my studies and be of good behaviour. She reached out her arms and hugged me. That was my undoing. Her arms were so comforting that I didn't know when I blurted out about the pain in my thighs.

"Your thighs are paining you?" she asked, promptly disengaging from me and holding me at arm's length, a worried look on her face.

"Yes, Mum, I have been experiencing the pain for some days now," I said dully.

"What could be responsible for that?" she asked, peering closely at me.

"I don't know," I said, almost bursting into sobs. She narrowed her eyes and looked thoughtful.

"Did you carry something on your lap, something heavy, especially for a relatively long time?" she asked, giving me a shrewd, baffled look.

"Ahh!" I squeaked as details of my sexual escapade came rushing back with an angry sting of remembrance. Good God! What had I done? I snorted in disgust. Disdaining my foolishness, I shrugged off the feeling with an effort and tried to dispel my mother's fears.

"Don't worry, Mum," I said in a careful voice. "It's nothing to worry about. I'm sure it's a normal pain that comes and goes. I remember now that I even felt it on my neck sometime ago and it stopped after a few days. I'm sure this one will soon stop, too. Besides, I can always go to the university clinic if the pain persists," I blabbed before bidding her a final goodbye and fled before she could ask further questions.

However, our discussion served to remind me of my earlier resolve to confront my roommate over my indiscretion since she more or less goaded me into it. I wanted to tell her about my experience in detail; that there was nothing enjoyable or exhilarating about it as she had made me believe. I quickened my steps. Thankfully, she was alone in the room when I got back. I didn't leave out anything, concluding that she had misled me. Again, she permitted herself prolonged laughter. She laughed and laughed until tears stood in her eyes. That was what I disliked most about her. She always laughed at my naivety and inexperience just because she was older than me. Finally, when she had calmed down sufficiently, she told me that it was normal to experience pain the first time. She said that I would find subsequent encounters so pleasurable that I would wish they would never end.

"If you knew what happened the last time my boyfriend and I got together," she said, grinning from ear to ear.

"What happened?"

"As soon as I stepped into my boyfriend's apartment, I reached for him with female fervour, no pretences and, of course, he had no power to resist my advances. Soon, we were both lost to sensation as he wound himself around me until we became a tangle of arms and legs and heartbeats. Anjola, by the time he lay on top me, his masculine angles fitting so perfectly against my feminine curves, I began to sing a sweet, delirious melody. Both of us were singing, actually; we were singing different tunes and our songs could have filled a whole   album. Believe me, Anjola, sex is sweet and delicious."

I allowed a smile to play on my lips but I didn't believe her. "Why do you like to exaggerate?" I asked.

"I'm not exaggerating. Why not trust me enough to have another go at it and come and tell me about it?"

I didn't respond. I just sat there facing her, silently chewing on my lower lip. As far as I was concerned, she wasn't to be taken seriously. In any case, I had decided what to do. I would not believe her or anybody else who tried to cajole me into having sex for as long as I was on campus. Instead, I would follow my mother's counsel. After all, I had known my roommate only a short while and had found most of the things she told me to be false, whereas I had known my mother all my life and there was nothing she had told me that I discovered to be untrue. It certainly made more sense to trust my mother. I sacked my campus boyfriend, refused to sleep with my supervisor and warded off other attempts in and out of the university to get me into bed with a man.

That was history. I was now a university graduate. More importantly, everybody said I was about to go into the world. Surely it must also be the right time to go into sex. It was with all this on my mind that I silently resolved not to believe everything my lecturer had said. I remained in a state of excitement until I received information that my call-up letter was ready. I promptly visited the campus. My palms were sweaty as I opened the letter. Lo and behold, I had been posted to Anambra. I didn't know how to feel. If rumour was to be believed, serving in Anambra would mean that I would not have the good luck of being spoiled silly by rich, generous but obviously much older boyfriends. But I parked these thoughts so as not to allow them dampen my enthusiasm. There was certainly nothing to be upset about, I reassured myself, as I prepared for my journey.

I had a dream on the last night before my departure. In the dream, I was standing on an airport tarmac. I had just disembarked from an aircraft and was one of many other people I saw around me who had also just arrived. I had no idea where we had come from or where we were headed, although it seemed that we were all going in different directions. I stood alone, seemingly rooted to the spot, while others kept moving. My luggage was placed beside me and in my right hand was a bowl of stew filled with orisirisi which I understood was intended to make my stay in my new destination hunger-free and generally pleasurable.

What kept me rooted to the spot was the sheer splendour of my new environment. I had never seen such beauty before. I was stupefied. Everything was whirling; every object was in bright, shining colours, including the tarmac. I saw an exquisite bus parked a few metres from where I stood which I understood was waiting to take me to my final destination. I lifted my face only to behold the road the bus would journey through, with me as special occupant. The road was well tarred, smooth and long with no bumps or holes that were the regular features of Nigerian roads. Beautiful flowers adorned both sides of the road with men in uniform taking positions apparently waiting and ready to wave in welcome as I passed. I had finally arrived in my new world and it was far more beautiful than I could ever have imagined. I stood rooted to the same spot and began to smile, a small smile at first which became a mild giggle. I was about to let out a loud shout of EUREKA when someone tapped me on my shoulder, jolting me out of my reverie.

"Welcome to your new world, Anjola," he said genially. His voice was husky. I swung around. He was broad-shouldered and heavily muscled. There was dignity about him, a quiet aloofness. I smiled.

"How did you know my name?" I asked, unable to hide my surprise.

"Never mind," he said, and added, "Do you like it?"

"Like what?"

"Your new world."

"I love it. It's captivating, absolutely fabulous."

"I'm glad you find it so."

He signalled to the bowl in my hand. I had been so overwhelmed that I had inadvertently loosened my gip on the bowl. All the stew, including the assorted meat, had emptied on the tarmac.

Suddenly I woke up. It had all been a dream, after all, but I felt certain that it would translate into reality for me. My face broke into a confident smile as I looked at the wall clock in my room. It was a quarter past five in the morning; time to get out of bed and hurry into the shower. Anambra was a far distance from Kwara and my journey must begin in earnest.

CHAPTER 3

My eyes twinkled in merriment and my gait was full of energy when I arrived at the central motor park to begin my journey into the world. After changing vehicles a couple of times, I eventually boarded an Enugu-bound bus from Benin City. A thrill of excitement ran through me. We were now making the long stretch of the River Niger Bridge that separated Bendel State from Anambra. Out of its own volition, my mouth suddenly flew open in wondrous appreciation as soon as I found myself on the bridge. Was I still alive? Or was I in heaven already? It was the longest bridge I had ever seen. I closed my eyes in momentary bliss and opened them again to assure myself I was actually alive. What a long and beautiful bridge! What a beautiful country I was fortunate to have been born into! I silently resolved to serve my motherland with all my zeal. Life was truly good, I muttered with a knowing smile. The smile was still playing around the corners of my mouth when, suddenly, I sighted her. I gasped in shock. My heart leapt to my throat, beating wildly.

"What?" I screamed in disbelief.

My fellow passengers shot me confused looks but my gaze was focused past their eyes to the object of my distress.

"Oh, my God! A woman? See, look, woman, ha, eh, ye!" I screamed like someone in a sudden fit of madness, abruptly seizing the man sitting next to me by the elbow and shaking him violently.

"What's it?" he snapped.

Confusion rent the air. While others looked bewildered, the man whose elbow I had grabbed looked angry. I couldn't say anything coherent until he summoned the courage to challenge me again.

"What is it? Why are you making a nuisance of yourself like this?" he remonstrated, his voice rising with each word. He attempted to free himself from my grip but I wouldn't let go.

"See," I began, "look at her, she is a woman, she is old, she is riding a bicycle on the highway. Isn't she afraid of getting crushed by impatient motorists?"

Rather than answer, he burst into derisive laughter. I straightened abruptly, deeply hurt by his reaction. I was mortified, awash with humiliation and embarrassment. I let go of his elbow, my legs shaking with fury. He noticed the sudden change in my demeanour and perhaps he felt sorry for me. He stopped laughing and peered curiously at me. I snorted my disgust, crossed my arms over my chest and looked out of the window. Silence stretched between us, and then he cleared his throat.

"I don't understand you. What do you say is wrong with an old woman riding a bicycle?" he asked tentatively.

"Why should an old woman ride a bicycle?" I retorted.

"What do you mean by that? Are you just seeing a woman on a bicycle?"

"Well, yes, it's the first time."

"You've never seen such before?" he asked, clearly stunned.

"How else do you want me to say it?" I said sternly, my mouth flattening in fury.

"Ah-ha, this is getting interesting. Is it your first time in this part of the country? Are you visiting the east for the very first time?"

"Well, yes, this is the first time an ..." I spread my hands in lieu of finishing my thought. I couldn't bear his ridicule. He rubbed absently at his beard. For reasons I couldn't fathom, he appeared to be ready to set aside his sarcasm. As his mood softened, a feeling of relaxation also came over me, especially as I noticed that other passengers had shifted their attention away from me.

"Oh, I see. What are you doing in the east? Visiting a relation, a boyfriend?" he asked in a voice so soft that I almost missed it.

"I'm here on national service. I am a youth corper. I'm on my way to the orientation camp."

"Great!" he exclaimed dramatically, stretching out his right hand as if I should grab it in a warm handshake. I ignored him. I didn't know what to think because I was still furious with him for making me feel like a fool.

"I understand now, Corper Shon!" he mouthed in mock salutation.

That did it for me. I laughed heartily, pleased to be so addressed.

"Now tell me honestly, are you seeing a woman on a bicycle for the first time in your life? Where are you from?"

"Yes," I admitted. His brows lifted at my candidness. "Old women don't ride bicycles where I come from. Young girls of school age, maybe, but certainly not mature women. I thought bicycles were for men and probably girls in their teens."

He stared at me uncomprehendingly for a moment then nodded several times.

"I see," he said. "In that case, I advise that you prepare yourself for a good number of culture shocks because what you have just seen is not likely to be the only thing that may surprise or even shock you."

"Really?"

"Really," he muttered, echoing my own incredulity. I stared at him in confusion, feeling suddenly overcome with weariness from the psychological trauma of this odyssey. I closed my eyes.

"You haven't told me where you come from. Where is this place that women are forbidden from riding bicycles?"

"I didn't use that word," I said tightly.

"What word?"

"Forbidden." My fury had returned. "What's the mockery in aid of?" I asked tersely.

23

"I'm sorry," he soothed. "Where are you from?" he repeated

"Kwara State. Have you ever been there?"

"No; but I know someone who did his youth service there."

"I am glad to hear that," I said, swallowing my misgivings.

"You schooled in Kwara?"

"Yes."

"All your education, from primary to university?"

"Yes."

"You never travelled outside Kwara until now?"

"No." My tongue felt sluggish. What was I doing? I gave a self-deprecating smile but my openness seemed to have touched a chord in him.

"Women don't ride bicycle in Kwara?" he asked in the gathering silence. With an effort, I shook myself out of my uneasiness and smiled brightly at him.

"I never saw old women riding bicycles on the highway. I don't think it's safe."

He sighed hugely and shook his head.

"What do you think?" I asked.

"Don't worry about what I think. What's your name?"

"My name is Anjola. And yours?"

"I'm Ifeanyi but you can call me Ify."

"Ify, I like the name," I said truthfully.

"Thanks, you'll get to know many more Igbo names that you may like even better. You are beautiful, you know?"

I clapped my hand to my mouth to suppress a giggle.

"Oh, thanks, you are good looking too," I said demurely.

For the first time, I took a close look at him. He was dark skinned and had an athletic body. He had a compassionate face with expressive eyes. There was strength about him. Yet there was also a certain shyness that was appealing. He was dressed in a pair of blue jeans with a stereotypical flannel shirt. The two top buttons were undone, revealing crisp chest hairs that vaguely pulled at my senses.

"But tell me more about yourself, Anjola."

24

"I have told you all there is to tell. I was born in Kwara, I grew up in Kwara, had my elementary and secondary school education in my home town, Ifelodun, and I attended the University of Ilorin. I've been posted to Anambra to serve my motherland."

Ify and I bonded immediately, like two people who had known each other for a long time. He accompanied me to the orientation camp and stayed with me until I was fully documented. I was happy since every indication so far suggested that my new world would be a joyous and fulfilling one. Although not in the way my dream had foretold I had nevertheless arrived happily, Ify by my side carrying my luggage and asking me if I wanted this or that. What could be more interesting to a young lady? Occasionally, he took my hand to lead me through a particular direction or guide me through a difficult path. It was all so interesting to be enjoying male attention. Besides, there was a caring edge to Ify. He was thoughtful and kind. He radiated physicality. He liked touching, not necessarily sexually but as a way to connect and say, 'I like being with you.' It pleased me to distraction. His manner of touching was full of unspoken loyalty. I felt like a new bride. We just stopped briefly now because he wanted to buy me something. It was a big bunch of bananas with groundnuts. He said it was good for me. I believed him and appreciated his kindness. I liked bananas. What I didn't understand, however, was why I had to eat them with groundnuts.

"The combination tastes great!" he said.

"I won't combine bananas with groundnuts." I said, shaking my head fervently.

"I think you should try it," he urged.

"They are strange bedfellows where I come from," I said.

He started to laugh again but, apparently realising that I might misunderstand his laughter to mean that he was making jest of me, stopped and urged me once more to try it

"I don't want .."

"Shhh. No protest."

"Ify!"

He held up his hands, warding off any further protests. Finally I agreed, not because I trusted his judgment but because I couldn't think of a way out. Shuddering slightly, I cocked my head and wrinkled my nose, like a toddler whose mother was about to give them bitter medication. I took a banana from the bunch, peeled it, took a bite and, before chewing it, added some groundnuts, then chewed them together, slowly at first, expecting that I would throw out the stuff in no time. But, no, the combination tasted good. I lifted my palms in surrender, adding more groundnuts and enjoying the taste even better. It was as if I had never eaten bananas before. He gave me another, adding a generous amount of groundnuts and muttering: "There you go," a smile in his voice. I grabbed it and kept taking more and more from the bunch and adding groundnuts until he cautioned me to keep the rest till after dinner.

"You see? Bananas and groundnuts are great friends!" he declared with pride, folding his arms across his chest and arching one brow, daring me to deny it. I chortled in delight.

"I wish to see you again, soon. Would you like to see me?" he asked softly.

His words disconcerted me. I glanced away momentarily.

"Your wish is my command," I answered with ill-disguised delight.

"I like you," he murmured.

"Thanks," I mumbled.

"I must be on my way now but I would like to come around tomorrow, if you don't mind," he said, peering intently at me. I smiled my consent. Then he made me promise I would learn to ride a bicycle before the end of my national service.

"Not on the highway," I said emphatically. He smiled his agreement. I assured him I was willing to learn after he promised to personally coach me.

He gazed at me from beneath his lids and I couldn't help feeling a treacherous stirring of emotion within me despite myself. I closed my eyes momentarily and sighed, my lips twisting.

"I'll see you tomorrow, Anjola," he murmured as he put a tender hand on my shoulder. For what seemed the longest time, although it was mere seconds, I stood in frozen delight.

My new world was sweeter than I could have hoped for, I thought, as I walked to my room. Presently, I was lying on my mattress and staring at the ceiling, my forehead tingling with the memory of Ify's tender touch. I was told that I would be sharing the room with three other girls, just as I had in the university. I was happily tired but as I lay there with Ify's male splendour etched indelibly on my mind, sleep eluded me. I couldn't help but juxtapose my experience with Ify with what transpired with Dr Agbebi back in Ilorin.

CHAPTER 4

The mutual respect that later characterised my relationship with Dr. Agbebi was not achieved without misunderstanding and a certain resentment. Before he became my project supervisor, he was just one of the many lecturers in my department. I knew little about him apart from the fact that he was married, had three children and was one of the most brilliant lecturers. Dr Christopher Agbebi gained the respect of many students, including me, because he delivered his lectures with the calmness and confidence of a true intellectual. He didn't go about with unnecessary airs. He seemed to be interested mainly in his job and never missed his lectures, never came late to class and was not lazy about marking students' assignment scripts - unlike many of his colleagues. He went about his job with incredible passion and seriousness. That was why I was surprised about what he told me in his office one hot afternoon during the first semester of my second year.

"I want us to have a romantic relationship," he announced grandly.

I shuddered and stared at him in stunned bewilderment, feeling the shock of his words and not knowing how to react. Why would Dr Agbebi want to sleep with me? Had I inadvertently given him the impression that I was loose? Everybody thought him to be responsible and ethical. We all believed he had integrity and honour. Even his outward appearance lent credence to this. He didn't have a randy look. Rather, he looked calm, decent, responsible and almost serene. Above all, he was married and his wife also worked in the university. I was angry but also disappointed. What was it with men and sex? I became angrier when he pushed back his chair, rose to his feet and came over to where I sat. He stood so close I could smell his peppery sweat. We exchanged glances, then, he smiled. Good God! This man was idiotically audacious. I stared at him wordlessly.

"I have always had a soft spot for you and I would like us to be close," he said with solemn seriousness.

I took a deep breath to calm my nerves. I felt outraged, frantic and unbearably humiliated but said nothing, just gazed at him with as much disgust as I could muster. He seemed embarrassed and I hoped he was. He said nothing more and returned to his seat, leaned back and continued to look at me. My anger was beginning to return but I made no comment.

"I don't want you to think there is something strange about my interest in you," he resumed, trying to sound responsible. "These things are normal and I don't want to go on pretending that I don't feel the way I do about you. I mean, I like you and want you to believe me because I really do."

A smile appeared on his face as he spoke but I was far from amused. My brain was spinning rapidly, making plans about how to deal with the situation. Silence stretched between us. Eventually, I responded.

"I'm sorry sir. It's obviously not right, sir," I said through quivering lips.

Tears started in my eyes. Was I afraid of him? Or was it rage and perplexity I felt? I didn't know but I didn't like what was going on. I desperately wished I could stop him from telling me the silly things he was saying. If he thought they were going to impress me, he was wrong; they would only upset me. Who would tell this man to stop being foolish? I stared at him blandly, silently willing him with all the power in my soul and spirit to stop making me miserable.

"Why did you say so?" he asked. I heard his voice from a distance. "What's not right about you being friends with me?" I noticed my hands were slimy with sweat.

"It's not right, sir," I insisted. "I don't know how to say this, sir, I ... I ... I'm ... I mean, you are my lecturer, sir and it's ... it's ... it's rather unethical, sir."

"What has ethics got to do with the way I feel about you, Anjola? I'm your lecturer, true. You are my student; nobody is disputing that either. I'm a lecturer, you are a student and I'm asking for your love. I could be a medical doctor, a lawyer, an architect or anything and still be interested in you. We have met in a university but we could also have met on the street, in a taxi, an aircraft or anywhere else. By the way, you know I'm married, don't you?"

He wanted to drag his wife into his foolishness?

I made a face. "I know you are married, sir. I even know your wife," I said accusingly.

"Good. Do you also know that I met my wife on this campus while she was an undergraduate?" He paused, obviously eager to get my reaction. What was my business with where or how he met his wife? The man obviously had no shame.

"Well, I didn't know that, sir," I admitted, shaking my head.

"That is what I'm trying to let you know now," he said triumphantly. "You need to understand that my being your lecturer or the fact that you are my student has nothing to do with the way I feel about you. Lecturers are human beings. They are capable of experiencing the same kinds of emotions as anybody else. Lecturers can like, they can dislike, they can envy, they can even hate. I like you a lot and I have decided it's no use pretending."

He looked at me inquiringly. I met his gaze, desperately trying to get my beating heart to slow down. I didn't want to feel like this. I didn't want Dr Agbebi to know how much he was devastating me. I sat straighter in my chair.

"I'm sorry, sir, but I still can't have a romantic relationship with you," I said with finality

"Give me a good reason why you think you can't."

Frustration gnawed at me. I muttered a sound of disgust. "Ehn, ehn, I'm sorry, sir, you are much older than me, sir. Look at me. I'm only nineteen and I ... I ... I have... I have not had sex before, sir."

"You mean you are a virgin? Oh my goodness! That is fantastic! Absolutely incredible! You are meant for me! Do you understand? You see why I'm crazy about you?" he babbled excitedly.

My lips parted in disbelief. I had to fight down the bile rising at the back of my throat. If he noticed my discomfort, he gave no hint of it. He seemed possessed of some strange energy. He couldn't stop talking.

"I have always known there must be more to the way I feel about you but I just couldn't put my finger to it. My angel, that's the more reason why you need an experienced man like me to gently guide you into becoming a real woman. It also means that I have not made a mistake about you. I like you even more now that I know you are pure. Something always tells me you are a good girl."

He started pacing about the office happily. I snorted my disgust, my legs shaking from outrage, but he took no notice.

"I don't need an experienced man. I need a green horn like myself, you lecherous old man," I exploded.

"Pardon?" His brows lifted in inquiry.

"No, I wasn't talking to you, sir. I'm sorry, sir. I don't know how else to explain it to you but I don't want to have sex with you, sir," I said flatly.

"There is no need for you to look and sound the way you do. There is absolutely no need to make it appear dirty or shameful. What I'm offering you is not just sex. It's an all-encompassing relationship. It will involve sex, no pretences, but it's also a relationship that will give you true love, genuine affection, support and protection. It is one relationship you need and one which you will not regret. You will cherish it forever and reminisce over it throughout your entire life, I assure you."

How the man disgusted me! But he was obviously having fun. He rose from his seat again and was now standing right in front of me, arms folded across his chest, ankles negligently crossed in front of him as he leaned against the edge of his table. I knew it was a pose meant to relax me, but how could I relax in the presence of a lecturer I had hitherto held in awe but who chose to shamefully proposition me?

I was now at my wits' end. I didn't know what more to tell him. What I knew, however, was that I wouldn't go to bed with him, not ever. I just stared at him now without saying another word because he had rejected my explanation. I was waiting for him to get tired of making a fool of himself so that he would tell me to go. I was determined not to say anything further because it seemed to me nothing I said would be agreeable to him.

"Do you need time to think about it as women always do?" he asked without making any effort to hide a smirk. He must have imagined he had convinced me already, I thought resentfully. How wrong he was! How foolish he truly was despite his high intellect. There must be absolute truth in the conventional wisdom that women were fools but men were even more foolish.

"I'm sorry, sir, my answer is still no," I said drily.

"Why?" he asked again as if he had not asked me before.

"I have told you. I gave you my reasons but you kept rejecting them. I don't know what else to tell you," I said defiantly.

He returned to his seat. His mood has changed. He looked strange and pale now.

"If I rejected your reasons, it could only be because they had no merit whatsoever. Consider my age, which was one of the reasons on which you based your objection to my proposal. Age has nothing to do with love."

My jaw nearly dropped but before my shock could register I gritted my teeth and let my face show only mild surprise. Why would a married lecturer profess love to his teenage student? It was unconscionable. I decided to tackle him.

"Love, I think you just mentioned that for the first time. Do you love me, sir?" I asked with a sardonic smile.

"Well, I ... I ..." He stopped. His lips tightened briefly then he shrugged and continued, ignoring my sarcasm. "What I mean is that I like you enough to want to sleep with you. What it means is also that there is something unique for us to share. What I feel for you is something I don't feel for the other girls in your class, for example. There is something intense, something noble, special, something to be proud of and to appreciate. What is love, after all? Love is likeness that is deep, intense and maybe unexplainable; and I think what I feel for you comes very close to all of that."

His sigh was long-suffering. I squirmed in my seat and felt heat invade me. Silence stretched between us. The thought of whoredom or explosions of lust had never crossed my mind and that seemed to me to be what he was throwing at me. He would have to try this on another student, certainly not me. I braced myself.

"I appreciate it all, sir, but I'm not interested in you," I said with a note of finality.

"Then you have to convince me to stop liking you. Tell me why I should stop feeling the way I currently feel about you," he said, giving me an angry look.

"Well, if you insist, sir, you don't attract me, I mean, I don't feel anything for you and I am sure you will not be able to excite me in bed, sir," I said sternly, rising to my feet.

"I thought you said you are a virgin. How then do you know men who can or cannot excite you sexually? Don't contradict yourself, Anjola."

He looked at me as if he were dealing with a moron. I wanted to interrupt him but he raised his hand.

"I am willing to believe your claim to virginity and I like you the more for it. I think what you need is time. Go and think it over properly and give me your answer at your convenience, which I am sure will not be later than one week from today. You may leave now."

He waved a hand in dismissal, swivelled his chair round and stared out of the window. Humiliation prickled my nerve ends and the lining of my stomach. Words failed me. With an effort, I rose to my feet and walked out of his office, feeling slightly sick and definitely depressed.

That incident took place in my second year. One week, two weeks, three weeks, four weeks after our discussion, I didn't go to his office to tell him my decision. As far as I was concerned, I had already told him my mind and it was entirely his business to accept or reject it. I wouldn't let him hector me. I attended his lectures as usual. I participated in class discussions alongside the others but avoided him like the plague outside the lecture room. I also ensured that I didn't mention what transpired between us to anyone. On his part, he treated me like any normal student, as if he had not held any private discussion with me. I waited for him to send for me for my final response but he didn't. He had told me he would expect me to come to him within one week to give him my final answer with a threatening voice, as if he was giving me a class assignment. His final words were proprietary and they carried the unmistaken tone of an instruction but I knew he had no sexual authority over me and I was determined to ignore him.

That was the situation between us until the first semester ended and we wrote the examination accordingly. He appeared to have graded my script without bias as my score seemed to have been commensurate with my effort. The second semester began; still there was no allusion to our discussion. I was surprised but pleased. Perhaps, he had decided to let the matter drop, I thought with relief, but I was jolted midway into the second semester when the department wrote letters to all students in my level informing us that the department had assigned project supervisors to each student and that it was in our interest to proceed immediately to holding preliminary discussions with our assigned supervisors with a view to getting our long essay underway. Expectedly, we collected our letters with excitement for it meant that we were on our way to becoming graduates but I almost had a heart attack when I discovered that Dr Christopher Agbebi had been assigned to me. Why? I couldn't discard the feeling that it was no coincidence. This was a clear mischief, I told myself sadly. Dr Agbebi had been biding his time all the while, knowing I would fall into his trap. I stood rooted to the spot for minutes, oblivious of the excitement around me. I tried to pull myself together and headed in the direction of his office. He wanted an answer. He had always wanted an answer. He had waited long enough for it and finally he was going to get it. Damn Dr Christopher Agbebi! I cursed under my breath.

"Anjola! Anjola Adeniyi! Where are you going?"

I recognised the voice even without looking back. It was Aisha.

"I'm going to the department; I will be back shortly," I shouted without turning. I had too much to worry about. Who the hell did Dr Agbebi think he was? What gave him the right to believe that he could get any female student to go to bed with him just because he had requested it? His wife was once an undergraduate in my department, he had told me proudly. Well, I didn't care whether his wife had consented to his marriage proposal because she had loved him or because she had felt intimidated. I wasn't bothered either about whatever punitive measures he might have decided to mete out to me. I wasn't going to sleep with him - or any other lecturer for that matter. That was my decision and it was final. I was practically racing to the department now. In my fury, I refused to greet known faces I encountered on my way, students and lecturers alike, and neither did I acknowledge greetings from them. Presently, I was standing at his door, panting like an athlete who had just completed a difficult race. I knocked and entered without waiting for his invitation. I still had my letter in my hand. I waved it at him angrily without bothering to greet him.

"What's the meaning of this?" I demanded. He looked up sharply from the book he was reading. His eyes flared.

"What's the meaning of what?" he asked.

"This letter says you are to supervise my long essay," I blurted out. He sighed hugely and nodded.

"I see, and what's strange about that?" His tone was without malice.

"Well, nothing is strange really. I just want you to know that this will not change anything," I stated tightly.

"How do you mean?" he asked quietly.

He looked at me with a reasonable amount of patience but I wasn't prepared to be taken in by his calm disposition. I stormed out of his office without another word but with even a greater resolve not to have a sexual relationship with him. As the semester wore on, I acted as if I had no care in the world even as my mates regularly held meetings with their assigned supervisors. I avoided my own supervisor like the plague, which was further made effective by the fact that I did not offer any of the courses he handled that semester. I knew the implication of my action but I just couldn't think of a way out. I was aware, for instance, that avoiding my supervisor would mean not writing my long essay, which would mean not graduating, but each time I ruminated over the likely consequences of my stubbornness, I always concluded that it was more honourable to have an extra semester or even an extra session than debase my womanhood. I took a firm decision also not to share my misery with any of my mates because I knew what advice most of them would proffer. They would tell me I had no option but to succumb. They would give me a thousand and one names of students, past and present, who had succumbed; that I should be 'realistic'. And so I kept the matter to myself. I was suffering internally; I was going through agony trying to think of a way out. Nonetheless, I managed to maintain a calm exterior as I went about my other academic activities.

Then, several weeks after our altercation, he requested to see me. Conflicting thoughts raced through my mind, including the possibility that he might try to rape me in his office. Some lecturers were infamous for sleeping with their students in their offices. I thought of how I could prevent this. Perhaps I should wear multiple trousers and ensure that I stood close to the door. No, Dr Agbebi wouldn't rape me, I thought. He didn't look like someone who could do such a thing but then rapists didn't look different from Dr Agbebi - or any other man on the street. Maybe he merely wanted to issue threats, tell me to grow up and face the reality of university life. Then I would tell him I was already grown; that I was a full grown woman now approaching my twentieth birthday. This thought was beginning to make me feel angry as I attempted to address him in absentia. Finally, I decided to go to his office to see him as he had requested, doing so with reluctance, of course, but fairly well prepared to safeguard myself from sexual harassment. I went to the common room and bought a packet of razor blades which I put in my jeans trouser pocket. If he tried anything funny, I would lacerate his body. This helped imbue me with confidence. I knocked on his door.

"Yes, come in," he answered. I turned the knob and eased myself in.

"Good day, sir," I mumbled, watching him for signs of passion, even lust. I wasn't about to drop my guard.

"How are you today, Anjola?" he said cheerfully, which only made me more suspicious. I felt the packet of razors in my pocket. I'm stronger than you think, you miserable maggot, I muttered under my breath. To him, I said:

"I am fine, sir. You wanted to see me."

"Yes, I sent for you." he said blithely. I remained expressionless. A little smile played on his face as he reached for his desk drawer and brought out some naira notes.

"Go and buy two bottles of Coca-Cola," he said with restrained heartiness, handing them to me. I didn't move a muscle. I was certain I was dreaming.

"I should go and buy Coca-Cola?" I asked incredulously.

"I know you are wondering what's going on but never mind. You will understand soon enough."

He spoke in a voice so friendly that I didn't know what to think. I took the money but even as I headed toward the door, I glanced over my shoulder. I returned shortly. He opened the bottles then said, in a mild voice:

"Sit down, Anjola."

As I did so I felt my anger melting. Suddenly, I began to see him in a different light. He looked quite harmless. He was calm, almost sober. How could I have imagined he would bring so much dishonour to himself as to want to rape a student? Moments passed in silence.

"I liked you and I still sincerely do but it's obvious to me you don't feel the same about me," he finally said.

"It's not that I didn't …" I began defensively but he held his hand.

"You don't have to apologise for anything. I didn't call this meeting to apportion blame or pass the buck. What I'm saying is that you don't like me enough to desire a romantic relationship with me and I don't think we should fight because of that."

I stared at him. He continued.

"Perhaps we would have been through with the affair by now even if you had consented to it. Life is dynamic, meaning that there are many important things friends can do together apart from having sex. I like you because I discovered you are brilliant. Your intelligence fascinates me. I thought that having an intimate relationship with you would guarantee that you would always be around me so that we could tap from each other like true intellectuals. Clearly, you do not share my sentiments and, as I have said, we need not be at war because of that. It would be selfish of me to engage you in a battle over your lack of interest in me. I have therefore invited you to call a truce and to let you know that I harbour no grudge toward you. On the contrary, I think you are a dignified and highly respectable young woman. I propose we drink to a new kind of friendship. Come on now, here we go, stubborn Anjola."

He chuckled and took one of the bottles. I shot him a look of gratitude and picked the other bottle. As we clinked, we burst into laughter. Life was as sweet as the drink. That marked the beginning of a new chapter in our relationship. It was amazing, almost unbelievable. He supported me at every stage of my long essay - lending me books and directing me to personalities whose views and intellectual input would enrich my work. He was like a father who desired the very best for his daughter. And it was in that fatherly spirit that he invited me to his office that afternoon to counsel me on how to face the world.

CHAPTER 5

I was jarred awake by the sound of a bell. I looked at my watch. I had slept off while reminiscing. It was daybreak. Corps members were being summoned for morning exercise. I must have been exhausted from the journey. I sprang up from the bed, rushed into the sportswear I had been given on arrival and made for the parade ground. We were divided into several groups, each one headed by a platoon commander. Mine was a staff sergeant. He was tall, well over six feet with a delicate, predatory face and eyes that had known suffering. Although only in his forties, his forehead was furrowed and his receding hairline made him look older. His voice boomed as he ordered us to run round the field six times, after which we did other exercises before settling down to learn how to march. All the while he was informing us that we were nothing but a bunch of lazy bones. I managed to endure the rigours but by the end I was panting badly. I felt queasy and was suddenly aware that my sport wear was soaked through and clinging to my body. My legs felt weak; I was certain I would collapse at any moment. I needed to sit down for a few minutes. I raised my hand:

"Excuse me, sir," I said hesitantly, "I'm feeling dizzy, sir."

He skidded toward me, eyes threatening. I swallowed nervously.

"Bloody lazy civilian!" he barked as he approached. Was he going to whip me? I was scared.

"You get belle?" he asked sternly. There was a ripple of laughter from my fellow corpers. I was silent.

"Answer me! You get belle?"

Still I said nothing. I found his question embarrassing. He was standing by my side now. I shuffled nervously from one foot to the other, praying that he would be merciful. Suddenly, the hint of a smile broke across his face and his real or pretended anger turned to amusement. He smiled and asked:

"What's your name?"

"Anjola."

"Anjola, jola-jola," he said playfully. He turned to my fellow corpers, shouting, "Big belle!" They looked momentarily lost, as if in anticipation of something dreadful. "Big Belle?" he repeated. They seemed to understand the game now as they all chorused:

"Something dey."

"Small belle?" he shouted again but in a more sing-song voice and again they responded:

"Nothing dey."

"Big belle?"

"Something dey."

"Small belle?"

"Nothing dey!"

"You are feeling dizzy, ehn?" he asked, still smiling.

"Yes."

"You wan fall?" he teased.

"No sir."

"Ah, ha, she dey feel dizzy true true. See her, she don dey sweat like Christmas goat. Go and sit down, lazy girl with local marks."

I let out an audible sigh of relief as I walked groggily from the line.

That was the end of my participation that first morning in the camp. I sat down and watched as my fellow corpers were taken through different kinds of exercises. I was still keenly watching when another corper came to join me. He sat down quietly beside me. I hadn't noticed when he left the line. I didn't know what must have transpired between him and the commander but I was glad to have company. We soon started to gist.

"How are you, Anjola?" he greeted as if we had known each other before.

"How did you know my name?" I demanded.

"You told the commander. Why, what's the fuss?"

"There's no fuss. What's your own name?" I asked, softening.

"Cyprian, but you can call me CY," he said blithely.

I took a closer look at him. He had a long, narrow head and a cheerful face. He had scars of old pimples on his face but they didn't undermine his good looks. His body was narrow, like his face, and he looked neat and pleasant.

"Where is CY from?" I asked in a playful voice.

"Imo."

"Oh, the state next door, right? You didn't want to travel far."

"What do you mean?"

"I mean you had your posting changed so that you could be close home."

He shook his head. "No, I didn't do anything to influence my posting. Besides, I don't know any big man or woman who could do that for me."

He spoke earnestly. There was no sense of offence in his tone.

"I was just joking, okay?" I said guiltily.

"I knew you were joking. Where are you from, Anjola?"

"I'm from Kwara."

"Oh, you are a northerner. Why do you have a Yoruba name? By the way, you also have Yoruba tribal marks. Why is that?"

"I'm not a northerner, I'm Yoruba."

He gave me a searching look.

"Come off it, Anjola, you can't be Yoruba if you are from Kwara. We all know that Kwara is in the north."

"Yes, Kwara is one of the northern states but I'm from the Yoruba ethnic group so I'm not a northerner," I said in a subdued voice.

"I don't know why people behave like this. The youth service programme is meant to educate people more, not to confuse them, okay? You can't claim to be Yoruba while at the same time you claim to come from Kwara. Or is it only one of your parents that is from Kwara while the other is Yoruba?"

I was silent for a moment, thinking of the best way to explain to him. "No, both my parents are from Kwara. They are also both Yoruba and so I am," I said calmly.

"OK, Anjola, but you are certainly Hausa or you want to deny that as well?"

I peered aggressively at him. "Look, you are making me angry unnecessarily. I have just told you that I'm not a northerner and you say I'm Hausa. What's your problem? Are you hard of hearing?"

Without realising it, I had leapt to my feet, my heart pounding. A worried look crossed his face as he mirrored my action.

"OK, sit down. I say sit down, OK? Don't mind me. The truth is that I don't understand what you are telling me but never mind," he said in a conciliatorily voice. "Please sit and let's continue with our gist."

He seemed inoffensive and eager to please. We both sat down and continued our conversation. I could sense that he was making a deliberate effort to avoid the vexatious issue.

The morning exercise ended soon after and we dispersed to return to our hostel to take our baths and breakfast. I spent the day with Ify on my mind although I hadn't decided what the nature of our relationship should be. What I knew was that I liked him enough to want to be his friend. I was looking forward to his visit and my heart jumped for joy when he arrived. Ify was reliable, I told myself happily. He wasn't like some guys who would meet a lady, treat her as if she was the best creature in the world and promise her heaven and earth only to disappear almost as fast as they had come.

"How has it been with you?" he asked me as soon as we shook hands.

"I'm very well, Ify, and thanks a million for yesterday. You made everything easy for me."

I got a whiff of his overpowering perfume.

"It was the least I could do. You know, this time last year, I was also a youth corper." My brows lifted in surprise.

"Really? Why didn't you tell me yesterday?"

"We didn't really have time to talk, did we? That's why I'm here today so that we can get to know each other properly."

His eyes twinkled warmly.

"Okay, then, let me go first. Tell me about yourself," I said girlishly.

"Well, I'm Ifeanyi. I'm from Anambra State," he began. "I hold a master's degree in civil engineering from the University of Western Ontario in Canada. I came back to Nigeria only last year for my national service. I served in the north, precisely at Bayero University in Kano and was retained as an assistant lecturer afterwards. I'm here to run an errand for my father. He lives in Jos."

"Impressive!" I said smiling.

"What about you? Tell me about yourself," he said. His eyes were filled with naked adoration. I couldn't help it; my smile widened into a laugh.

"What else do you want to know? I already told you my name and my state and where I went to university. All right, I haven't told you what I studied. I hold a bachelor of arts degree in English."

"OK. I want you to tell me about your facial marks. Why do they resemble Yoruba tribal marks when you are a northerner?" My mood immediately darkened but he evidently didn't notice as he continued. "Northerners don't have that type of facial mark."

"I'm not a northerner, I'm Yoruba," I stated curtly.

"No, you are not Yoruba. Didn't you say you were from Kwara? By the way, why do you have a Yoruba name?"

I tried to check my irritation.

"What's wrong with you people?" I asked, my voice rising.

"Which people? You look angry. What's getting you worked up?" He was clearly baffled.

"Why shouldn't I be angry? Did you listen to yourself? Do you know the implications of what you've just said?" I was losing my temper again.

"What did I just say?"

"You've just implied that I'm ashamed of my roots."

"Come on, Anjola, is there something else to this matter?"

He peered down at me, his forehead creasing into tiny folds. Then he put his hand on my shoulder and turned me around.

"I'm sorry, OK? It really doesn't matter to me where you come from. You are a Nigerian and even if you were not, it still wouldn't matter. What matters right now is that we are friends and intend to go on being friends. Aren't we?" He looked flustered. I must have overreacted. I thought regretfully.

"Yes, we are, Ify," I said softly and tried to explain.

"It's just that it troubles me when people call me what I know I'm not and it drives me crazy when people argue about what they don't know."

"Which people? Who have you been talking with?"

"Don't ask me. All I know is that you are not the only person who has tried to make me feel that I don't know which ethnic group I belong. Believe me, Ify, I neither understand nor speak a word of Hausa. I'm Yoruba through and through."

"Let's talk about something else," he mumbled as he fixed me with a penetrating look. I blushed. I didn't like the way he was beginning to affect me. Perhaps, the problem lay with me. He took me by the arm and guided me in the direction of the football pitch, stopping every now and then to peer at me, perhaps to confirm that my temper had indeed cooled.

"Tell me about your experience during the early morning exercise today. Remember you are talking to an ex-corper shon."

I told him what had happened and we laughed. Then he told me about his job. He said he was twenty-six and was already thinking of getting married. He also said he planned to leave the university to seek employment in the industry. He planned to relocate to Kaduna, where he hoped to actualise his dream.

"I'm a highway engineer," he said proudly, adding that, as a civil engineer, he would feel a lot more fulfilled. He liked the university, he said, and even liked most of his students, but he insisted he wanted something more physical to be truly happy. I listened to him pour out his mind and, as he spoke, I liked him even more. He seemed thoroughly real to me. He appeared to be without false airs. It seemed to me also that he possessed a great heart, was hardworking, focused, results-oriented, responsible and peaceful. He took my hand and looked directly into my eyes without saying anything. I also mirrored his action with our eyes interlocking for what seemed a long moment. Neither of us spoke. Then he released my hand gently as if I was a baby to be handled with care. This made me feel special. I smiled secretly. There was surely no better way to enjoy my new world.

Ify wanted us to take a walk around the camp, after which he said we would go to town on a date. I visualised him making love to me and felt wet between my legs but I wasn't sure he was the kind of person I really wanted as a boyfriend at the moment. He was kind, calm, reasonable and persuasive. He looked too much of a gentleman for me. I wanted fun; I thought the time had come to experiment with sex. I desired life. I desperately needed to explore my new world without the encumbrances of a 'serious relationship.' I felt certain that I didn't need commitment yet. But why did I need to bother myself about what the man wanted or did not want, anyway? He hadn't proposed marriage, for goodness' sake. He hadn't even asked me to be his girlfriend. I quickly cautioned myself. What was important was what I was getting at the moment. We were enjoying each other's company and it was only reasonable that I left things the way they were. I went out with him thereafter and we had a great time. He took me to some important places in the city and told me he would not be visiting the next day because he had a lot to do. However, he would definitely come at the weekend. He then escorted me back to the camp, following me to the gate, where he gave me a passionate hug before bidding me goodbye.

CHAPTER 6

I was ecstatic as I made my way to the hostel. This was truly a new world. I had absolutely no reason to be in dread of it as my supervisor had suggested. I was exhilarated. I instinctively began to hum a local song composed to admonish young maidens who were about to enter matrimony.

Iyawo o, tio ba nre'le oko	Oh you new bride, headed toward matrimony
Ori ni omulo, ki o ma ma se mewa lo o	Take along with you good fortune, not beauty
Oojo o oun 'lewa mbowa'le	The day of your nuptial is the same day the beauty evaporates
Ori eni l'on bani gbe'le oko	It is your higher self that enhances your ability to enjoy your matrimonial home.
Eleda iwo Iyawo agbe e de 'jokole e o	Your maker will keep you permanent in your matrimonial home.

Chorus

Ile oko l'ere o	There is reward in matrimony
E se	We thank thee O Lord
Ile oko l'ere	There is reward in matrimony
Yarabi funwa l'omo	O Lord give us children to reward this matrimony
Ile oko l'ere	There is reward in matrimony

Like a new bride who was urged to go into her matrimonial home with good fortune, I no longer had any doubts that I had indeed come into my new world with extremely good fortune. Hence, I happily substituted my name wherever there was iyawo in the song. Then, with incredible ingenuity and creativity, I realised I had suddenly become dramatic and had radically altered the original lyrics to suit my joyous situation. I raised my voice and sang louder.

Anjola o	Oh Anjola
nigbati mon lo s'aiye tuntun	when I was going into my new world
ori ni momulo o	I went with good fortune
Emi o ma mewa lo o	I didn't go with beauty
nitoripe	because
oojo o oun l'ewa nbowa'le. Sugbon,	beauty is transient and it evaporates in no time, but

ori mi l'obami d'aiye tuntun	my good fortune has accompanied me to my new world
Eleda emi Anjola	Me, Anjola, my higher self
ti gbe mi d'aiye igbadun o	has elevated me to the level of bliss
Aiye tuntun l'adun o	This new world is more delicious,
se e gbo?	have you heard?
aiye tuntun l'adun	This new world is delicious
Oluwa lo mu mi de be	Almighty brought me there
aiye tuntun l'adun o	This new world is delicious

Life couldn't be better, I thought. I sang as I walked. Most corpers cast curious glances but I couldn't be bothered. My happiness was beyond their comprehension. A smile which had earlier broken out on my face had spread and become a wide grin. I was singing loudly.

"Hey! Anjola, what's amusing you?"

It was a girl I had nearly bumped into without realising it. I didn't recognise her and was surprised she knew my name.

"Hello, what's up?" I greeted with exaggerated familiarity.

"Nothing much, I'm just going out," she said.

"Going out to town? What's happening there and don't tell me you are going alone," I said jocularly.

"Who else should I be going with?"

"Don't mind me jor, how long are you staying out?"

I noticed she was holding what looked like a jewellery box. "What's that you are holding?" I reached out to take it from her before she could respond.

"It's nothing much, it's just a small piece of jewellery," she said.

I took it from her and opened it. Inside was a set of earrings and a pendant.

"Wow!" I exclaimed. "This is beautiful. Is it yours?"

"Of course, it's mine; who else's could it be?"

"I'm sorry, where are you taking it to?"

"Nowhere in particular; I just feel like taking it out with me."

"Very well, then, just be careful not to misplace it because it's too beautiful to get lost."

"Thank you. Let me run along before it gets dark."

"All right, see you later."

I walked confidently to my hostel, thinking about the rollicking time I was having, contrary to my dad's fears. He hadn't been enthused about the prospect of me having to go so far for my national service and had tried to nudge me into agreeing to his plan to use his influence to change my posting to a neighbouring state like Oyo or even serve in our own Kwara, but I wouldn't hear of it. I refused to yield to his persuasion, citing the need to broaden my horizons. On his part, he explained that he was worried about the dangers inherent in long-distance travel. Any right thinking Nigerian should avoid unnecessary journeys on our roads, he said, but I insisted my quest for more learning through travelling was necessary. I wanted to learn about the culture and traditions of other people. In the end, he consented on condition that I was not to visit home during the entire year. I was also banned from travelling to anywhere else. I agreed.

"Anjola!" I swung around. It was the girl in the room next to mine.

"Florence, how are you doing?"

"You've been having fun, huh?" she asked. I nodded in joyous agreement and smiled at her benignly. A bolt of lightning flashed across the sky. I wanted to have my evening shower and spend the rest of the evening 'gisting' with my roommates. I was learning a lot from them. One was from Benue, another from Niger and the third from Cross River. Each had stories to tell me; stories that intrigued me. The one from Niger was the oldest and obliged us with her 'wealth' of experience. The only problem with Halima was that she worried too much about the need to find a life-partner before the end of the service year.

"I can't go back home a spinster," she kept saying as if it was our responsibility to find her a husband.

"I'm already twenty-six," she would invariably add.

"What would you do if you failed to hook a man?" I asked, determined to take her to task.

"Don't curse me, Anjola. I will hook a man. I must hook a man, otherwise, I'm doomed."

"You are not doomed. You cannot be doomed simply because no man asks you to marry him. Listen, Halima, you need to take things easy…"

She cut me short. "Don't even try to preach at me, OK? I don't expect you to understand. After all, you are not from my place and you are not twenty-six…"

"You think I don't understand but I do. Honestly, I do but I still believe you need to take things easy and comport yourself so that the man you seek will not think you are desperate," I said.

"I don't care what he thinks. Let him propose marriage to me, shikenna. Besides, I'm really desperate, Anjola. I am."

"You don't have to be," I insisted.

"I have to be desperate to be determined. I have to be determined to be able to achieve my ambition. You are just a small girl of yesterday, I don't blame you."

I was about to protest her labelling me a small girl when noise filtered into our room from the corridor. A girl was shouting at the top of her voice that somebody had stolen something from her wardrobe. We rushed out of our room. A crowd of fellow corpers had gathered. The girl whose valuables had been stolen was crying and swearing. Everybody seemed to be talking at the same time. Some were asking her where she had kept them; others were appealing to her to pull herself together. I moved closer to her.

"What kind of valuables?" I asked.

She stopped crying. "It's a set of earrings and a pendant," she said.

"A set of earrings and pendant?" I echoed and described what I had seen earlier.

"That is it!" she exclaimed as she wiped away her tears. "Ah, thank you. You saw it. Can I have it, please?"

My face clouded in confusion. "I saw it quite alright, but it's not with me. I actually saw it with someone and I'm trying to recollect who it was."

Her eyes flared. "Eh–hey! What? What's the meaning of that?"

The spontaneous reaction from the crowd caught me unawares. The jewellery owner wanted to speak but several people were talking simultaneously. Finally, she gained control and addressed me directly:

"What do you mean you saw it with someone but you don't remember who it was? How come you remember that you saw it in the first place?" she demanded, twisting her mouth in disgust.

"I wonder o," many chorused as if on cue. I suddenly felt stupid but I was still struggling to rack my brains. I should at least be able to describe the girl I had met at the gate only a few hours before.

"What's her name?" the jewellery owner asked no one in particular.

"Anjola," a few girls chorused.

"Well, Anjola or whatever your name is. Listen to me." She took a few steps toward me. "Call the name of this girl you said you saw my jewellery with in the presence of everybody here or you produce my jewellery. Something tells me you are the thief."

I couldn't believe what I was hearing. Was she out of her mind? I felt the blood rush to my face and my stomach tightened in anger.

"How dare you accuse me of stealing? I was only trying to help," I thundered.

"You were only trying to help whom, you bloody thief? Is everybody here listening to this foolish thief trying to play smart?"

I tried to shout back but the evident disgust in her eyes rendered me speechless.

"Look, Miss Thief, release the poor girl's jewellery and save yourself further trouble. What do you thieves gain by stealing, ehn? How do you have the heart to take what you know does not belong to you?" another girl said from the crowd.

I couldn't believe what was happening. Things were getting out of hand. I felt helpless. I braced myself.

"You must be a bloody idiot," I lashed out at the girl. "Did you see me steal the jewellery?" I demanded. But despite my outrage I sounded pathetic, even to my own ears.

"Go and report her to the authorities if she refuses to release the jewellery. She appears to be a hardened thief," another girl said aloud, her eyes challenging mine.

I couldn't believe those words were being said about me. I was surprised my roommates didn't come to my defence. They appeared to be weighing their options. They looked sad, alright, which probably meant they sympathised with me, but they also seemed not to trust me enough to declare openly for me; that I was their roommate and an honest and upright person. Worst of all, I was angry with myself. I still couldn't recall the girl whom I had seen with the jewellery. Ironically, I could vividly recall the particular spot where I had almost bumped into her. I could also remember our conversation. I began to sob.

CHAPTER 7

I was summoned by my platoon commander the next morning. He said the matter had been reported to the state NYSC director. I was to write a statement about what happened, after which I would be informed when I would appear before a panel.

"Theft is a serious offence in the camp, Anjola. Why did you do it?" he asked.

I wanted to talk, to explain to him that I didn't do it, but I couldn't find my voice. Instead of articulating my side of the story, hot tears streamed down my cheeks. I could not have imagined that my new, exciting world could turn upside-down so quickly. My commander put his hand in his pocket and brought out a handkerchief. I took it gratefully and wiped my face but, as I made to return it, fresh tears cascaded down my cheeks. He took me by the wrist and led me to the football field and told me to sit down. He remained standing and urged me with as much tenderness as he could muster to tell him all about it. I told him I had seen a girl going out of the camp with a jewellery box. I had even taken it from her and admired it but couldn't recollect who it was. He repeated that stealing was a serious offence and that the offender could even be denied their NYSC certificate. I started to cry harder. My shoulders shook. His countenance became more thoughtful. He assured me that he was likely to be a member of the panel and that he would ensure that justice was tempered with mercy. I rose to my feet, mumbled my gratitude and started for the hostel. Back in my room, I threw myself on the bed and thought about Dr Agbebi's warning. I decided to write him a letter.

Dear Dr Agbebi,

I have to write this to give you horrible news of myself, sir. I met a fellow female corps member one evening as I was walking back into the orientation camp from a social outing. She was holding a small box that contained a piece of jewellery. I asked her if it belonged to her and she replied in the affirmative. We had a light conversation around the jewellery as I admired it and admonished her to keep it safe. A few hours later, an alarm was raised by another female corps member that a box containing a piece of jewellery had been stolen. I asked for the description of the stolen jewellery and realised it was the same box of jewellery I had seen earlier. Unfortunately, however, I could not remember the particular girl in whose possession I had seen the jewellery. I explained, innocently, to the owner of the jewellery and the crowd that had gathered that although I had sighted the jewellery with a corps member, but that I could not recall the identity of the person. My honest disclosure became my undoing immediately as I was promptly accused of being the thief. Things have since turned awry for me, sir. I have even been informed that the matter has been reported to the NYSC authority and that a disciplinary committee will be raised soon.

I feel world weary and utterly awful. You don't know how much I miss you and our wonderful talks. I realised now than ever how much of a friend you were to me. I miss the university, and, most of all, I miss the protection and bliss of being a student. At this point, I would gladly choose to be a student again. No matter how much reading I would have to do, or how many assignments, tests and examinations I would have to write. I am beginning to realise that there is too much turmoil outside the campus.

Once again, I miss you and your wise counsel and guidance.

Your former student and friend,
Anjola.

When I finished, I clutched the letter to my bosom and sobbed, rocking back and forth. I cried so hard my stomach hurt.

In the end the panel decided that I pay the full monetary value of the jewellery to be determined by the owner. The amount she quoted was six times my monthly allowance, which she was to collect in full at the end of each month. That frustrated me. How would I survive in far-away Anambra State for six whole months without an allowance? I remembered my father's warning not to visit home throughout the duration of my service year. Even if I did so, how would I explain what had transpired?

From the day I was falsely accused of stealing, I observed a radical change toward me. No one seemed interested in my company. Ify came to see me at the end of that week but only to tell me he was returning to the north. Although sympathetic and supportive, he couldn't continue to be around since his casual leave was over. I was left to brood over my misery alone. As for my roommates, they had grown distant and cold. They talked to me only when absolutely necessary. I moved about in a fog. My only bright moments were with Cyprian Ugbechie, whom I had grown to calling CY. He was fun to be with. He knew a lot of jokes, which helped to cheer me up. Moreover, he seemed to trust me without any evidence. He simply refused to believe that I was a thief.

CY and I grew very close. Within one week, we began to date. The ease with which I fell into his arms was partly because I needed a shoulder to lean on and partly because he generally fitted into my earlier design as regards what I wanted as a corper. Unlike Ify, who was in search of commitment, CY just wanted fun. I could be free as I wanted. Besides, Ify lived in the north while CY was around and understood the terrain. He took me to party after party and, within a short while, I got my groove back. I even took to treating my resentful roommates with the same coldness with which they treated me. I only felt sad when any of them was in the room with me. Otherwise, I was as happy as any corper could be. Moreover, the orientation was coming to an end, with our endurance trek and party slated for the last week of our stay. We all looked forward to trekking a long distance outside the city. We were told that the exercise would take us to a certain village approved by the NYSC secretariat and that an ambulance, medical personnel (some of whom would be corpers themselves), medications, food and drinks would accompany us.

Finally, the day of the long trek came. Hand-in-hand with CY, I joined the others. Just as we had been told, the sweet memories of the exercise would last us a lifetime. Although a few people fell sick along the way, most of us made it to the village, where we fell on the refreshments. As we ate and drank, disco music blared from the powerful speakers in the ambulance. When we finished eating, CY seized me by my hand and all but dragged me to the impromptu dance floor. As we were digging it out, he told me he would out-dance me. Soon it became a competition between us. Perhaps I was having fun; maybe I was finally shaking off what remained of my misery from the jewellery saga. In any case, we were having fun. Suddenly, without warning, a girl walked up to us and said:

"No be the girl wey thief earring dey dance so? Miss Thief, Original Designer Face, so you sabi dance like this?" She sniggered. "Oh, don't look so glum, Miss Thi-e-e-e-f," she added before turning on her heels and walking away.

"You are nothing but a low-life nonentity. I didn't steal any earring," I retorted. I was going to say more but CY took my hand and led me away. I was boiling with rage.

"See what you are doing to yourself," he said as he folded his arms around my neck and drew me gently to himself. "You shouldn't give anyone the privilege to upset you. She saw that you were happy and wanted to spoil your fun. Now you have given her the chance to do just that; a chance she didn't deserve."

He stared at me, his hands warm and protective as he

continued to hold me. I lowered my head on his shoulder and closed my eyes. I couldn't hold back the tears. CY was right. We spent the remaining time just talking. I appreciated his love and affection. What would I have done without his support?

It was now two days to the end of the orientation. The following day was our orientation party. The next morning corpers would be given letters of posting to their places of primary assignment. I went to the party but I stayed close to CY, not wanting to be embarrassed or upset by anyone. CY had also spoken to me at length about how to ignore mischievous people and how not to allow anyone to ruin my happiness.

"You are the only one who can permit others to make you unhappy," he had said tenderly, adding that I did not have to give such permission. It was amazing how much I had come to depend on him within such a short time. He had become more than a boyfriend; he was like a guardian, a big brother and a protector. Our platoon commander was walking toward where we sat. We thought he hadn't seen us but we were wrong.

"Good evening, sir," we greeted in unison.

"Good evening. I hope you people are enjoying the party," he asked.

"Very well sir, thank you," CY said.

"Then why una no dance?"

CY and I exchanged glances because it just dawned on us that the man was tipsy.

"We like it this way, sir. We are OK," CY said.

"Ha-ha-ha, una no sabi enjoy life o. Anyway, as you no wan dance, CY, you go gree make I dance with Anjola?"

"No problem, sir," CY said.

"Anjola, you go dance with me?"

"Very well, sir."

I followed him to the dance floor. He was trying to dance but he was too drunk to make much success of the attempt. He swayed drunkenly and smiled at me sheepishly.

"I dey dance o," he said, drawling on each syllable. He looked like a comic character; watching him was fun. He suddenly moved close to me and said:

"Even if I die tonight, at least I have danced with a university graduate." I laughed and used the opportunity to guide him from the dance floor. As we made our way through the crowd, he kept saying, "I have danced with a university graduate; I have danced with a youth corper. I have danced with a corper."

CHAPTER 8

There were no exercises for us on our last morning. I was glad. I no longer had to endure our platoon commander's persistent complaint that I didn't know how to do the march past.

"Anjola Adeniyi! Stop dancing and march for me! Anjola, I said you are dancing, not marching," he would scream repeatedly. Sometimes he would rush at me threateningly, as if he wanted to release his dreaded whip on me, although he never did. Day after day I struggled to up my game. I never succeeded. Perhaps I lacked the skill, or maybe the concentration. No amount of practice or determination could get me near-perfection. Now it was over and I was relieved.

I had woken up that morning with great enthusiasm to begin the actual service to my motherland. Letters of posting to places of primary assignment were being distributed and, surprisingly, a new kind of drama was unfolding. I couldn't understand it. I watched without interest at first but, as the scenario became more entertaining, my curiosity grew. I watched with amazement the reaction of some of my fellow corpers to their posting. Some celebrated while others lamented their ill–luck. A few of the latter even went to the ridiculous extent of throwing themselves on the ground and weeping like children.

Most corpers wanted to be posted to Enugu, the state capital. Those who were not posted there talked about how they would get their respective employers to 'reject' them after having done their 'homework'. This involved securing the consent of an organisation of their choice they already had an understanding with. I found this curious. I didn't know that corpers could wield that kind of influence. At the other end of the spectrum were those who seemed to think nothing of their posting other than a call to service. I was one of them, as was CY, although his could be described as good since he had been posted within the Enugu metropolis. I, on the other hand, was posted to a secondary school in a village thirty kilometres away. We decided we would alternate our weekends in order to maintain our affair.

"Anjola, there's something I'd like to tell you," CY said softly. The calmness in his voice commanded my attention. "You're a very special person. Don't change."

I took a deep breath and nodded. He continued talking, fixing me with a concentrated gaze. "It's usually easier to lie to people than to tell the truth about them or their situation, even though they know you are lying. The reason for this is because people live in illusion and fantasy and don't want anyone to disturb their world of comfortable lies. But let me assure you that your honesty will make you stand above so many others although that honesty will sometimes make you seem foolish or even cruel. You must continue to be who you are."

How deeply he felt the things he said, I thought. Neither of us said anything for a moment.

"One more thing," he continued. "Each moment of your day must be positive and worthwhile. From this moment on, don't let any opportunity slip through your fingers. Promise?"

"Promise," I mouthed.

"It's been wonderful and it's just the beginning," he added, then kissed me and pressed me to him. My throat was so choked up, I couldn't speak.

"Thanks for your words and more thanks for believing in me, trusting me even without evidence. You are an amazing guy, CY," I whispered when I finally found my voice. He nodded, his eyes twinkling with joy as we parted.

The journey to real national service began in earnest. I got to the village soon enough and discovered that ten of us had been posted to the five secondary schools in the village, two to each. Two of them were government schools while the others were private. I had bagged one of the government schools, as had one of the male corpers, Henry Okonta. The principal welcomed us warmly and assured us that our stay would be rewarding. The school had a permanent apartment for corpers within the compound, he told us. The school had also appointed one of the regular teachers to be in charge of our welfare. He would be introduced to us presently and we were to channel all our enquiries or complaints through him. After what seemed like his welcome address, we were taken to the coordinator of corpers' affairs who was introduced to us as Mr Chudi Nweke. He was a slim man, almost thin, with a bald head. He looked harassed but nevertheless seemed like an optimistic person judging by the way he smiled broadly. He extended his hand to Henry.

"Welcome, Miss," he said to me genially without attempting to shake my hand. I smiled my response. He told us to follow him, dragging Henry with him from the waist like a friend or relation. I was amused. Henry looked back to wink at me and I did the same as I followed closely behind.

"Let me take you to your apartment first," he said. "Thereafter, I will show you other places." We went through a football field and I could sight from a distance an array of small bungalows that looked like the staff quarters. We kept following Mr Nweke, who had begun to speak again.

"I'm your neighbour," he said.

"Really?" Henry said, apparently more out of courtesy than from a genuine feeling of excitement.

"Daddy, daddy wait for me."

A girl of about five emerged from one of the houses and ran toward us.

"Princess, go back to the house, you hear? The sun is too

much," Mr Nweke said but she ignored him. She took his hand as she joined us.

"Is she your daughter?" Henry asked.

"Yes, she is my third daughter," he said proudly.

"She is very beautiful," Henry commented.

"Ah, this one? Na govanor go marry am."

"You are a very funny man," Henry said.

"No be you talk am now say she fine?" Nweke asked, suddenly stopping in his tracks to look at Henry, who was now laughing.

"Na lie I talk, Miss? I think you yaself don see say my daughter na fine gal," Nweke said to me. I smiled in agreement.

"Your daughter is beautiful, no dispute; but what if she doesn't love a governor or she doesn't even get to meet one?" I queried.

"Governor must find her come o," Nweke said with the conviction of someone who had the gift of clairvoyance. Neither Henry nor I pushed the argument further. The seriousness with which he spoke did not leave us in doubt that it was in our own interest to agree with him or let the matter drop. We reached our apartment, which consisted of two rooms with an adjourning door permanently bolted with a heavy iron rod. Each room had a three-and-a-half spring bed with a foam mattress. There were two lockers put together to serve as a table; there was a chair and a clothes' rack in each room. This had always served as the school's permanent corpers' lodging, Nweke told us enthusiastically, adding that as a rule the school never accepted more than two each year because it lacked the facilities to accommodate more. He promised to cooperate with us in every way necessary and ensure that our stay in the school was pleasurable. To demonstrate his readiness, he promised to take us on a guided tour of the village later that evening. He explained that it was necessary to acquaint us with important locations, including the palace of the paramount ruler of Obodonwayi autonomous community. Every community in Igbo land was autonomous, he explained with pride, promising for the umpteenth time that our service year in the state would be memorable. Again, he shook hands with Henry and laughed heartily as he took his leave, promising to return in two hours' time. He had hardly taken a few steps when he turned back abruptly and walked directly to me. He lowered his voice almost to a conspiratorial tone:

"Look, Miss, you are going to enjoy Obodonwayi. Go and write it down. Write it down, that I, Nweke, promised you that you would enjoy yaself in Anambra as you have never done before."

"I'm convinced already. I mean, the reception we got here is quite warm; and I'm happy," I said, smiling sweetly.

"You haven't seen anything yet. See, emm, Miss, I know good men who will appreciate ya beauty. Look, unm hem! I swear." He put the index finger of his right hand to the tip of his tongue and then raised it heavenward. "I will connect you with men, I mean, men who are real men, men who will pamper you."

I frowned but if he saw he pretended otherwise. I just stared at him wide-eyed but said nothing. I was puzzled. I didn't know what to say and it appeared he didn't expect a response. He went on:

"See, ehn, I don see you, well, well. You are a very beautiful gal. I can see you are hairy; although I'm yet to see ya legs. No worry, inugo? I dey for you."

Then he turned back abruptly as he had come and walked away. I didn't think Henry overheard our discussion but we both watched him leave.

"This one is a character," I said as soon as he was out of earshot.

"Yeah, he is a character with a good heart," Henry said, adding that we should try to settle down by unpacking our luggage. I agreed with him, knowing that Mr Nweke would be back before we knew it. I went into my room and took a look around. The place looked desolate. I felt suddenly lonely but tried to shake it off by telling myself that this was my first time of really being on my own. It wasn't going to be easy at first. I saw a broom in a corner and dusted away the cobwebs on the ceiling. Then I made the bed and lay down for a nap before Mr Nweke would come to take us for our outing.

CHAPTER 9

A gentle knock on my door after what appeared to be just a few minutes woke me up. It was Henry. He said Mr Nweke was waiting for us. I sprang up and the three of us started off. As soon as we got to the gate of the school, Mr Nweke suddenly stopped to address us.

"Where do you want us to start from?" he asked.

"You are our guide, wherever you take us first is where we want to go first," Henry said.

Nweke looked at me and I nodded my agreement.

"Let's start with the Market Square."

Neither Henry nor I said anything. We hadn't walked far when we fell into step with an elderly man and a young woman with a baby strapped on her back. Mr Nweke gestured to us conspiratorially, as if he wanted us to take more than a casual look at them. We followed his hint and did as we thought he wanted us to do. Mr Nweke increased his pace. Henry and I took longer strides so as to match his own. I looked back involuntarily and noticed that the pair was now a few metres behind us. I couldn't help observing that there was something unusual about them. They looked somewhat out of place. There was an air of melancholy about them; they seemed wrapped up in their separate worlds. Henry and I exchanged puzzled looks but said nothing. Meanwhile, Mr Nweke looked at us in turn before clearing his throat.

"It's a good thing that even strangers like you can observe that there is something abnormal about them."

"Who are they and why do they appear so strange?" I asked.

"The elderly man is the biological father of the young woman. Well, she now doubles as both wife and daughter. The baby also doubles as his daughter and granddaughter."

"What?" I screamed in horror.

"You are screaming, even when you have not heard the whole story."

I kept quiet and he resumed talking.

"You see, my dear corpers, wonders, they say, will never end in this sinful world of ours. The man did not lose his wife. His wife is alive and well and was living with him at the time he committed the abomination. Together, they had six children, of which the young woman you now see with him is the eldest. They were doing well and living happily, or so everyone thought, until his first daughter became pregnant. Efforts to find out who was responsible proved difficult initially until all manner of pressure was put on her, following which she finally disclosed that her father had been having carnal knowledge of her since she was eight and long before she saw her first menstrual cycle. It became a huge embarrassment to the entire village. The matter was reported to the Igwe. The man's wife hurriedly packed her belongings, took the remaining five children with her and left to settle in another town. In case you are wondering if the community did not mete out any punishment to the accursed couple for committing such an abomination, I can tell you that their punishment is what even you, total strangers who have not spent a full day in the village, can notice. The entire community is forbidden from talking to or having any dealings with them. As you see them now, even if they want to buy the simplest of items such as table salt they must travel to the next village. Nobody is allowed to talk to them. They are condemned to a life of solitude. They are rejected by the living and cursed by the spirits of our ancestors," Nweke concluded.

"Sorry, Mr Nweke, how old was this young woman when she became pregnant?" I asked.

"Fourteen."

Fourteen; I said under my breath, and to Nweke: "Don't you think the community was unfair to this girl? Why do we even call her a woman? She is a mere child who could not stop her father from sexually abusing her. What she needed was help, not condemnation, certainly not rejection. Mr Nweke; don't you think so?"

"That's very wrong, Miss; she was enjoying what her father was doing to her. Didn't you hear what I said? She said her father had been sleeping with her since she was eight. She got pregnant at fourteen. This means she had been enjoying sex for good six years without telling her mother. She is a bad gal, Miss, and she deserves to suffer."

Anger blazed through me.

"What I'm asking is this: Didn't the Igwe and other elders of the village ask her why she didn't report the matter to her mother or anyone else? Didn't they try to find out if she was afraid of her father?"

"Nobody asked her such irrelevant questions."

"Poor girl, misjudged and condemned in a hurry by those whose responsibility it was to protect her from shame and degradation," I said, fuming.

"Whose responsibility is it to protect her, if I may ask you, Miss?"

"It is everybody's responsibility, including the Igwe, the entire village and, most important of all, her irresponsible mother who abandoned her daughter when she needed her the most."

"What? You blame her mother? Would you rather she waited and engaged her own daughter in an abominable rivalry?"

"That is exactly the point, Mr Nweke. The foolish woman saw her daughter as her rival rather than as a defenceless child who had the misfortune of having her innocence violated and who needed a mother's love and support."

"You've been reading dangerous books, Miss, and I don't think it's good for you."

"What books?"

"I don't know the books you've been reading but I know they will serve you no useful purpose if they make you talk like this," he said disapprovingly before addressing Henry who, up till then, had remained silent. "I think you should advise Miss, otherwise she may fail to get a suitor the way she is going. No man wants to put a woman with dangerous ideas in his house."

Henry said nothing. He appeared to be deep in thought, uninterested in our argument. We walked on in silence.

My day was ruined. I followed the two men mechanically but was hardly aware of the goings-on around me. My thoughts kept hovering around the young girl but I had no idea what to do about her situation. This was a girl who had been subjected to indignity and abuse at an age when she ought to have been in primary school. As if that was not enough, she had now been ostracised by her community and rejected by her own mother. What a life! What a fate! I was particularly saddened by the realisation that the man who had done this appeared to be about sixty. What would become of her and her unfortunate baby when he died? Where would she find compassion and support?

I woke up the next morning still feeling traumatised by the events of the previous day. I discussed the matter with Henry but he said he didn't think I was in a position to do anything about it. I told him I wanted to request to see the Igwe, to ask him what he and the elders of the community planned to do to save the poor girl, but he advised me to take my mind off the couple and concentrate on my national service. Perhaps he was right, I thought miserably, especially as I noticed that my mental faculties were beginning to be troubled. Finally, I managed to convince myself that I hadn't seen any odd couple, that it was all a bad dream and that I probably had malaria or typhoid. The next day was a Saturday. Henry and I had agreed to spend it looking up other corpers in the village. I was also expecting CY later that day so that we could spend the weekend together.

There were indications already that Henry and I would get on well. He hailed from the Igbo-speaking part of Bendel State and had studied agricultural economics at the University of Port Harcourt. He appeared easy-going, although not particularly voluble if playful enough to be interesting. He told me that I came across as an interesting person and that he, too, believed we would make great friends. I was happy. I told him. I also told him everything about CY and me. He said CY was lucky, which made me even happier. I thought I was the lucky one. The important thing was that CY and I thought we were both lucky to have found each other.

There was a knock on the door. It was Mr Nweke. As soon as we had exchanged pleasantries, he said that he had come to find out how we were settling down.

"We are doing very well, Mr Nweke, and we truly appreciate your friendship and comradeship," Henry said.

"Miss, Miss," Nweke hailed me, while at the same time raising his right hand to touch the tip of his right ear in mock salutation.

"Mr Nweke, the Great!" I responded, laughing,

"Ehn, ehn, you must stop reading those dangerous books o. You are a beautiful gal, I like ya colour and ya shape, uph."

He brought together all five fingers on his right hand and placed them on both lips in a cackle of amusement. Henry and I watched, grinning.

"Ehn, let me tell you people the purpose of my visit this morning. You remember I promised you yesterday that I would take you to other places."

"Yes, you did say so," Henry said.

"Yes, that's why I have come; I want to take you people to see your land."

"Land?" I asked, both surprised and confused.

"Yes, we give our corpers land to plant crops of their choice during their service year. You two will come with me now so that I will show you ya own land and you can start to clear it immediately."

"I don't need land to farm, Mr Nweke, I'm not a man," I said without preamble.

"What do you mean you are not a man? Who told you farming is only for men?"

"I don't need land because I won't farm," I persisted.

"Let's go and see the land, Anjola," Henry said in a conciliatory tone, giving me an encouraging smile.

"You need the land, Miss," Nweke insisted, and went ahead to explain why he believed I did as the three of us set off.

"You need the land. You are free to plant what you like on it. If you don't want to plant yam or even corn, you may, for instance, plant vegetables like ugwu, water leaf and other small things that will be of benefit to you," Nweke said.

I didn't understand what he was saying; I had never owned a farmland and no one had ever told me of the necessity for it. But Henry was enthusiastic, which amazed me. He was a youth corper, for goodness' sake. Could he have possibly forgotten? Yet here he was, engaging Nweke in a discussion on methods of cultivation and types of crops that yielded good harvests in the area. We soon got to the land, which was all covered with weeds. Mr Nweke happily pointed to where ours began and ended. We were to share it equally, he said, encouraging us to start the clearing as soon as possible in order to take advantage of what remained of the rains. What an odd world! I was now completely out of tune with what was going on. Was I supposed to become a farmer overnight? That was certainly not what I had envisioned. It must be some sort of joke, I thought miserably. Meanwhile, Henry and Nweke seemed to have noticed my sad countenance and started to tease me.

"Cheer up, Anjola, you are not a lazy corper, are you?" Henry said.

"Don't mind Miss, let her continue to pretend as if she has truly never farmed before," Nweke said.

"I have never farmed, Mr Nweke," I said, almost with hostility.

"You mean you never worked on ya mother's farm?"

"My mother doesn't own a farm. Women don't own farmlands where I come from. We only go to the farm to help the men harvest the crops. We don't even help them plant," I said, beginning to get hysterical.

"All right, but ya mother surely owns a garden, doesn't she?"

"Leave me alone, Mr Nweke, I don't know anything about farming," I cried, tears suddenly forming in my eyes.

"Very well then, women own their own farms here. They work as hard as the men. This is ya farmland; you are going to clear and cultivate it," Nweke said.

I shrugged and said nothing. Henry tried to encourage me. He told me it was magnanimous of the school authorities to have dedicated a portion of land for their corpers. I wasn't persuaded but I didn't want to prove difficult. In the end, I nodded in agreement. He suggested we cancel our earlier plan of visiting our fellow corpers. He wanted us to return to the farm after breakfast and start clearing it. I couldn't understand his eagerness but I decided against arguing with him. Mr Nweke, for his part, was happy. He said he would give us tools and promised to send them immediately.

After breakfast, I reluctantly followed Henry to begin the clearing. We worked till three in the afternoon before returning home for lunch. Henry suggested we work again the next day, which was Sunday, but I rejected the idea. CY came to the village later that day to spend the weekend as planned. I narrated to him all that had happened so far. He laughed at what he termed my laziness, confirming to me that women in eastern Nigeria worked as hard as their men.

"Women work hard in Kwara, too," I retorted.

He looked at me with amusement but I pretended not to notice.

"Let me tell you," I continued. "The only difference is

that women in Kwara channel their energies into other life endeavours. They are definitely not lazy."

"Hey, easy, see who is fighting an ethnic war," he said, cupping my lower jaw in his left palm and using his right hand to draw me close. I felt ashamed that I was already getting all worked up over such a trivial issue. I rested my head on his chest and allowed him to hold me tenderly.

"Every part of my body aches," I told him.

"It's because you are not used to manual labour," he whispered tenderly. I was grateful he had come. However, the following morning I couldn't get up from bed. It was as if my whole body had been thoroughly pounded and rendered immobile. CY attempted to lift me up but I simply couldn't stand and broke down in tears. Was I paralysed? Was I dying? This was a nightmare. I saw fear on CY's face. He told me to stop crying but I could see he was at the verge of breaking down himself. Henry ran to Mr Nweke's house to inform him. In no time he had arranged for the school bus to take me to the village health centre, where I ended up spending the rest of the weekend.

CHAPTER 10

When I returned to the school on Monday morning, I gave my own portion of the land to Henry to farm. No one said anything about it afterwards. I also wrote to Dr Agbebi, briefly describing my out-of-camp experience so far but, more importantly, letting him know my postal address so that he too could write to me. I found a friend in the music teacher. Her name was Adanma Nwazue. Although she was a few years older than me, I could regard her as my contemporary in many significant respects. She was single, carefree, bubbling with energy and as playful as I wanted in a friend. We started to 'gist' as if we had known each other all our lives. She told me about herself, her family and her dreams. I told her about mine as well and by the time we had spent an hour getting to know each other, our 'gist' veered into what both of us had been itching to talk about.

"Do you have a boyfriend?" she asked, eyes twinkling mischievously.

"Yes o, I do," I answered happily and told her about CY. She expressed reservations about my preference for a fellow corper, arguing that I ought to have taken my time to find a more mature guy who would take me more seriously.

"Anyway, if he likes you as much as you say he does, nothing can change the feelings you have for each other," she added a little doubtfully.

I told her she was wrong about her assumption of immaturity concerning CY. I went on and on telling her how wonderful he had been to me and how fond we were of each other. She warmed up to my story after a while and went on to tell me about her own boyfriend.

"Nduka is a wonderful man," she quipped.

"Really? He must be taking good care of you," I said, impressed.

"Oh yes, Nduka is a fantastic lover. I'm so lucky to have found a man like him."

"I'm green with envy," I said with a laugh, feeling genuinely happy for her.

"You know what, Anjola?"

"What?"

"I want you to meet him."

"That will be great, where is he?"

"He works with a manufacturing company in Obodo Nna. It's just twenty kilometres from here. We can visit him after school tomorrow."

We did so the next day. She had insisted that we not have our lunch before leaving; assuring me that Nduka would spoil us with the kind of food we would never have been able to afford. Even when I was thirsty and wanted to buy a soft drink as we waited for our bus to fill up she refused to let me, emphasising that doing so would amount to a waste of money.

"You don't know what you are going to enjoy today. Just relax and bear whatever inconvenience there is for now. Na me dey tell you something."

"OK, now, I gree your own," I said, dismissing the hawker.

Nduka received us warmly, as she had said he would. He looked fortyish, tall, light-skinned and handsome. I liked his sideburns: classy and elitist. I was a little surprised that he was still a bachelor at his age. Well, I hoped he would soon propose marriage to my friend. He moved briskly to raise the window blinds in his sitting room, ostensibly to allow more fresh air into the room even as he repeatedly said welcome to us. Adanma started the introductions immediately.

"Anjola, this is Nduka, the man in my life. You have heard a lot about him already."

"Yes, indeed," I said. "Thanks for taking good care of my friend."

"Nduka, this is my friend, Anjola. She is a corper newly posted to our school."

"You are welcome, Anjola. I can see the two of you have hit it off. This is very good. Are you familiar with the east?" he asked, taking a seat directly opposite me.

"Not at all, it's actually my first time here."

"You mean it's your very first time in this part of the country? You've never been to the east since you were born?"

"No, I have never been here."

"Ehn, hen, this NYSC is good o. So, if not for NYSC, you may never come to the east. Where are you from?"

"Kwara."

"Oh, I see, you are Hausa," he stated flatly.

Oh no, not again. I mumbled under my breath, but to him, I said: "I'm not Hausa. I'm Yoruba."

"Ha-ha, you are Hausa now, from Kwara, no be so?" he asked.

I smiled but shook my head firmly. "I'm from Kwara but Yoruba, not Hausa," I said softly.

"What are you trying to say? You can't be Yoruba if you are from Kwara now." His eyes twinkled amusingly.

"Well, I'm from Kwara and I'm Yoruba." I said calmly.

"You must be kidding. Kwara is in the north, everybody knows that," he insisted.

"I don't dispute that Kwara is in the north, but what I'm saying is that my ethnic group is Yoruba, not Hausa. I don't speak Hausa. I don't understand a word of Hausa language. My name is Anjola Adeniyi, a Yoruba name."

"You don't make sense to me, young woman. If you are

from Kwara then you are Hausa," he said, picking his words carefully; and added: "I don't think it is right for you to try to be an impostor. It's not good at all." Disapproval was evident on his face. He amazed me.

"I'm not trying to be anything, Mr Nduka. I think you should try to understand me. I'm merely making a statement of fact," I said as softly and calmly as I could but there was anger in his eyes.

"What statement of fact? It's funny, isn't it? I was actually going to accord you some respect because I liked your personality. What a pity." He now spoke with a raised voice and was acting rude.

"You are embarrassing me. You are not being fair to me at all." I said for want of anything better to say. Frankly, I didn't know the appropriate response to give him.

"You asked for it. I don't like people who tell wicked lies about their ancestry. You might as well tell me that a man from Nnewi is not Igbo," he said, eyes flashing; then, turning to Adanma: "You must be careful how you choose your friends. You have no business being friends with people who have no integrity. You shouldn't associate yourself with people who are ashamed of their roots."

I sat there dumbly.

He rose to his feet and made for the refrigerator. I shot Adanma a questioning look. Using her eyes, she pleaded with me to remain calm. Nduka brought out a bottle of Fanta and started drinking. He looked visibly angry. My forehead was now dripping with sweat. I felt queasy. I brought out a handkerchief from my bag and began dabbing my forehead and cheeks. Nduka was yet to offer us a drink. I suddenly became aware that my blouse was soaked and was clinging to my body. I became infuriated. I was boiling with rage now. Why should I stay silent while a total stranger cast aspersions on my character? Come to think of it, this was the third time I was being taken up on the same issue. What was going on? It seemed clear to me now that there was a problem, a misunderstanding, perhaps a misrepresentation. I took a deep breath to calm myself as I prepared to explain the status of my state.

"Have you ever visited Kwara?" I asked softly.

"No, but did you have to visit the east to know that the people there are Igbo? Don't insult my intelligence, young woman. I'm not your mate."

"Why not give me a chance, Mr Nduka? I just want to explain certain things to you."

Adanma said something to him in Igbo which made him calm down a little. I cleared my throat and began to speak.

"There are different ethnic groups in Kwara, including the Bororos, Yorubas, Nupes and Barubas but no Hausa-speaking indigenes. For instance, news broadcasts are read in the major indigenous languages in the state, apart from English, but Hausa language is not one of them. However, probably due to the proximity of the state to the north, many indigenes have acquired proficiency in Hausa language. However, you will agree with me that you would not claim to be a Yoruba man because you found yourself in Lagos and learnt to speak Yoruba. I am aware that a common source of ignorance about the ethnic composition of Kwara is that it is in the north. What is important is that citizens of the state are of different ethnic groups but the dominant one is Yoruba. You don't have to believe me. Do your own research."

I smiled broadly. I thought I had given a brilliant presentation which would have erased all doubt in his mind. I was wrong.

"You are nothing but a pathetic liar, Anjola, or whatever you call yourself and you should be ashamed," Nduka thundered. I opened my mouth in astonishment. I was still wondering how to react when I saw him turn his attention to Adanma and begin yelling at the top of his voice:

"You really need to watch out for the company you keep. Do you understand? I'm a man and I can tell you that only bastards get confused about their roots."

I was a bastard? This was the limit. Unrestrained anger

welled up inside me but, again, I struggled not to give vent to it. I was an ambassador for my state, I tried to counsel myself. It was an opportunity to set the record straight. No, I wasn't going to allow myself to get angry. Doing so would serve no useful purpose.

"Why should I lie about where I come from?" I asked with a forced smile.

"That's precisely what you should be telling me, Miss fake Yoruba girl. You gave yourself a fancy Yoruba name because you imagine you are smart." His voice rose with each word. I opened my mouth to say something but he held up his hand and resumed talking.

"Look, I know people play pranks and behave foolishly, especially when they are young, but it's sacrilegious for anyone to deny their roots. What you are doing amounts to cursing yourself. You don't have my sympathy."

I realised it would be a waste of time and energy trying to explain anything to him. He was basking in contented ignorance.

"It's a pity, Mr Nduka. You are absolutely blind; your ignorance makes you utterly blind. Who do you think you are? What do you know about Kwara? What do you know about me and my people? Nothing, but you act like one who knows it all. Now, who should be pitied?"

I allowed myself a prolonged, contemptuous hiss and rose to my feet. I had had enough. I was already at the door when Adanma tried to call me back.

"Anjola, come back. This is a minor issue."

I ignored her. I didn't know how to find my way back to the school. I went down the street, half-walking, half-running. What a day! What an impossible fellow! How on Earth did Adanma come to regard him as a wonderful man? What could be wonderful about a man who was so self-opinionated that he didn't think he could be wrong about anything? I increased my pace and soon began to sweat. I needed to walk in order to clear my head.

"Anjola, Anjola, wait for me," Adanma called after me but I refused to stop or even look back. It wasn't as if I blamed her but I didn't see how we could cope together in the prevailing circumstance. She caught up with me and held me by the shoulders, forcing me to a halt.

"I'm sorry for everything, do," she said.

"You don't have to be sorry for anything and you know it. You've done nothing wrong."

"You are not going anywhere; you are coming back with me. I don't even know what you people are arguing about. Come on, let's go and enjoy ourselves."

"Then it's my turn to be sorry because I'm not going back with you. Go and enjoy with him. He is your boyfriend, not mine."

I freed myself from her grip and resumed walking, this time less agitated. Adamma fell in beside me. I asked for directions on how to get back to the school but she refused to tell me. She said she had brought me out and it was her responsibility to take me back.

In the event, our afternoon was ruined but not our friendship. If anything, we bonded more and soon became inseparable. One Friday afternoon, as we were preparing to leave the school, she said:

"Anjola, I would have loved to invite you to my church this Sunday if not that you are a Muslim."

"What makes you think I'm a Muslim? I don't remember telling you my religion."

"Ah ha, you are from Kwara now. Everybody from Kwara is a Muslim."

"You amuse me, Adanma. Yes, Islam is the dominant religion but many full-fledged indigenes are Christians. In my town, the Evangelical Church of West Africa, the Baptist Church and the Seventh Day Adventist Mission had all taken firm root long before I was born."

"Is that so? Are you a Christian or Muslim?"

"You don't need to know my religious inclination to invite me to your church. I'm used to accompanying both Muslim and Christian relatives and friends to their places of worship. That's the way in my place."

"Na wa o. I'm truly sorry, Anjola."

"You don't have to be sorry, Adanma. I just told you what you didn't know."

"Would you come to church with me this Sunday, then?"

"I'm warming up already. Where do you worship?"

"I'm a Catholic. Come and celebrate Mass with us and you would be glad you did."

"Sure, why not?"

I went to church with her that Sunday. I enjoyed the brevity and near-solemnity of the service and the dexterity of the young, immaculately dressed seminarians who sang heartily and guided parishioners to the Altar when it was time for Holy Communion. Before long, I became a regular face although it didn't curb my restlessness. I wanted 'real' fun. I decided to teach myself how to ride a bicycle. Although Ify had promised to coach me, he was obviously unavailable. I spoke to one of the male teachers whom I had observed was very friendly. He said we could start practising as soon as I was ready. I told him I was ready any day. He explained that bicycles were available for rent at the Market Square and that he would pick the bill. I was ecstatic. I hadn't expected him to be so generous.

"It is easy," he began on our first day. "You place your hands on the neck of the bike. Put your left leg on the lower side of the pedal and the right on the upper part. Press the pedal with your right leg and as soon as you do this, the left leg will respond automatically and the bike will move," he said, making it sound easy. He continued:

"Now, how do you bring the bike to a halt? There are two brakes attached to either side of the neck. The right brake is used to reduce speed but to stop you have to press the two brakes at once. We can now go into practical bike riding," he concluded.

I clapped with excitement. He lowered the bicycle and told me to mount, which I did with trepidation.

"One thing you have to guard against is fear," he said seriously.

I nodded doubtfully. He mounted behind me, placing his strong hands on mine and taking me through the rudiments of bicycle riding. I was thrilled. We did several trips round the football field before he told me it was time for him to return the bicycle but that we would continue our practice the next day. I thanked him and went to Adanma's house to 'gist' her before returning to the 'Corpers' Lodge', where I regaled Henry with tales of my exploits. He laughed loudly and encouraged me to continue. I left school as soon as the bell sounded for closing the next day; eager to resume my lesson. I got to my room and quickly made lunch. I had just finished eating and was lying on my bed, trying to take a brief nap, when my instructor knocked on my door. I was pleasantly surprised at his enthusiasm.

"You are a wonderful person, Mr Nnamdi," I said.

"It's the least I can do to make our dear corper happy," he teased. I laughed. He had gone ahead to rent the bicycle. Surprisingly, however, we hadn't practised for more than a few minutes when he suddenly brought the bicycle to a stop.

"Is there any problem?" I asked.

"No, there is no problem. It's just that there is something I have been meaning to tell you."

"Go on, I'm all ears," I said.

"You know, Miss," he began. "I don't really know how to say this but you know now."

"I'm sorry, I don't understand."

"What I mean is, ehn, you be my type."

"I be your type? What does that mean?" I asked, genuinely puzzled. I had no clue whatsoever what he was trying to say. I urged him to make himself clearer but he appeared to have developed cold feet.

"I mean that you are my type of woman. I like you," he

blurted out.

I burst into derisive laughter before asking him if that was why he had agreed to coach me.

"Well, it was not the only reason but it was part of it."

"I see. You had better save your time and money because this lady here no be your type at all, Mr Nnamdi." I let out a long, contemptuous hiss before walking away..

"No vex, Miss. Come, make we continue."

I turned back and walked toward him.

"Pardon my manners." I said. "I ought to have thanked you for your time and money. However, I'm sorry, I won't continue since it's clear now that the kind of reward you want for your effort is one I can't give. Besides, I think I have learned enough. I'm sure I can ride on my own now."

He stared at me as if he hadn't quite anticipated my reaction. Why was he acting surprised? I wondered as I walked away.

"I'm sorry. Come back and let's continue."

"I no be your type o."

"I said I'm sorry, OK? It was a mistake. Just come back."

"I no be your type o, yeye man."

"Come now, Miss. Na so you dey vex?"

"Go find your type o."

CHAPTER 11

The next day, I went to where bicycles were on display for rent and paid for an hour. I didn't try to mount it immediately. Instead, I wheeled it along the road as I searched for a convenient place. My heart was beating hard but I was determined to become my own instructor. Just then, I sighted two male students from one of the private secondary schools. They appeared to be talking about me as they looked at me intermittently and pointed in my direction. I kept walking with my bicycle and wondering whether it would make sense for me to call them and ask for assistance. One of them crossed the road and came toward me. I slowed down my pace, relieved that I was about to get some help.

"I want to tell you that there are two types of love. There is natural love and there is artificial love. You see, I want to give you the natural love, if you understand what I mean."

He recited the line in a rush, as if he was afraid he might forget some of the words. I could almost hear his heart beating. I would have been thoroughly entertained if I hadn't had enough problems of my own. As he stood there, waiting for my response, I could only gaze at him. When it became obvious that he had no more to say, I began walking away, still dragging my bicycle along.

"Okay, expect a letter from me later today," he shouted. I didn't look back. I soon got to a part of the road with a slight slope and made a brave attempt at climbing my bicycle. I did it successfully and, just like a dream, was gliding down the tarred road. I smiled as I saluted my courage. I, Anjola Adeniyi, was riding a bicycle in Anambra State. What an achievement! I would never have thought I could do it. Then, all of a sudden, a lorry approached from the opposite direction. Although there was no chance of it hitting me, its sheer size and speed intimidated me. I didn't know when I started yelling: Mogbe o! Egbami o! Mo daran o! Mo ku o! Ye! Ah! Eh! Temi bami o! No one appeared to notice me until I crashed by the side of the road. There was a spontaneous rush of people toward me now. Nne, sorry o. Ndo. Are you hurt? Are you okay? They were all talking simultaneously but shame and embarrassment prevented me from responding. I nodded courteously as they brought me to my feet and dusted my dress. I dragged the bicycle back to where I had rented it.

"But the time never reach for you to carry am come back now," the man said, looking surprised.

"I know, I be wan rush go somewhere before. I come forget but as I remember now, na im I say make I go come," I lied.

"You for go where you wan go with am now," he pursued.

I smiled sheepishly, not knowing what fresh lie to tell. I made my way quietly back to school, warning myself to desist from further dangerous adventures. From then on, I concentrated on teaching my students and making friends among them. The girls and the younger boys called me 'Miss' while most of the older boys addressed me by my first name, apparently convinced that I was their contemporary. They also spoiled me with gifts - mostly fruits - and paid me unsolicited visits. I didn't discourage them. We shared information about our respective states. They told me a lot about the Igbos and I told them about the Yorubas. They and Henry and Adamma became my regular companions in the village as CY's visit gradually became infrequent. I never saw Mr. Nduka again because he and Adanma ended their relationship shortly after our visit.

One evening, I was taking a walk around the school

compound when I passed through the house of one of the teachers. His name was Onuorah. He taught history and was generally regarded as a friendly person. He enjoyed chatting and believed he had had a lot of experience, which he was eager to share. He looked like a happy man and had a positive disposition toward other members of staff, including Henry and me. I greeted him and he responded warmly, asking me where I was going. I said I wasn't going anywhere in particular.

"I'm just taking a walk to enjoy the cool evening breeze," I told him.

"That is very good. In that case, why not come and sit with me for a while so that I can entertain you with fresh palmy?"

I enjoyed drinking palm wine, which I discovered to be in abundance in eastern Nigeria. Henry and I frequently bought some and it was always delightful. Onuorah called out to his wife to bring a chair for 'corper.' She came out immediately and we exchanged pleasantries. His six-year-old daughter emerged from the apartment and sat on her father's lap.

"She looks so much like you," I said for want of anything better to say but my observation appeared to mean a great deal more than an idle comment. He smiled broadly, drawing the little girl closer to himself as if he had suddenly been struck by a sense of foreboding. I smiled in amusement.

"My son looks like me, too," he said, eyes glinting with pride.

"Oh, you have a son?"

"Yes, I have a three-year-old son but he is sleeping now; otherwise, I would have asked his mother to bring him."

"You are a fulfilled man, Mr Onuorah, and I'm truly happy for you." I said good-naturedly.

"Thank you, my sister. But, you know, all these things that make us happy do so only while we are here on this earth."

"I don't understand you."

"I mean that we feel fulfilled looking at our children and marvelling at what precious gifts they are. The joy we feel tends to suggest that our children will go on being our heritage even after we have died. In reality, the benefit, so to say, does not go an inch further. As soon as we depart this world, it no longer matters whether or not we have children. Every achievement of ours, including our children, will no longer be relevant. That is why we must permit ourselves as much happiness as we can while we are alive and prepare our minds for the revelation that having or not having children means nothing once we bid the world farewell." He said all this in a careful, subdued voice.

"You are very perceptive, Mr Onuorah," I said, again for want of anything better to say. Then I started searching for nicer words to describe him but he suddenly exclaimed dramatically:

"Oh yes! That's right!"

"What's that, Mr Onuorah?" I asked, startled.

"A car has just driven in there at full speed," he said, pointing to a nearby bush.

"A car just drove into a bush? How can a car drive into a bush? Besides, I didn't see any car and I'm here with you."

"That's because you don't have the third eye."

"Third eye?" I said, confused. "What's a third eye?"

"That is the power to discern, to see what ordinary mortals can't see," he said.

I stared at him blankly.

"Let me tell you a story to help you understand. One day, I went to Onitsha market with my wife. Markets are full of all kinds of creations; but only people with the third eye can recognise them for what they truly are. Did you know that markets are not only patronised by human beings? Are you aware that spirits and other kinds of creatures also patronise them?" he asked excitedly, obviously enjoying my discomfort.

I said nothing. I felt like leaving but I didn't know how he would react. What was my business with spirits and strange creatures? I summoned the courage to cut him short.

"I think it's getting late and I still want to go for a walk," I said.

"No, corper, there is still time. Besides, you have to let me finish my story. So, as I was saying, my wife and I were busy shopping when I noticed a spirit walking toward us. You know, my wife could not see him because she doesn't have the third eye. This spirit was coming toward us. He was walking on his head, of course, because, you know, spirits don't walk like human beings. He had his legs up, his head to the ground, looking fearsome and was coming toward us. He was focusing directly on my wife. Somehow, I suspected what it was planning to do. Can you imagine? The spirit was targeting her breast! He wanted to touch my wife's breast and probably fondle it. God forbid! How could I allow anyone play with her breast - even if it was a spirit? That would have amounted to a slap on my face. I decided to act fast. Do you know what I did?"

"No, Mr Onuorah," I said, terrified and now sitting on the edge of my chair.

"Ah, I positioned my hand near my wife's breast, the very breast the spirit wanted to touch, and waited with full concentration. As the spirit's hand was about to touch it, I hit it with all my strength and sent him staggering away. I can tell you something, though. Spirits are powerful in their own strange way. Before I got home that day, my hand was so badly swollen that it took the village dibia to heal it. But I was proud I hadn't allowed the spirit to fondle my wife's breast. That was how to be a real man."

"Well done, Mr Onuorah. I want to go now," I said, rising to my feet.

"Corper, corper, I don't think you enjoyed my story."

"I did. It's just that it scared me," I said.

"Don't be scared. By the way, what's this I'm hearing about your leader?"

"Who's leader?"

"I mean the leader of the Yorubas, Obafemi Awolowo."

"What about him?"

"I hear he is sick. The news is everywhere that he is no longer strong."

"I don't know anything about him," I confessed. He released a short, high laugh.

"You don't know about your country's history? You don't know how Nigeria got her independence and those who fought for it? You are not aware that Obafemi Awolowo is to the Yorubas what Nnamdi Azikiwe is to the Igbos?" he asked, his eyes fixed on me so that I couldn't look away

"Oh, you are talking about Nigeria's nationalists?"

"I'm saying that my own great Zik is still strong, kakaraka," he bragged, eyes twinkling with amusement.

"It gives you pleasure, doesn't it? Congratulations!" I said, eager to leave the topic.

"Ntorrr, Anjola."

He threw his head back and cackled.

"Nttorr, to me, why? Wetin I do you now?" I asked, beaming.

"Ha, ha, ha, this one is ignorant o. How old are you?"

"Twenty-one. Why did you ask?"

"Ha, ha, ha, no wonder. I have been talking to a baby. Go, you no go know."

"Good night, Mr Onuorah," I said and walked rapidly away. I had lost interest in my planned walk. It was actually getting dark and, with Onuorah's talk about spirits driving cars and fondling breasts, I thought it was better to return to my room.

Henry handed a letter to me when I got back. He said a student had brought it. It turned out to be from my 'lover boy.' I was intrigued that he actually wrote as promised. I tore the envelope open and began to read:

Dear Sweetie,
Ditto...
Time and ability plus double capacity have forced my pen to dance automatically on this benedicted sheet of paper. I hope you're swimming in the wonderful pool of Mr. Health over there, if so, doxology! I'm also perambulating in the cool breeze of wellness here. Sweetie Pie, the reason why this miraculous

thing is happening is because, honey, I love you spontaneously, and, as I stand horizontally parallel to the wall, and vertically perpendicular to the ground now, I only think of you. Since you're a fantastic and fabulous girl, put together as fantabulous, I implore you to decipher this anthem of love oozing out from the innermost pendulum of my thoraxial cavity. Darling, please stop haranguing with the feelings in my heart because I love you more than a snake loves rat. Believe me; I start each day by dreaming of you. Each time I see you, my metabolism suddenly halts and my peristalsis goes in reverse gear. My medulla oblongata also ceases functioning.

Crazy, crazy, crazy, you may say, but this is verily veritable. If only you knew what is going on in my encephalon, you would prostrate. That's why I need to see you vis-à-vis soon for a better elucidation through tête-à-tête. No hyperbole and onomatopoeia, simple candidness. Only you and I are protagonists in this subtle affair. As I cogitate and ruminate over your beauty the last time I saw you, I genuflect before the Omnipotent and implore Him to let this affair emulsify. By the way, I was bamboozled, scintillated, exhilarated, and left in a state of prolonged euphoria by your ravishing beauty which was quite edifying and exalting. It left my bio-chemistry in paradise-like equilibrium.

Empirically speaking, I love you chemically. I don't ever want to see gloom and doom looming over your angelic live portrait. Let my appellation be scribbled across your heart, with indelible ink. If any boy tries to ask for your companionship, tell him that you are leased and caveated.

I think I have to pen off here, because I still haven't finished studying electrolysis polymerisation. But before I evaporate, I like to revitalise your memory with those encapsulating lyrics which proclaim that your catarrh is my butter, your piss is my mimbo, the world's greatest lover is me. Catch you later, sleep tight and don't let those bed bugs bite you because you are too sweet for them.

Goodbye for now,

Yours in love,
Your pillow, your cushion,
Chukwudi Wonder.

I burst into laughter. "Oh my God!" Well, the fear of spirits deserted me. Meanwhile, the time was fast approaching for the final-year students to sit for their West African School Certificate examination. Some of them had requested me to give them additional coaching in English, which I gladly obliged. I also gave them assignments to test their competence in such areas as letter-writing, comprehension, essay-writing and summaries. I found it particularly amusing that, each time I gave them an assignment on letter-writing, especially formal letters, some would copy a famous author, S.M.O Aka, and would present it to me as theirs. I would laugh heartily before explaining that the worst mistake a student could make was to copy from textbooks - or anywhere else for that matter. Chances were that the teacher would have also read the same material.

"I also read S.M.O. Aka for my WASC," I would tell them amidst laughter and explain that textbooks were there to serve as a guide only. It didn't come as a surprise, therefore, when three final-year students showed up at my door that afternoon. I thought they had come to request for extra lessons. They bore more fruits than usual: oranges, pineapples, watermelon, as well as a small gourd of palm wine. I was happy. I knew they appreciated me. I also knew that, besides being their teacher, they seemed greatly enamoured by my personality and carriage, hence the affectionate nicknames. I was enjoying my service year and truly serving my motherland. However, unknown to me, they had come on an entirely different mission.

"We want you to cooperate with us, Anjola," one of them started without preamble. He spoke with such seriousness that it almost sounded like an order. I was taken aback but decided not to make an issue of it.

"How?" I asked coolly.

"The day we are going to write the English exam, you will stand outside the hall by the window. One of us, who will sit close to the window, will pass the question paper to you. You will come to your room here and answer the questions. You will then come back to the same window and hand it over to the same person. That's all."

"Really? How very simple!" I remarked sarcastically but they didn't seem to get my drift.

"That is just all; it's very simple," the same boy said with relish.

"That's all right but you know how far Kwara is from Anambra, don't you?" I asked. They looked confused. "Now, tell me, if I'm locked up here who amongst you will bail me?" I added calmly.

"Who would lock you up?" the same boy asked.

"If I am arrested for aiding exam malpractice and put in prison, how will my relations back home know my whereabouts?"

"Which one you dey now? Na today? You want tell us say you never do this kin' tin before?"

"I have never done it before and I don't know how to do it, OK?" I said honestly.

"Guys, make we go bo, e be like say na pretence this one dey so," he told his friends.

I called them back and gestured to the fruits. They took them quietly as one of them said: "Na like this you come spoil yourself, ehn? We think say you be correct person. See as you spoil yourself for nothing."

I closed my door gently and went to lie on my bed. Moments later, Mr Nweke brought a letter for me. He said it arrived after I left school. It was from my former supervisor, Dr Agbebi.

Dear Anjola,

How are you and how is the national service coming on? I am hopeful you are doing well and have since put the unpleasant experience of the stolen jewellery behind you. I thank you for notifying me of your postal address; I hope you will do the same when the service year ends and your address changes again. This is very important to enable us stay in touch especially in view of recent development from my end. Oh yes, Anjola, I have been at the receiving end of human treachery of late. It sounds curious, doesn't it? Well, let me save you from undue suspense.

A few months ago, I received a car loan and proceeded immediately to purchase a 504 salon car (SR Model). Everyone around me, in and outside the university community, congratulated and rejoiced with me. They seemed genuinely pleased with what many of them mouthed as my progress. How could I have known I had unwittingly attracted the envy of some of them? Perhaps, they merely wanted to punish me especially knowing I couldn't have afforded the car without a loan and that it would take years to offset. Anyway, two weeks later, I came to the office and placed my car key on my desk as had become usual with me. Moments later, I stepped into the HOD's office to have a word with him only to return less than fifteen minutes later to discover that my car key had vanished. First, I thought I had misplaced it, so, I searched elsewhere and everywhere. The key was nowhere to be found. Then, I thought I might have forgotten to remove it from the ignition. I dashed to the car park, and that was where reality hit me like thunderbolt. My car had disappeared into thin air, driven away by someone who must have come stealthily into my office and picked its key! Of course the police were alerted immediately, but even as I write this, they have neither succeeded in tracing it nor have a clue about its whereabouts.

I have applied for my sabbatical leave and have made arrangement to spend it in the United States of America. When I leave, I do not intend to return to Nigeria; I will take up a permanent appointment in an American university and I have made plans to relocate my family as well. I will be spending the rest of my life in America where, I hope, I can at least be me, Christopher Agbebi.

Now, enough of stories about me; write and give news of yourself but whatever you do, be safe and look after yourself.

Your friend,

Dr Christopher Agbebi.

I folded the letter and stared unseeingly about the room. Thinking about what happened to Dr Agbebi brought heaviness to my heart and made it feel like a lump of lead in my chest. I sighed.

CHAPTER 12

The service year was fast coming to an end. Mr Nweke and the other teachers continued to support Henry and me. Nweke was a frequent visitor. Sometimes he came alone just to 'gist.' At such times, we would sit together for long hours talking about anything and everything that caught our interest. At other times, he would come with a strange man and launch into a long tale about how he had told the man about my extraordinary beauty and how the man had insisted on meeting me with a view to becoming friends with me. The man would smile and nod his head vigorously as Nweke spoke and there would be a lot of drama. However, I took a decision from the beginning not to have anything to do with anybody Mr Nweke brought to me. I resolved to treat every man that accompanied him with distant politeness. Mr Nweke seemed determined to get me a boyfriend. He cajoled, teased and even mocked me but I remained adamant. When CY was visiting me regularly, he would make fun of me for going out with an ordinary corper instead of rich business men. When CY's visit became irregular, he admonished me to grow up and be realistic. He said he had always known that my relationship with CY would not last more than a few weeks. He was just a young man in search of fun. I always replied that I was equally a young woman in search of adventure.

"What kind of girl are you?" he would ask me. "You don't want to enjoy your youth? You need men who can give you what you need and deserve. You won't remain young and beautiful forever, do you know that?"

"I know, Mr Nweke, but I don't like any of the men you bring to my doorstep. I really do want to have fun but not with the old men you bring."

"That is the point, Miss. That is what I have been trying to explain to you but you still don't understand."

"What don't I understand?"

"You don't have to like a man to sleep with him. Just let yaself go, OK? For instance, you can be plaiting ya hair when he is doing it."

"You are kidding me, right?"

"Of course I'm serious."

"I can be plaiting my hair when a man is making love to me? I'm sure I can even be watching television while he is at it."

"Now you are the one who is not serious."

"OK, seriously speaking, what's fun about the picture you just painted?"

"That is what I'm saying, you try it and see. I just want to help you."

"Well, it's just like you to say something like that but I don't need that kind of help."

We would go on and on arguing about the propriety or otherwise of having unmitigated fun to celebrate one's youthfulness and what constituted enjoyment. Although we never got tired of arguing; neither of us ever got angry. And he never stopped bringing men to me, none of whom I agreed to date. I knew he thought me conservative and foolish but I didn't care. There was something about his judgement that left me free and he himself was not hurt or diminished in any way by my attitude although he would point it out from time to time.

The service year was finally drawing to a close. Some of us who felt we were having the fun of our lives openly expressed our unhappiness at what we regarded as the brevity of the programme. That particular service year had run too fast, we complained. We felt sad when we realised that, all too soon, we would be holding the passing-out parade, after which we would return to our respective states. However, not all of us seemed to be having a great time. Some were anxious for the programme to end. They complained about everything from their places of assignment to the people they had to interact with. CY was one of those despite his good fortune to be serving in Enugu. He said the arrangements made for them at the state secretariat were shoddy. He told me how things were better organised in Imo, his home state. He also claimed that Anambra people were not as hospitable as his own. I couldn't understand him and I told him so as often as he brought it up.

"What's the difference between Anambra and Imo?" I challenged him one day, tired of his incessant complaints.

"You will never understand," he said angrily.

"I will never understand because you know there is no difference. Both states comprise Igbo-speaking people, the same people with the same history."

"God forbid!" he retorted sharply. "It is only ignorant people like you who could make such a baseless comparison. The Imo people are far more elevated; they are superior in every respect. But, as I have said, I don't expect you to know." He was boiling with rage. I was bewildered.

"Like hell I won't," I shouted and walked away.

Anyway, the service year was coming to an end. All of us posted to Obodonwayin got together to brainstorm on one last activity to make it memorable. In the end, we came up with organising a tour of all the eastern states, which we took to comprise Anambra, Imo, Cross River and Rivers. Many openly admitted having never visited the east prior to their posting; others expressed doubt about the likelihood of having the privilege to visit the east again. The few shirkers were bullied into agreeing with the majority. We took permission to be away from our respective schools for one week and set off to actualise our plan.

The tour was more exciting than we had anticipated. In each state we visited, we went straight to the NYSC secretariat, where we collected the addresses of corps members in some previously determined organisations and secondary schools. We then went in search of them. They instantly became our hosts. They showed us around and shared their experiences. One particular corps member was especially happy when he discovered that Henry hailed from the Igbo-speaking part of Bendel State. He said there was something that had been bothering him, a kind of mystery he had been trying to unravel. He had taken an interest in one of the girls in the secondary school where he was serving and had invited her over to his apartment. The girl readily obliged and their understanding grew to the extent that she consented to share his bed. But what always baffled him was that, midway into their sexual session, which he believed the girl was enjoying judging by her performance; she would shout "Chere! Chere! Chere! According to him, this excited him further. He intensified his efforts to impress her. But what baffled him was that, instead of louder cries, he received a deafening slap. The next thing the girl was hurrying into her dress. What had he done wrong? What was the meaning of chere? He wanted Henry to tell him, especially since the girl had refused to talk to him ever since and he had not been able to summon the courage to ask around. By this time, Henry was rolling on the floor with laughter. Without knowing the reason, the rest of us were laughing along with him. Finally, Henry brought out a handkerchief and wiped his face. We all kept quiet now, waiting for him to speak as if our lives depended on it.

Chere means 'stop', he told his bemused audience, and we all broke into a fresh round of laughter. "You see, you must have been hurting her. What you assumed to be ecstasy was actually a cry of pain."

Henry then advised him to make another attempt to speak with her; an effort, he warned, that should not be aimed at getting her back into his bed but at apologising and genuinely seeking her forgiveness. We all supported him, especially as the service year was about to end. At the conclusion of our tour, we all agreed that it had been a worthwhile undertaking and congratulated ourselves accordingly.

Two days after I got back, Ify showed up. I had never been so glad to see him and bask in his energy and laughter. He told me he had taken part of his annual leave because he had an important project to execute in the east. Was he building a house? I asked, surprised at the possibility that he might have made sufficient money in less than one year.

"What I have come to build will last much longer than a house," he told me enthusiastically. My curiosity was further aroused.

"OK, Mr Dramatic, you have succeeded in what you set out to do, which is to make me anxious to know what is so important that you have to take part of your annual leave. Would you be out with it now?"

"Don't be too eager," he warned playfully. He took my hand and led me to where I had my soup pot; He gestured for me to open it.

"Who cares about what you are about to build?" I said in mock anger. I opened the pot to show him it was empty.

"By the way, is it true?" I asked, changing the subject.

"What?"

"Is it true that the Igbo people in Imo are better than those in Anambra? That they are more hospitable, better organised and generally more elevated?"

"Who in heaven's name has been feeding you with such wicked lies?"

"Wouldn't it be more useful if you answered the question?"

"Of course, it's a blatant lie and you know it. Haven't you been in Anambra all this while?"

"Yes, I have, but I haven't been in Imo to compare. Perhaps the Imo people are truly superior."

"Look, let me tell you. The Anambra Igbos are not just good, they are far better than the Imo Igbos. The Anambra people are the genuine and authentic Igbos. Besides, look around you, nearly every great Igbo person in this country is from Anambra – Nnamdi Azikiwe, Chinua Achebe, Odumegwu Ojukwu, Emeka Anyaoku; the list is long. You have spent close to one year in Anambra and you have tasted their hospitality. What further proof do you need?"

I was disappointed by his answer. A sigh of regret escaped me. I held my head in my hands.

"Well, I have been in Anambra for close to a year and have had the good fortune of interacting with people from both, all of whom have shown that they possess incredible humanity. All Igbos look genuine and authentic to me and it doesn't seem as if one state is superior or inferior to the other," I said, smiling lightly.

"Don't allow anybody to poison your mind, Anjola. That is my point because it's the last thing we need now."

"We? What are you talking about?"

"I am talking about why I have taken part of my annual leave and travelled all the way down from Kano to see you. I'm talking about us and the long-lasting relationship we are about to start building."

I gulped. Was he kidding me?

"You've been drinking, Ify, and it's obviously not good for you because it's making you say things you wouldn't have said if you were clear-headed," I accused.

"I haven't touched alcohol in weeks."

"Then try and make sense to me. I don't understand you."

"That is what I'm telling you."

"What are you telling me?"

"I want to marry you. I want you to be my wife. I want you to give me the privilege to love and cherish you for my entire life," he said, looking inquiringly at me.

"You are kidding me," I said in a disbelieving voice.

"Do I look like a jester to you?" he said in a tone that made his eyes sparkle.

"No, you don't look like a jester but you are acting like one. You certainly can't be serious."

"What makes you so sure that I'm not serious even when I insist that I am?"

"Well, what are you going to tell your people?"

"Tell them about what?"

"How would you justify the decision to go as far as Kwara to pick a wife when there are pretty, well-behaved spinsters all around you?"

"That's my worry. Why don't you leave me to sort out things my own way?"

"I'm your friend. I should show concern."

"Thanks, but I can deal with it. It's my life."

"Well, I expect you to know that I can't possibly agree to marry you."

"I see. Why did you have to make it appear as if getting my family's approval was the only problem we would have to contend with?" he said, somewhat peevishly.

"I can foretell the reaction of your people the same way I can predict my family's reaction."

"Would your parents object to your marrying an Igbo man?"

"Object? That's putting it mildly. They would disown me for life." I paused to collect my thoughts, then added quickly: "See, Ify, I think we are wasting our time talking about an issue that will lead us nowhere."

"I don't share your pessimism. On the contrary, I believe we have a noble ambition which we can translate into reality if we are steadfast."

"I won't encourage you to go on using the word 'we' because I'm not in it with you. I won't even consider it."

"That's a pity because I won't give up on you. I take it that we have started then."

"What have we started?"

"The struggle or is it the battle now? All I ask is that you give me a chance and see how it goes."

"I don't believe your claim that you don't have alcohol in your system."

For a moment I was unable to move. Ify's words were so revealing and I was frightened by the depth of feelings he obviously had for me. What had I done to cause it? I fixed him a penetrating gaze, hoping to find answers. He had crossed his legs, his hands folded over them as he sat comfortably in the lone chair in my room, his mouth open in a gentle smile, his eyes never looking more warm and bright. He looked casually elegant in his white shirt and black trousers. I sat on the bed and continued to gaze at him. Finally, I asked:

"Why do you feel so strongly about me? I mean, it's not as if I'm the prettiest girl around."

"There's something different about you," he said.

I started to blush. He rose from the chair and sat beside me and put his hand over mine.

"Don't change," he said so fiercely he surprised me with his vehemence. "Be yourself and don't let others make you over into what they expect or want you to be. You are a very special person so continue to be your own special person."

Was I really sitting here listening to Ify tell me these things? I closed my eyes and opened them but he didn't disappear. He was still there, sitting beside me, gazing at me with enough admiration to make my heart pound. His eyes were laughing, full of sparkling lights as he templed his fingers beneath his chin. I didn't know how to feel.

"You look like you're about to cry," he observed. I swallowed back my tears of gratitude.

"It's just nice to hear you talk to me like you just did," I said. He nodded and leaned back, gazing toward the door.

"Anyway," he continued, putting his hand over mine again. "I feel like I've known you all my life."

I rose from the bed and pulled myself into a stern posture.

He mirrored my action and we stood staring at each other. He looked so much taller. His face had lost its innocent softness. It was firm and full in a mature way. He stood tall, radiating confidence. As he looked down at me, warmth flooded through me. I struggled not to let it show. Then he sat back on the bed, a lot more relaxed. He seemed so different, so calm and strong. I took a deep breath.

"Anyway," I said, "I can't marry you." His face registered disappointment for a moment then he nodded slowly, his lips pressed together with understanding.

"You don't think there's anything we can do to make your family accept me?" he asked.

I didn't respond. Instead, I insisted on knowing why he was bothering with me when he could easily find an Igbo girl.

"Because you are different," he repeated, and then blushed when he realised how emphatically he had spoken.

"That's very kind of you to say, Ify," I said.

He stared at me and smiled. I shook my head this way and that and wiped a lingering tear from my cheek.

"Do you really want to know what I plan to do?" he asked. Without waiting for my response, he continued, "I intend to be patient and hopeful until you realise how much I care about you. You are the only woman I have ever loved like this."

He looked away quickly, embarrassed by his confession. For a moment, I was speechless. I thought it was best to simply pretend that I hadn't heard. He took a deep breath, his shoulders rising and falling. Neither of us said anything for a moment. I was afraid he might explode with anger.

"So," he said, his eyes filling with a mischievous twinkle as he placed his hands gently on my shoulders. Shuddering all over, I silently cursed my weakness but I was powerless to do more than stare back. I felt so starved for the sight of him that I blushed. I felt the heat rise in my neck and when I looked at him, I saw a silly, satisfied smile on his lips.

"We can make it happen," he said firmly.

"I don't think so," I protested.

"I love you, Anjola," he said with a wry smile. I nodded, my tongue refusing to form any words.

"And I know you love me, too. I can see it in your eyes," he said, his smile spreading.

"My family won't approve," I said with a clear and sharp determination.

"We won't rush things. We'll appeal to them and make them see how strongly we feel about each other. I'm helplessly in love with you."

Tears shone in the corners of his eyes. "I know, but ..."

"Shhhh." He placed a finger over my lips. I hushed instantly, undone by the feel of his flesh against my mouth.

"Anjola, I love you," he said urgently. "I want to be with you. I need you," he stressed. "Please ..., please..."

After he left, I stood there, my thoughts whirling around in my head, making me dizzy. I had to lean against the wall and catch my breath. Was I dreaming? My heart was racing so fast that I thought I might faint and have to be taken to hospital.

Hours later, when calm returned, I thought about the things he had said. I might not have known his people and might therefore not be certain about their reaction toward our proposed union, but I could make an intelligent prediction based on precedent. Inter-ethnic marriages were generally frowned upon. Most who did so had unhappy stories to tell. Some made one shudder in horror. I knew my own people. I knew our history and all the reasons why marrying outside my local government area was unthinkable. I was the last child of my parents and the only female and saw how married daughters temporarily relocated to their parents' home to look after their ageing mother till death. I witnessed my mother do it for her own mother. It was not a rule; it was not a piece of legislation. It was simply a tradition but well-entrenched. It was not one I was prepared to break. As a growing child, I was aware of how parents took exception to their daughters going to faraway places to marry.

They had no problems with their sons going as far as they wished to pick other people's daughters and bring them back as wives, but they wanted their daughters to stay close.

Nonetheless, Ify seemed to me to be a dream man for any young woman. He was amiable, kind and gentlemanly. He was a man of few words and I had heard it said that such men were the best. I ought to have congratulated myself on having had the good fortune to meet him and even receive a marriage proposal. He was also a decent man; he never attempted to take undue advantage of me. Above all, there was something about his personality that seemed to hold much promise. I knew all of this and more yet I couldn't do otherwise than discourage him. I didn't agree to marry him not because I was unreasonable or lacked affection for him but because I was conscious of the prevailing reality. Whatever promise and good qualities Ify had been endowed with would have to be the gain of another woman, who would probably be more deserving than I was. The only problem was that his silhouette lingered on the inside of my eyelids.

CHAPTER 13

By now, I had begun to prepare my mind toward returning home, where I was certain I would secure a job with the foreign affairs' ministry. Looking back, I concluded that life had been good to me and that things could only get better. As an undergraduate, I never spent any of my long holidays engaging in meaningless ventures. Rather, I always secured a holiday job with the Federal Ministry of Works, where my father held sway. Although the pay was meagre, it kept me from mischief. That was my life as a student. Peering into my future, it seemed reasonable to look forward to happier times. It was the only logical thing to expect. It was my destiny and the destiny of all young people of my generation who had had the good fortune of a university education. It was our heritage and I was glad to be alive in my country to partake in a glorious time. I looked at myself in the mirror. The girl who gazed back at me had changed radically. I had sharper look in my eyes now, more pronounced cheekbones and a tighter jaw. I was a woman!

Meanwhile, I had ensured that I obeyed my father's instruction not to visit home throughout my stay in Anambra. However, we corresponded regularly through letters and I was nearly as knowledgeable about happenings at home as I would have been if I were actually at home. And now it was almost over. Already, corps members who would take part in the passing-out parade - including CY - had begun to practise for the event.

I had also gone to the bank to withdraw all the money I had saved. Because I served in a village and lived among a people who were hospitable and regularly supported my feeding; and because CY and Ify kept their separate promises of assisting me financially due to the problem I had had during the orientation, I had succeeded in saving some money and had made plans on how to spend it wisely.

From my monthly allowance of two hundred naira, I had religiously saved fifty naira. Even when one hundred naira was being deducted from my allowance from source following the allegation of theft, I stuck stubbornly to my resolve. The result was that, in ten months, I had saved a whopping five hundred naira. I was proud of my achievement. I pleaded with Henry to accompany me to the market, where I made the biggest purchases of my life. I bought a three-point gas cooker with the intention of buying a cylinder on my arrival back home. More impressively, I bought a three-in-one sound system with radio, cassette player and recorder. I was thrilled. I couldn't wait to get home to show off my possessions. I was particularly eager to thrill my cousin with uninterrupted music.

My cousin would envy me. I was sure about it. Tunbosun would wish he was like me: a graduate just completed National Youth Service Corps programme and, above all, about to take up a plum job with the Ministry of Foreign Affairs. Well, I was the lucky one and I was determined to flaunt my new possessions. He would envy me no end and I would savour the pleasure. I hadn't bought recorded cassettes yet. Henry had advised me against buying cassettes originally recorded by artists.

"Just buy empty cassettes and take them to record stores where they will record different songs into them for you. That way, you will spend less because you could have as many as three albums in one cassette."

I thanked him profusely for his advice. I loved the songs of King Sunny Ade, Ayinde Barrister and the sassy lyrics of the one from my own state, Kollington Ayinla. In the meantime, I would content myself with just listening to music played on the radio, which I did as soon as we returned from the market. Edna Ogoli was playing on the radio. I became so enthralled that I started to sing along with her:

The world is going bad
Situation getting bad
Many people getting mad
No ideal situation
Starvation biting harder
 Many people suffering in the land
Bribery is one of the cankerworms
Corruption not left out
Yeha! Woyo!

The world is going bad
Situation getting bad
Many people getting mad
There is no human sympathy
Some of the youth into ritual killing
Brothers where are we heading to
Sisters where are we going from here
Yeha! Woyo!

The world is getting bad
Situation getting bad
Many people getting mad
All that the children need is peace and love
O God save us from this situation
The world is going bad

I didn't know Henry had entered my room until he tapped me on the shoulder.

"Anjola," he called. I was startled.

"I...I didn't know when you entered," I stammered.

"Of course you didn't know. How would you know with your loud music?" he said smiling. "Nweke's daughter brought this letter for you. She said her father said it came this afternoon."

I recognised my dad's handwriting. I was surprised. I had received a letter from him just the previous week and had thought it would be his last. I hadn't even bothered to reply since I knew I would soon be home. Anyway, I was glad he cared enough to write again. My father's affection for me was incredible. I smiled as I tore open the envelope.

My dearest daughter,

It must come to you as a surprise that I'm writing again having just posted a letter to you a few days ago. It was not my intention to write again, especially as I was aware that you would soon come home. However, two unhappy events have occurred and their nature demanded that I inform you immediately. Your cousin, oh yes, the one who had lived with us since his childhood, Tunbosun, died suddenly earlier this week and his death has thrown the entire family into grief. The second event is that two days ago, the new military government announced an embargo on employment.

I couldn't read the rest. I felt suddenly dizzy. I managed to get up to switch off the radio. Then I felt a rumbling in my tummy and ran to the pit latrine in the compound.

"Oh no!" I cried as my bowels rampaged. I washed myself and went back to my room to continue reading the letter. Moments later, my stomach began to rumble again. I barely made it to the latrine. I returned to my room and fell back against the pillow, too weak and defeated to bother with tears. Tunbosun had died earlier in the week. What could have killed him? Was that how people died? Tunbosun was my age-mate. He was hale and hearty when I left him less than a year before. He also had great plans for his future. He had a mission to accomplish, heights to attain, and I could tell that he had the perseverance to pursue his dreams. How, then, could all that end so abruptly? No, there must have been a mistake somewhere; life could not be so cruel as to slam an undeserving death on a promising young man.

Fresh tears streamed down my cheeks as my stomach started to rumble yet again. Back in my room some minutes later, I sat pensively, thinking about events since my graduation. How confusing and complicated the world was once you left that realm in which you dwelled as a youth. I realised that I had been living in a bubble. I was now being forced to look around and see that pain and suffering were not part of some make-believe that would disappear with the blink of an eye. What a difficult world to navigate! How I longed for the simpler times of my studentship! I wish I could go to sleep and wake up a student again. Oh how I wish... I sighed. Dear God, how would I cope with life as an adult? I began to wail loudly. Then I remembered the second part of the letter. The new military government had placed an embargo on employment. In my confusion and misery, I forgot the meaning of the word. What did it mean?

I went to Henry to break the sad news of the untimely death of my cousin. He was full of sympathy but urged me to take heart and pray for the repose of his gentle soul. Was that all? Just pray for the repose of his gentle soul - whatever that meant - and move on? I thought about it and concluded that it would not be so easy. People prayed for the repose of the souls of their aged ones after happy and fulfilled lives, not youths who had not even started. I broke down again. Henry reminded me that anybody could die at any time.

"Life is unpredictable, Anjola. We have no choice but to accept it as such. It could have been any of us. Nobody can stop anybody from dying," he said.

I was somewhat pacified. Henry was right. It could have been anyone. I wiped my face with the handkerchief he had given to me and forced a smile, then asked him the meaning of 'embargo.' He said it meant putting a temporary stop to something. Government had put a temporary stop to employing people. How could that be? As far as I could remember, employment had always been a routine activity of government. It was one of its responsibilities to the citizenry. How could a government place an embargo on it? What would such a government expect its teeming youth to do in the meantime? How could I have anticipated that there would be slings and arrows falling on my bubble of joy and optimism all too soon? The weight of reality was too heavy for my youthful fantasy to bear. Events in my short life were teaching me never to count on anything. I turned these things over and over in my mind as the walls of my heart quivered but thinking about them exhausted me. In the end, I gave up trying and sought solace in sleep. I didn't want to keep my eyes open for it was only in sleep that I hoped to find relief from the harsh reality that had befallen me. If I wasn't sleeping, I accepted sadness and despondency as my companions and moved about like someone in a trance. Goodbye to being carefree and young, hopeful and energetic. I could see the clouds moving over the sun and dropping shadows like torrents of rain.

On the day of the passing-out parade, I stood like a statue among my obviously happier fellows. CY tried to snap me out of my melancholia but it was no use. Finally, he told me to disbelieve my dad's letter and hang on to my earlier belief that I would pick up a job as soon as I got back. I told him that would amount to an exercise in self-deception and that only a self-hater would do so. We were still arguing when I saw her walking toward us. I didn't recognise her immediately because she had put on weight but it was her all the same. It was Halima, my roommate during the orientation.

"Oh my God! Halima, you look changed!" I screamed. "It's so nice to see you again," I added whole-heartedly, putting behind the animosity that characterised our last days at the camp.

"Good to see you, too," she said, embracing me warmly. Then I noticed she was a bit careful about the way she held me. She allowed more space than necessary. I detached myself to take another look at her.

"Halima, am I imagining things?" I held my breath as the full ramification of what I was seeing became even clearer.

"You are very correct, Anjola. I'm five months' pregnant."

"Whoa!" I exclaimed. "Who is the lucky man?"

"I'm the lucky woman," she said, eyes twinkling warmly.

"I still don't understand. Who is he? Where is he? What does he do for a living? Where did you find him?"

"Easy, Anjola, I know you are happy for me. My husband is a medical doctor. He is also one of us. He is a youth corper passing out today but I didn't know him when we were in the orientation camp. We were posted to the same town and that was where we fell in love."

"You made him fall in love with you?"

"My husband is a grown man. He knew what he wanted." She smiled enigmatically.

"Halima, I fear you o," I said, laughing and temporarily forgetting my misery. "You said you must hook a man during the service year and you did exactly that. How did you do it?"

"Determination, focus and optimism. I was set in my ways and positive that life would give me whatever I asked for. You are a great girl, too, and can achieve whatever goals you set as long as you have faith in yourself and work toward achieving them."

I gave her my full attention. I didn't just listen to her; I watched her countenance as she did so. I paid attention to her body language. She looked and acted like someone whose life was truly at a plateau. I concluded that she meant every word she uttered. I found her conviction inspiring. What a girl! What bravery! What audacity! I felt a sudden gaiety come upon me as I watched her, mesmerised by her slightly protruding tummy. I shifted my gaze from her momentarily to look at CY. He gave me a wink, and, for the first time in many days, a genuine smile broke out on my face.

PART TWO
SEPTEMBER 1986 – JUNE 1989

CHAPTER 14

Two days after the passing-out parade, I was on my way to Ilorin. Although the happiness and enthusiasm that had accompanied me to Anambra had since deserted me, I struggled to brighten up. Apart from drawing inspiration from my encounter with Halima, I was hopeful I would happily reunite with the few friends I had in Kwara, for instance, Kike Tomori, if I overlooked the constant bickering. I didn't remember the details of our last quarrel, which occurred a few weeks before I started my final exam at the university; but I remembered that she had written an offensive letter and given it to a messenger to deliver to me. One of the high points in the letter, which I also found offensive, was that I was "below her standard" because she was a working-class lady, and that she regretted our friendship. I wasn't one to lose out in a war of words so I sent her a swift reply stating that I didn't know she was a coward. Couldn't she have summoned the courage to insult me to my face? That had been our last contact before I left school and I remembered assuring myself that I could do without her friendship for the rest of my life. The new reality, however, was that I needed a friend around me when I got back because I wasn't sure of the kind of life that awaited me in view of recent developments. The twin incidents of my cousin's death and news of the government embargo made the prospect of returning home dreadful. I would apologise to her.

Finally, I arrived home. There was no rousing welcome, just as I had expected. My parents were pensive; they looked solemn and withdrawn, apparently still struggling to come to terms with Tunbosun's death. They didn't pay me much attention. I understood. I spent the first few weeks feeling confused. Thankfully, Kike and I resolved our differences when she came to sympathise with me over my cousin's passage. However, I found out soon afterwards that we could not spend as much time together as I had hoped because she had a job. I woke up each morning realising that I had no worthwhile engagement planned for the day. I spent most days either loafing around the house feeling miserable or visiting Kike at her office. The situation was threatening to drive me crazy and I wondered how long I could tolerate my unemployed status.

Then, gradually, life appeared to return to normal as my parents seemed to be coming around. Weeks after my arrival, my dad noticed for the first time that I had brought back a sound system. My mum also congratulated me on my new three-face table gas cooker. Both commended me for not being a spendthrift. This raised my morale and I started to look forward to getting a directive from my dad to write an application for employment, which I still hoped he would submit on my behalf. I tried to veil my anxiety, knowing how grief-stricken he was. I resolved to wait patiently until he raised the matter. I was still biding my time when I found my mum in my room one night as I prepared to go to bed. I had been with my dad in the sitting room watching television and had imagined my mum was already fast asleep in their bedroom. I was taken aback. What did she want? I had my suspicions but thought it was better not to pre-empt her.

"You are no longer a child," she began.

My suspicions were confirmed. "You want me to get married," I said with forced politeness and pleaded with her not to compound my frustration.

She left without another word. I was glad. I wasn't even

twenty-two yet. What was my mother's problem? Afterwards, however, I ruminated over her visit and concluded that her attempt to broach the subject might not be without some advantage, after all. Hadn't she reminded me that I needed to take definite steps toward finding my feet? Perhaps it was time to call my father to a meeting over my job search. What was the point of waiting until he introduced the subject?

I told him over breakfast the next morning how terribly frustrating my continued stay at home had become. He was quiet for a long time. Had I been insensitive? But by the time he started to speak, I wished I had not bothered him. With visible anguish, he told me how sad he was watching me loaf about the house. I was his only daughter, he reminded me. I was also the only one among his children still at home as my older siblings were happily employed in different parts of the country. No one knew how long the present embargo would last, he said sadly. He wondered if I could modify my ambition and try the few private secondary schools in Ilorin for a teaching appointment because the government secondary schools were also affected by the embargo. Life was going to be tougher for me than I had anticipated and I needed to brace up for the challenges ahead, he concluded gravely,

I felt my world crumble. He said he wished he had a company of his own where I could work as director or enough money to set me up in a profitable business, but he was a civil servant fast approaching retirement. I sat moping. It was as if I had fallen into a trance. The picture he had painted was completely at odds from what I had envisaged. What had happened to my dreams? I was supposed to be among the millions of youths widely acclaimed to be the hope of the nation and not her misery. The youth are the leaders of tomorrow, as the popular saying I grew up with and believed in fervently had it. Would I ever become a leader in my country?

I went to the bathroom for my shower but I was hardly aware of what I was doing. I then found myself in my room, dressing up. I didn't have any idea where I was going. I came out to the sitting room, fully dressed, to find my parents sitting dejectedly. They looked at me expectantly. I managed to mumble something about wanting to go out. My mum protested that I hadn't finished my breakfast but I ignored her. My dad said nothing. I was out of the house in a jiffy, walking toward the bus stop with tears cascading down my cheeks. I didn't have a handkerchief so I used the back of my hand to rub my face. Where was I going?

I tried to think of someone I could visit that early morning without betraying my distress. Kike was the only one who came to mind but I was aware I had been visiting her too often. Suddenly, I noticed a car slowing down. I watched until it came to a stop a few metres away. It was an SR model Peugeot 504 saloon with only one occupant. I shifted my gaze and watched the oncoming traffic, ostensibly to flag down a taxi. Meanwhile, the man in the car started to hoot his horn in a bid to attract my attention. He was reversing now. I acted as if I didn't care although I needed a free ride. Finally, the car was beside me. He opened the passenger door without talking and I eased myself in.

"How are you?" he said.

"I'm fine," I responded.

"You don't look fine to me," he said.

I said nothing in response.

"So how far are you going?" he asked.

That was the problem. I hadn't had the time to think about where I wanted to go. I had to decide quickly now. Kike remained the only person on my mind. I told him I was visiting a friend at Kwara State Chamber of Commerce and Industry. He tried to nudge me into further conversation but it was no use. I was too wrapped up in my misery. Expectedly, Kike was not excited to see me but I couldn't be bothered. I drew a chair in front of her and sat down, ignoring her unwelcome countenance. One of her colleagues came to discuss a job-related issue but suddenly burst into a prolonged laughter on sighting me. Kike and I frowned and waited for him to finish.

"Anjola, so you are here already, ehn? I think it's high time we get you a permanent seat in this office," he said and burst into laughter again.

Kike looked at me as if expecting me to react but I didn't. As soon as her colleague left, she said:

"Seriously, Anjola, I think it's time we did something about your situation. Your frequent visits to this office are an embarrassment to me as well. You are the butt of jokes among my colleagues but I didn't expect Wale to make fun of you to your face."

"What do you want me to do?"

"I want you to get a boyfriend."

"A boyfriend?"

"Yes, someone you can spend time with."

"Maybe you are right. But how do you suggest I go about it? Place an advert in the papers?"

"Don't be ridiculous. Leave it to me. I will handle it."

I surrendered to Kike's plan. In no time, she introduced me to Deinde Komolafe, a paediatrician at the University of Ilorin Teaching Hospital. He became a God-send. Our relationship blossomed so incredibly that I wondered if God was about to grant my mother's wish. Deinde came from the same local government area of the state; his village was less than thirty kilometres from mine. It was the kind of arrangement I knew my mother would be excited about. I forgot about the ordeal of being a job-seeker.

Curiously, also, I discovered I no longer needed much of Kike's attention. I was always with Deinde. Soon, my entire world was wrapped around him. He became my very essence; dictating and controlling my every movement. He was a fantastic lover. He made love to me as if I was the most precious creature in the world. He described his training, his friends and some of the things he had seen and done, including his past relationships. He was unequivocal that I was the woman of his dreams. It was incredible how I had found love so easily and so soon. I became the envy of my other friends, especially because Deinde treated me almost like an orphan. He provided my every need. He made budgets to buy me a dress every month and, accordingly, took me out for shopping as soon as he received his salary. He monitored my shoes to know when they were due for replacement. My mood was of great concern to him. Did I look happy or sad? What was happening to my complexion?

My parents soon found out about my relationship and expectedly gave their tacit support because they could identify with his background. My mother did not ask me probing questions about him but I knew she was anxiously waiting for me to announce our engagement. Deinde had not proposed marriage although we both appeared not to be in doubt that marriage was to be the ultimate climax. In the meantime, I concentrated on getting all the fun and thrills of our relationship. I knew all the pepper soup joints in Ilorin. We went out for pepper soup in the evenings he was not on duty and our choice of which joint to patronize usually depended on our preference for the night. If we wanted fresh fish pepper soup, the Adewole Housing Estate was our port of call but if cow tail was our preference we headed in the direction of Tanke.

Deinde described himself as a 'social drinker' when I met him and I assured him I had no problem with it. However, when he told me he also smoked, I protested vehemently. He promised to make an effort to stop and I believed him but I also made a plan to assist him overcome his habit by refusing to kiss him whenever he smoked. He contrived to suppress the smell by licking sweets but it never worked for him and he eventually quit the habit. I didn't complain about his alcohol but I stuck to soft drinks. Soon, he began to complain that drinking was no longer enjoyable for him due to my lack of participation. The effect was that he started to take less of alcohol and more of soft drinks.

That was the situation that particular Sunday evening as we ordered our drinks and pepper soup. Once our order had been taken, we began our usual talk about everything and nothing.

We talked about how we felt about each other, how deep our love was and how certain we felt that neither of us would be able to live a normal life if we failed to make it to the altar. We made a promise to love each other for ever. We would surmount all obstacles to ensure that nothing ever separated us. He cupped my jaw in his palm and I drew closer to him. He gave me a tender kiss, beginning with my lower lip until he gradually held my tongue between his teeth. I gave my tongue to him as I usually did and his saliva tasted so sweet that I swallowed it. Then he began to release my tongue and later my lips as gradually as he had started. I hadn't realised my eyes were shut. I found myself opening them to behold that one of the attendants had brought our drinks and was waiting to know if he could open them. Neither Deinde nor I felt any embarrassment. We told him to go ahead and thanked him profusely.

Deinde was now regaling me with tales of his exploits in the medical school. He told me how brilliant he was and how his professors were very impressed with him. Then he remembered an incident that happened to one of his colleagues whose area of specialisation was gynaecology. He said the practice was that, upon their attaining a certain stage in their medical studentship, they would be allowed to attend to patients under the supervision of their professors. On this particular day, a student training to become a gynaecologist was to attend to a set of patients. He started well and was making a good impression until it got to the turn of a certain beautiful woman, who had to strip naked to be examined properly. The woman was told to take off her undergarments. She complied without making a fuss. However, hardly had she taken off her clothes than the professor noticed that his student began to shiver rather strangely. It became the lot of the perplexed professor to examine his own student and upon, a closer look he saw he had developed an embarrassing erection.

"My friend, would you pull yourself together and do your job?" the professor barked. The offending organ shrank with immediate effect. The medical profession is very interesting, he told me after we had recovered from laughing. Our pepper soup had just arrived. As we got ready to eat, I warned Deinde to spare me laughter-inducing stories because pepper soup and wild laughter had never been known to be friends. This produced another round of laughter.

We were still laughing when one of his friends showed up at our table. He was also a medical doctor, a gynaecologist at the same teaching hospital. They had been friends for a long time, having graduated the same year. Deinde had told me a lot about him and I always felt very comfortable around him. The only problem with Dr. Kolade Durotoye, Deinde told me, was his excessive drinking. Aside from that, he was a fantastic person with a good heart. Laughing boisterously, Kolade signalled to a waiter to fetch him a chair. Even from across the table, Deinde and I detected he was reeking of alcohol. We exchanged knowing glances. Deinde offered him a plate of fresh fish pepper soup but he declined, insisting that all he wanted was a bottle of beer. As soon as he made his order, he got up from his seat and began to dance to Ebenezer Obey, which was blaring from two speakers, one of which was adjacent to our table.

"Alowo ma jaiye, eyin lemo/ It's a pity some people have money but deny themselves enjoyment.

"Awon t'o laiye l'ana da won tiku won tilo/those who were alive yesterday are dead today.

"Awon   t'olowo tan ole nan/those who have money but don't spend

"Ao ma wara ti won o fowo da/let us see what they will do with their money.

Kolade threw up his hands in the air, gyrating vigorously and singing excitedly. Curious eyes were attracted to our table. I lowered my head in embarrassment.

"Sit down!" I heard Deinde shout at his friend. The waiter arrived with Kolade's order. He seized the bottle with mock animosity, opened it to his mouth, taking a generous quantity in one gulp.

"You are drunk already. Why do you want to go on drinking?" Deinde challenged.

"No, no, no. I'm not drunk at all," Kolade protested.

"Are you saying this is your first bottle today?"

"I didn't say that, I only said that I'm not drunk. This is just my seventh bottle and I came because I thought you might be here and you can see that I'm right. It means that my reasoning faculty is still intact."

He raised the bottle to his mouth again and downed about half the remaining contents before putting it down. Then he turned to me, as if he had just discovered my presence.

"Our wife, I salute you."

"Good evening, Uncle," I said politely.

"You are taking good care of my friend and I thank you for that. When a man is looking as happy as my friend, the woman in his life deserves commendation," Kolade said.

I smiled shyly. Then he got up abruptly, saying he wanted to go and pee.

"What are you going to do about your friend?" I asked as soon as Kolade was out of earshot.

"Honestly I don't know. I feel sad about it. He is a good guy. I mean, he is too good to allow alcohol to ruin him like this."

"Does he have a girlfriend?"

"Kolade has no time for a serious relationship. He drinks and plays with several girls. My worry is that his drinking is beginning to affect his medical practice. Some patients object to having him attend to them at the hospital."

"That's a dangerous sign. You should act fast as a friend."

"I know. It's just that I haven't been able to figure out what to do."

All of a sudden, all eyes across several tables appeared to be turned in a particular direction. Kolade was walking toward us. As he did so, everyone stared at him, mouth agape. He was holding up his trousers with one hand and clutching his organ with the other. He stood in front of us and said, laughingly:

"Ai mo ye obo t'aw a tido, oko yi nan ni/ What an innumerable number of women I have slept with, it is this same penis that did it all."

I shuddered in disgust. Deinde got up abruptly, gripped me by the wrist and headed for the car park. We only managed to say good night to each other when I alighted at my parents' house.

CHAPTER 15

My dad came back from work the following day with a letter addressed to me. It was from Ify and had been posted six weeks earlier. The letter didn't give much news except to say that he had relocated to Kaduna as planned, was working with a construction company and was "alright generally." What dominated the letter was his concern about my job search and how I was faring. If I had not found a job in Ilorin, would I consider coming to Kaduna to try my luck since I had earlier informed him that I had an uncle who lived there? He reminded me that Kaduna was a big city. There were many manufacturing companies. He went on to explain that northerners were generally kind people and eager to assist others. I tried to detect a veiled interest in the letter but couldn't. I thought it was better to take it at face value. I told my father the letter was from a concerned friend but he just shrugged his shoulders. I mused over Ify's suggestion for a few days but decided to ignore it. However, I thanked him for his suggestion and promised to consider it. I assured him that I was doing well although I had not gotten a job yet. I also hinted that I was in a serious relationship that was keeping me occupied.

A few weeks later, however, I found myself mentally appraising my relationship with Deinde. What I wasn't sure about was whether it was in my interest to allow the relationship to take precedence over my job search. My dad acted as if he was not aware I was in any relationship but my mum could not contain her excitement. There were times when I wanted to genuinely share her happiness. At such times, I tried to convince myself that getting married was the best way to solve the frustration that threatened to overwhelm me. The truth, however, was that I often found myself trying too hard without much success. As loving and caring as Deinde was, I had secret fears about our compatibility as husband and wife. One of the things that worried me was the way he treated me as if I was bereft of reasoning; that he alone was capable of giving me direction. He wanted to be the one teaching me how to walk, talk, bathe and even brush my teeth. I couldn't understand that aspect of him, especially when he ranted and raved if I didn't do as directed. We were in the middle of a conversation one afternoon when he suddenly asked me how I normally brushed my teeth.

"How do you mean?" I had asked, feeling slightly embarrassed that I had mouth odour without realising it.

"No, it's not as if your mouth stinks but I need to be sure that you know how to brush your teeth properly," he said.

"I see, go on then, tell me."

"You start with the lower teeth; then you take the brush to the upper teeth before moving into the corners. Finally, you take the brush to your tongue and ensure that it reaches far inside without feeling afraid that you might vomit. Now, the essential thing to note in brushing the teeth is to ensure that the tongue is not coated," he lectured.

On another occasion, he complained about the way I walked. We had gone out on a leisurely ride along Ibrahim Taiwo Road. We were talking about food and I reminded him that he needed to buy bread. He parked by the side of the road and gave me money to dash across to buy it. When I returned, he started berating me for my manner of walking.

"I don't like the way you walk, Anjola. I have said this time without number."

"You have told me several times that you don't like the way I walk but you are yet to tell me precisely what you don't like about it and, more importantly, what I should do about it."

"Your problem is that you don't like to be criticised and that scares me. I don't want to marry a woman who would not listen to me."

"You haven't answered my question. How do I walk? How do you want me to walk?"

"I can't really describe how you walk. I don't know whether it's your legs or shoes that make slap-slap sound that I find irritating. Can't you walk differently, for God's sake?"

"I will try to change the way I walk but I suggest you also try to accept me the way I am."

"You are my woman and I have the right to make you do what I want."

"Why do you like to pick quarrels unnecessarily?"

"I don't just pick quarrels. I say what I don't like. I'm categorical about the things I won't tolerate in a woman."

"Have you considered that you might have a problem?"

"You have a problem, Anjola. Why not admit it."

"Like hell I do," I yelled in exasperation.

That aspect of him worried me greatly. He was petty, quarrelsome and difficult to please. He made me happy by taking care of me and showing me off to his friends and colleagues but he made me miserable by being almost impossible. I laboured to satisfy his every whim and make him agreeable and pleasant to be with, but the more I tried the farther it seemed I was from achieving my objective. He made me wonder if living with him would not be hellish.

Another thing that worried me was that he never wanted to mention the subject of my job, let alone suggest how I might find one. Each time I attempted to broach the subject, he cleverly manipulated me into dropping it by introducing another. I didn't initially realise this was deliberate. I imagined it was just a coincidence and felt certain there would be another opportunity to discuss it. However, after what I observed to be too many coincidences, I began to suspect that Deinde was dodging the issue. One evening I insisted that we talk about it.

"What are you doing to help me get a job?" I asked.

"What should I do when your father is already making enough of an effort?"

"My father can't make any effort and you know it. He says there is an embargo on public service employment."

"How can I help you, then?"

"You told me you have friends in high places, remember? You said you have a large network of chief executives of corporations as patients. These companies are not affected by the embargo. I'm convinced you can use your influence to get me a job in one of them."

"You make a mistake by thinking that private organisations are not affected by the policies of the government. All organisations, no matter their size, are affected by the government's Society Adjust to Poverty Syndrome. The economic climate is cloudy. No one can tell when - or even whether - it will become clear again. However, I'm not keen on your getting a job. I don't even want you to."

"You don't want me to get a job?"

"No, I don't."

"That's cruel."

"What do you need a job for?"

"What do you mean by that?"

"You are going to be my wife."

"Have you proposed marriage to me? Even if you have, why should my becoming your wife stop me from having gainful employment?"

"Do you plan to be a career woman?"

"What's wrong with that?"

"Everything; I hate the idea with a passion."

"I see. I thought you had women who studied medicine with you in the university and are now practising."

"Yes, some of my course mates were women but I sympathise

with the men who had the misfortune to marry them."

"You know, you truly disgust me when you talk like this. Was it necessary for me to have gone to school?"

"Well, it was good you went to school but you didn't go to school to stop you from being a woman."

"What does being a woman mean to you?"

"You know what it means to be a woman, why the pretence?"

We ended up quarrelling over the issue but he insisted that I didn't need a job. He said I could do as my father suggested and take up a teaching appointment in a private school since I was still a spinster but warned that I would have to leave the job and become a full-time housewife as soon as we got married. He said he would buy me a motorcycle and when I asked him why not a small car instead he accused me of wanting to compete with him. That aspect of him also worried me but the one that actually gave me the greatest jitters was his feeling of insecurity. He didn't seem to trust me. He also imagined that the only thought that went through the mind of any man I encountered was to sleep with me. That made me sad. I couldn't understand why he felt so insecure despite all my reassurances and in spite of the fact that he monitored my movements. He was also a thoroughly loyal and extremely devoted lover. Why would any woman in a relationship with such a man choose to be different?

There was a particular incident that kept on nagging at me and making me wary of agreeing to marriage whenever he proposed. I had run into one of my old school mates at the university and we had naturally got talking. He asked me if I had the contact address of one of our mates whom he wished to contact but whose forwarding address he had forgotten to collect before we left school. I told him I had the address but that it was at home. He asked if I didn't mind his following me to collect it and I said I didn't. We went to my parents' house together but he declined to come inside. I explained that my parents trusted me and would even entertain him as their daughter's old school friend but still he refused. Finally, I left him standing outside and went to fetch the address. I was walking him to the bus stop when I saw Deinde's car approach. He brought the car to a halt and demanded to know where I was going. I told him I just wanted to see a former school mate to the bus stop and would be with him shortly. However, as soon as he drove off, my friend asked me if Deinde was my boyfriend. I said yes. He told me to go back quickly to meet him because he sensed he was angry. I laughed and assured him he was wrong. I told him Deinde couldn't have been angry because there was nothing about the situation to warrant it. Nevertheless, I decided to take his counsel by returning home immediately. I reached home to find Deinde sitting calmly in our sitting room, waiting for me. My father wasn't home; only my mum was.

"Go and pick your handbag and let's go," he commanded.

I saw my mum beam with satisfaction. I wasn't sure whether to congratulate her or be sorry for her over her eagerness to see me marry. I fetched my handbag from my room preparatory to going out with him. When I returned, he and my mum were exchanging what I imagined must have been their second round of pleasantries for the day, my mum urging him to partake in the meal she was preparing. He thanked her profusely and promised to ensure that I returned home shortly.

He said nothing until we reached his apartment. I still didn't suspect that there was anything amiss. I thought he was preoccupied with private thoughts and that I should not intrude. I started to suspect something only when we got to his apartment and he still wouldn't talk to me. I tried to begin a conversation but gave it up when he simply responded in monosyllables. I decided to keep myself busy by cleaning his bedroom. I picked up some washed clothes carelessly dropped on the bed and began arranging them in the wardrobe. I noticed that some of his shoes were scattered in the room and I started to dust them. He came to me now and seized me roughly by my shoulders, forcibly making me to face him. A ripple of apprehension shot down my spine.

"Who was he?" he demanded tersely.

"Who was whom?" I asked in return.

"Who was the guy I saw you with in your house?" There was a clear tone of accusation in his voice.

I burst into laughter, relieved that he was angry over a minor issue. I was going to tease him but my joviality was short-lived because a thunderous slap landed on my right cheek, making me stagger and fall. He stood over me and rained blows on me. I struggled to get up but it was no use. He pushed me down with devilry and kept on beating me. The punches were vicious and unending. It was a nightmare. Finally, I stopped struggling. I just lay on the floor and received the punches as they came in torrents. Perhaps my end had come. Maybe I would pass on to the so-called great beyond without a chance to live my dreams or even say goodbye to my parents. How I sympathised with my mother. If only she knew that the man she was anxious to give her only daughter was a demon. I decided to surrender to my misfortune.

After some time he realised that I was making no attempt to fight back. He stopped beating me although he was still boiling with rage. Not wanting to do anything that could further fuel his anger, I made no attempt to get up. Besides, I wasn't sure he was satisfied yet. I lay there whimpering like a tortured animal. He shouted at me to stand up. I obeyed. He ordered me to make the bed. I discovered I had forgotten how to do so. I perambulated momentarily while trying to recall what exactly I was required to do. In my confusion, I forgot that there was a bed sheet on the bed already and that I only needed to straighten it. I ran to the wardrobe and started to look for another. He came over and slapped me from behind, pointing to the bed and ordering me to re-make it. I stifled my sobs by pressing my lips together and holding my breath while I did as he directed. A robot couldn't have performed better. Afterwards, he said I should go to the bathroom to wash his undergarments, which he had soaked in detergent. I nodded in tears and went to do as he ordered. I was washing his pants now and crying as I did so. How and when would I be able to make my escape? I decided to bide my time in the hope that he would go out soon. I cautioned myself against attempting anything hasty because I was convinced that he could kill me if he caught me trying to escape. I was sobbing hysterically and my heart was thumping against my chest, shortening my breath.

I had just finished washing his pants and was drying them when I noticed him pacing about the bedroom. He called out to me to ask if I had finished and I said yes. He told me to come to the bedroom. I took staggering steps, trembling and weeping uncontrollably. I hadn't had a chance to look in the mirror but I could imagine how awful I must have looked. He came close to me, as if he wanted to touch me. I shuddered in fright. This seemed to have an effect on him. He moved closer to me. I tried to summon my courage, knowing that there was nothing I could do even if he wanted to start beating me all over again. I was in his house.

Surprisingly, he took my hand and gently led me to the bed. It was at that point that I noticed he was holding a balm ointment in his hand. He carefully guided me to a sitting position and began to apply the ointment to all parts of my body, the same body he had pummelled mercilessly less than an hour before. I watched him in awe for he had also started to weep. He was pleading with me to forgive him. It was because he loved me and was afraid of losing me to another, he said. He also pleaded with me not to let my parents know what had happened, promising that he would never lay his hands on me again.

Well, I didn't tell my parents but I wanted to call off the relationship. However, the different ways he tried to make it up to me, and the responses I got from my friends when I told them, dissuaded me from carrying through with my plan. I actually contemplated telling my mother but the seriousness with which my friends counselled me never to divulge information about the way my partner treated or mistreated me to my parents put paid to that. Also, Deinde went to great lengths to assure me that the ugly incident would never recur. His remorse seemed genuine as he took practical steps to demonstrate greater tolerance of my male associates, in addition to buying me gifts. He blamed his blind jealousy on immaturity and expressed the conviction that his behaviour would normalise as he grew older. He was twenty-seven and I had just turned twenty-three.

CHAPTER 16

Things returned to normal between us after the incident but in my private moments I kept pondering over our relationship and asking myself critical questions to which I was getting unsatisfactory answers. Nevertheless, there didn't seem to be a way out of the confused state of affairs in my life. As far as my mum was concerned, I had no problem at all because Deinde would walk me down the aisle and nothing else mattered. She was merely waiting for me to announce our engagement. Should I articulate my concerns to her and ruin her happiness? Or should I just pretend that all was well? I weighed the options and their consequences and in the end decided to concentrate on Deinde's positive attributes. I resolved also to agree to marry him whenever he proposed to me. My mother was right, after all; I was no longer a young girl, especially as I had turned twenty-three. If I wasn't careful, I just might clock thirty still a spinster. God forbid! I shouted aloud and spat out in superstitious rejection of such a fate: PPF! Every young girl of Yoruba descent in my generation would reject the fate of the unfortunate maiden who remained in her parents' home until her thirtieth birthday. No, I would not be one such. PPF! I spat out again forcefully at the mere thought of it. I was a reasonable girl who knew how not to over-stretch her chances.

Many things worried me about Deinde but he was all I had. I had no job and the prospect of finding one soon was practically non-existent. What else was there to do? I decided, therefore, to savour every moment of the good times he could give me. He had promised me, for instance, that we would be having dinner in the newest restaurant in the city that evening and I was eagerly looking forward to it. That was one of the things that gave me joy about him. I smiled with satisfaction as I got up to take my evening bath. Deinde would pick me up at seven and he was a man of his word. I had already told my mum that I wouldn't be home for dinner. By the time I finished dressing, my mum came to tell me that Deinde was already waiting for me in the sitting room. I hurried up and we were soon in his car, driving toward Tanke.

"I can't wait to taste the special meal you promised," I said.

"I'm going to surprise you tonight," he said, smiling.

I wondered if he wanted to propose marriage. I felt happy at the prospect.

"I'm taking you to the newest and biggest hotel in town. I bet you've never seen anything like it."

"Are you kidding me?"

"Never mind, you will find out for yourself."

"Who owns it?"

"Maj-Gen Taye Olokoba."

Deinde was right. The land on which the hotel sat could not have been less than ten acres. Everything was in a whirlwind: the array of lights, the uniformed workers and the flooring all enraptured and transported me beyond my environment. Was I still in Nigeria? He led me toward the restaurant but, as we walked, I missed my step on the slippery floor and almost fell. He held me by the waist and gently guided me until we got to where he wanted us to sit.

Dinner was served in various courses. I relished every one of them even as I waited anxiously for the magic moment when he would pop the question. We chatted excitedly as we ate but our conversation was largely on inconsequential issues. I was surprised when he suddenly told me that the night was far spent and asked if I was ready to go back home. I told him I was although I was fighting hard not to show my disappointment I bore my disappointment in silence and wished for a happier occasion.

Deinde pulled up abruptly as soon as we had exited the hotel, muttering something about feeling pressed. I sat in the car waiting for him. Suddenly, I heard his raised voice as if he was arguing with someone. I got out of the car and found him shouting at a kid hawker. I looked on for some time, trying to take in the situation. The child, about twelve years old, was wearing a ragged buba and sokoto and a pair of bathroom slippers. On his head was a tray of boiled groundnuts with empty milk and tomato tins. He looked as if he had not had a bath in days. I looked at Deinde, who was still boiling with rage.

"What's the problem?" I asked.

"Can you imagine that this little rat had the audacity to ask me for money?"

"He asked you for money? What money?"

"Search me. This imbecile, this ordinary son of a goat actually had the guts to stop me in my tracks and ask for money. What an insult!"

Deinde was raving.

"Calm down and explain it to me, okay? He asked you for money. Money for what?"

"Tell the little idiot to explain why I have to give him money to eat. Tell him to explain how it is my problem that he has not eaten since morning."

"Oh, I see, you mean he begged you for alms?"

"Yes, the fool is looking for a free meal. I said if he has not eaten since morning as he claims, why can't he eat what he is carrying on his head?"

"You mean you got so angry because a kid hawker begged you for money to eat?"

"What gave him the nerve to ask me for money? Do I look like someone in his miserable class? You know, the problem with

143

them is that they don't want to take their time."

"I don't understand. What time?"

"They are in a hurry to enjoy. They don't want to suffer at all."

"Somebody said he has not eaten since morning and you asked him to take his time?"

"What's your point, Anjola?"

"My point is that this boy doesn't deserve your vituperation. Why don't you leave him alone if you are not willing to help him? Why harass him?"

"It's stupid of you to say what you have just said. How dare you talk to me in that manner?"

"Is there wisdom in stooping so low as to engage a kid hawker in a street argument, especially when you are the only one talking?"

I turned to the boy and told him to wait for me while I dashed to fetch my handbag. Deinde followed me. I had hardly taken my bag when he roared the engine into life and zoomed off, leaving a trail of red dust. Well, it was just as well, I thought angrily as I walked back to where the boy was still standing. By driving away in anger, Deinde had given me time to interact with the kid hawker. I wanted to know if he truly hadn't eaten since morning and why. I took his hand and led him to an adjoining street, where I knew there were local restaurants. We located one. I helped him bring down his tray and asked him what he wanted to eat. He said he wanted rice and stew. I gave his order and asked him questions in Yoruba when I found out he couldn't speak English. As soon as they brought his food, I knew there was no need to ask him whether or not he had eaten that day.

His name was Dele. He was fourteen and lived with his maternal aunt. He was the first child of his parents, who had five other children in one of the rural communities in the state. His parents could not afford to put him in school and pleaded with his mother's younger sister to take him with her to Ilorin and help to educate him. Her aunt had promised that she would but as soon as they arrived she told him he would have to contribute toward his education by hawking since she also had her own children to feed, all of whom, Dele said, were in school. She also told him that he would have to wait for her children to finish school before he could start. Dele had now been on the streets every day hawking groundnuts for five years. He said he had reminded his aunt at the beginning of every school year that he, too, wanted to go to school but she always told him to be patient; that he had not made enough money from hawking to finance his education. Neither of his parents had visited Ilorin and he believed they were not aware that he was not yet in school. He had not eaten that day because his aunt told him that he would be entitled to food only after he had sold all the groundnuts. On the days that sales were poor, he went to bed hungry. He had therefore taken to begging. His aunt's children didn't hawk and, although his uncle appeared unhappy about the way he was being treated, didn't seem to be in a position to do anything about it. I gave Dele the little money I had on me. I also bought the remaining groundnuts and urged him to return home immediately.

I was still asleep, going through several disjointed dreams the following morning, when I heard a knock on the front door. The person must have been knocking for a while and had grown impatient, I thought, as I dragged myself out of bed to see who it was. I was alone in the house. My mum and dad had both gone out without alerting me. They must have decided not to bother me, having remarked my melancholy mood the previous evening.

Deinde was at the door. It was clear from the way he looked that he had come for a fight. I wasn't surprised when he brushed past me. I closed the door calmly and joined him in the sitting room.

"What was yesterday's show about?" he challenged me before I could speak.

"What show?"

"I'm talking about your shameless performance before

145

the hawker. You must have enjoyed yourself playing the role of philanthropist."

"It's a pity you saw it that way."

"How else was I supposed to have seen it? You are so despicable. I feel sorry for having taken you seriously all this while."

"Have you come to my house to insult me?"

"Why wouldn't I insult you? Do you know how painful it is for me to realise that I have been wasting my time treating a miserable low-class pretender with respect?"

"You are the miserable wretch, Deinde. You are the truly pathetic low class who ignorantly arrogates an imaginary social status to himself. I sympathise with you."

"You don't deserve somebody like me, Anjola. It's a pity it took me this long to find out."

"Don't be so conceited, lover boy. I didn't beg you to date me," I said disdainfully.

"I shouldn't expect you to understand since you are daft and unintelligent? You don't even know simple arithmetic that could give you an idea of how much I have spent on you, you miserable ingrate."

"I wish you would listen to yourself. How could you reduce what we have shared to money? I thought we had a relationship we both cherished."

"Don't you dare preach at me. I came here to tell you it's over between us and that I will have you return every single thing I have ever bought for you. I'd rather burn them to ashes than you continue to use them. Do I make myself clear?"

"I suppose you expect me to burst into tears and fall down on my knees begging you not to leave me, ehn? I'm sorry to disappoint you; it's actually good riddance to bad rubbish. Now leave my house."

"You haven't told me when you will return my things."

"What things?"

"The clothes, shoes, handbags and jewellery; you must

return them all."

"Ha, ha, ha, you have forgotten to mention the cars, the houses and the aeroplanes. You are a bloody fool and I think you are beginning to show that your mental faculties are impaired. You deserve a place in the asylum."

"I give you two days to return all the things I ever bought for you," he said as he made for the door.

"Go to hell," I said, closing it behind him.

CHAPTER 17

I felt strangely relieved that Deinde had walked out of my life but I wasn't sure how my mum would take it. I braced up to the challenge of telling both her and my dad after dinner. Dad said little; my mother expressed deep unhappiness with what she described as my foolish behaviour. She said there was nothing unusual about the situation of the kid beggar as there were thousands of them scattered all over the country. She also said she had no harsh words for Dele's aunt; rather, she believed his mother should take the blame for foolishly trusting that her sister would help her shoulder her responsibility. It was an exercise in self-deception to assume that your relative would care for your child the way you would, she said. What difference did I think I had made in the hawker's life? She berated me for arguing with Deinde and insisted it was foolish of me to have traded my future happiness for a momentary show of kindness to a child whose life I was not in a position to turn around. She urged me to take steps toward getting Deinde back into my life by apologising to him. I told her it wasn't necessary. How could she be certain that my break-up with Deinde amounted to trading off my future happiness? What if it was a future misery I had prevented, in which case she ought to congratulate me?

We argued back and forth but I refused to budge. I was determined to chart a new course to sustain my happiness. I hadn't had the courage to make the decision I had always known was important but I was grateful it was forced on me. So, the following day, I decided to visit a fellow job-seeker. As I approached the gate leading to our compound I saw two of our neighbours talking excitedly. I greeted them and they responded well but I had scarcely taken a few steps when I heard one of them telling the other:

"There goes our dear Miss University Graduate. After all the fuss, she can neither find a job nor someone to marry. Her boyfriend has just dumped her."

"That is double jeopardy o," the other responded.

I turned back abruptly to face them. "Why are you two gossiping about me?" I demanded.

"Who is gossiping about you? Did you hear your name?" the first voice asked with undisguised animosity.

"Leave our poor graduate alone, jor. Can't you see she is still smarting from the break-up?" Then she turned to me and said, "Anjola, pele o. Good luck as you go in search of another bobo."

They burst into derisive laughter. I stood watching them, contemplating what to do. Perhaps I should be grateful to them for subjecting me to open derision. Maybe it was what I needed to propel myself to the next decisive step in my life. What should I do? I kept asking myself that evening. By the time I returned home, I had come to a decision. I resolved to take up a teaching job in a private secondary school, as my father had suggested. I was now determined more than ever before to build a career for myself in whatever area of human endeavour was available to me. If my ambition to become a career diplomat was unrealisable, what was wrong with becoming an eminent teacher? It was clear to me now that my primary ambition was far-fetched. The only realistic option left was to teach. I resolved to do it with the same zeal as if it was what I had always wanted to do. After all, I had already gained experience during my national service

I told my father of my decision. His face lit up in relief. I got a teaching job less than a week later. I took time preparing for my first day. I paid particular attention to my appearance because experience had taught me that appearance had a lot to do with delivery. I decided I would always dress smartly as a teacher and would avoid anything that could make me feel encumbered and sluggish. For my first day at work, therefore, I selected a pair of black pant trousers and a simple, short-sleeve blouse. I wore sandals rather than high-heels. No elaborate make-up, just a simple application of white powder. No lipstick, no eye-pencil, no eye-liner and no necklace. I wore a wristwatch, in addition to the smallest earrings I owned.

Dad dropped me off on his way to work, wishing me a joyous first day. My appointment letter didn't give details of my remuneration; it only asked me to report to the principal's office at seven-thirty in the morning. I was there at seven-fifteen. I was impressed that he was already at work. However, I had hardly entered his office when I observed he was looking at me with disapproval. I was perplexed but I tried to convince myself I was only imagining things.

"You are the new English teacher," he said coldly.

"Yes sir."

"Well, you are welcome but I must let you know that this school does not allow any form of indecent dressing, either by students or teachers. A situation where a female teacher wears trousers to school is highly embarrassing. What kind of moral lesson does she intend to impact on her students?"

"I'm sorry, sir. I didn't know trousers constitute indecent dressing."

"Alright, apology accepted but after this meeting you will go home and change. Is that understood?"

"Yes sir."

"Ehn, Miss Adeniyi, details of your engagement are still being worked out but I can give you some basic information. You will be on a monthly salary of fifty naira but your appointment will initially be on probation for two terms, during which you will earn half that. You will be entitled to your full salary only upon confirmation of your appointment."

"I don't understand, sir. Did you mean I will be on an initial salary of twenty-five naira per month?"

"That's right. I will take you to the proprietor shortly but I want to inform you that there are a few extra-curricular activities our teachers do in this school. For example, we have a roster for female teachers with respect to rendering assistance to Mummy, the proprietor of this great school."

"I don't understand, sir."

"As a teacher in this great school, you will be required to take turns with your fellow female teachers to render domestic assistance such as washing of clothes and other household chores at her residence."

"Excuse me, sir, is this some kind of joke?"

"Watch your tongue, young woman! Why would I wake up early in the morning to start sharing jokes with an over-pampered little girl? Have you met the woman I'm talking about? You would be glad to wash her clothes."

"I'm sorry, sir."

"You had better be. Now, come and meet her but don't forget that you go back home immediately after to change into something decent, OK?"

"Yes, sir."

I genuflected as a mark of respect for Mrs Ololade Kalejaiye as soon as I was ushered into her office but she told me to get fully down on my knees. I complied. She gave me a long speech on the conduct expected of a good teacher and asked the principal if he had briefed me fully on the terms of engagement, to which he replied in the affirmative. I went home to change but was again sent home on the grounds that the skirt I had changed into was not long enough.

"Your students can see your underwear when you bend down to pick chalk with this length of skirt," he fumed.

I later discovered that no teacher addressed the proprietor by name or official position. Everyone called her 'Wonderful Mummy' because she insisted on being so addressed. I joined the fray. My name was also put on the roster and I visited 'Wonderful Mummy' weekly to do her laundry. I concentrated on teaching my students and equally learning from them. The experience was a good one. However, my morale was slightly dampened when I didn't get paid at the end of the first month. I sought an explanation from the principal and he said new employees received their first salary three months after joining the school. However, he assured that I had nothing to worry about as the school would open a bank account for me, into which my accumulated salary would be paid. Four months later, there was still no sign that I would be paid. Again, I asked the principal. He blamed the delay on logistics, promising that it would be rectified the following month. When I didn't receive my salary at the end of that month, I decided to give another month's grace before complaining. Perhaps the problem was being taken care of. Six months of diligent teaching and part-time laundering later, I lost my patience.

"Is someone playing games with me?" I fumed. The principal remained surprisingly calm.

"No one is playing games, Miss Adeniyi. The school is having some problems."

"What problems? Are the students not paying school fees?"

"All I can tell you is that the school is having some problems. You need to be patient."

"Until when? When will I be paid?"

"I can't tell. I don't know myself yet."

I left his office without another word and quit the school. Once home, I went straight to my mother's room to take a close look at my reflection in the mirror. I stared at myself. My face had lost all its youthful plumpness. My cleavage was now deeper with a shadow at the bottom. It was time for me to begin to live like the person I had become, a grown woman. I retrieved Ify's letter and read it over again. He had written that I had a better chance of employment in the north because the embargo was not being strictly enforced. I made my decision and waited for my father. He had a cousin in Kaduna. All I wanted was for him to get his cousin to allow me stay with him while I searched for a job with the promised assistance of Ify. I wanted to put the past truly behind me: Deinde, my neighbours, Success Assurance Secondary School, all.

PART THREE
JULY 1989 – DECEMBER 1989

CHAPTER 18

I felt a wave of relief and calm descend on me as I got down at the Mando Motor Park in Kaduna. Here was a chance to put the past behind me and make a fresh start. The warm welcome I received from my uncle and his family thirty minutes later further ignited my hope. For the first time in three years I prayed; thanking God for rescuing me from the hellish experience in Ilorin. My uncle's wife was plump, ample-bosomed and pleasant-faced. I soon became aware that she was genuinely pleased for my company. I felt a warm friendliness each time she smiled at me. How I wished my happiness could last. I knew Ify wouldn't delay broaching the subject of my relocation and I wasn't surprised when he told me there was an important issue we needed to discuss. What I wasn't prepared for were the things he told me.

"There's something you need to do quickly," he announced and fell into a deep silence.

I peered at him closely, trying to decipher what was on his mind but I couldn't. I gave up the effort. He looked as if he was wondering how to broach a difficult subject.

"This is rather awkward for me," he began hesitantly.

I wrinkled my nose.

"You need to learn the strategies for getting a job in the north," he said softly.

"What strategies?" I asked, puzzled. He was beginning

to ignite a fresh sense of foreboding in me. Nothing would go wrong here, I said firmly under my breath.

"One of the first steps you must take is to change your name," he said with a downcast face.

My jaw nearly dropped but before my shock could register, I gritted my teeth and let my face register only mild surprise. "Change my name? Why?" I asked, hoping that I sounded calm.

"You are a fresh graduate with little knowledge of the dynamics of your country. The northerners are good people but you've got to be ready to identify with them, demonstrate that you are a part of them, before you can benefit from their kindness," he said and stared at his feet. It took some time before he raised his head, and when he did, he looked troubled and shifted his eyes away quickly.

"I don't get your drift."

"You have to claim to be a northerner to get a job in the north," he said in a rush. I gasped.

"I have to change my identity to become employable?" I queried, my lips parting in disbelief.

"Don't misunderstand me. It's just about recognising that certain things are necessary and then doing them," he said persuasively. I blinked and sat straighter on my seat.

"I still don't understand. Why do I have to pretend to come from a particular part of my own country?" I asked, rage beginning to roar through my veins. He must have sensed my anger.

"You want to work in the north, don't you?" he asked but I didn't respond. I stared blankly at him.

"Well?" he pursued.

"Yes," I said.

"That's why you mustn't see it as pretence. You have come to the north because you want a job. Changing your name will facilitate the process. That's the way to look at it," he said in a soothing voice.

"You are an Igbo man earning a living in the north. Did

you have to change your name to get your current job?" I asked, watching him accusingly.

"I was going to explain that but you wouldn't give me the chance."

"Well, I am sorry. Perhaps your story will guide me in this city," I said, not bothering to hide my impatience.

Ify was born and raised in Jos, Plateau State. He had his primary and secondary education there before a military government paved the way for some Nigerian youths to travel to either Canada or the United States of America for higher technical education in the 1970s. The government sponsorship was for a two-year diploma programme, after which they were to return to Nigeria. However, Ify stayed back in Canada and, with the financial support of his family, obtained both a bachelor's and a master's degree in civil engineering before returning home for his National Youth Service Corps programme. He was the eighth child in a large, monogamous family of ten children. Although his parents, Mazi Ugochukwu Jeremiah and Rebecca, hailed from Anambra, they had both lived in Jos from childhood before they met and married. Mazi Ugochukwu was a great entrepreneur, dealing in automobile spare parts and the city was the only place Ify and his siblings knew as home. It was Gwete and Towon Acha they knew as their native food; it was Hausa language they spoke as their 'mother tongue' and it was the people of Plateau they related with as kits and kin. Ify and his siblings never visited their parents' native home until the civil war broke out in 1967.

It was also the war that gave them the opportunity to learn the Igbo language for the three years it raged. As soon as the war ended, however, they returned to Jos, where their father built their family house as well as all other properties he owned. Jos was where his business was domiciled and it was the only city he could function properly in. All his friends were there. Even with all Mazi's children being fully mature, with many of them already married, they remained in the north. Some of them lived in Kano, some in Bauchi, Maiduguri, Sokoto and there were those who stayed back in Jos. Ify and one of his older siblings, Cajethan, lived in Kaduna. Sadly, however, despite their full acculturation in Plateau, all Mazi's children had had to hide their links with Anambra to be accepted. They were educated to believe that they had to renounce their father's native name and state of origin and acquire Plateau State Citizenship certificates before they could advance their interests. They had also had to discard their Igbo names - at least officially - and adopt Plateau-sounding, English, or Biblical names. Hence, Ify and some of his siblings used their biblical names rather than their traditional names. Their father also used his Biblical name, Jeremiah. Ify's was Joshua.

"Only my family members and close friends know me as Ify," he finished with a sudden drop in tone, depressed by some reality he believed he knew but I didn't.

"You need to change your name, after which I will arrange a Kaduna State Citizenship certificate for you," he concluded with a sigh.

I hung my head in confusion. I was silent for a while, turning over his suggestion. No, this was one advice I didn't need, I told myself.

"I don't think that will be necessary in my situation," I said, raising my head and making an effort to sound cheerful.

"You don't understand," he said unhappily.

"I do. I'm from Kwara and Kwara is one of the northern states," I said triumphantly.

"Don't be naive. Kwara is one of the northern states in Lord Lugard's book and for northern political exigencies only; you have to belong to the core north to be regarded as a true northerner," he said in a lecturing tone.

"You confuse me."

"Don't get confused. It's the way of the country. Look at me, was it fair that I had to go through the psychological trauma of hiding my traditional name, acting as if my parents were not Igbo and paying bribes to obtain the citizenship certificate of a state in which I was born and raised and where I have lived all my life?

What was wrong with being an Igbo? Why did I have to conceal the fact? My family is not the only one that has gone through the trauma; other families from other parts of the country also had to change their names and alter their identities before they could be incorporated into the scheme of things. It's the reality. That is not even the only problem you have in your own case. You don't speak the language, which is a huge problem. It's difficult to forge ahead in the north if you don't speak Hausa but I have friends around who can assist in shielding you from scrutiny, at least initially. The bottom-line, however, is that you have to learn the language," he concluded, peering at me closely and sticking his face almost in my chest.

I leaped to my feet, my heart pounding. Why was he tormenting me this way? I looked at him in momentary confusion.

"The same can't apply to me. I'm a northerner by birth," I said shaking my head securely.

"Don't waste your time, Anjola. I have it all planned. The people from southern Kaduna are Christians and that provides you with some leverage. You can, for instance, change your name from Anjola to Angela and I will get a Kaduna State Citizenship certificate for you."

"What about my surname?"

"We will find a way around it."

"How?"

"We can modify it to something like Adnoyi which means that your name will become Angela Adnoyi and you can claim to have come from southern Kaduna, also known as southern Zaria."

"That would be criminal. I could get myself arrested or even imprisoned," I said, arching him a perfect eyebrow.

He laughed. "Nobody will arrest you because you will do everything legally."

"I beg your pardon? What's legal about obtaining a certificate of citizenship under false pretences?"

"You don't understand. First, we will get a sworn affidavit of change of name duly signed in a court of law."

"You mean I have to go through such illegalities to get employed?"

Ify smiled sadly. I could read his mind. I knew he believed I had no choice if I wanted to work in the north but I disagreed. I came from Kwara, which is in the north. How more northern could I possibly be? Why should I pretend to come from another northern state? All northern states were equally northern. I braced myself.

"Don't do me such favours, Ify, I won't forge certificates. I won't claim Kaduna State. I'm from Kwara and that's northern enough to earn me a job in the north," I said finally.

"I don't blame you for being ignorant. You will learn your lesson soon enough and that's why I will go ahead to assist you - with or without your consent," he said with forced triviality and cheerfulness.

"You amuse me. Is it some kind of sport for you?" I asked.

"What do you mean?" he asked, smiling weakly at me.

"I said I don't need forged documents and you are insisting on procuring them. Why?" I asked haughtily.

"Never mind, I will do what I have to do," he said, injecting a manly gruffness into his voice.

We argued until our throats became dry. True to his word, he announced the following morning that he was going to the Kaduna State high court for an affidavit of change of name. I reiterated my earlier position and he insisted on going ahead with his plan. I decided to go with him for want of anything better to do. We didn't need to enter the court premises. As soon as we got within its vicinity we were surrounded by touts who jostled to outdo one another enquiring if we wanted an affidavit. Ify talked to one of them, brought out his wallet and counted some naira notes, which he handed over along with a piece of paper. He told us to wait for him and disappeared. A man pushing a trolley filled with sugar cane nearby announced his wares. Ify asked if I wanted and I said no. He urged me to try, explaining that sugar cane in the north was special. As we watched him peel it the tout reappeared clutching an old copy of New Nigerian newspaper. He opened the paper and brought out the affidavit. Ify looked at it briefly before handing it to me. I marvelled at its glamour and official finesse. At the top of the paper was printed, in block letters: IN THE HIGH COURT OF KADUNA STATE HOLDEN AT KADUNA, followed by a heading underlined:

Sworn Affidavit of Change of Name

It read:

1. That my name is Angela Adnoyi
2. That from birth, I was named Angela
3. That my father's name is Adnoyi
4. That Adnoyi is my surname / family name
5. That Angela Adnoyi is the name everyone in my family knows me by
6. That teachers and authorities in my primary, secondary and university days ignorantly   used Anjola Adeniyi as my name.
7. That I am now known and called Angela Adnoyi after the necessary correction
8. That all previous documents bearing Anjola Adeniyi remain valid
9. That.I make this declaration in good faith believing the same to be true and correct with the provision of Kaduna State Statutory Declaration Law of Nigeria.

Sworn to at the High Court Registry, Kaduna this 28th day of July, 1989

Two weeks later, Ify gave me a citizenship certificate titled: CLAIM TO KADUNA STATE ORIGIN

I confirm that Miss Angela Adnoyi whose passport photograph appears below is a native of Zango Kataf in Zango Kataf Local Government Area.

Her father's name is Zecharia Adnoyi of Zango Kataf.

Her mother's name is Esther Adnoyi also born at Zango

Kataf.

She is therefore of Kaduna State origin.

Ify told me to write an application for employment to the Ministry of Information and Strategy. He said interviews were conducted between November and December. Since I had arrived in July, this meant that I had to wait a few months. He suggested I spend the time acclimatising myself and learning the language. He went ahead to enrol me at a local language coaching centre. I was amazed at his strong organisational ability and what I reckoned to be his deep affection for me. He urged me to be hopeful, assuring me that it was still possible for me to live my dream. I believed everything he said except the one bordering on my change of identity. I shared his optimism that a fulfilling job was on the horizon and permitted myself a generous dose of my pre-NYSC fantasies.

There were two passengers in the taxi we took on our way from the high court. One of them was well acquainted with Ify, going by the camaraderie between them.

"Meet my wife," he said, putting his hand on my shoulder. I cut him an eye but he acted as if he hadn't noticed. The man smiled pleasantly and Ify continued his introduction.

"Anjola, this is Kingsley. We have known each other since childhood. We used to live in the same neighbourhood."

I smiled back at Kingsley, quietly warming up for a fight. Imagine him introducing me as his wife without my having agreed to marry him. I let him have it as soon as we were alone in his apartment.

"Did you need to make such a bogus claim to impress your friend?" I challenged, cocking my head to one side and arching a perfect eyebrow at him.

"What's bogus about what I said?" he retorted, winking at me.

"Oh, so you agree it was false?" I pursued, my blood singing in my veins. He appeared prepared to play my game judging by

164

the way he was struggling to stifle a laugh.

"What was false?" he asked, his lips curled in a half smile.

"When did we get married? You haven't even proposed to me."

"Now see who is making a false claim. I proposed to you way back in Obodonwayi, remember?" he said triumphantly.

"Did I say yes?" I asked, still trying not to show my exhilaration.

"Very well then, I suppose it's time we revisit the issue. How and where do you want me to do it? Here at my place or under the cosy atmosphere of an exotic restaurant?" he asked with his trademark smile.

"You must be the least romantic man God ever created," I commented, a wide-mouthed grin on my face.

"What are you waiting for? Why not get me started on romantic lessons?" he asked without attempting to hide a smirk.

"You are nothing but a naughty engineer," I teased and we laughed. He gathered me in his arms, smooching me and I surrendered to him happily. I was being melodramatic and no matter how hard I tried, I was aware I could never have succeeded at veiling my excitement. Ify and I had bonded so well that neither of us needed to convince the other about what we both wanted. It was clear we wanted each other. We were not just in love; we understood each other and didn't find it difficult to accept our negative sides as well. We had mutual respect for each other and he gave me good reason to look up to him. I loved his honesty. It was a quality I had despaired of ever finding. There was a dignity about him, a gentleness that I found appealing. He amazed me by the way he tried to direct my path, yet never failing to constantly express faith in my ability and potential. He encouraged me to believe in myself and trust my own judgment. He was always willing to counsel and offer advice and suggestions whenever necessary, yet he held no grudges when I chose to assert my individuality.

Ify was a confident person, self-assured and not afraid that my success could devalue his achievement. It was obvious he wasn't in competition with me. He viewed our association as one that would compliment him and make his life more complete. He was the man who would let me be who and what I wanted without being apologetic about it. If he disagreed with me on any issue, it was because he wanted me to see it from a different perspective. His criticisms were aimed at opening new vistas so that I might be a better person. He didn't criticise me or forcibly bend me to submission. He supported me financially, not because he felt he owed it to me but because he wanted to share. He didn't concentrate on my character defects; he dwelt on my positive attributes and made his assessment of my personality believable. He was not a frivolous person. We hadn't seen for a while prior to my relocation to Kaduna, for instance, but rather than distract me with issues about us, he focused almost strictly on the subject of my relocation, believing that we would have plenty of time for ourselves afterwards.

What I cherished most about us, however, was the informality that characterised our relations. Ify was a man like no other. He was a great friend, a dependable ally and the man on whose shoulder I could truly lean on. I felt comfortable with him; I felt loved, appreciated, protected and cherished. I agreed to marry him but impressed upon him that we would do so only after I had secured a job. He accepted. I also insisted that he propose more romantically, on one knee, in a cosy restaurant. I didn't want to miss the fun of the moment and I was right, he was a spectacle on his knees. I had a good laugh just watching him.

When we returned to his apartment, he removed a bunch of keys from his pocket and inserted one of them into the lock. He turned it slowly and pushed the door open, fumbling around for the light switch. I preoccupied my mind with my plan, making no attempt to help him. Finally, he flicked on the switch. I began to execute my plan immediately by slowly running my fingers down his chest to the top of his trousers. I smiled seductively at him and began to undo the buttons. Then I pushed him away gently and lifted my skirt to reveal that I was wearing nothing underneath. He made a face but I pretended not to notice his embarrassment. I waited expectantly for him to make a move but he continued to stare. I leaned forward and pulled down his trousers, then removed his shirt.

"Let's go to the bedroom," I said.

"You lead," he said.

I took him by the hand and we turned in the direction of the bedroom, taking small paces. He seemed dazed but I took no notice. Now in bed, I climbed across him and lowered myself gently onto him. I began to move slowly up and down, my head tossed back. I took his right hand and placed it on my breast. He left it there for a while, still not moving even though my rhythm became faster. Then, suddenly, he pulled me down and started kissing me. Long after he had rolled onto one side and fallen into a deep sleep, I lay there, thinking about the journey we had just begun.

CHAPTER 19

Meanwhile, the time was fast approaching for my selection interview with Kaduna State Ministry of Information and Strategy. The interview would hold in November and successful candidates would assume duty in January. Before then, however, Ify would take his annual leave in December and we would travel to Jos and Ilorin to announce our engagement to our respective families. My thoughts about both upcoming events gave me indescribable joy and the assurance of a happy future. Ify gave me books on the history of Kaduna State and the Nigerian civil service. He also gave me a compendium on the duties of an information officer. He gave me endless tutorials on how to pass the interview. I felt confident I could face the world. I had everything going for me, I assured myself for the umpteenth time. I would pass the interview and earn my selection on merit, I told myself yet again as I got my Kwara State Citizenship certificate and other documents ready for the day.

"Don't go to that interview with your Kwara State Citizenship Certificate," he warned.

"I see no reason why you have to revisit an issue we have discussed exhaustively," I said stubbornly.

"You reduce your chances of being selected with it. Why don't you want to believe me?"

"Because you are an engineer, you have poor knowledge of political science. Would you take me to the interview venue, please?" I asked, feigning exasperation.

"Your stubbornness has no cure," he said, shaking his head dramatically and starting ahead of me with a show of reluctance. He took me to the ministry, where we met the other candidates in the conference room. Most offices were locked, apparently because their occupants had not yet reported for duty. Workers began to trickle in from nine o'clock and we were eventually provided long benches on which we sat quietly, in obvious apprehension of what lay ahead. An official came to us at about ten o'clock to announce guidelines for the interview. He gave us specific instructions on how to arrange our documents for presentation to the screening committee.

"May I have your attention please?" he bellowed. Immediate silence descended on the crowd. "This is the procedure for the interview: You are to carefully arrange your documents, placing your Citizenship Certificate in front, followed by your Degree Certificate, NYSC Discharge Certificate, West African School Certificate and any other certificate you wish to present to the panel. You will present these documents to the screening committee, which has power to vet and determine whether or not you are qualified to attend. Any candidate who fails to meet the criteria will not be allowed to face the panel of interviewers."

There was a flurry of movement as we hurriedly arranged and re-arranged our documents. We formed a queue on his instructions and waited for about an hour before three people we immediately recognised as members of the screening committee appeared. A long table was placed with three chairs in front of one of the offices and we were told to start our presentations one after the other. One of them appeared to be the leader of the committee and another seemed to be the secretary. The one I presumed was the chairman received the documents and scrutinised them before passing them to the other man, while the man I believed was the secretary recorded the names of the candidates who had scaled through. The process went on smoothly until it was my turn. I was number four in the queue. I genuflected as I handed my documents to the chairman. He was a small, exhausted-looking man. He responded to my greeting in the quick, courteous way of an official. He frowned as soon as he saw my documents. He raised his eyes momentarily to look at me, then, shifted his gaze to my citizenship certificate before addressing me without bothering to look at the other documents.

"You are from Kwara?"

"Yes sir."

"You are not qualified for this interview," he said promptly.

"Sir?"

"You are not qualified to attend the interview."

I felt suddenly faint and gripped the edge of the desk for support. "Why?"

"Your state is not covered by the pre-requisites for eligibility. Your state excludes you from this process," he said flatly.

"I thought the interview was for applicants from the north, sir."

"Yes, from the north."

"I'm from the north, sir. I'm from Kwara, sir."

"When we talk of the north, we refer to the core north," he said unapologetically.

"Sir?"

"You heard me."

"You confuse me, sir. I don't understand you."

"It's obvious you don't. Don't waste our time, young woman. We have a busy day ahead."

"Excuse me, sir, I... I...am qualified. I...am from the north. Kwara is one of the northern states."

"Next person."

I walked away angrily when it became obvious I was making a fool of myself. On my way to Ify's office, I noticed that my mouth was dry. Good God, what was happening to me? I was still angry, confused and tired when I got to Ify's office but he burst into wild laughter on sighting me without waiting to hear what I had to say. The mockery in his laughter was like a physical slap.

"Welcome, your royal northern majesty," he said, still laughing and genuflecting in mock obeisance.

"This is not funny. I have lost the only opportunity I probably ever would have to get a job," I said miserably.

"No, you haven't. I knew it would not work but it was good you satisfied your curiosity. I don't blame you. You don't know your country but then many of us also wallowed in ignorance for a long time."

"What am I to do?"

"You will attend another interview with the documents we procured."

"Is there another interview coming up?"

"Yes. This is the time all state ministries in the north conduct interviews. I knew this one wouldn't work."

"There is still a chance for me?"

"The Ministry of Interior holds its interview next week. Just pick your documents and go for it."

I was weak with relief.

"You know what?"

"No."

"We will get fresh documents. We will take it a step further this time. I won't claim Southern Kaduna, I will claim 'core' Kaduna. I will change my name to a proper northern name; I mean a real Muslim name. I will even wear hijab to the interview," I said determinedly.

"Are you that desperate? Tell me about it, ha-ha-ha."

"Stop laughing and let's think of a good Muslim name," I said impatiently. The thought of me as Hajia gave me a delicious thrill.

"No, you will tell me this time. Angela was my idea, remember?"

"OK. What about Zainab? Hajia Zainab."

"Ehn-hen, so you are Hajia Zainab now?" He put his arm around me and tickled my midriff. I pulled away from him and moved languidly toward the rest room.

Ify and I returned to the vicinity of the high court the next morning and, in no time, were in possession of an affidavit that claimed my name was Hajia Zainab Abubakar from Magaji Ngeri Local Government Area of Kaduna State. Two days later, he got another Kaduna State Citizenship certificate in my new name. I was ready for another interview. I hated the lies; building one false story on another to create a foundation of deceit, but I told myself they were good falsehoods because they were making it possible for me to achieve my goal, which was fair and legitimate. I didn't forget to wear the hijab I had bought specially for the day. Apart from the hijab, Ify took me to the Central Market the previous day where I bought good lavender and had a gold cap fixed on one of my front teeth. I was satisfied with the preparation I had made as I dabbed a generous dose of the lavender that morning.

The interview did not begin until about noon but I was lucky to be one of the first candidates to be called after successfully passing the screening, which took the same procedure as the one conducted by the ministry of information. Only two candidates had been interviewed before I was called and they didn't come back to where the rest of us sat, waiting for our turn.

"Hajia Zainab Abubakar! Zainab Abubakar!! Zainab Abubakar!!!."

"Yes sir, present sir, I'm sorry sir."

I sprang clumsily to my feet and followed the official.

"Haba, Hajia, have you forgotten why you are here?"

"I'm sorry wallahi," I said apologetically.

"No problem, Hajia, just come with me," he said, leading me into the conference room, where I was confronted with the panel comprising three men and a woman. The man who brought me in remained standing in a corner, arms folded across his chest. I could identify the chairman by the way he took control of the proceedings. He was fat and handsome. He was white-haired, not from age but because he was born that way. He gestured to me to take a seat as soon as I greeted them. Then he stretched out his right hand and I gave him my documents but rather than look at them he stared at me intently. I readjusted myself to convince myself that I wasn't nervous. Why was he looking at me like that? Suddenly, he averted his eyes and looked at my citizenship certificate, which was foremost among my credentials, having been instructed to arrange them in that order. I was relieved he was now ready to face the business of the day. My heart, which was thumping furiously, began to calm. I readjusted myself again in my seat; this time feeling relaxed. Suddenly, he started looking at me again. Not knowing how to react, I stared back at him. We stared fixedly at each other for some moments before he asked:

"Your name is Zainab?" he asked. His voice was friendly.

"Yes sir," I mouthed, nodding vigorously and hoping I looked convincing enough.

"You are..." He paused, his brow wrinkled in thought. "Are you married?" he asked. My brain began to spin but I maintained a calm exterior.

"No, I'm not." I tried not to stutter.

"Where are you from?" he asked.

Why did he ask me where I came from when he had my citizenship certificate in his hand? My legs quivered, my head thundered and my palms were slimy with sweat. Don't panic, I told myself silently; keep calm. Then I braced myself and met his gaze.

"I'm from Magaji Ngeri, Kaduna," I said valiantly.

He forced a smile but didn't look convinced. He gave me a scrutinising gaze, his eyes full of questions.

"Zainab Abubakar from Magaji Ngeri, how did you come about the Yoruba tribal marks on your face?" his voice rang out but I tried for bravery.

"Actually, sir, my mother is Yoruba but my father is from Magaji Ngeri, Kaduna," I said, surprised at how easily the lies fell from my mouth. "I was taken to Ibadan a few years after my birth for the tribal marks, sir." I continued, embellishing on my fabrication.

He continued to stare at me, now with interested, gimlet eyes.

"You were taken to your maternal home for tribal marks in Nigeria? You have to think of another lie because this won't help you," he said, trying not to laugh.

I realised that I had goofed but I didn't know how to correct my mistake. I stared at him dumbly for a moment then bowed my head in defeat.

A wild laughter erupted among the panel members. Everyone, including the official that led me in, was laughing. One of them dangled his head from side to side and was almost falling off his seat; the other one was banging his fist on the table with frenzy. The only female member of the panel didn't join in but just sat there, seemingly morose. She cupped her jaw in her right palm, looking at me but I couldn't decipher what she was thinking. I wanted to seize the opportunity of their laughter to think what to say in my defence but my mind went blank. I hadn't prepared for the chairman's question. Neither Ify nor I had given a thought to my tribal marks. Suddenly, the chairman stopped laughing and the others took their cue.

"Who are you and where are you from?" he asked, leaning back in his chair. His eyes grew small and watchful.

"Actually sir, in actual fact sir, let me explain sir..." I couldn't string a sentence together. I gave up the effort and sighed.

"Ezekiel!" the chairman called. "Come and count the number of marks on her face for proper documentation."

Other members of the panel, apart from the woman, were now trying not to smile

"Yes sir," he responded. He ordered me to stand up. I could feel beads of sweat beginning to trickle down onto my nose but I obeyed.

"One, two, three, four, five, six, seven, eight, nine, ten, eleven, twelve, thirteen, fourteen, fifteen! Oh my God! There are fifteen tribal marks on her face, sir. Her right cheek has eight marks and there are seven on the left. They wanted to kill her wallahi. Her parents didn't like her gaskiya."

Surprisingly, I seemed to have gathered my ravaged senses because I now looked defiantly at the panel members. Tears stood in my eyes but I blinked them away. I was determined not to weep or betray any emotion.

All the members of the panel, except the woman, had started laughing again. They seemed even more excited and I watched them as if I was enjoying their show. How dare they turn me into a spectacle? What did they know about my travails? I would have loved to scream and tell them to go to hell but I knew I mustn't so I threw a baleful glance in their direction and inclined my head. I saw the woman cover her face with her hands as if she was sharing in my humiliation. It saddened me to see her feel so bad but I was far from being remorseful. The chairman cleared his throat and everyone stopped laughing.

"Fifteen marks on one face? What cruelty! Why did your parents have to go that far? To prove what point? Anyway, that's not our concern here. I'm contemplating handing you over to the police for impersonation and forgery but I want you to answer a few questions first. Where are you truly from?"

"I am from Kwara State."

"What's your real name?"

"My name is Anjola Adeniyi."

"You are obviously Yoruba by descent."

"Yes."

"Why did you lie and forge documents?" he asked. Something in his manner of approach commanded my respect. I knew it was time to tell him my story.

"I'm in desperate need of employment. I tried to take part in a selection interview in Kaduna here with my real name and correct state of origin but was disqualified on the grounds that Kwara does not belong to the core north. I was informed that the only way to get a job in any state of the federation is to claim to be an indigene of that state. I wish to live and work in Kaduna and the only way to achieve my dream seems to be to lie that I'm an indigene."

I watched him as I spoke and saw his expression metamorphose from anger to compassion. When I was finished I sat back, exhausted. I waited for his final pronouncement. He smiled enigmatically at me.

"Well, you are not from Kaduna State and you can't take part in this interview. On compassionate grounds, however, I will let you go, but don't ever try this kind of gimmick again because you may not be so lucky next time," he said.

Looking grave, he tore the forged citizenship certificate into shreds, handed my other documents to me and instructed Ezekiel to escort me out. I rose groggily to my feet and made to follow Ezekiel but the woman called me back.

"Let me advise you, my daughter," she said tenderly.

"Yes Ma," I said courteously

"Go to Ibadan. I have it on good authority that Oduduwa International is on a recruitment drive and will hold a selection interview in December," she said, giving me a comforting smile.

"Thank you, Ma," I said gratefully as Ezekiel led me out.

I was surprised that the panel members chose to poke fun at me because of my tribal marks. They all belonged in the category of the older generation Nigerians, like my father, so, I expected them to be familiar with Nigeria's trajectory. It was my father who told me, for instance, that in pre-literate Nigerian society, tribal marks served as a means of identification of family lineage so that wherever members of the same lineage found themselves, they could connect easily and be of assistance to one another. Perhaps, this was partly what Achebe had in mind when he insisted in Anthills of the Savannah that "it is the mark on the face that sets one people apart from their neighbours". My father even said that facial marks were given for the purposes of identification during the slave trade and also during intra and inter-tribal wars so that soldiers would be able to identify themselves and forestall the likelihood of friendly fire. Another reason was that it served as a mark of royalty. He told me how they were a source of pride in Yoruba land, and how those who didn't have them were jocularly referred to as ko rowo kola - not wealthy enough to have marks. When I queried him about the rationale behind his giving me facial marks since I wasn't born at that time and none of my brothers had tribal marks, he said he thought they would accentuate my beauty. Good heavens! Anyway, my father admitted that in modern society, many parents, especially those with Western education no longer practise it on their children. Sounding contrite and somewhat apologetic, he said he had become aware that facial marks could cause people discomfort, especially as other people often make jest of them, calling them 'designer face', which he also said he knew could engender a feeling of low self-esteem. He gave me a quizzical look, ostensibly to detect how my facial marks made me feel but I put up a brave effort to make my face blank. I acted that way not because I wanted to be petulant, but because his reasons for supporting the eradication of facial marks were not quite the same as mine.

I had appraised and re-appraised the role of tribal marks and concluded that although, they had served very useful, life-saving and probably aesthetic purposes in the past, the current realities suggested that they were no longer necessary. Apart from the fact that they disfigured faces, education had brought better ways of identification. For instance, like other people in different parts of the country and around the world, Yoruba people had since devised a new way of identifying themselves which was through family name. Also, there were no more intra or inter-tribal wars, so what did we need tribal marks for? Most importantly, I envisioned a movement toward a common Nigerian culture in which tribal marks would have no place. I remained optimistic that we would evolve a common national identity that would suppress ethnic particularities. I supported the eradication of facial marks wholeheartedly and wished I could remove the ones on my face so that I wouldn't feel and look different from people from other parts of my country. What I didn't understand was why Ezekiel would suggest that my parents gave me facial marks because they didn't like me. Part of my humiliation, I supposed.

Anyway, Ezekiel's assumption was wrong but his mischief and the attitude of the panel served to deepen my meditation on the issue. The more I thought about it, the happier I felt about my engagement and the more excited I became about how my marriage would bring greater unity in my country. I was an agent of positive change. I thought happily and smiled secretly in self-congratulation. With our planned marriage, Ify and I would be counted among other progressive elements in my motherland. I closed my eyes momentarily and inhaled deeply as I visualised the positive transformation from mutual mistrust to mutual love and respect that would reign supreme in my country. In my mind's eyes, I saw how our union would offer hope and engender greater harmony between our different ethnic identities just as the marriage between the parents of Maj-Gen Ike Omar Sanda Nwachukwu did. Nwachukwu was born to an Igbo father and a Hausa-Fulani mother and he grew up in Lagos. In no distant future, Ify's blood and mine would form a formidable connection and we would have adorable children who would be true specimens of Nigeria. Through our children, a new generation of Nigerians with a common identity would evolve and it would be difficult for people to take up arms against one another.

Going to Ibadan in December fitted into the earlier plan Ify and I had made. For reasons I couldn't explain, I felt toughened by the series of disappointments and humiliation that had been my lot since I had started searching for employment. The more difficult it seemed, the more determined I became to get into the scheme of things in my country. I had also begun to write notes on the policy changes I would use my position to propose to government when, eventually, I got a job and climbed the career ladder. There were many aspects of our national life that made me uncomfortable. I would go to Oduduwa International, where I would not be rejected, and from there begin the task of reforming my country. The thought of my mission made me walk taller and straighter. I was disgraced but unburdened.

CHAPTER 20

Our journey to Jos was smooth. We left Kaduna early in the morning. Ify wanted us to arrive early so I could see the beauty of the city. At Mando Motor Park in Kaduna we sat very close, feeling proud and chatting endlessly as our vehicle loaded passengers and their luggage. There was noise everywhere as drivers and Motor Park touts jostled for passengers and hawkers shouted their wares. I wore my hair pinned firmly in a bun to give me a confident look. I also tried to radiate outward calm but I was preoccupied with thoughts of what lay ahead in Jos. What if my future in-laws didn't like me? I had been told that the Igbo people were blunt; that they made no pretences about their likes and dislikes. What if they said to my face: "Young girl, we don't like you and don't consider you good enough for our son?" Would I try to convince them otherwise? Or would I accept their decision with equanimity? Ify didn't share my apprehension. He gave me a long lecture on determination and optimism and concluded that I would be his wife regardless of what anyone said or wanted. I wished I was as confident.

"Please help me in the name of God. There is nothing to eat. I'm married, have five children but no job. I need your help my brothers and sisters. God will help you, too."

Ify and I turned simultaneously to a middle-aged man standing by our bus. We listened to his solicitations for a brief moment, as did most other passengers, before resuming our 'gist.' We didn't give him money. The man went to the other side of the bus and repeated what he said earlier. Again, some of the passengers who were engaged in conversation stopped momentarily to listen to him but soon went back to their conversation. He returned to our side of the bus and started all over again:

"I beg you in the name of God. I have lost my job. I have a wife and five children. I have no money to feed them. Please help me. No amount is too small, please."

There was still no response. Ify was telling me there were things I needed to know before we got to Jos. Although I tried to listen my eyes were on the persistent beggar. He appeared to be getting exasperated judging by the look on his face and his now slightly raised voice.

"I don't know what else you people want me to say. I can't say it more than that. I didn't go to the school of begging. I…"

Everybody burst into laughter as the beggar turned his back on us and began to walk away. Ify resumed his talk.

"I was trying to tell you that my mother is a very strong woman."

"That's interesting," I said.

"She is also very strict. She is widely regarded as a no-nonsense woman and a great disciplinarian."

"You think she may not accept me?"

"I'm trying to tell you to be strong. You must stand by the decision we have made no matter what happens."

"You scare me."

"Okay, let me narrate the experience of a few of my married siblings so that you understand my drift."

"Yes, yes."

"My eldest brother, Benjamin, is in Jos; you will meet him soon. His wife, Auntie Cecilia, comes from a village very close to our own. It was like a man from Abacha taking a wife from Abatete. In fact, the distance between her father's compound and ours can be covered in less than thirty minutes on foot. However, when Benjamin brought Auntie Cecilia to my mother as his intended, my mother objected and categorically told Auntie Cecilia she wasn't accepted. My brother patiently explained that Auntie Cecilia was the woman he loved but my mother wouldn't hear of it. My brother took a series of measures aimed at placating her; he begged, cajoled and even threatened but nothing worked. He sought the assistance of elders of our mother's church; he visited her natal family but no one could make her change her mind. In the end, he just went ahead and married her with the support of our father and most other members of our family. We thought the war was over but it turned out to be the beginning. My mother took to visiting my brother's home whenever he wasn't around, threatening his wife. She would seize Auntie Cecilia by the elbow with intent to physically drag her out of her matrimonial home, shouting on top of her voice: "You are not my daughter-in-law; you will leave my son's house by force. You are not good for my son."

"Are you exaggerating?" I demanded, raw panic beginning to seize me.

"Why would I do such a thing? You'd better listen."

"Why didn't you tell me this before now?" I asked but he ignored me.

"As I was saying, Auntie Cecelia would report to her husband, who would visit our mother in anger to warn her to desist but she would repeat it all over again. This continued until Auntie Cecilia gave birth to her third child. It was only then that she started to treat Auntie Cecilia as a daughter-in-law."

"It's scary," I said but again Ify acted as if he hadn't heard me.

"I respect Auntie Cecilia's doggedness and perseverance," he continued. "There's another of my older siblings, Cornelius, who lives in Bauchi with his wife and children. When he wanted to marry his wife, Auntie Ngozi, he took her to Jos but my mother rejected her on the grounds that she was from Mbaise. By the way, Mbaise people are considered wicked. When my mother again withheld her consent, Cornelius made no attempt to appeal to her. Interestingly, Auntie Ngozi didn't suffer undue persecution from my mother because they live outside Jos. However, when they had their first child, they mailed the photograph of their little bomboi to our mother, hoping that she would be happy that another grandchild had arrived for her. To their shock, however, my mother sent back the photograph with a note stating that she did not wish to know, much less accept, the child of a woman she did not approve of as her daughter-in-law. Ha, ha, ha, I have almost forgotten the most interesting of all involving another of my siblings who…"

"Save me the rest please. I feel dizzy," I cried in terror. Imagine him telling me all this for the first time and on our way to go and meet this 'strong woman.' This is wicked, to be mild about it. What would I do now? I wondered.

"Don't be scared," he said, interrupting my introspection and using his index finger to raise my jaw so that our eyes locked for a long moment. Then he took my right hand and gently squeezed it. My heart was thumping; my head was in a whirl. I wanted to say something but couldn't find the words.

"You need to know what to expect," he said.

I looked blankly at him.

"I'm the only one among my mother's children taking a wife not just outside Igbo land but also with tribal marks. The challenge before us is not for the lily-livered but it's also simple if we are determined. That's what I'm trying to impact into you. Don't expect a warm welcome," he concluded. I managed to nod. Our bus was filled. The journey began.

We got to Jos at about 1pm but I didn't get to appreciate the city. The terminus was on the outskirts, from where we took a taxi straight to Mazi Jeremiah's family house. Besides, I was too concerned about my mission to give consideration to aesthetic pleasures. We had hardly driven for ten minutes when Ify told the cab driver to stop in front of an old building directly overlooking the road.

"We are here," he announced with an encouraging smile. "Don't worry, the most important thing is our own decision," he added, looking at me, his eyes narrowed with firmness. I took a deep breath and nodded.

I alighted from the taxi and sighted an old woman of about seventy sitting on a padded chair in front of the house. She must be Ify's mother, I said to myself. She smiled broadly as soon as she saw Ify and I knew I had guessed right. As Ify and I bent over to remove our luggage from the boot, he whispered to me conspiratorially:

"Don't forget that no woman is good enough for her son."

I smiled weakly as we walked toward her. "Good afternoon, Mama," I greeted with a smile and genuflected simultaneously.

"Ibu onye Igbo?" she asked. I turned to Ify. He smiled and said:

"She wants to know if you are Igbo."

I cast a nervous glance at her, wondering whether there was anywhere in Igbo land where they had my type of facial marks. I wanted to respond to her question but I couldn't form the words so I shook my head this way and that.

"O bu onye ebee?" she asked, directing her question this time at her son and staring fixedly at him.

"Mama wants to know where you come from," Ify interpreted with a mischievous smile. My mouth dried as I digested her question. Was my worst fear about to be realised? I had to fight the choking fear clawing in my heart. I forced a smile and managed to find my voice.

"Oh, Mama, I'm Yoruba, from Kwara state," I said, feeling numb in both legs. She stared impassively at me now, her face unreadable. Silence stretched between us. Then, as if she suddenly came to a decision, she lowered her gaze and my legs felt free.

"Welcome," she said in English and rose to lead us into the house, the corners of her mouth drooping. Mama was dark-skinned, slim and tall with long, graceful fingers. She was the only one at home. She and Ify started chatting cheerfully while I sat quietly, occasionally casting worried glances in his direction. He ignored me. I noticed Mama was looking at me intermittently, too, which made me fidgety. By and by, she left the sitting room. I felt momentarily relieved. I wanted to ask Ify for his mother's impression but I was tongue-tied. I was perspiring and he seemed to be enjoying my discomfort. He sat smiling mischievously without as much as a casual glance in my direction. I felt like hitting him. I realised that I had to pull myself together. I got up in search of Mama without asking for directions. I found her in the kitchen making food. I offered to help but she wouldn't let me. She said I had just come from a long journey and must be tired. Well, at least she was now talking to me, and in the language that I understood. I refused to leave the kitchen despite her telling me to.

Anyway, we eventually started talking properly. Mama spoke good Pidgin. In less than an hour we were chatting like two relatives. Her frail body was deceptive. She regaled me with tales of her strength. She said she took exception to being treated like an old woman or someone not able to do house chores. She dramatised her strength and agility with deft movements as she lifted one heavy object after another. Mama was thoroughly entertaining. I was amazed at the fluency of her Pidgin, too. Didn't Ify say she never went to school? She allowed me take the prepared food to the sitting room.

The sitting room was sparsely furnished. There were four old-fashioned cushion chairs in different colours. There was no dining section but in the corner to my right was an old centre table. On the other side of the room were three old plastic chairs. Behind the chairs were shelves filled with old cassettes and records. My gaze fell on an old framed photograph of my parents-in-law. I loved the sense of homeliness. Well, I chose to affirm it was my home. She dished her own food separately but used one plate to dish for Ify and me, asking me if the quantity was enough. We sat down to eat. Mazi Jeremiah came in much later and warmed up to me as soon as we were introduced. He seemed thrilled by the novelty of having a Yoruba daughter-in-law. He told me stories about his family and asked me endless questions about mine.

"I like you," he said with a smile. "I can see you love my son. The only thing is for you to accept us as we are. You are welcome to our family," he said. I smiled.

Papa and I went on chatting until Mama brought a plate of garden eggs and groundnut paste and placed it on a stool between us.

"Eat garden egg, my daughter. Me and you go talk; inugo?"

"No Mama, let's talk now. I can always come back for the garden egg," I said, fear welling up inside me.

"Come make we go," she said, leading the way. She took me to her bedroom. I wanted to sit on the couch but she insisted I sit on the bed with her.

"Ify report me to im Papa," she started.

I was taken aback.

"He did? Over what?"

"He say I no wait make you enter house before I begin ask whether you be Igbo."

"Ah! Sorry Mama. How could he have done a thing like that?"

"No worry my pikin. Na true he talk. Me ma don tink am say e no good as I do. Him Papa say make I beg you, make you no vex."

"Beg me? Mama, it's your right to know the company your son is keeping."

"No worry, my pikin. My son don tell me everytin. He say na you he wan marry. I tell am say I like you but I no like as you no be Igbo. He say e no mean, sake of say na you he want."

"Ha, Mama."

"I don tell am say I gree."

"You mean you accept me?"

"Wetin I go do? But e get something' wey I wan ask you."

"Go on, Mama."

187

"You go fit take care of my son like say you be Igbo woman?"

"Is that all, Mama?"

"E don finish."

"I will do my best. And you go help me too. Teach me small, small."

"God go bless you, oh. Ify no be trouble-maker. Come make you go chop your garden egg."

No. I didn't bathe with any special soap. I was tongue-tied. Ordinarily in such a situation, I would have had muscle pull. But I got up and my legs also responded. I hugged my, yes, mother-in-law and we returned to the sitting room.

Ify and I set out early the next morning. It was the only day we had to go round his relations; we were scheduled to leave Jos for Ibadan the next day. Our first port of call was the house of one of his two brothers, Uncle Ikechukwu. He didn't seem excited to see us but he made an effort to be civil. His wife offered us food but we declined, explaining that we had just eaten. Ify and his brother chatted in Igbo. I didn't know at what point he told him our mission. Uncle Ikechukwu was distant. He seemed to be struggling with himself as he served us drinks. At one point he said something in Igbo and they abruptly left the sitting room. His wife promptly came to join me.

"Congratulations, my sister; you are marrying the best of them."

"Thank you, Auntie."

"Don't take what I said as a mere compliment. You will enjoy your marriage because Ify has a good heart."

"Thank you, Auntie."

"I understand you are Yoruba. Where are you from?"

"Kwara State."

"That's interesting, we will …"

We heard footsteps. Ify emerged from one of the bedrooms and told me brusquely to get up and follow him.

"Ikechukwu doesn't like you," he said as soon as we were out of the house.

"What does he have against me?"

"He said I must be insane to have gone to Yoruba land to pick a wife."

"Why?"

"He said only a senseless man marries a woman who cannot communicate with his mother. When I told him you and Mama have been talking since we arrived, he asked me in what language and I said Pidgin. He started to insult me. He said Pidgin is not a language and can never be an ideal medium of communication between a woman and her mother-in-law. He told me the only time he speaks even proper English to his wife is when they quarrel."

"Is that why you are so angry? Doesn't he have a right to his opinion?"

"You've not heard everything."

"Okay, go on."

"He described my plan to marry you as unacceptable. He even told me never to bring you to his house again."

"Is that all?"

"What do you mean is that all? Who gave him the right to dictate to me who to marry?"

"You know you surprise me when you talk like this. Didn't you lecture me on how not to expect every member of your family to dance around me in jubilation?"

"You have a point. It's just that I didn't expect that kind of reaction from someone who claims to be enlightened. Ikechukwu is a senior lecturer at the University of Jos."

"It doesn't matter; even professors are entitled to parochialism. Besides, life is a mixed bag."

CHAPTER 21

We headed for the house of his eldest brother, Uncle Benjamin. He received the news of our engagement with enthusiasm. He told me a long story about the cosmopolitan outlook of the Jeremiah family and how their stay in Jos had broadened their minds. He said he supported inter-ethnic marriage as a weapon of peace and harmonious co-existence among the numerous ethnic groups in Nigeria. He promised to protect me and the children I would have for his kid brother and urged me to cultivate a positive attitude toward my in-laws. You needed to have seen my face. I couldn't hide my joy.

"There is one more piece of advice I will like to give you, Anjola," he said as Ify and I rose to leave.

"I am appreciative, Uncle," I said.

"You must learn to listen more and talk less."

"Yes Uncle."

"Always bear in mind that people will misinterpret, most times deliberately, what you say to suit their personal purposes."

"Thank you, Uncle."

"Every woman needs the wisdom of Solomon to guide her as she interacts with her in-laws."

"Yes Uncle."

"Don't give people the opportunity to twist your words and the best way to achieve that is by keeping quiet most of the time."

"Thank you, Uncle."

"May God uphold your marriage."

"Thank you, Uncle."

We left Uncle Benjamin's house feeling like a married couple. The feeling remained with us for the rest of the day such that we hardly took notice of the countenance of the other relatives we visited afterwards. Our mission had been accomplished. Before we left Jos, Papa and Mama wanted to know when they would be required to visit my parents. We told them it wasn't time yet. Ify explained that he hadn't met my parents and that we planned to visit them after my job interview in Ibadan later in the week. Papa gave us a note to the leader of the Igbo community in Ibadan to accommodate us. We left Jos feeling happier than we thought was possible, I much more so.

In Ibadan, we were warmly received by Chief Ogbonna Amadi, whose son also drove us to Oduduwa International Headquarters at the famous Dugbe the following morning for my interview. I was left to interact with the other applicants with a promise that they would come back to take me home. I met a huge crowd, each clutching a big envelope. Everybody was looking anxious and the atmosphere almost made me afraid. My attention was drawn to a particular area where the applicants seemed to be converging. Perhaps we were being summoned by an official of the corporation. I looked at my wristwatch; it was just a quarter after seven. I joined the others and saw a man who seemed to be the object of attention. He could have been mistaken for an official of Oduduwa International judging by his appearance but he wasn't. He was dressed in a pair of striped black trousers, a white short-sleeved shirt and a blue bow-tie. His black shoes shined and his hair glittered with what might have been too much Morgan pomade. He had a plump face and held a suitcase. He was addressing the crowd of applicants, who were listening with rapt attention. I moved closer.

"I'm a motivational speaker of great repute. I have positively turned around the lives of many young people in this city, especially the students of the University of Ibadan. Anybody who is based in Ibadan and comes to the campus frequently can also attest to the power of my tongue. I got information that Oduduwa International will hold a selection interview this morning and I decided to come and offer my God-given talent to all of you. I have not come here to talk about religion. I'm here to give you practical guidelines that work. I will introduce myself only because most of you are visitors in Ibadan. My name is Tobi Olusanya, an inspirational and motivational speaker par excellence, the man ordained by God and sent to mould, encourage and direct young people. I know your goal this morning and I have been sent by God to help you achieve it. Now, I want all of you to repeat after me: I will not be put to shame in this interview. I will not be disgraced in this interview. I will leave the venue of this interview with my head high."

I joined other applicants in repeating every word he said.

"Without much ado, I will proceed now to releasing the secret of success. Let everyone take a pen and a sheet of paper and write down what I'm about to dictate. The title is: THE SECRET OF SUCCESS. Write the word SUCCESS in vertical order and put a hyphen after each letter.

S – Start with a prayer
U – Utilise your knowledge
C – Curb your anxiety
C – Conquer your fear
E – Endeavour to be extraordinary
S – Speak with confidence
S – Stand out

"You have just received the secret of success which is what you need this morning. It behoves each and every one of you, therefore, to show appreciation for what you have been given by putting a substantial amount of money in the envelope that will be passed round shortly. Let me emphasise that you must put something substantial, something commensurate with what you have received. Remember that God hates an ingrate. And, in all things, give thanks."

"What? You are a beggar," someone in the audience shouted.

There was wild laughter and murmuring. People began to walk away, some laughing excitedly and 'hailing' him as a smart crook; many others abused him: ole, fraudster and yeye; but there were those who were patiently waiting for their envelope. When it came, they put money in it. My feeling was mixed but I opened my handbag and brought out money in readiness for my own envelope. I put the money in it and passed it before joining the other applicants to await the interview.

"Guys, this one is a professional beggar o, but seriously, more and more people seem to be taking to begging these days; why now?" asked a tall, thin man with myopic eyes.

"Well, maybe because they think begging is lucrative. I mean, think of it, a guy wakes up in the morning, takes a walk round town and comes back home with money," someone offered.

"Begging is not as easy as you think," another man countered fiercely. "Have you considered that a majority of them take to it as a last option?" he asked perceptively.

There was silence as we turned over his observation in our minds.

At exactly nine o'clock, an official came to explain the modalities for the interview. They were similar to what obtained in Kaduna. We formed a queue for certificate screening.

"Yes, next person."

I handed over my documents.

"You are from Kwara State?"

"Yes sir."

"Why are you here?" he asked, peering at me aggressively. He had a dark, dusty-looking skin with pigmented spots. His teeth were square, white, slightly protruding with little spaces between them.

"Sorry?"

"You are not eligible for this interview."

I stared at him in stunned bewilderment.

"I am eligible, sir," I muttered when I finally found my voice.

"Didn't you just say you are from Kwara?"

"Yes."

"This is Oduduwa International. This interview is for applicants from the western region, not for northerners."

At first my tongue refused to form words, but as the silence became uncomfortable I swallowed and cried out: "I'm Yoruba! I was born and raised in Ibadan here. Look at my tribal marks. I'm a full-fledged Yoruba girl."

"Nobody is interested in where you were born or raised. Or your facial marks. Are your parents from the western region? Are they from Ogun, Ondo, Lagos or Oyo?"

"My parents are from Kwara."

"That means you are from Kwara and your citizenship certificate rightly states it. That also means you are from the north. You are a northerner. This is Oduduwa International. We don't employ aliens into our workforce," he said, eyes blazing furiously.

"Sorry?"

"I said aliens are not allowed to attend this interview."

"You called me an alien in my country?" I asked, wrestling down the note of hysteria that wanted to invade my soul. Something about him hinted that it would be useless trying to make him see things from my perspective.

"What are you in Ibadan if not an alien? Take your documents and go. We are not here to play," he said with a repulsive smile.

I collected my documents and left without further argument. I was determined to handle his hostility with quiet dignity. I also didn't think it was necessary to wait for Ify or Chief Amadi's son; I knew I could find my way. Besides, I wanted us to leave Ibadan at once so I could see my father. Surely there were many things I didn't know about my roots that only he could explain to me. I felt the stares and whispers behind me but my focus was to exit the premises without betraying any emotion.

"Excuse me! Hello sister! Please stop!" I heard a voice calling behind me.

I spun around. I recognised the caller as one of the applicants in front of me at the queue.

"Sorry about what happened," he said.

"It's no big deal but thanks," I said, forcing a smile.

"I don't want you to feel bad. I know it's painful but you are not the first person this kind of thing is happening to."

"Thanks for your concern but, believe me, it doesn't bother me at all," I lied.

"You must be a strong person then because it bothered my uncle's wife when they did it to her."

"Who did what to your uncle's wife?"

"She was a high court judge in Ibadan when the western region was a bloc. She is also an indigene of Ibadan. However, when the western region was split into states, she fell under Oyo, as you know, and that became a problem."

"How?"

"Because she and my uncle didn't fall under the same state; my uncle is now from Ogun."

"So?"

"The new states that were created from the old western region formed their independent civil services and this meant that my uncle's wife was to become an employee of Oyo."

"She was lucky, wasn't she? She's from Ibadan and already working in her state."

"That's exactly the point. She kept waiting for her new posting in the newly created state but it seemed as if she would wait forever. When she got tired of waiting, she went to the Oyo State Ministry of Justice to enquire why her posting was being delayed. Do you know what they told her?"

"No."

"They said she wouldn't be posted; that she could no longer continue to be a high court judge because of her affiliation, through marriage, with Ogun State."

"What about her right to employment as a citizen of Oyo State?"

"Well, the state government insisted that being married to a man from Ogun made her a potential enemy."

"What did she do?"

"I haven't finished. The Oyo State government advised her to go to her husband's state to work because that is where she belongs."

"Did she go?"

"She did; and you know what happened?"

"No."

"The government of Ogun State also refused to give her a job, claiming that they couldn't guarantee her loyalty since she is from Oyo State."

"What?"

"Now you understand what I have been trying to tell you. Don't look at your travails as a north-west problem. It's a national problem. The country needs help."

I thanked him and made my way to the residence of our host, where I narrated my experience to Ify, telling him how determined I was to clarify the confusion surrounding my identity with my father. I saw sincerity in the countenance and demeanour of my 'Good Samaritan' friend. I believed the story he told me about his uncle's wife but I couldn't help feeling that I needed to find out more about myself and the position of my state. Where was I from? Was I a northerner, a Yoruba or neither? Why was I being tossed about and humiliated in every part of my country?

It was during our journey to Ilorin that I realised I hadn't thought about the best way to introduce Ify to my parents. We had discussed it and agreed to simply take our chances, as we had done in Jos.

My parents were surprised but happy to see me. They received Ify courteously, apparently suspicious of our mission. My father said I had come home at a good time because my two older brothers were on leave.

"Broda Lanre and Dayo are in town? Where are they?" I asked excitedly.

"They went out but I'm sure they will be back soon. Why don't you go and eat your food? It's a full house," my father said, grinning.

"There's something I need to tell you alone, Father."

"Right away then," he said, leading the way to his bedroom."

"I'm getting married."

"That's a pleasant surprise. To the gentleman you came with?"

"Yes Father."

"Who is he? Where is he from?"

"His name is Ifeanyi."

"That sounds like an Igbo name."

"He's Igbo, from Anambra State."

"I can see where this is coming from. You met him during your national service, didn't you?"

"You are right. Actually, that's the main reason why I came home."

"I see."

"I don't like it when you sound like that. What do you think?"

"I think of your happiness and will support whatever will make you happy but I have my worries."

"Let's talk about them," I said.

"The Igbo people hold their tradition and culture as sacrosanct. Are you sure you can cope? Even more importantly, do you think they will accept you, an outsider that knows nothing about their tradition?"

"I'm willing to learn as much as I can of their tradition and way of life. As for acceptance, I have already met his parents and some other members of his family. Most of them seemed to like me."

"Ah-ha, you have obviously gone far. I'm happy and have

no need to withhold my consent. Let me be the one to break the news to your mother and brothers."

I was relieved. My father told my mother first and promised to call a meeting of the extended family early the following morning. I had expected my mother to be unhappy but she was excited. She, however, wanted to know about my encounter with Ify's parents and relations and what their disposition was. I did a good job of narrating my experience without exaggeration.

After lunch, I went to visit my friends, leaving Ify alone with my father in mock revenge for what he had done to me in Jos. I couldn't contain my excitement, especially because of the ease with which my parents took the news. I had no reason to entertain fears about my brothers. They were young, cosmopolitan and civilised. Surely they would be happy for me. As for my extended family, I could predict negative reactions from many but it didn't bother me. What was important was that I had secured the support of my immediate family, just as it happened with Ify. That was something to celebrate. As it turned out, my friends heightened my near-state of delirium when they started asking questions about Ify. They wanted to know if he had a car and were disappointed when I said he didn't. Then they asked if he was tall and handsome, broad-shouldered and sexy. They were interested in whether he was light or dark. They said most Igbo people were 'yellow' and that 'a real man' ought to be dark. I told them my Ify was dark and they hailed me: "Omo, you are lucky o!" I laughed boisterously.

"Oya, give us proper 'gist' now; Iyawo Yanmirin," Kike said jocularly.

"Isn't that what I'm doing? What else do you want to know?" I asked.

"Describe him."

"Why do I need to bother? Come to my house tomorrow and see him for yourself."

"At least tell us what to expect," Ireti insisted.

"OK. OK. Ify is tall, dark and very hairy. He has dreamy

eyes."

"Eh he! You'd better do your home work well o; otherwise, they will snatch him from you."

"Nonsense! Ify has eyes for me only," I boasted and we laughed.

"Eyin girls, it's like my period is late o," I said.

"The guilty are afraid. Have you been eating the forbidden fruit?" Arinola asked.

"I don't know about the forbidden fruit but I have been eating a particularly sweet fruit for some time now."

"Trust Igbo people with action. They don't waste time. Have you told him?" Ireti asked.

"No, I haven't. I wanted to be sure."

"It's double congratulations then. Pray for us too o."

"I'm praying and I know yours will come sooner than you think."

We agreed to see the following day at my parents' house. I was intoxicated with happiness.

CHAPTER 22

I was still filled with a sense of euphoria when I arrived home but met my mother sitting on the cement slab outside the kitchen door, looking agitated. She said my father had gone out with Ify because Dayo, my immediate elder brother, wanted to make trouble. She said Dayo was categorical in his rejection of Ify because he was Igbo and had threatened to ensure that the marriage never happened.

"Unfortunately for him he's not in a position to do that," I said but she looked downcast. I couldn't understand. Was she not the same woman who, only a few hours before, had shown tremendous excitement at the news? Why was she so upset by Dayo's ranting? Although it came to me as a shock that Dayo wanted to play the spoiler, there could be nothing more to his outburst than a mere threat. My mother said there was something disturbing about the way he spoke; she said she detected a level of vehemence that was worrisome. I refused to believe her. Dayo was the brother I felt closest to on account of the closeness of our age. I thought I knew him. I even believed he was the one to count on to help me push a difficult idea to my parents. I stood rooted to the spot, struggling to come to terms with what my mother was telling me. Was this what people called betrayal of trust?

Only my mother and I were at home at the time. I sat pensively, looking at my feet as her intermittent appeals filtered through my troubled ears. Finally, everybody was home and all hell was let loose. Dayo's vituperations astounded me. He accused Ify, whom he had just met, along with the entire Igbo race of innumerable wrongdoings. His sister would not marry an Igbo man, he vowed. Did my parents know the implication of their daughter going to Igbo land to marry? Were they aware that it would make her incommunicado with her kith and kin? Were they prepared to lose their only daughter to a miserable Igbo man? He said all these things in Ify's presence. Bemused, I realised that my mother's fears were genuine. Dayo was truly playing the spoiler. My father looked confused. Was he reconsidering his earlier position?

My mother used eye contact to appeal to Ify and me to be calm. The only person who engaged Dayo in verbal exchange was Lanre, my other brother. First, he tried to pacify him, but when Dayo proved difficult he called his bluff and told him he was being unreasonable. Why would he want to impose his ideals on anyone? Didn't he know that it was insensitive of him to be throwing tantrums in Ify's full glare? A hot argument raged between them while the rest of us looked on. Dayo eventually stormed out of the house, after telling me he would do everything to frustrate my marriage plans. He even went as far as placing a curse on me; that happiness would elude me if I went ahead. My father tried to call him to order, demanding that he retract his curse but he refused. My father thereafter drove my fiancé and me to a hotel and paid for three nights. He told us to ignore Dayo and concentrate on building a happy relationship together.

The extended family meeting held as planned. One of my father's younger brothers, Uncle Gboyega, also expressed his opposition but no one paid him any attention. I told Ify about my pregnancy that night. He suggested we do a registry wedding immediately we got back to Kaduna in order to legitimise our union pending when we could perfect our traditional and church weddings. To my consternation, Dayo came to the hotel later in the evening saying he wanted to talk to Ify alone. I told him to say whatever he wanted in my presence. Ify intervened quickly, telling me to stay out of their conversation and assuring Dayo he was prepared to grant him audience any time and at any place of his choice. I was speechless. Dayo wanted them to go outside. Ify agreed. They left immediately. Ify came back two hours later and told me Dayo had nothing new to tell him other than to restate his opposition and warn him again to stay away from me.

"Your brother is an angry man," he said, shaking his head slowly.

I looked at him quizzically. He said Dayo didn't mince his words telling him how much he hated the Igbo people. It apparently began the day he had an encounter with an Igbo man in Lagos during traffic congestion. As commuters struggled to outsmart one another, Dayo unknowingly stepped on the toes of another commuter, who pulled him roughly by his shirt collar.

"Why did you step on my toes?" the Igbo man demanded tersely.

"Sorry, I didn't know I stepped on you," Dayo said apologetically.

"Cut the crap, you lying son of a bitch."

"I'm sorry, my brother, I didn't know. Why would I step on you deliberately?"

"Don't you dare address me as your brother; God forbid that I should be a brother to an ngbati-ngbati. I'm a proud Igbo man."

"I said I'm sorry. I didn't do it on purpose. What more do you want from me?"

"I want you to keep your miserable foot in check next time, do you understand me?

Do I have to take the punishment for the limitations of your race? You don't travel. You merely rotate from your local village to Lagos and back, never venturing outside your land. That's why you can't conduct yourself in a civilised manner."

"You have no right to insult me."

"What would you do, fight me, uh?"

"Are you looking for a fight?"

"And are you ready for a fight? Have you pulled your shirt, shoes and wristwatch, you bloody coward?"

"I didn't know you are not a responsible person. I won't stay here and bandy words with you," Dayo said and turned to walk away but the Igbo man forcibly pulled him back and spat directly into his face. Dayo was stunned. He stood rooted to the spot, wiping his face with his palm and trying to spit out the Igbo man's saliva that had found its way into his mouth. Igbo people were rash, arrogant and inhuman, he told Ify maliciously, threatening that he would stop at nothing to prevent his sister from marrying one and warning him for the umpteenth time to stay away or risk losing his life.

"Dayo is very bitter but I don't think we should worry about him. Let's talk about us, about the progress we have made so far," Ify said and I agreed.

My pregnancy became common knowledge the following day but it was also the day I almost had a miscarriage. Ify and I had gone to my parents' house for our breakfast, after which my father was to accompany us to Ifelodun to see the village folk. I had scarcely taken two slices of bread when I felt the urge to throw up. I got up swiftly and ran toward the toilet but I wasn't fast enough. I left a trail of vomit along the corridor and my mother ran after me, sprinkling water on my face.

"Pele, don't worry, it's normal," she kept saying, as if I had told her I was pregnant. She guided me back to the sitting room and suggested we postpone our planned trip until I was strong enough to travel. I disagreed. My father drove us to the village but it was after we had returned that it happened. I felt pressed to pee and went to the toilet, only to find blood in my undergarment. I raised the alarm. My father rushed me to the hospital, accompanied by Ify and my mother. The doctor diagnosed my condition as threatened abortion and said I had to be under observation for twenty-four hours. Ify wanted to stay with me but the doctor wouldn't have it. He said I needed to be left alone.

I woke up the following morning feeling stronger. The doctor examined me again and said the pregnancy was no longer in danger.

"The doctor said my condition was stable," I told Ify excitedly when he came but I observed he was also eager to tell me something. I paused, watching him set the food on the bedside table.

"You won't believe what you are about to hear," he said, smiling.

"What?"

"I stumbled on something that will surprise you."

"Then out with it. You know how I hate suspense."

"Dayo thinks you have suffered a miscarriage."

"Too bad for him."

"That's not surprising, is it?"

"No. It's normal for anybody to think that I must have lost the baby given what happened."

"Would it surprise you to know he's organising a party to celebrate your presumed miscarriage?"

"You are not making sense."

"I saw him talking in hushed tones with two men outside the gate. The way he was trying to keep his voice low made me curious so I went after the men to find out more. They didn't know who I was. They said Dayo was treating them to a bash tonight to celebrate the deserved miscarriage of his sister, who foolishly got pregnant for an Igbo man."

I stared at Ify in disbelief. I was discharged from the hospital later that evening and told my father when he came to take me to the hotel that Ify and I would be leaving the next day but that there was an important matter I needed to discuss with him.

"How did Kwara come to be a northern state?" I asked.

"Kwara has always been in the north since its creation."

"Let me tell you a story, Father. I could neither speak nor did I understand any other language apart from Yoruba as a child.

I recall that when you enrolled me in our community primary school in Ifelodun, Yoruba was the language of instruction. I didn't understand a word of English in my first few weeks in secondary school and had to depend on my seniors to interpret the principal's speech after morning assembly each day. Today, the only indigenous language I speak is Yoruba. Doesn't that suggest we are Yoruba and not northerners?"

"Don't get confused, Anjola. I haven't said we are not Yoruba. Of course we are but our state is in the north and religion is a major reason why Kwara has remained associated with the north."

"Tell me about the origin of the Kwara people."

"Let me start with Ilorin since it is the capital."

"Yes Father."

"Ilorin town is made up of about six different ethnic groups: the Kannikes from the far north like Bornu; the Gobirs, or Gobiriwa, also from the far north; the Nupes; the Barubas; and the Hausas and the Fulanis made up of Town Fulanis and Cattle Fulanis known also as the Bororos. In other parts of the state, there are the Yoruba people who came from different parts of Yoruba land, including the Egbas, the Oyos and the IIjeshas."

"In other words, Kwara is multi-ethnic?" I asked.

"Yes."

"How did one tribe dominate the others such that Kwara is now believed to belong to the Fulanis only?"

"The Fulanis that came from Mali for trading had settled in Ilorin before the establishment of an organised administration there. This made it easy for them to dominate other tribes. Another reason was because the Alafin of Oyo never exercised control over Ilorin, as he did over most towns and villages in Yoruba land. For instance, Ilorin never paid tribute to Oyo."

"Was the Yoruba population in Ilorin insignificant?"

"Not at all, remember that Ilorin is popularly known as Ilorin Afonja, meaning: Afonja's land. Afonja was a prince in Alaafin of Oyo's palace and dynasty. Even before Afonja came to settle in Ilorin, there was a Baba Isale who also came from Oyo and settled in Ilorin so that when Afonja came he met an already settled Baba Isale. In Ilorin till today, there is Afonja compound."

"How were the Fulanis able to dominate Ilorin if two Oyo people had previously established their presence?"

"Let me tell you the full history."

"Please do."

"Before he relocated to Ilorin, Afonja contested the Alaafin kingship with Alaafin Aole but lost. When Aole became the king, he appointed Afonja the Aare Ona Kakanfo, meaning War Commander. As War Commander, Afonja was not supposed to live in Oyo but it was only a strategy by Aole to push him out so that Aole would enjoy his reign. That was why and how Afonja as a warrior came to settle in Ilorin with some of his soldiers. Meanwhile, Ilorin was like a transit town for the cattle Fulanis when Afonja arrived. He immediately liaised with the Fulanis, who were Jihadists led by Alimi, to help him fight Oyo in revenge for his technical expulsion from the Oyo dynasty. With the help of the Fulanis, Afonja defeated the Oyo Army but could not capture the Alaafin. After the war, what had then come to be regarded as the Ilorin Army became a force to reckon with. Also, after the Jihadists of Alimi had assisted Afonja to defeat the Oyo Army, they wanted to convert him to Islam but he refused. He gave out his children to learn Islamic studies and become Muslims but he remained a traditionalist. Alimi, the leader of the Jihadists, had no intention of becoming a ruler but one of his sons, Abdulkalam, was ambitious and organised the Jihadists to wage war against Afonja so as to eliminate him and take over Ilorin. Afonja was so powerful that no one thought he could be subdued, let alone killed, but the Jihadists succeeded in killing him. In view of his acclaimed powers, however, the Jihadists wanted to assure themselves that Afonja had indeed been killed; hence they burnt his body to ashes. That's why, till date, the descendants of Afonja do not use ashes. After killing Afonja, the Jihadists fully established the first administration in Ilorin in

1837 and began to overrun, one by one, all the towns and villages in Kwara. Some of the towns willingly surrendered but those that refused were forcibly conquered."

"What about us, Father? What and who are we? Fulani? Yoruba? What?"

"We are Yoruba but Ifelodun, where we come from, was overrun by the Jihadists, just like all the other towns in Kwara."

I sighed. It wasn't an encouraging revelation.

"Why didn't the Yorubas outside Kwara come to rescue their people from the Fulani Jihadists?"

"There were series of wars in Yoruba kingdom at the time, including the Ijaiye War that led to the dispersion of the Yoruba people."

"Okay, if we have all been conquered how come Yoruba remains our language? Why are we not speaking the Fulani language?"

"Yoruba was retained as the language of communication because the Fulanis had no culture in the sense that their culture is Islam, their language is Arabic. What the Fulanis do is to adopt the most popular language wherever they go."

"Your story implies that the Yoruba people were in the majority, hence, Yoruba became the choice language of the Jihadists."

"Yes, indeed."

"I still find it difficult to understand why a majority of people in an environment would allow themselves to be easily overrun by people who were not only in the minority, but who merely used the town as a transit camp in the course of trading."

"War was ravaging the Yoruba enclave and other empires during this period. People were looking for a safe haven to run to for refuge. People from various settlements came to Ilorin to settle because it was considered safer than most other places. This unhappy situation gave the Fulani Jihadists the opportunity to perfect their strategy of domination and control."

"From your narration, some indigenes of Ilorin originated

from the north, while some came from the Oyo Empire."

"Yes."

"What about us? Where did we come from?"

"We are from Oyo. We are wholly and originally Yoruba."

"Why does Ilorin dominate other parts of Kwara, including our own Ifelodun? Why is it that anyone that comes from Kwara is regarded to have come from Ilorin?"

There was a long pause.

"Ilorin dominated and has continued to dominate other parts of Kwara because all other parts were conquered, coerced and forced to pay taxes to Ilorin. All other towns and villages in Kwara were paying what was called tributes to Ilorin. These villages and towns were small and disorganised. Besides, Oyo had been weakened and had disintegrated so that the Jihadists had complete control," he said.

There was another long pause. I thought I had never heard anything so sad.

"It's a sad story," I murmured, crestfallen.

"Don't feel bad about it. Kwara is a force to be reckoned with," he said after a while.

"That seems like an exercise in self-deception, Father. Who truly reckons with us? Is it the Yoruba people who push us away as northerners or the northerners who will never accept us?" I felt distraught, angry and demoralised.

"We are well respected in the country," he said uncertainly.

"I disagree. I think Kwara is a state in search of its soul."

"What's responsible for this pessimism?" There was anguish in his eyes.

"I can't find a job, Father. No one seems to know where to place Kwara in the comity of states in Nigeria; and it tears my heart to think that I'm lost in a country of my birth, I'm a complete stranger in my own country," I said, chewing on my despair.

"You will get a job, be hopeful."

"It's been over four years since I graduated and there is no hope yet that I will find one soon. Can you tell me when, Father? Can you truly tell me when?" I asked, tears streaming down my cheeks.

In spite of my efforts to control myself, the anguish that had tightened my chest since my job search began overcame me. My father was looking blankly at me, perhaps searching for words of encouragement which would be at variance with his demeanour. I waited for him to answer my question, a little light of hope flickering inside me but after staring at me for a long moment, he hung his head and stared at his feet. Perhaps he was racking his brains for the appropriate response. Sighing resignedly, I pulled myself together, pushed my worries aside and changed the subject.

CHAPTER 23

We left Ilorin the day after I nearly miscarried and we resolved to formalise our union at the Magaji Ngeri Marriage Registry immediately. Throughout our journey, however, my mind was preoccupied with Dayo's party, which I had gone to see the previous night against Ify's advice. I secretly wished the talk about my brother hosting a party was a ruse. I wanted to assure myself that Dayo would not organise a party to celebrate my misfortune, notwithstanding our disagreement. I was wrong. The hall was almost filled to capacity when I arrived and people were gyrating to the music of the Commodores. I stood in the crowd, watching in sheer perplexity. A tall guy sporting an Afro came, smiled at me and asked for a dance. I declined. He shrugged his shoulders and walked away. Soon, Dayo's voice came blaring through the microphone. He looked fabulous in his glimmering shirt and white bowtie. He thanked everyone present for honouring his invitation at such short notice. He said the party was the first in the series of activities he had planned to celebrate his vindication of his opposition to his kid sister's wrong choice of spouse. His words hit me like a thunderbolt. For minutes on end, I stood perfectly still, my brain strangely frozen. With an effort, I strode across the hall to convince myself that the person speaking was indeed Dayo.

"Ladies and gentlemen, I have invited you here to rejoice with me tonight because even God is in agreement with my

211

position," he said to loud applause. "I have been vindicated." He grinned from ear to ear as thunderous ovation rent the air. "As I speak to you, my foolish sister has not only lost the bastard she was carrying but she is also lying in hospital savouring the consequence of her disobedience. God is teaching her a well-deserved lesson which is worthy of celebration."

The crowd applauded yet again. He urged everybody to make merry, assuring them an adequate supply of drinks. My shoulders slumped in grief. I left shortly after with my head hung down. In retrospect, I wished I had taken Ify's advice and saved myself the heartache. Dayo's attitude afflicted my soul and left me utterly confused. He was the one I was always eager to share my innermost thoughts with. I had thought that family was the most important thing. I was wrong; blood wasn't always thicker than water. I merely loved illusions. Why would my own brother gloat over my misfortune even if he had adjudged me headstrong and stupid? It was unconscionable! Recollections of Dayo's words and action made me shudder and squirm with grief and despondency. With the benefit of hindsight, I realised that certain things were better left unseen, unheard and undiscovered so as to avert the absolute finality of some fights and the unforgivability of some blows. No, I ought not to have gone. I should never have found out that he felt such monumental ill-will toward me, I thought, blinking back my tears. Closing my eyes, I inhaled a long, healing breath.

Anyway, I was in Kaduna now, married to the love of my life and with my pregnancy still intact. Visions of my growing foetus provided me pleasurable moments. I foresaw only good things after my baby's birth. My uncle agreed to stand in for my father at the marriage registry, although reluctantly, while Ify's brother who lived in Kaduna, Uncle Cajethan, stood in for their father. Two days later, Uncle Cajethan visited and said it had become necessary for my husband and me to join the Kaduna branch of their town union, the Zelachi Development Union. He said I was required to present certain items to the women's wing to formalise my entry. They included five cartons of malt drink, five packets of Cabin biscuits, five plates of garden egg and a plate of kola nuts. Ify was to ensure that all the items were taken to the venue before my appearance. I was thrilled by the prospect. I saw it as a step that would give me a greater sense of belonging and cement the bond with my in-laws. My excitement was heightened by the warm attitude of some of the women I had met informally.

On my first day, I observed that I was the only non-Igbo. The leader of our union, whom we called 'chairlady', Auntie Emily, introduced the members one after the other. She said my husband was a likeable young man and that I was welcome in their midst. She explained that the gift items were a symbol of my interest in their association and assured me of the friendship and cooperation of all members. Other members giggled and made friendly interjections as she spoke, after which they sang a welcome song and pronounced me a worthy wife of Zelachi. I was ecstatic. Speech over, Auntie Emily said it was time to eat the things I had brought but that someone had to 'break' the kola nut before other consumables could be shared. However, there was a problem, everyone agreed. I looked confused. I didn't understand.

"What does it mean to break the kola?" I asked.

A woman sitting to my left explained that tradition forbade people from eating kola nut without first offering a prayer to the ancestors. How could I have forgotten Chinua Achebe's books? She said there was a problem still. How? Let someone 'break' the kola so the meeting could progress. She said only a man could do it. There was no man in the gathering. Couldn't the chairlady or the oldest woman in the meeting 'break' the kola? The woman laughed so loud her body shook.

"Women don't break kola nut in Igbo land. Only men do," she said.

"But this is an all-female gathering. A woman has to 'break' the kola since there is no man," I pointed out.

"A woman can't 'break' the kola, irrespective of the situation. It's either we get a man to do it or we keep everything until a later date," she explained.

Suddenly, I saw a smile of relief on the chairlady's face.

"How could we have forgotten there is a man in our midst?" she shouted triumphantly.

I looked around; there was no man but the chairlady was still talking.

"Cordelia's son is here," she said and a cheerful laughter erupted. Cordelia was asked to bring out her sleeping baby strapped on her back.

"Be careful not to wake him. He is our husband; we want him to help us, but we have no right to disturb his sleep," Auntie Emily said as Cordelia loosened her wrapper and brought out her son.

The chairlady raised his right hand, gently placing his palm on the kola nut and everyone, excluding me, clapped with frenzy. The kola nut, garden egg, biscuits and malt were thereafter shared and the meeting progressed. The chairlady was now addressing members about the qualities of a good wife but my attention was distracted by a woman talking in low tones to Cordelia.

"My husband no dey near me again," the woman, whom the chairlady had earlier introduced as Nneoma, was telling Cordelia.

"No be only you, my sister. My own husband dey do like say I rub shit for body," Cordelia muttered knowingly, nodding several times.

"You mean am? Your husband wey I been dey think say na correct man wey dey do im wife well," Nneoma said, relief spreading across her face.

"For where? He no dey like to touch me so tey I tire I go tell im Mama," Cordelia said seriously.

"You get mind o! You go tell your mother-in-law say im pikin no dey near you?" Nneoma asked, her brows lifted in surprise.

"Wetin you wan make I do? I don talk tire. He no gree do."

"Nack me tory," Nneoma said, adjusting herself in the chair.

"You know e get as these men dey behave wey dey make person wan craze. Nothing wey I no do make he look my side. Na so he dey do like say I no even dey."

"Cordelia! You sef too do. Your pikin still dey small now. E never too tey when you born," Nneoma challenged, regarding Cordelia with a narrow-eyed glare.

"Na you dey talk like this? Who no know say no be only pikin them dey take the thing born. You wey don born finish, why you wan make your husband still dey do you?" Cordelia retorted, shooting Nneoma a dark frown.

"No mind me. Wetin im Mama talk?" Nneoma asked conciliatorily.

"He say make I get patience; say im go talk to am."

"He don change?"

"Nneoma, na so he come house one evening come tell me say I no know when person dey do me well."

"Wetin that one mean?"

"He say na pity im dey pity me na im make he no dey near me; say I no get the kin power wey the small small girls wey im dey carry for outside get. He say the small small girls get power so tey dem fit do any style wey im want whether na dog or any style at all; say na im make he think say make im leave me jeje as im know say I no get that kin' power."

"Na wah! Women don suffer for this world. Your husband dey take him mouth tell you this kin' thin'?" Nneoma said, fuming.

"Wetin my eye never see?"

"You try o, Cordelia; so you stand there dey look am?"

"My body dey hot; e be like say I wan craze. I come cool down small. I tell am say I get power; I say make he do me as he dey do the small small girls."

"He do you like that?"

"Nneoma, na so we start. He say make I turn, put my face

for pillow, put my bum-bum for up. I do as he tell me. Na so he come enter me from back. My sister, as he enter, na with force, e come pa-a-a-i-i-i-n me. Na so I no come know how one heavy pollute come comot for my body gbgbgbrrrraaa!"

Involuntary laughter escaped me before I knew it. All eyes turned on me. I felt embarrassed but not as much as Cordelia and Nneoma, who exchanged knowing glances and ended their 'gist.' As soon as the chairlady declared the meeting closed, I hurried out, afraid that people might come to ask me why I almost disrupted the meeting.

PART FOUR
JANUARY 1990 - JULY 1998

CHAPTER 24

I continued to attend the monthly meeting of the Zelachi Wives' Association. Each one gave me a new experience, some of which I shared with Ify, who had become a member of the male wing. I also put my job search temporarily on hold and concentrated on my pregnancy. Ify gave me money every month specifically for shopping for our unborn baby. It became a major activity I looked forward to every month end and made friends with the young members of our meeting, most of whom were traders. Some of them assisted their husbands in their trades; many had businesses of their own; a few were civil servants, while others were into vocations such as tailoring and hairdressing.

Joy and Ebere became my closest friends. We visited one another frequently and shared our marital thrills and woes. My major challenge in the first few months was that I was being regularly confronted with situations that tried my patience. Ify's older brother, whom I called Uncle Cajethan, seemed particularly determined to provoke me. He took to coming to our house when he knew Ify was at work. I had no problem with that. As a full-time house wife, I needed company and a friendly brother-in-law would be of great value. What I found worrisome, however, was his reckless, unguarded utterances. I was reclining on the sofa, dozing off when he came one afternoon. I sat up and adjusted my blouse to cover my protruding tummy before lifting myself clumsily to open the door. I genuflected and remained standing for a while, enquiring after my nephews and nieces in-law and their mother; then disappeared into the kitchen to bring him cold water. I went back to the kitchen to prepare a meal of cassava and egusi soup and invited him to the dining table and returned to the kitchen to wash the dishes. I returned to the sitting room to clear the plates. I had just finished washing them when he called me.

"Thanks for the food, Anjola."

"You are welcome, Uncle."

"So how is the baby?"

"Very well."

"Is it kicking? You know it's important the baby moves from time to time."

"Yes, Uncle."

"If the movement suddenly ceases, you must seek urgent medical attention."

"Yes, Uncle."

"Thank you for the food. You see, this life is not predictable at all."

"You are right, Uncle."

"I expected you to ask me why I spoke like that."

"Why?"

"I never thought I would one day eat a meal prepared by an ngbati-ngbati woman."

"I see," I mumbled, my mood darkening.

"You know your people are very dirty."

"Thank you, Uncle," I said, determined not to allow him hurt me.

"You don't like what I have said but you know it's the truth, don't you?"

"Thank you, Uncle," I said with forced cheerfulness.

"There is no need to act as if you are surprised at what I have said. Your people are dirty. I know it because I have them as neighbours. Whenever they bring food to my household during festivities, I don't think twice before I tell my people to throw it into the garbage. Why would I eat a meal prepared by someone who keeps a bowl in the corner of her room to defecate in at night?" he said. I blinked and lifted a hand to my brow. The next moment, I dropped my hand.

"Thank you, Uncle," I said with an effort.

"This is a fact but what I'm also telling you is that the unpredictable nature of life is another fact to recognise. Look at me; in the house of an ngbati-ngbati woman, not only eating but even enjoying her food. God is wonderful," he said, flashing me a grin.

I was filled with indignation but managed to keep muttering, "Thank you, Uncle," to every statement he made, no matter how offensive. Uncle Cajethan was a reckless talker and, although Ify dismissed most of what he said as the utterances of a clown, they got me upset some of the time.

There was another instance during Christmas. He and his family came to share with us the joy of the season, as we had done with them the previous day. We had an exciting time with much to drink as their children bustled about until sundown, when he announced it was time to leave. As Ify and I got ready to see them off, he said it was necessary for us to pray together. He led the session; starting with a general prayer for the Jeremiah family. He then prayed for all of us individually by laying his hand on our heads in turn while we chorused, "Amen." It reached my turn.

"Oh Lord, our God, we pray for Anjola and her pregnancy; we pray that you grant her safe delivery, oh Lord."

"Amen!"

"Our father and our God, we ask that you cure Anjola of her Yoruba stubbornness! Our merciful father, we know that Yoruba stubbornness is a serious disease; it is a disease that is difficult to cure but we trust in your supreme power, oh God, because you are the God of possibilities."

Pure shock bolted through me. I opened my eyes to look at Ify. His eyes were closed but a sardonic smile was etched at the corners of his mouth. I shifted my gaze to Uncle Cajethan. His eyes were firmly shut and he was gesticulating with all his strength. I folded my arms across my breast and waited for him to finish. I was boiling with rage and had decided to confront him for the first time.

"What was that in aid of, Uncle?" I challenged, my heart thundering.

"How dare you talk to me with a raised voice?" he demanded tersely.

"I'm sick and tired of the way you look for every opportunity to insult and cast aspersions on my people," I declared tautly.

"Are you challenging me? Do women in your culture challenge their in-laws?"

"You know I'm trying my best to respect you but you are not being fair to me," I said, spreading my hands.

"Now I see you have no home training. I will teach you the lesson of your life," he threatened, flicking me a look.

"It's unfortunate you threaten your brother's wife like this. What wrong have I committed?"

"By the time I'm through with you, Anjola, you will be sorry." He turned to Ify. "So you stand there like a castrated he-goat while your so-called wife insults me, ehn? I will deal with the both of you," he vowed. He glanced briefly at Ify and stormed out of the house, his wife and children trailing behind him.

Ify said nothing while his brother was around but he told me later he was surprised I took Uncle Cajethan seriously enough to challenge him. His brother was a jester, he reiterated, advising me strongly to henceforth learn to control my anger. I asked him what he would have done if he were in my situation. He said he would have laughed it off as a joke but that he would go and apologise to his brother on my behalf. He challenged me to check the word 'stubbornness' in the dictionary to discover if it was attributed to any one tribe, race or colour. Cajethan was a jester, he repeated. I resolved to take his counsel. I also decided to ignore all innuendoes, intentionally or otherwise, directed at me or my ethnic group. I stood by my resolve to the extent that, even when my fellow women at Zelachi Wives' Association said things that normally would have gotten me agitated, I either acted as if I hadn't heard or I just smiled vaguely.

I was at a meeting one day when one of our members was telling another about a certain girl who lived in their compound and had just committed an abortion

"What tribe is she?"

"Yoruba."

"Ehey hey, I knew it! I just didn't want to take the word from your mouth. Yoruba people don't know God. They do anything that comes to their mind."

"You have just hit the nail on the head. That's why I have pleaded with my son not to marry a Yoruba woman. In fact, I told him not to marry from any tribe other than Igbo. I don't want trouble."

As they chatted, they cast glances at me intermittently. They stopped chatting after some time.

My daughter arrived soon after. Ify named her Athena. Her birth further exacerbated my loss of concentration on job-hunting because there was always so much to do. There were days when I literally wished there were more hours. My day usually began at five in the morning - if Athena permitted me to stay in bed that long. First, I would prepare and feed her with her baby formula as she would have fed on my breast milk during the night. If I was lucky, she would drift off to sleep shortly afterwards, which would enable me start on the house chores. I would wash her feeding bottles, boil water for her flask and do her laundry before progressing to the general chores such as sweeping, cleaning and washing dishes. There were days when I had no free moment to eat breakfast until afternoon but I couldn't have been happier. It was amazing how my daughter's arrival had stifled my job hunting urges.

Meanwhile, I wrote to my family informing them of their new grand-daughter. My mother visited to help me for some time. Ify's mother also came. Our house was filled with happiness. How I cherished those few months. It took a considerable time for the euphoria to wane. Mama returned to Jos first, after which my mother also left. I had no time to brood over my lack of employment. Athena's rapid growth was providing me with all the joy I needed. Before long, it was time for her to start school. My daily routine was re-ordered. I now had to do the school run, especially as Ify had not been able to buy a car since the entire family was surviving on his salary. Ify also had to send money to his parents. I suggested it was time for me to renew my job search and he agreed. I wrote several applications.

I was still awaiting a response when Ify came home with a letter of termination of appointment. What offence had he committed? He said his sack was not on account of any misdemeanour. Many of his colleagues were affected. The company was downsizing as a result of the economic downturn. Things changed fast in our home except the love we shared. I went into petty trading, buying adire and selling mostly to office workers. Ify was optimistic he would soon get another job.

In the meantime, he bought a motorcycle and started using it commercially. On his first day, he didn't return until 11pm. He placed his earnings on the centre table and started counting, ignoring my repeated appeals for him to take his meal, which had already gone cold. He chatted as he counted, telling me about the attitude of some of his passengers, the behaviour of some policemen, his poor knowledge of certain routes and sundry other tales I was hardly interested in. I sat half-listening, half-pondering over what lay ahead. When Ify noticed I was paying scant attention he squeezed my shoulder.

"Everything will be okay, Anjola," he sermonised. "Things will be difficult for a while, I agree, but we will pull through because of the stuff we are made of. Besides, I'm confident I will get another job sooner than we think. There is no need to despair," he assured, looking at me imploringly.

I rose from my seat and curled up in his lap, feeling the

warmth of his body. The money he was holding fell to the floor. I put my arms around him and let my hands slide down his body. I pressed my hips against him, making slow, small circles. The money we had and didn't have had been perfectly forgotten now. My soul mate, the love of my life, how could I watch him go through such anguish? I marvelled at his gorgeousness as I rose and slipped out of my dress. He was watching me; there was passion in his eyes. I returned and started to undress him. There was a sudden urgency in him as we were both naked and our bodies were pressed together. He stroked me, his fingers lightly touching my face and neck, and down to the swell of my breasts. I began to moan softly as his hands moved to my legs.

"Take me, Ify." I whispered. Our sleep was good, our hope intact.

CHAPTER 25

I was jolted awake by a knock on the door. I sat up. A chilly harmattan wind rustled through the curtains. Ify was fast asleep, his mouth wide open, his tongue hanging out as he snored thunderously. I heard the knock again. I tried to shake Ify awake. He swung his arm around my waist and mumbled something incomprehensible. I made my way to the sitting room and checked the time on the wall clock: quarter-to-five. I opened the door with some trepidation. Uncle Cajethan stood impatiently outside. I was overtaken by mixed feelings of relief and panic. What could have brought him so early?

"Ha! Uncle, I hope there is no problem?" I asked, stepping aside to let him in.

He scowled at me and stormed into the house.

"How dare you ask me such a silly question? Have I lost the right to visit my own brother when I please just because he puts a miserable woman in his house?"

I was staggered by his hostility but tried to pull myself together, muttering: "I'm sorry, Uncle. I didn't mean it that way. I was only trying to find out if all is well."

"What can you do if all is not well and who are you to worry about me?" he roared.

"I'm sorry," I muttered.

"You had better be, you gold-digging wretch," he bawled.

I made no further attempt to respond, knowing that once

he got into his full stride there was little point interrupting him.

Ify emerged from the bedroom.

"Ha, Ibolachi, nno."

I left them.

I expected Uncle Cajethan to exaggerate what transpired between us but I wasn't prepared for what I heard. He told Ify I was rude and hostile; that I questioned his mission to our house so early and that I even went as far as telling him he had disturbed our peace. He also said that I accused him of making excessive financial demands on our family and that I was tired of his constant meddling in our affairs. I stared blankly at Ify as he reeled out many more rude and disrespectful utterances I had supposedly made. Finally, he told me that he pleaded with him to forgive me but that Uncle Cajethan threatened to report me to the Zelachi Development Union. I said nothing even when he said that his brother actually came to ask for money, and that he had given him half of what he had made the previous day in the hope of pacifying him. It took a long time for Ify to coax out of me what had truly transpired.

A few days later, two members of Zelachi Development Union summoned me to their meeting to defend the allegations of grave disrespect brought against me by my brother-in-law. I hadn't realised the seriousness of the problem until I received the notice. If what happened was a deliberate calculation to throw me off-balance, Uncle Cajethan had succeeded. I was dazed. How did I get myself into this mess? How was I supposed to deal with what I couldn't understand? Ify advised denial. I was to deny all the allegations no matter how many and maintain a straight face.

I asked him, in exasperation: "What in heaven's name had I done wrong?"

He told me to stop worrying myself about being right or wrong. He said all I needed to do was simply insist that I didn't say any of the things credited to me.

"I did say something, Ify. I specifically said that I hoped there was no problem."

"That's precisely the statement Cajethan wants to twist to suit his purpose. Can't you see? The only way out is to deny you ever made any such statement."

"Wouldn't that amount to lying? Wouldn't it be more honourable to admit making the statement and going ahead to explain the rationale behind it?"

"You don't understand, do you? Somebody wants to persecute you and you talk about honour?" he asked perceptively, adding quickly: "The wise thing is to wriggle out of the trap he has set for you. That is my candid advice."

I dropped to my knees and sat back on my legs, tossing my hair over my shoulder and folding my hands on my lap. I was counting my heartbeats. No, I had to find a way to deal with the situation on my own. I rose groggily to my feet and told Ify I wanted to go for a walk to clear my head. The street was silent. The only sound was the slap-slap of my slippers. I saw a mallam hawking sweets and beckoned him and then realised I had come out without my purse. I smiled my apology and resumed my walk. I got to a bend that led to another long street. The harmattan wind teased my face. This was not the first time I would find myself in this kind of quagmire. I remembered way back in primary school when I stole. I must have been about seven at the time. It was my first time of stealing and I didn't know where the urge had come from but I saw my grandmother's purse lying carelessly on her bed and, realising that no one was around, hurriedly put it in my school bag.

I went to school the next morning feeling pleased with myself. Curiously, it didn't occur to me to open the purse to see what it contained. I was happy I had grown big and smart enough to steal without being caught. I went out at break time to play with my friends. My mind kept going back to my conquest; the more I thought about it, the happier I became. But my happiness didn't last. Soon, I was told my auntie was looking for me. I ran across the field to her with excitement. She asked me if I had seen my grandmother's purse. I told her without hesitation that I took it. She asked me where it was and I told her to come with me to my class. I opened my bag, brought it out and handed it to her. Suddenly, a loud slap landed on my right cheek. I staggered twice but the roll of benches prevented me from falling. That was when it dawned on me that I was in trouble.

When I got home, the entire household seemed to be waiting for me. My grandmother told me my initial punishment for stealing was that I had forfeited my lunch, but that the family might consider allowing me to eat dinner if I could satisfactorily defend my misdemeanour. I explained that I had no specific motive for stealing the purse, hence neither did I open nor tamper with the contents. I told them it was something I did as a sport, which had given me a thrill. I told them how good it made me feel to discover I had grown so big and become smart enough to steal without being caught. I could read on their faces that they knew I was telling the truth. They gave me my lunch. Afterwards, my grandmother explained that taking what did not belong to one was stealing and that stealing was a dreadful offence which could attract imprisonment and even death. She made me promise that I would never steal again. I never stole again.

Another time I found myself in trouble was during my third year in secondary school. It was a boarding school and it was the tradition to set aside one day during term, known as Open Day, for parents and guardians to visit. It was an important activity in the school which most parents didn't miss. There seemed to be an agreement between my parents that my mother would always come. My mother had also established a pattern of behaviour each time she did so. She would painstakingly scrutinise my notebooks one after the other, stopping here to check my score in a class assignment and reading my notes, there to ensure that I had copied correctly. She would study the dates from the commencement of the term to detect possible gaps that might suggest I had missed classes. If she found any laxity, however minor, she would scold me in the full glare of my classmates. I dreaded Open Day.

During this particular term, I had missed some classes because I had fallen ill and had been admitted to the sick bay for a week. When I recovered, my mates had written long notes on geography which I didn't have the chance to copy before Open Day. I therefore resolved to borrow the notes of one of my classmates who understood my plight. My mother's eyes widened in surprise when I gave it to her.

"This handwriting is strange, Anjola," she said. I stayed silent, thinking of what to say. All of a sudden, she tore off the old calendar wrapping I had used to disguise the origin and her eyes settled on my classmate's name. Without another word, she got up and marched to the administrative block, clutching the notebook. I knew there was no use running after her to plead for forgiveness. I sat dejectedly, tears streaming down my cheeks. A disciplinary committee was set up the following week to hear my defence and recommend the appropriate punishment.

When I was summoned by the committee I admitted my offence. I explained my mother's harshness, how my illness prevented me from updating my notes and how my classmate had agreed to lend me his. The committee reported that although my offence attracted two weeks' suspension, my honesty was commendable. It recommended I weed the grass for two days. They further recommended that I undergo counselling to understand that lying was always wrong

I was jolted by the honk of a car. My walk had taken me far. I turned for home. I passed a sign, 'original honey sold here,' and wondered how "original" it really was. I remembered the one Ify brought from his office shortly before his sack and its funny taste. We poured it away. I looked up at the sky. The fading sun was sinking on the horizon. I had decided on my line of defence. I felt confident that I would be able to answer every of the union's admonitions.

Ify was standing in the middle of the sitting room with Athena when I walked in. He looked at me q uizzically. I flashed him a reassuring smile.

"Zelachi Kwenu!"

"Kwenu!"

"Kwenu"

"Kwenu!"

Ify whispered to me that the man speaking was the secretary of the union. I nodded and readjusted myself in the chair.

"Ehn, we are all gathered here today to hear an important matter involving the family of Cajethan and Ifeanyi Jeremiah. I will now call on the President, Mazi Okenwa, to take over the proceedings."

There was loud applause as he got up to speak.

"Zelachi Kwenu!"

"Kwenu!"

"Kwenu!"

"Kwenu!"

"Thank you, my people. As the secretary has said, we are all aware that today has been set aside to hear the complaint brought before us by one of our own, Cajethan, in respect of a misunderstanding between him and his brother's wife. Men of Zelachi are wise. We do not follow the foolishness of the world for it is only a foolish person that pronounces judgment after listening to the grievances of only one party to a dispute. A wise person will always give the other party the opportunity to state their own side. Today, Cajethan is in our midst; Ifeanyi is in our midst and so is his wife, Anjola, who has been accused of showing disrespect to her brother-in-law. Ifeanyi is only an observer here because he was not present at the scene of the altercation and will not be able to tell us what happened. We will now call on Cajethan to tell the wise men of Zelachi what really happened between him and Anjola."

Loud applause rent the air, which took time to subside. Eventually, Uncle Cajethan rose to his feet.

"Zelachi Kwenu!"

"Kwenu!"

"Kwenu!"

"Kwenu!"

"It is a known fact that Ifeanyi is my blood brother. What many of you may not know is how I suffered to contribute to his education. This boy spent six years in Canada, studying engineering while we toiled day and night to make sure he achieved his dream. We did this in the hope that our brother would come home after his training, get a job and help our family. But wonders, they say, will never cease. Rather than show gratitude to the family which made him, Ifeanyi came back, got a job and announced that he wanted to get married immediately. We were all shocked to our bone marrows. Was this how to pay back the hand that had fed him? Where was his sense of gratitude?

"Our elders say that when the rabbit is old and weak, it feeds on the breast of its babes. We didn't expect Ifeanyi to treat us the way he has done but what could we do? We left him and accepted his wife even though we were not happy he went to Yoruba land to marry. As if we have not suffered enough, our brother's wife does not want to see his family near him. Like the parasite that she is, she alone has been feeding on my brother. Anytime I go to their house, it is as if I have committed the worst offence in the world. Na so this woman go dey waka de jam wall; all because I have come to visit my brother. Now, to the matter at hand, I went there recently for an important family discussion. I went in the morning so that I would meet Ifeanyi at home. What did I get as soon as his wife opened the door? She squeezed her face in anger. She did not even try to hide her feelings. I was willing to ignore her, as I have been doing, but then she threw the bombshell by asking me: 'What is the problem again? Can't we have our peace?' "

Condemnation and outrage rent the air. The secretary appealed for calm. Ify glanced at me. There was anxiety in his eyes. He wanted to make a point of order but I signalled for him not to. Some people were born liars. I rose to my feet.

"My in-laws, I thank you for the opportunity you have given me to state my own side of the matter."

"Just say what you want to say, don't waste our time," someone shouted. He was greeted with laughter. The secretary called for silence.

"I have always respected my in-laws, including Uncle Cajethan. When I opened the door and found him standing there early that morning, I panicked. I was afraid that something bad had happened. It was out of genuine concern that I enquired if all was well."

Uncle Cajethan leapt to his seat and punched the air as he shouted: "Liar! Pretender!"

There was pandemonium. Everyone was talking at once but I couldn't make out what they were saying. I looked at Ify. He was shaking his head sadly, muttering to himself. Uncle Cajethan was still standing, shaking violently. The president appealed for calm. Eventually, order was restored. The president turned to Uncle Cajethan and asked him if there was something he wanted to say. He nodded in the affirmative.

"Zelachi Kwenu! The woman you see standing before you is the epitome of Jezebel. If you are looking for the proverbial green snake in the green grass, look no further. She is a liar, a pretender and a bitch. As you see her, she is stubborn, arrogant, selfish and intolerant of her in-laws. I tell you, I have never seen a bad woman like her but that's not all. Since she came into my brother's life, she has brought nothing but bad luck. We all know that Ifeanyi is a Canadian-trained engineer with bright prospects but this woman has used her cursed destiny to ruin her husband to the extent that Ifeanyi has lost his high-paying job."

He paused for effect and then continued: "I'm happy that she has revealed to all of you what she is. A mere woman stands before the gathering of wise men and audaciously admits to asking her brother-in-law what problem brought him to his younger brother's house. Can you imagine the cheek? What point was she trying to prove? That she is bold? I leave the judgement to the wise ones."

He grimaced in disgust and sat down. The president cleared his throat. "I think we are approaching the resolution of the conflict. I just want to ask Ifeanyi's wife one last question and the elders will put their heads together to arrive at a judgment. Our wife, did you or did you not ask your brother-in-law what problem brought him to your husband's house?"

"That was not the way I asked him, my elder."

"How did you ask him?"

"My exact words were: 'I hope there is no problem, Uncle?'"

Pandemonium broke out again. I read anger and disgust on their faces.

"Ibu ajo nwunye/you are a bad wife!" someone shouted and hurled an imaginary object at me. Ify folded his arms across his chest and stared fixedly at me. I was unperturbed. I knew I had been found guilty. I awaited their judgment. I didn't have to wait long. The president again took the floor.

"We have heard both sides give account of what transpired and even the gods of Zelachi have not abandoned us in this onerous task. Cajethan, you have done well by bringing the matter to Zelachi Development Union. You have shown that you do not own yourself in Kaduna and that you put your people first in all your actions and decisions."

He turned to me.

"Our wife, you are a small girl of yesterday and do not know many things. You also do not understand the customs of your in-laws, hence you have used your own mouth to state your side in a dispute and have pronounced yourself guilty. A woman is not married to her husband alone but to his relations, friends and associates. You did not do well. When you asked your husband's elder brother, the one who contributed to training him and making him a man fit for you to marry what problem brought him to your house, you were indirectly saying he had no right to visit your home whenever he chooses. This is unacceptable. We have seen many bad wives banish their husbands' parents from their lives. May God not allow our son, Ifeanyi, suffer such a calamity. Ehn, the elders understand your limitations and are willing to be lenient. What you did was wrong but we have a consensus opinion that you did not plan to cause offence to your brother-in-law. For this reason, our judgment is that you have to tender a public apology and promise this meeting that this kind of report will not be made against you in future."

Uncle Cajethan got up swiftly, raising his hands. The president obliged him.

"My people, it comes to me as a surprise that even the elders don't seem to realise that this woman is not yet ready for marriage. Yes, she may have all the physical requirements of a full woman which have enabled her to give birth but it is obvious that she lacks the manners expected of a wife. My suggestion, therefore, is that she goes back to her parents for a period of twelve months to learn how to be a proper wife."

Ify sprang to his feet.

"I thank all respected members of Zelachi Development Union and I'm particularly grateful to the elders for your intervention in this matter. I have appealed to my brother in private to forgive my wife but he insisted on reporting her to the union. As you have rightly observed, she does not understand the customs of our people. I thank you for forgiving her. However, I want to state here and now that my brother has no right to suggest to me to send my wife to her parents even for one day. Anjola is going nowhere over this matter but she will apologise for her mistake."

The president gestured to me to apologize but Uncle Cajethan was having none of it. I was on my feet, eager to say something. After a while, the president was able to restore order and I had the floor.

"My in-laws, I thank you for forgiving me and, as you rightly pointed out, I didn't disrespect Uncle Cajethan on purpose." Then, glancing in his direction, I said: "Uncle, please forgive my mistakes. I'm sorry."

I turned back to the president.

"One thing bothers me and I'd like to be educated. Uncle said he wants to send me home, in his words, 'for a period of twelve months to learn how to be a proper wife.' And I would like him to explain to me which home he is referring to. I'm married to his brother, therefore, their family is now my family, their home is my home as well and I.."

He didn't allow me to finish before jumping to his feet. "Mba, mba, desperado, na by force?" he yelled. "Get it into your thick skull, woman, I made it clear where I'm sending you to, don't twist my words. I said you are going to your parents. Who told you my family is now your home? Did you really think that being married to my brother and having a child by him could confer on you the status of citizenship? Wake up from your dream, your village in Kwara State is where you belong, that's your home, and you're going back there, no question."

He was trembling with rage but there was something dishonourable about him, jeering, boastful and trampling on everything sacred. Ify had grown gloomier. In the end, the president said we should go home and allow tempers to subside. He also promised to talk to Uncle Cajethan. The meeting was adjourned. Ify thanked the elders. He took my hand and we escorted them out amidst shouts of Obidiye – husband's heart. We were about to cross the road when we heard footsteps behind us. We turned instinctively to find Uncle Cajethan approaching us.

"The battle lines are now drawn, you miserable couple!" he spat menacingly.

CHAPTER 26

I sat pensively in an Ilorin-bound 504 station wagon at Mando Motor Park in Kaduna. I straddled Athena, now eight and in primary three. She had no care in the world; she was busy munching on a Gala and sipping from a bottle of Coke. I wished I could have been that young and happy. Ify stood by the window looking morose but making an effort to chat. A woman well past middle age solicited alms. We looked at her but said nothing. She turned away but just then a young girl called her back and gave her a five-kobo coin. The beggar made no move to collect the money. Surprised, the girl glared at her.

"You want to give me five kobo?" the beggar finally asked, visibly outraged.

The girl was taken by surprise. She opened her mouth but nothing came out.

"I won't accept five kobo!" the beggar continued angrily, saliva dribbling from her mouth. The girl looked even more baffled but didn't withdraw her outstretched hand.

"Do you have hearing defect? I said I will not accept five kobo from you."

"What's wrong with five kobo?" the girl asked, suddenly finding her voice. "Is this how to reward a compassionate gesture? How many people offered you anything despite your long solicitation?"

"I was once a successful businesswoman. If you knew my

shop before 1985 you would be lucky to be my customer."

"This is 1998. You are now a beggar and beggars don't choose."

"I don't blame you. Na condition make crayfish bend. If not, why should I be begging a small girl like you for money?"

"You are an ungrateful old wretch who deserves no sympathy," the girl said, withdrawing her hand abruptly.

"If I look like a riff-raff, do I speak like one?" the beggar fumed.

"Does it matter?" the girl retorted.

"I can see you are just in the kindergarten of life. You will mature in due course," the beggar said and walked away.

Our vehicle was now fully loaded. The driver shut the doors. I stuck out my head for a goodbye peck. Ify waved at us effusively until we were out of sight.

After reviewing the issues surrounding the misunderstanding between Uncle Cajethan and me, and the animosity it had created between him and Ify, we had agreed on my temporary relocation to Ilorin. Initially, he had insisted that I wasn't going anywhere because sending me away would be tantamount to allowing his brother run his life for him.

"No member of my family has sent his wife away on the advice of even my father or my mother, much less a sibling," he fumed.

We agreed that Uncle Cajethan was merely acting in character – clowning. However, we were concerned about what seemed to be the general assumption that I lacked initiative. Uncle Cajethan had openly accused me of laziness. He said I was content with being a layabout, one who liked to depend on someone else. He had insinuated that I lacked dignity. We were also unhappy about his labelling me a gold digger. These were weighty issues.

"Anjola wants to milk my brother dry," Uncle Cajethan had yelled. "All she does is sleep and wake and sleep again while Ify works himself to death," he had added as I stood with my head hung low, taking all the insults. I was convinced that Uncle Cajethan's overriding motive for reporting me was to remonstrate against what he perceived as my decision to be a full-time housewife. It was unfortunate that my inability to secure gainful employment portrayed me as someone who would be content to lie in the gutter and watch while others climbed mountains. I recalled how I had expressed reservations about the prospect of my staying idle while waiting for the Kaduna interview and how Ify had agreed with me, although his concern had been how I would spend my mornings when he was at work since my language lessons held in the evenings. He had suggested that I take a temporary teaching job to forestall boredom. I was delighted. It meant much more to me.

"Ingenuous JJ!" I hailed, in reference to his official name of Joshua Jeremiah. "How come you always have a ready solution to every puzzle?" I teased, jabbing him in the kidney.

"Experience is the best teacher," he bragged, savouring my compliment.

The next morning, he came to my uncle's house to take me to a private coaching centre, advising me that there were certain things I needed to know about the proprietor before I made up my mind. I told him I was determined to cope with any circumstance provided it would give me a sense of being busy earning a living.

"The man likes to be respected," he said.

I laughed derisively. "I don't have a problem with that. I will respect him."

"You don't understand. He wants more than that. He likes to be worshipped."

"Is he God?"

"He's self-opinionated and believes himself highly knowledgeable. He believes he has read more books than any individual and expects people to show him reverence."

"Would it make him happy if I punctuate every phrase with 'sir' whenever I speak with him?"

"He will enjoy it but you will have to do more than that. You will have to demonstrate that you recognise the feat he imagines he has accomplished."

I was eager to meet the curious fellow.

The centre occupied a bungalow with a small compound. Apart from the name: ONUOHA COACHING CENTRE written boldly in red on one wall, there was nothing to suggest it was an academic centre. There was no signboard outside and there was little academic paraphernalia inside. We entered a passage with rooms on either side. One of them served as Onuoha's office. He was sitting calmly behind a small table. Two bookshelves were crammed to capacity. More books were piled up on the floor. He responded to our greetings with encouraging smiles, rising from his seat to take a book from one of the shelves. Ify and I followed him with our eyes until he returned to his seat. He was not tall. He was dark-skinned with a bony face and deep eye sockets. His cheeks were long and slightly hollow. I didn't detect any arrogance in his mien. He was young, maybe Ify's age, and appeared unassuming. I thought Ify must have misunderstood him but decided to tread with caution all the same.

"Good morning, sir," I greeted. He smiled luxuriantly and gestured for us to sit down.

"Ify mentioned you to me. What's your name?"

"My name is Anjola, sir. Anjola Adeniyi."

"I suppose he told you my name."

"Yes he did, sir. You are Mr Onuoha, sir."

"Very good, Miss Adeniyi. Where are you likely to be at about nine o'clock on Sunday morning?"

"I'm likely to be in Church, sir. I'm a Christian and I go to Church every Sunday, sir."

"Splendid! You have passed the interview."

Interview? I wondered but said nothing. Onuoha was still talking.

"You see, I studied education, psychology, sociology, anthropology, philosophy, classics, political science and many other fields. I can tell you confidently that I have read enough books - even on religion - and they all confirm Christianity to be supreme."

Ify and I exchanged glances but I quickly averted my eyes when I noticed he was fighting to suppress a laugh. We nodded vigorously in agreement and Onuoha told me to see him the next day, by which time he would have worked out the details of my engagement.

When Ify and I reached the passage, we rushed out, both of us swallowing our giggles.

I went to see Onuoha the next day, basking in the euphoria of my engagement to Ify. I radiated extraordinary warmth to everyone I encountered that morning. I felt incredibly pleased with life. Onouha had made good his promise to get details of my terms of engagement. He said I would teach English language and literature for three months, two sessions per day, one in each of the respective subjects, Monday through Friday, ten sessions in all. He said the centre paid a fixed salary but didn't disclose the amount. He said it was mandatory that I engage my students for two hours each time and charged me to be diligent and up to date by consulting relevant materials that could enrich my knowledge and enhance my delivery. Thereafter, he gave me the timetable and wished me well. I contemplated asking about my remuneration but didn't.

Ify was unhappy when I told him I didn't ask Onuoha how much he would pay me. He said I was making a mistake if I allowed Onuoha to get the impression that I was afraid of him. I must never show him fear, adding that he only wanted me to understand the way his mind worked so that I would be able to tolerate his excesses. He told me more about Onuoha to underscore his point. Onuoha was the first son of his parents but they could only educate him up to secondary school level. His educational deprivation created a thirst for knowledge in his young mind and made him enrol at a college of education soon after he got to Kaduna. He subsequently obtained the National

Certificate of Education. He established his coaching centre thereafter but continued to live in perennial fear of ignorance. He became the victim of a desperate obsession for relevance, trapped in an endless struggle to convince everyone that he had overcome his childhood adversity. He was a pathetic victim of both superiority and inferiority complexes.

Listening to Ify made me resolve to study Onuoha within the three months I would work with him as a way of enriching my understanding of personality types. Ify reiterated that I had the right to know the amount I would earn for the service I had been contracted to render and that I should ask him the following day. I was still excited about my engagement and decided not to start with an argument over wages. I would concentrate on delivering a good lecture first, I said under my breath as I went in to teach. I had an exhilarating experience with my students. The more I taught, the more convinced I became that teaching was as much of a service to the teacher as it was to the taught. I was equally thrilled by the responses I got from my students, which suggested that they enjoyed my delivery. Now in a more pleasant mood, I felt confident to approach Mr Onuoha to discuss the matter of my salary.

He was having an argument with a man when I got to his office so I sat and waited patiently. The man was talking at the top of his voice. "The military government has announced plans to create two political parties as a step toward handling over to a democratically elected government. I say a military government has no business showing us how to go about democracy. Why not leave the formation of political parties to politicians?"

The man's submission seemed to have angered Onuoha, who thundered:

"You see what I have been saying? The kind of education this country is giving its citizens is dismal. I studied education and political science. I have travelled outside the shores of this country. I have lived in Birmingham, Oxford, London, New York, Texas and Atlanta, to mention only a few." He paused for effect and then continued. "I know how things are done in advanced societies. The people over there don't argue the way you are arguing because they have good education which..."

"Good afternoon, sir," a middle-aged woman greeted as she walked into the office, interrupting Onuoha.

"Good afternoon, madam. Yes, yes, quickly, I have forgotten what you said you wanted me to do for you."

"Yes sir, it's about my brother, sir. He is looking for a job, sir. I came here to ask if you can help him find a job. I know you know big people, sir."

"Where is your brother?"

"He is in Calabar, sir. He finished his NYSC since three years ago, sir, but hasn't found a job, sir."

"Tell your brother to come to Kaduna."

"Ah, thank you, sir. God bless you, sir. I have always known you can help me, sir."

"Hold it, woman. Don't get excited unnecessarily. I haven't said I have a job to give your brother. I want you to bring him to Kaduna because he needs counselling."

"I don't understand, sir?"

"The most important assistance he needs is counselling, which I'm going to give him free of charge."

"Ehn, thank you very much, sir, but actually, sir, I want you to help him more than that. He is very unhappy, sir, and his unhappiness makes me very sad."

"My training in psychology tells me you, too, have a problem and need counselling."

"Sir?"

"Yes, you have a psychological problem. That's why you worry about other people's problems. As for your brother, he needs counselling to understand that if things are not moving in the direction he wants, he needs to do environmental scanning and SWOT analysis. Your brother needs counselling more than he needs a job but you people are so ignorant. Many of you have sleepless nights worrying about how to make money when the principles for getting rich are at your finger tips. The principles for acquiring riches are contained in Napoleon Hill's Think and Grow Rich but you don't know because you haven't read the book. I sympathise with you people and your ignorance."

"Thank you. Goodbye," the woman said and hurried out of the office. I had grown tired of waiting and decided to broach my own subject before Onuoha could resume his argument with the other man.

"Excuse me, sir," I started.

"Yes, Miss Adeniyi."

"There is something I will like to discuss with you, sir."

"Go on."

The man rose to his feet, telling Onuoha he would see him again soon. It was just what I wished for. I wasted no time in asking Onouha how much I would be paid.

"I hope you don't mind my asking, sir. I need to make financial projections for the future," I began courteously.

"That's okay," he said. "Ehmnn, you will be entitled to one naira per session. That is, you will get one naira for each teaching session of two hours."

"Excuse me?"

"What's surprising about what I have just said? How much were you expecting? There are millions of university graduates like you looking for an opportunity of this kind. I will like to attend to other clients if you will excuse me," he said brusquely.

I left his office without another word.

Ify was furious when I told him.

"Is the man insane?" he fumed, telling me to forget about the entire idea. "Why should you teach for two whole hours and receive one naira as remuneration? He must be truly out of his mind."

Ify went on and on and it became my lot to convince him of the need to continue with the teaching since I had already started. I told him I had strong reasons to want to continue. I wanted to be productive. Another reason was my desire to study Onuoha's personality. He had developed certain qualities for his assault on life and its vagaries – sharpness, smartness, determination, arrogance, and self-praise. He was a steadfast braggart and there was concentrated passion in all his statements. I needed to interact with someone like him to prepare me for the challenges of managing human relationships in the future. More importantly, I explained that I enjoyed teaching because of its potential to enhance my intellectual capacity. I would teach for the entire three months Onuoha had contracted me regardless of the miserable pay that awaited me at the end. He told me it was unnecessary but I saw a look of admiration on his face.

I took my teaching engagement seriously. I bought books, visited the National Library frequently for relevant materials and deployed my utmost energy to imparting as much knowledge as I was gathering to my students. I derived tremendous joy from the positive responses I received from most of them. I felt sad when the three months elapsed, even though there were times I was angered by Onuoha's antics. What I found particularly objectionable was sending people to sit in on my class to watch me teach and report on my performance. Ify said Onuoha was only acting the trained teacher that he was. He reminded me that the man was the product of a teachers' college where teaching practices were held for embryonic teachers while older teachers watched. He told me to ignore them and carry on as if they were not there. Once or twice, Onuoha himself sat in on my class and I had to restrain myself from expressing my reservations.

There were also other minor incidents during which he demonstrated almost intolerable arrogance. However, I felt tremendously entertained each time he found a reason to talk about the numerous fields of study he had had training in and how he had visited 'advanced societies.' He was a curious one. Finally, it was my last day. I was surprised when he asked me the total amount I was expecting. I had done my calculations but since he liked to be respected, I decided to let him be the one to mention the amount so I told him I had decided to respectfully leave the calculation to him. He grinned from ear to ear and told me to come back the following morning to collect my money.

"I want to thank you, sir, for the privilege you have given me to teach at your centre," I said as soon as I sat down in his office the next morning.

"That's alright. That's okay," he said.

"So, how was my teaching?"

"I can't say anything about your teaching for now."

"That's a surprise."

"Well, I can't evaluate your contribution until the students write their exams. Only then can it be said that their teacher has or has not taught them well."

"Very well then, let me once again thank you for giving me the platform to test my teaching ability."

"That's okay, that's alright."

He opened the left drawer of his table, brought out a small exercise book and opened it at a blank page. He stretched it toward me with his right hand. I looked at him quizzically. He was making leering faces.

"Write that you collected the sum of one hundred naira being teaching fee for the period of three months at Onuoha Coaching Centre."

"One hundred naira? Why?" I asked calmly, placing the exercise book on the table.

"Actually, you shouldn't get as much as that but in our magnanimity we decided to make it up for you," he said with insincerity.

"I see. That's very kind of you, sir, but I will like to know the precise amount I'm entitled to get, sir."

"Don't bother yourself, Miss Adeniyi. We are humble in our service to humanity. It's not in our character to praise ourselves by giving details of our magnanimity," he said and pulled himself into a stiffer posture. I tried not to laugh.

"I appreciate your kindness, sir, but I want to satisfy my curiosity. How much did you say each teaching session was worth?"

"One naira."

"Thank you, sir. I did two sessions per day, five times a week. That gives a total of ten sessions in a week sir."

"That's correct," he said, giving me a shrewd look.

"Thank you, sir. Ten sessions in a week ought to translate to ten naira each week. Am I right or wrong, sir?" I asked.

"You are right," he mouthed. I smiled wryly at him.

"Now, if I taught for three months and each month consisted of a minimum of four weeks at ten naira per week, it brings my remuneration to forty naira a month or one hundred and twenty naira in three months. Besides, there were thirteen full weeks in the three months that I taught, which should earn me an additional ten naira bringing my total pay to one hundred and thirty naira. Sir, if you are paying me thirty naira less than what I legitimately earned, how much is your magnanimity worth?" I demanded. My voice was mild and gloating.

"So you knew?"

"Knew what, sir?"

"You knew the precise amount due to you."

"Meaning what?"

"Be smart next time?"

"I see, so swindling is synonymous with magnanimity," I said contemptuously.

"Don't take our humility for granted. Our policy is to resolve all misunderstandings in favour of our client. We will pay you the amount you mentioned but we don't tolerate insolence," he said reproachfully.

"Go tell that to the dogs, Mr Onuoha," I said scornfully.

He picked the exercise book and pointed it toward me but I fixed him a malicious gaze, ignoring the book.

"Take and write that you have collected the sum of one hundred and thirty naira from me."

"You are at your game again; aren't you? Why should I write that I have collected what you have not given to me?" I asked ruefully.

He placed the exercise book back on the table, pulled out the left-hand drawer and brought out some naira notes. He began to count. I counted with him and recounted again when he finally handed the money to me before I signed. I left his office without the usual courtesies. My heart was filled with thoughts of Dr Christopher Agbebi as I made my way to Ify's house to recount my experience. Of course, he was furious but I had taken everything in my stride. I sighed heavily and was pulled back to the present but memories of that ugly experience threatened to blight my mood.

My brother-in-law obviously didn't know me or what I represented, hence his erroneous summation of me as a layabout. I tolerated Onuoha's cant and hypocrisy because I genuinely wanted to be meaningfully engaged. I was merely a victim of the glaring state of flux of the economy. I wasn't a layabout, I told myself for the thousandth time. In spite of everything, however, I resolved not to indulge in unwholesome self-righteousness. Rather, I decided to consider that there might be some merit in my brother-in-law's accusations. Ify admitted he had felt uncomfortable, too. This meant that Uncle Cajethan was right to some extent. He was right about my not contributing to my family's upkeep. He was not wrong that I had truly been looking up to my husband to provide for all my needs. For how long did I want to continue to live that way? Where was my dignity as an individual? As Ify and I went over these utterances and the issues that occasioned them, I pointed out that Uncle Cajethan probably deserved to be given a chilled bottle of wine by us, not only as an apologetic gift but more to thank him for re-awakening in us the need to plan our marital life.

I told my husband I wanted to return to Kwara to make another effort at finding a job. The prospect seemed brighter in the sense that we were in 1998. The military government that placed an embargo on employment had since gone into hibernation, passing the baton to another military government which went the extra mile to put the country at the edge of the precipice for five years. Three months earlier, and perhaps as a result of what some citizens described as divine intervention, the head of the military junta died in controversial circumstances. A new military government had again taken over and hope was high among the populace that the new government had a genuine desire to return the country to democracy. There was hope, also, that the economic fortunes of the country would soon witness a positive turn-around, especially as the country had regained membership of prominent world bodies that ostracised it in the wake of military dictatorship. I explained to my husband that the time might just be right for me to get a job and that it might be easier to do so in my state since we lived in a country where citizens' rights were doled out according to where one came from. Besides, my temporary relocation would also help to douse the tension between him and his brother. It was not as if we didn't recognise the challenges our temporary separation would bring. We knew, for instance, that it would create a void in our individual and collective souls. We were even aware of the negative implications it would have on our daughter, including her having to change school. However, we also knew, and observers of our love life were quick to agree, that what bound us together was extra-terrestrial. We were acknowledged by those who watched us keenly that we were one of those rare couples whose marriage was truly made in heaven and handed down to humanity as a gift. We knew we would pull through. Suddenly, my heart began to pound in anticipation because the road signs announced that we were drawing close to our destination. Finally, my eyes fell on the 'Welcome to Ilorin' sign.

"We have arrived." I mumbled to Athena, but I might as well have been talking to myself. She was deeply asleep, looking absolutely adorable. I smiled down at her and took a deep breath.

CHAPTER 27

I held Athena in my right hand, our luggage in my left to cross the road to where I could hail a taxi. Because my parents had relocated to Ifelodun following my father's retirement, I had made plans to stay with my Ilorin-based paternal uncle, Uncle Gboyega. I got a taxi to his Coca-Cola Road residence. His wife, Auntie Labake, hurriedly opened the door as soon as she confirmed it was us. She was a heavyset woman with a flashy face, dyed hair and a loud, raucous voice. She was loaded with jewellery, as if she was just about to set out for a party. Her eyes brightened with surprise and a small smile formed on her lips.

"Welcome, my dear, it's so good to see you. It's been ages. Ha, ha, ha, see the pretty girl you have here. Welcome," she enthused, patting Athena on the back, who rewarded her with a smile.

"Thank you Auntie" I'm happy to see you, too," I said.

My uncle emerged from one of the rooms as my nephews and nieces wrapped their arms around me. He looked shrunken, diminutive, pale, a shadow of what he once was. I knelt down to greet him. He patted me on my back and asked me to rise.

"Ah!" he exclaimed, appearing to notice Athena for the first time. "Come, come, come. What is your name?"

"Athena."

"Ante what?" he sniffed indignantly. "What kind of name is that? Antenna, why not call her television or ante-natal?" he queried sarcastically, pushing Athena roughly away.

"Her name is not Antenna, Uncle, it's Athena, the founder of Greece and the goddess of wisdom," I explained, making an effort to laugh although I was upset by the manner in which he pushed Athena and the fear I saw on her face.

"You see your life, Anjola? When you came home a little less than ten years ago to say you wanted to marry a yanminrin, I gave you a piece of my mind without mincing words but, like the proverbial dog destined to get lost which ignores the whistle call of its hunter master, you turned a deaf ear. Now you have seen the result, you have a child that has been named after an object, antenna or a goddess in far away Greece." He laughed a loud, booming laugh that could be heard across the street. Athena burst into tears.

"Uncle, antenna has no bearing with my daughter's name. My husband is a detribalised man who is also not selfish. That's why he chose a name that is neither Igbo nor Yoruba. Athena is a distinguished name. You are just not familiar with it," I explained, trying to lighten the tone.

"Really? Tell me about it, madam philosopher," he challenged, barking out a humourless laugh before continuing. "Is television a Yoruba word? Does it change the fact that television is the name of an object? And when did you begin to bow to a foreign god or goddess? You are a lost child, Anjola, and I weep for my brother. How can this kind of misfortune befall him?"

His voice was venomous. I was trying hard not to be disrespectful but he was spoiling for a fight that appeared to have been well rehearsed. I wasn't going to play his game.

"It's a pity you have chosen that perspective, Uncle," I said blithely.

"Your so-called marriage is a sham. Your father told me you haven't found a job till now and that your husband has lost his. What else do you need to know that your marriage isn't working? I'm glad you have finally accepted your failure. That's why you are home to make a fresh start." His voice was gloating. I wouldn't let that pass unchallenged.

"Aren't you prejudiced? What has my marriage got to do with my job search?" I asked, amazed at how the purpose of my homecoming was being misunderstood.

"Don't be argumentative. You mean you can't see the link? I'm sorry for you," he said self-righteously. I knew there was nothing I could say or do to change his mind set. Weariness invaded every pore. I flopped down on the rug, my head pounding.

"Why not allow her take a rest? Why start this kind of talk now?" my auntie queried, eyeing her husband disapprovingly. He got up, shoved Athena aside and headed back to the room without another word. I felt downcast but my auntie put her hand on my shoulder, slowly helping me to my feet and urging me to come with her to the guest room. I followed her, Athena trotting behind us while their children tip-toed to the couch and sat down.

The next morning, Uncle Gboyega told me to write an application for employment and address it to the Permanent Secretary, Ministry of Youth Affairs and Social Development. We went together to his office, where he reported for duty before taking me to the office of the Secretary to the Permanent Secretary. Uncle Gboyega led me down a flight of stairs. He gave a deferential knock, opened the door and we ushered ourselves into the secretary's office. He was a small man, no taller than five feet. His hair had silvered. He had an austere face, almost hidden by a large pair of spectacles. He received us warmly and told us to take our seats.

"Eh-r, Mr. Olufemi Azeez, this is my niece. She needs a job and I told her that..."

The phone on the secretary's desk gave a shrill blast. "I'm busy," he snapped into the receiver, leaned back in his chair and signalled for my uncle to continue.

"I told her you are the only person who can help us," my uncle concluded, smiling sheepishly. He told us to give him a few minutes to peruse my application, stretching his right hand toward me. I handed it to him and genuflected. Then, I saw furrows line his brow as soon as he began reading. I panicked. What could be wrong again? He took off his spectacles and cleaned them with the end of his tie then fixed them firmly on the ridge of his nose and beckoned my uncle to come over. I followed him.

"I need to be completely honest with you, Mr Adeniyi," the secretary began and turned around, hands on the arms of his swivel chair. I shuffled from one foot to the other.

"Of course," Uncle Gboyega said.

"You see, things are a little more difficult than you think."

My mouth went dry but I made no attempt to interrupt.

"You mean it will be hard for my niece's application to go through?"

"Ehn, not exactly. What I'm saying is that it may not be as easy as you expect because of certain reasons," the secretary said without making eye contact.

"I don't understand."

"What I'm saying is that her local government may make things difficult for her."

"I still don't understand," my uncle said.

"I'm saying that this application shows she is from Ifelodun in Ifelodun Local Government Area."

"Yes, of course, she is from Ifelodun Local Government."

"You see, Ifelodun is in Kwara South, but if she were to come from any of the local government areas in Kwara Central, things would be easier for her."

A flash of anger began to smoulder as I stood watching for my uncle's reaction and not getting one. He didn't appear surprised. On the contrary, he seemed to have anticipated it.

"I see, so what can we do now? How can you help me, Mr Azeez?" he pleaded. I noticed a slight tremble of his hands as he placed them on the secretary's desk, peering solicitously at him. The secretary nodded.

"There is a way out," he announced grandly. My shoulders

slumped in disbelief.

"What might that be?"

"She has to write another application, then, you have to get her a local government certificate of any of the local government areas in Kwara Central, say from Ilorin West or Ilorin East, for example. If you can get her a citizenship certificate from Ilorin and she writes another application claiming to be an Ilorin indigene, her application will be processed very quickly."

"Oh my God! Nigeria needs help!" I said involuntarily. What was going on? I had been vaguely aware of the emergence of a disturbing trend in our national life but I couldn't have imagined that things could degenerate so badly. What if my uncle failed to secure a false citizenship certificate for me? What if he succeeded and I ended up with a repeat of the Kaduna experience? How would I explain to Uncle Cajethan that I could not find a job in my home state? Would he believe I made an effort? Or would he conclude that I merely came home to while away time only to return to Kaduna with intent to go on depending entirely on his kid brother? My whole body was suffused with pain and humiliation. I began pacing the office frantically, dripping in sweat. My uncle cut me a malevolent eye. I tried to calm down.

"My country needs help, dear God; come down and deliver your people!" I muttered.

"Anjola, one more foolish utterance from you and I will give you the dirtiest slap of your life!" my uncle remonstrated; then, turning to the secretary, said: "Thank you very much, Mr Durojaiye. I truly appreciate your openness. I will do as you have advised and we will come back with another application."

I was nearly knocked over by him when he stepped backward.

"You are not in tune with reality, that's why you are still not employed years after your graduation," he said, glaring at me as soon as we were out of the office. Then, softening a little, he assured me he would get an Ilorin citizenship certificate before the end of the week. "It's always about where you come from; it can't change," he told me with an ironic smile that spoke volumes about his own loathing of the way things were. I wanted to ask questions but he held his hand up to indicate that I should be quiet.

"It's about where you come from; it can't change," he repeated with a grimace. He instructed me to return home, assuring me that I would get a job before long. I crossed the road absent-mindedly and was about to hail a taxi when I noticed a Mercedes Benz 230 parked a few metres away. The driver was beckoning to me through the side mirror. I recognised him instantly.

"Dr Kolade Durotoye!" I screamed and sprinted toward him. He came out of the car, smiling, with his arms outstretched. We embraced warmly.

"It's been ages, Anjola."

"Quite so, doctor. How have you been?"

"Very well, thank you."

"I can see you look great," I said matter-of-factly.

"You don't look bad either," he said.

"You look exceptionally good, doctor. Are you married now?"

"I'm married."

"That's it then! Someone is taking good care of you!" I said triumphantly.

"Oh yes, let me answer your unasked question. I have quit drinking."

"Oh! Good to know, doctor."

"I thank God for everything. I now run my own hospital but your friend, Deinde, is doing much better than I am. He left the teaching hospital to start his own private clinic long before I did. He now has branches of his hospital in almost every part of Ilorin. He's doing really well."

"That's good to hear. I'm happy for the both of you."

"Are you in town to visit your parents? I understand you are married and live in Kaduna with your family"

"You heard right, doctor. I'm home to see my parents but

also to see if I can get a job here. My story is not as pleasant as yours. I haven't been able to get a job and my husband recently lost his."

"Oh I'm so sorry but you know what? I think Deinde can be of help."

"I don't think that is possible. What help can he possibly render, employ me in his hospital?"

"I meant he can render financial assistance. What are friends for and who knows whose turn it will be to need help tomorrow?"

"I see, I understand but that will not be necessary at all. I'm very hopeful I will get a job now that I have come home. My natal family has started a process toward that."

"I'm not saying you will not get a job but there is nothing stopping an old friend from offering some sort of palliative to relieve you in the interim."

"I appreciate your concern but I insist it's not necessary at all."

"Don't give in to foolish pride. You are in financial difficulties but fortunate enough to have an old friend who I just told you is now stupendously rich. Why would you refuse help from such a person?"

"It's not about pride. There is no dignity in a married woman crawling to an ex-boyfriend for money. Besides, it's morally unacceptable."

"What has morality got to do with it? Both of you are married and it's not as if you are about to rekindle the old relationship. As for one person crawling to the other, I will handle everything. It's obvious you need help and I want to ensure you get it. That's all. By the way, are your parents still residing where Deinde and I used to come to visit you?"

"No, they are not. Actually, my father is now retired and has moved back to Ifelodun. I'm putting up with my uncle at Coca-Cola Road."

"Very well, then, give me your address and leave the rest

to me," he said. His voice was soft, his command given with a caring tone, yet I hesitated. I wasn't comfortable with the idea. In my mind's eye, I pictured Kolade pleading with Deinde to save his ex-girlfriend from starvation. I shuddered in disgust. Perhaps I was indeed the victim of foolish pride, as Kolade said, but wouldn't it be preferable to be guilty of that than shamelessness? It would be better if I encountered Deinde directly and he offered to assist me of his own free will.

"By the way, are you going home? I mean to your uncle's house."

"Y-y-yes," I stammered, coming out of my reverie.

"In that case, I will drop you off," he said good-naturedly. I contemplated again for a brief moment, opened my mouth to say something but nothing came out. I smiled my thanks and got in. We spent the ride talking about Ilorin and the developments that had taken place over the years. We agreed that it was gradually emerging into a mega-city. Athena sat huddled in a corner when I got to my uncle's house. My nephews and nieces had gone to school; my auntie to her shop at Oja-oba. Athena was with the house help. I lifted her and planted a peck on her cheek.

"You are so pretty, my angel," I cooed.

"Mummy."

"Yes, sweetheart."

"When will I start school?"

"Very soon. Mummy will start working soon and you will start going to school, too."

"What of Daddy? Is he coming?"

"Yeah! Daddy will come to see us soon. Come, let's take a walk so that you can see how beautiful your mummy's state is."

My daughter was missing her father. What I couldn't tell her was that I was missing him as well. Being away from Ify was lonely, a feeling that a part of me was missing. Being with him was warmth, a celebration of life, a chasing away of darkness and ugliness. Sometimes, I had the terrifying feeling that if I lost him, I would be lost irretrievably. I needed my husband badly and no matter how many years passed, how many suns set, I yearned to be with him. There was dependability about him that I cherished. He was sensitive to my moods, my needs, and my all. He was intelligent and entertaining.

I was surprised that, by the time Athena and I got back, Kolade had come to look for me and had left a note stating that Deinde would be waiting for me at 5pm in one of his hospitals. He had written the address in the note. I read it over and over again, trying to make up my mind whether or not to go. In the end, I decided to give it a try.

CHAPTER 28

Many cars were parked around the premises of the hospital. Deinde must have done well for himself, I thought, as I made my way through the entrance. The young lady on duty gazed at me wordlessly, brows lifted in inquiry. I told her I wanted to see the medical director. Was I a patient? Did I have a previous appointment? I told her no but that he was expecting me. She went to announce my presence and came back to inform me that I should wait as he was busy attending to patients. She led me through a flight of stairs and we arrived at a door with the inscription 'Medical Director.' There was an array of long benches filled with patients. I sat down, waiting and watching as people went in and came out at the sound of a bell. While I waited, different attendants brought more hospital files and cards with people in tow. I got tired of sitting at some point and decided to take a walk down the corridor. A nurse was just emerging from Deinde's office when I returned. I quickly stopped her and pleaded with her to help me remind him that I was still waiting. Perhaps he had forgotten I was around. The nurse came out and told me Deinde said he knew I was waiting and that he would see me after he had attended to all his patients that evening.

At about 9.30pm, a nurse informed me the medical director was ready to see me. I knocked gently on the door; Deinde called for me to enter. He sat behind a large table; the back of his head on the chair's head rest, a smile quivering around his mouth. He was now gray-haired. His forehead had deep furrows and there were webs of wrinkles at the corners of his eyes, but he sat firm and had an air of authority about him.

"Hello, Deinde, good to see you."

"Same here, Anjola, take a seat."

"Thank you," I said, sitting directly opposite him.

"Yeah, let's make it snappy. I'm a very busy person as you must have discovered. How many hours did you spend waiting?"

"Four-and-a-half."

"You are lucky. I understand things are not going on well with you," he said with a pleasure he had trouble disguising. I was surprised by his demeanour. I became so nervous that I didn't know what to do with my hands. First, I folded them on my lap. Then, I thought that looked silly, made me look like a school girl about to request for school fees, so, I put my right arm over the back of the chair and dropped my left over my lap. I crossed and uncrossed my legs. He must have sensed my discomfort.

"Just make yourself comfortable," he said, flicking me a scornful glance.

"Oh, yes, thanks," I said, pulling myself straight. "Well, I'm in Ilorin to find a job," I added. He looked as if he was going to laugh.

"That's it. That confirms you are not doing well," he said, his words sharp and cutting. I could think of nothing to say. My brain just shut down. He continued: "Come with me, let me show you around." He got up abruptly, laughing merrily and leading the way. I started after him. The walls were bare except for his portrait. He took me round all the departments.

"You must be doing very well for yourself," I commented.

"Isn't that an understatement? I'm the epitome of success," he exclaimed theatrically.

"I agree. Congratulations," I said as we returned to his office.

"You would have said it much louder if you knew how far I have gone in life. This is only one of my hospitals. I have replicated what I have just shown you in five other locations in Ilorin and I haven't got to my target yet."

He folded his hands and leaned forward on his seat, his eyes boring into mine. I embraced myself and leaned back.

"I'm happy for you," I said, genuinely impressed.

"Of course you have to be. I'm one of the greatest achievers of our generation. No one takes a decision in my town without asking for my opinion. I'm not just a solid rock but the proverbial cornerstone itself," he bragged and immediately started to laugh.

What was I doing in Deinde's hospital? Why had I chosen to ridicule myself this way? What was I thinking? I covered my face with my hands and closed my eyes. I felt as if fate had pulled me through a knot hole and stretched me out, thin and flat. I trembled and had trouble organising my thoughts. It was as if I had lost everything I ever represented and I would be trapped forever. When I removed my hands and opened my eyes to gaze at him, he flicked me a scathing glance and then laughed again as he looked about his consulting room. I covered my face again with my palms but this time I didn't close my eyes. I saw the smile of satisfaction around his eyes.

"Congratulations, you have done well indeed," I said.

"Nobody can dispute that and I'm glad even you have admitted it," he said.

I nodded and bit down on my emotions.

"Nobody can fail to recognise your achievement. I congratulate you once again," I mouthed.

"You know the best part, Anjola? I owe my success to the brave decision I made to call it quits with you," he said disdainfully, his face filled with disgust.

"Is that right?" I asked dryly. I listened to him humiliate me, my face frozen in a smile.

"Oh yes it is. With you in my life, I wouldn't have had focus."

I gasped as anger blazed through me. Was he out of his mind? If he saw my reaction, he pretended otherwise. Well, I wasn't going to let him go on that way.

"What do you mean by that?" I demanded. A small smile, tight and cold, met my question. No, it was not a smile, more of a sneer.

"These things are not easily explainable. I know men whose lives are dogged with strife because they married the wrong woman," he said, turning his sneer into a smile of victory. My mouth fell open. I stared at him in disbelief but again he acted as if he hadn't noticed what his harsh words were doing to me. Why had I come? I queried silently again. He was having fun at my expense. Whenever he looked at me now, it was at some particular part of me. He didn't see me as a whole person but in sections that seemed to convince him that my life had taken a turn for the worse. He gave me that tight, firm, gloating look again.

"I didn't reckon I could be a harbinger of bad luck," I said, trying not to raise my voice.

"You don't have to be so hard on yourself," he sniggered. "After all, you didn't create yourself, which is why I sympathise with the man you eventually married."

A flame of anger travelled up my spine and whatever pride I had left came back in full dress parade. What had I done to deserve the insults he was hurling at me?

"Did you agree to see me just because you wanted to insult me?" I roared in a loud voice.

"No. I agreed to see you to show you what I have done with my life," he said with that cold smile on his lips. I felt a wave of calm momentarily descend on me. I realised just then that it wasn't about me. I thought he was someone more to be pitied than despised.

"Well, now I know you have done well. Once again, accept my congratulations. I'd like to be on my way now," I said, putting as much restraint in my voice as possible. But he wasn't done with me yet. He appeared to be determined to provoke me.

"Don't get yourself worked up, okay? There's no need to allow your frustration to get the better of you," he said icily.

"Well then, thanks for your advice," I said and made to take my leave but, again, he wouldn't let me.

"You see, Anjola, in the course of my practice, I have come across many frustrated people and I can diagnose your ailment right away. You are manifesting the initial symptoms of a nervous breakdown. Take it easy. All I'm saying is that I have worked hard in life and have got a lot to show as reward for my labour."

"Did you actually tell your friend to ask me to come and see you?" I asked, my tears burning behind my eyelids. I was trying with all my might to keep them from bursting forth. I didn't want him to have that satisfaction.

"Oh yes, I did. He wouldn't have given you my address without my consent."

"Is he also aware you would be telling me these things?"

"No. He gave me a long lecture about helping an old friend in distress and I told him I would see what I could do."

"I see. And this is what you can do?"

"Do you want to hold me responsible for your woes?" His words like a whip striking my shoulders.

"Don't think that because you have money makes it all right to insult me," I said, driving my words into him like needles. He did flinch but he didn't lose his demeanour. Instead, he widened his smile.

"The economy is still bad, as you know, so I can't promise anything. I don't deny that I'm wealthy but my expenses are huge. By the way, I forgot to tell you that I have four wonderful children. All of them are schooling in the United States of America. I just replaced my wife's Mercedes Benz after she complained about the one she was using before. You know you women are a handful. You would have done the same if you had had the privilege," he said without changing his expression. His smile was beginning to look like a mask.

"Congratulations," I snapped.

"OK then, take care. As I have said, I might have been able to help if not for my children's overseas school bills which are very high because, trust me, I give them the best. All the same, I will see what I can do to revive you." He started to laugh again. No, Deinde had gone too far. I wanted to handle his rudeness with equanimity but he seemed to think he could go on tormenting me. I stood beside him and looked down at him.

"I have never in my life wanted to say goodbye to anything as much as I want to say goodbye to you right now. Deinde, goodbye and good riddance to your hateful face; good riddance to your making me feel evil and despicable when you are the most evil and despicable thing in this world. Good riddance to your pretence of being clean when you live in the muck of darkness. And, do you know, you are more horrid than Satan?"

I wrinkled my nose in distaste and marched out, leaving him with his mouth open and his eyes frozen wide with shock.

Outside, I stood for some minutes to once again behold the magnificent edifice. There was no denying the fact that Deinde was successful but what about being a compassionate human being? It was contradictory how you could know someone almost all your life and not really know them. It saddened me to realise that the man I had once loved and respected, even desired to share my life with, was so full of evil. Good looks and charm were only thin, surface deceptions hiding evil and cruelty. Intelligence, talent, wealth, status, power, whatever people thought were blessings didn't always mean the person was good.

As soon as I stepped into the road, I became aware of the noise around me. As I made my way through crowd with the horns of vehicles and motor cycles blasting away, I thought to use the long walk home as therapy. I would be fatigued by the time I arrived at my uncle's house and would be able to sleep soundly.

True enough, I was labouring to remain on my feet when I knocked on my uncle's door. My auntie hurried to open it but hardly had I entered than I was greeted with the agonising cry of Athena. My auntie was saying something about being worried about my whereabouts but I shoved her aside and rushed to the sitting room. Athena was drenched in sweat and tears. She was sitting close to the dining table, far away from my nieces and nephews, all of whom sat on the couch watching television. As I ran toward her, arms outstretched, I expected her to rush into my arms but she didn't move. I had never seen her in such anguish. I attempted to lift her but something seemed to hold her back.

"Athena!" I screamed in panic. "Get up!" I commanded but she didn't respond. Instead, she started wailing. I tried again to lift her and then I saw that she was tied by her left leg to a chair with electric wire. I untied her leg and she rushed into my arms. I carried her, tears freely streaming down my face. I turned to find my uncle's wife standing directly behind me.

"You allowed your husband tie my daughter like an animal?" I accused.

"You know your uncle, I couldn't stop him," she muttered with a certain amount of sympathy. Uncle Gboyega emerged from his bedroom, eyes burning with fury.

"What's the difference between a yanminrin and an animal? Can the offspring of a hen be a duck?" he roared.

"What could an eight-year-old have done to warrant such cruelty?" I challenged him, unable to hide my anger.

"Your daughter does not fear anyone. You needed to have seen the way she talked to me without fear or respect," he said with a grimace.

"Is that all?" I asked.

All this while my uncle's wife sat at the dining table, crouched over the day's sales, making her calculations and small marks on a piece of paper. Every once in a while, she lifted her head and glanced at us. It was curious. A clock ticked loudly in the sitting room.

"Isn't that enough? I won't allow any child under my roof grow up with impudence. I know where she got her behaviour from. It's in her genes. She has to be tamed," he declared, looking violently angry.

"What you did wasn't right, Uncle. It's inhuman to tie up

a child," I preached, adding quickly, "I can't believe you are this callous."

My uncle's wife rose swiftly and marched toward us before my uncle could react to my harsh words.

"I won't watch you insult your uncle; I thought you were well raised," she said, fixing me a spiteful look. I glared back defiantly.

"You ought to treat my daughter like one of your own," I said. My auntie threw her head back and laughed the most hideous laugh I had ever heard. Then she gazed at me, her eyes cold and narrow.

"Your daughter can never be one of our own, you dreamer," she said.

"Then it's unfortunate," I commented, hugging Athena more tightly and backing out of their presence. I wanted to retire to our room. I was exhausted but I had just taken the first few steps when my uncle pulled me back rudely, a look of annoyance on his face.

"You have been very rude and disrespectful tonight," he said, shaking his head slowly, his mouth curling into a smile of loathing. "You and your yanminrin daughter don't deserve another night under my roof. Get out of my house this minute!"

Something exploded inside me. All the pain and anger I had held in, all I had shut up in my heart came pouring out. Every harsh and cutting word he had said to me and the way he had treated my daughter, as if she was lower than the lowest form of life was finally regurgitated like the sour things they were.

"In your eagerness to be characteristically uncharitable, you labelled my daughter and her ethnic stock animals, Uncle. You forgot that we are all animals. What you have done tonight was merely to prove to me that you are far more dangerous than I thought," I said contemptuously.

"Get out of my house!" he bawled and headed toward his room.

I packed our bags and left. We walked to a nearby kiosk. I

wanted to get my breathing under control and think about where we could pass the night. It was well past 11pm. I decided on an old course mate at the university. We could spend the night with her and travel to Ifelodun in the morning, from where I would seek my father counsel. It was about time I charted a new course in my life.

CHAPTER 29

We met my father at his front door, ready to go out. My mother rushed out of the kitchen when she heard my voice. She looked even younger to me. It was as if time had had no effect on her. She was immune to aging. She had a childlike quality with a healthy tint in her cheeks. She jumped on me so violently that I almost lost my balance. I never saw her face light up so quickly or her eyes seem so bright. She lifted Athena off her feet, shouting:

"Anjola, is this you? Athena, you came all the way from Kaduna to see your grandma? Ah, God, I thank you o, I'm blessed," she crooned joyously. A healthy flush came to her face. She sparkled; her eyes dancing with a youthful glint. I wished I could bask in her euphoria but her display of affection toward my daughter and me was my undoing. The walls of my heart quivered. I held the tears within and swallowed the cries that tried to emerge from my throbbing throat, but my legs betrayed me and began to shake. I couldn't hold back the tears any longer. She looked at me quizzically for a moment.

"Let's go inside," she said, patting my hand. My father stood still to contemplate me, looking thoughtful. I told him there was an urgent matter we needed to discuss but he said the compound people were already waiting for him. He told me to eat and rest but, sensing my unhappiness, changed his mind and told me to come with him. Athena appeared comfortable staying with my mother and was already bustling about the house.

"The compound people will be glad to see you after such a long time," my father said as we walked to the larger compound behind. I said nothing.

"There are two important matters for the extended family to deliberate on today. Well, one of them is not serious," he said. My father sure knew how to arouse my curiosity.

"What's it about?"

"It's about Baba Tayo and one of his daughters. She is bringing her would-be husband home today for the introduction."

"Ah, that's good."

"Yes, it is good. The only problem is that Baba Tayo can't remember her mother."

"I beg your pardon?"

"You know Baba Tayo and his numerous wives and children. He has forgotten which of his wives gave birth to this particular girl and he is shy to ask the poor girl. Our prayer is that she comes with her mother to save the entire family from embarrassment."

There was a spontaneous eruption of "Anjola, welcome." Most members of our extended family were seated, including my uncles, aunts and cousins who lived at home. It was interesting to find them in a single setting, particularly since I had almost forgotten how some of them looked. People were asking why my mother didn't come. My father explained that she had to stay behind to take care of my daughter. I spotted Baba Tayo immediately. He was decked in a resplendent flowing white agbada and grinning from ear to ear. I saw a radiant-looking young woman and a young man sitting close to her. I presumed they were the couple but I couldn't figure out if her mother was present. They all looked like village women to me. I held my breath and sat beside my father. One of my uncles, whose name I couldn't recall, got up to announce the reason for the gathering and the order of events.

"How come Baba Tayo can't remember his daughter's mother? He was never married to her?" I whispered to my father.

"He has been married to too many women and his children are so numerous that he doesn't know some of them," he whispered back.

"Does that mean he hasn't seen this girl in a long while?"

"I don't think he was aware of her existence at all; well, not until a few weeks ago when she came to tell him the man she wants to marry wants to know her father."

"Is the girl's mother here?"

"No."

"How will Baba Tayo go about things?"

"He always has a way around. Be patient."

Baba Tayo was now being asked to introduce his would-be son-in-law. He cleared his throat.

"It is a thing of great joy to me today that one of my most cherished, most beloved, most adored, and, in fact, most favourite daughters, Omolere, is here with her fiancé. Her mother..." He started acting as if there was a lump in his throat and was making a protracted effort at clearing it while also ostensibly repairing the Agbada, which seemed to be falling off his right shoulder. His daughter obviously got the message and came to his rescue by supplying the name: Atinuke.

"Yes, as I was saying, her mother and my beloved wife, Atinuke, is unavoidably absent. I don't have much to say other than let my son-in-law know that my daughter, Omolere, is not just the apple of my eye; she is my eye itself. I love her so much and will miss her. That is why her husband must take good care of her otherwise he will have me to contend with. Omolere is my life. I have suffered and sacrificed a lot to raise her decently and make her a woman to be loved and adored by any man."

Baba Tayo's speech was greeted with loud applause, after which my uncle, as MC, began to introduce all the family members present. It was now time for the second issue of the day.

"You will recall that Ayilara brought it to the attention of the family that his new wife was giving him problems. I'm sure we all remember that Ayilara told us that his new wife has refused to let him come near her at night. For the benefit of those who may have a poor memory, I take it upon myself to remind us all of how Ayilara gave a vivid account of what was happening between him and his new wife each night when he attempted to do his duty as a husband. He said his new wife was in the habit of screaming and punching him each time he attempted to see her undergarment. After several unsuccessful attempts, he cried out to the family. We all met here to deliberate on the matter. We reasoned that Ayilara's new wife may be one of those young women who are afraid of being deflowered as a result of the stories she may have heard. We asked Ayilara if he met his first wife a virgin and if he understood how to mate with a virgin. He said his first wife was not a virgin when he married her and that he has never mated with a virgin. We therefore mandated his cousin, Babatunde, who we all know is far more experienced in these matters, to assist Ayilara deflower his second wife. Babatunde has three wives and they all came to his house previously untouched. Today, Babatunde is ready to give us a feedback on how far he went in executing his assignment."

I pricked my ears and shifted uncomfortably in my seat. Babatunde's father was a full brother to Ayilara's father. However, both were half-brothers to my father. I was still trying to figure out the appropriate way to describe my relationship with them when I noticed Babatunde had gotten up to speak.

"I greet everybody here present. In accordance with the wishes of the family, I visited Ayilara's bed at night to help make his wife a woman. However, I regret to inform you all that for the three consecutive nights I tried, she didn't allow me to lift her wrapper, let alone get between her legs. Any attempt was met with violent resistance. Her attitude is puzzling. I have never come across her type."

Loud murmur rent the air. I was about to ask my father a question when one of my uncles started to speak.

"There is no doubt that the D-day has come. We have applied utmost caution in handling this matter because we didn't want to offend our new wife but we can no longer continue to act as if all is well in our son's household. Why did Ayilara marry a new wife? It is because he wants to have more children. This is the reason his family cannot look the other way. We will now call on our new wife to tell the family of her husband why she doesn't wish to bear our children."

Ayilara's wife, who was not in the gathering, was summoned. She was a young woman of about twenty-two. She was asked to stand in the middle of the gathering. She tried to talk but burst into tears instead. Two of my aunts got up to put their hands on her shoulder, while gently patting her on the back and urging her to dry her tears. Finally, she gained her composure. She wiped her face with the back of her hand, darted her eyes across the audience and began.

"I'm sorry. I'm very sorry. I have no hole," she said, barely audibly and burst into fresh tears. People exchanged confused glances. One of my aunts asked:

"What do you mean you have no hole?"

"My vagina has a smooth and bare surface. There is no opening."

There was naked agony in her tear-filled eyes.

"You are a bloody liar! Whoever has seen a vagina without a hole?" one of my uncles shouted but his outburst was greeted with condemnation.

"Be careful! Be patient! Let her explain!" different people offered. At this point, one of my aunts, who appeared to be the oldest female in the family, took charge.

"My daughter," she started; "if you say your vagina has no hole, how then do you pass urine?"

"I urinate through my anus."

I squirmed in my seat.

"You urinate through your anus?"

"Yes."

"When did you notice your vagina has no hole? I mean, when did you start to urinate from your anus?"

277

"I have been doing it like that for as long as I can remember."

"Does your mother know?"

"Yes, she knows."

I couldn't take it anymore. I rose to my feet abruptly.

"I'm sorry to interrupt this meeting. I know I'm a mere child who doesn't even deserve to be here but I will like to respectfully ask one or two questions and thereafter make a suggestion as to the solution to this problem."

They said I should go ahead.

"My fathers and mothers, the decision of the family to send Babatunde to go and mate with Ayilara's wife baffles me. If Ayilara's wife had not had this problem, does it mean that Babatunde would have actually had sex with his cousin's wife?"

Everybody burst into laughter. I sat down, feeling indignant. One of my uncles took the floor.

"Anjola is indeed a child of yesterday, so trivial issues trouble her." He turned to me, still smiling, and said: "To answer your question, we knew that sending Babatunde to Ayilara's wife meant he would have sex with her. We even knew that such a singular sexual encounter could put Ayilara's young wife in the family way but it is the same blood. What would be the difference between Ayilara's child and Babatunde's child?   Both   are products of the same blood. You said you have a suggestion to make. Let's hear it."

"Thank you. I'm not a medical doctor but I strongly believe that Ayilara's wife has a medical condition that can be corrected through surgery. Therefore, I suggest our family send an emissary to her family to inform them that she needs medical attention. I also want our family to take full financial responsibility of treating her in addition to giving her all the moral support she needs." The meeting agreed. I felt a small frisson of satisfaction.

My father and I didn't have time to talk until after an early dinner. First, I told him what had transpired between Uncle Gboyega and me. Next, I explained the problem with my brother-in-law. Finally, I told him the reason why I came home – to seek his advice on a new direction. I had reached my wit's end and no longer knew how to forge ahead in life. He said nothing. I was exasperated.

"Well, it seems you have nothing to say," I concluded. "That leaves me with the option my old school mate suggested last night."

"What option?" he asked, looking sceptical.

"She suggested I seek a political office in next year's general election," I said. A small tight smile appeared on his face.

"Did she also advise you on the party to join?" he asked.

"Well, y-yes, we did consider a few of them and we agreed that the National Equity Party may be the one through which I can actualise my political ambitions."

His eyes narrowed and his smile evaporated.

"What position did you have in mind?" he asked with a far-off look in his eyes.

"Membership of the House of Representatives," I said.

He sighed. "The two of you are children; you know nothing about politics in Nigeria," he said with a pitying look.

"Why did you say so?" I asked. He didn't reply immediately. He sat there, simply staring ahead; shadows deep and dark were in his eyes.

"Talk to me, father," I pleaded, desperation stealing through my soul. His body trembled and his eyes were bleak, warning me I was about to be shocked. Forewarned, I still wasn't prepared for what I heard.

"Things the rest of humanity take for granted are rare for us in Nigeria," he began, scrunching up his face and shaking his head. I frowned. He allowed his eyes to meet mine. "Politicians in Nigeria are not concerned with ideas, issues or programmes and I can assure you there will be no justice in the so-called National Equity Party you mentioned."

My frown deepened, but remembering that it made wrinkles if you frowned too much, I rearranged my face and inclined my head.

"There are only two things that 'qualify' an individual to even nurse a political ambition in our country," he continued. "These are money and the strong backing of a godfather."

My heart began to thump alarmingly.

My father went on. "I tell you the way it's done: People who intend to contest start to 'work' toward actualising their ambition long before the election. First, they register and obtain the party's membership card at the ward level, which is their village or town as the case may be. This ought to be free but it is not. Not only are they required to pay, they will not be recognised as 'serious' if they fail to dole out money on a consistent basis to their wards. Next, depending on the position they desire, they must 'service' the party financially at all levels, local, state and federal. Above all, the aspirant must seek political favours from those at the centre because the federal has a stake in what goes on in the state. This explains why the powers in the centre plant their loyalists in the state and can dissolve the state exco at will.

"As the election approaches, all aspirants go through what is called the primaries, where what actually takes place is the coronation of the highest bidder. What this means is that the fact that an individual has been spending money does not guarantee them their party's ticket, unless they are fortunate to be the highest spender. In addition to doling out money, a politically ambitious individual must regularly make themselves visible in their community by building a cottage hospital here, sinking a borehole there and constructing township roads in their locality long before they declare their ambition."

He paused to make sure his words had sunk in.

"Is it that bad?" I demanded bitterly. He nodded gravely, the lines of his mouth tightening, a glint of anger or sadness or both taking over his face. I sighed and hugged myself closely.

"As I said earlier," he continued, "the other way is to go through a godfather. This is even more expensive but more certain. Godfathers are very powerful to the extent that they impose their candidates. No one can challenge them. Most times, they charge a fixed amount for a specific office. You want to become a senator? Go and bring fifty million naira. Ha! I don't have fifty million, Chief, but if I sell my father's house, my mother's land and my friends form a fund-raising committee in my honour, I'm sure I will be able to bring thirty million. Please help me, Chief. You have to help yourself. Thirty million is for the House of Representatives."

"Once the individual finds the money and pays and is willing to enter into an agreement as to how they will share the spoils of office, victory is assured regardless of what the electorate does or doesn't want. In Kwara State, as in all other states in the country, you would be wasting your time, Anjola, if you joined a political party. All political offices are shared according to the whims of so-called political leaders. You can't make headway in politics, my dear daughter, because I don't have any contact with notable political leaders. Worse, we have no money, no political pedigree and no track record of political versatility," he concluded, looking despondent.

I felt my blood drain down into my feet; a stinging sensation began behind my ears. I raised my head heavenward. Large drops of tears coursed down my cheeks. I knew he had spoken from the depth of his heart but where would I go from here? What would I do with my life? Meanwhile, it was now dark. I got up, staggered and nearly crashed into a group of aluminium buckets as I groped in the dark.

"Be careful," my father said compassionately. My mother must have heard him. She called out to us:

"Is there no lantern where you people are?"

"No, it's very dark here," he said.

"It's very dark here," I echoed but I barely heard myself. My voice seemed to have been reduced to a whisper.

In my mother's room, I found the bed and lay down, perching my head gingerly on the pillow and going over all that my father had told me. I tried to arrive at a decision, my decision. Perhaps I could start by working for a political party, as my father had suggested. I would willingly serve in whatever capacity they might find me worthy. I would serve the people as well. I could teach if they would let me since I had no money to put at their disposal. Maybe I would impress them enough to earn their respect. All I ever wanted was to make my contribution to my motherland but I was overcome by a sense of futility. I wanted to reach out for my file and make more notes on the changes I would propose if I ever got the chance but I lacked the energy to stand right now. I was tired of even narrating my own story. What didn't I do right? When and where did I go wrong? Well, with my last scrap of will power, I would go to Ilorin in the morning, not to my university mate, but to my old friend, Kike, who had been in the civil service for many years. I would plead for her assistance; together, we might be able to strategise on how to make my dream come true. As for my father's concerns, they would form part of the issues I would address seriously once I became a member of the hallowed chamber, I thought, promising myself to summon the energy to make additional notes in my file in the morning. My mind drifted to the day Uncle Cajethan told me I was stubborn although he had been quick to add that there was virtue in it. For the first time since I met him, I realised he might be right. The time had come for me to put my alleged obstinacy to the test, I thought wearily as I dragged my body to bed.

PART FIVE
SEPTEMBER 1998

CHAPTER 30

Anjola woke up early the next morning and began to make preparations for what she hoped would be a life-altering journey to Ilorin. First, it was her father she roused from sleep, carefully articulating her thoughts, which included her understanding and trust of his perception of the political situation. Then she went on to express her determination to take her chances even as she would bear in mind all that she had been told. She also dwelled more extensively on the circumstances surrounding her journey home and her brother-in-law's pointed accusation against her as a layabout.

"I don't want to go back without trying, Father," she said with a note of finality. He took a long, deep breath.

"What do you have in mind, specifically?"

"I intend to do as you suggested which is to be ready to work for a political party and, by extension, the society. From your explanation, I've become aware that it would be unrealistic to hope for a chance to contest in the current dispensation so I'm willing to work toward the next four or five years. That way, I will demonstrate my commitment. When I get to Ilorin, I hope to find a link to the man you described as the most important personality in the National Equity Party. All I would ask of him would be to be given a chance to be useful," she said seriously.

"Things are far more difficult than you imagine," he said gravely. Anjola sighed and paced the room, looking high and low.

"I've come a long way, Father, travelling all the way from Kaduna, leaving my husband and inconveniencing my daughter. The most painful part is that we are already in September, the beginning of a new academic year when Athena ought to be going back to school. I have to find my feet quickly so that I don't truncate her education." She squeezed her eyes shut and swallowed hard. Then she went on and on, trying to make her father see things her way. As he listened, he realised that he needed to set his cynicism aside and embrace her optimism. In spite of what he knew, it was difficult not to be encouraged by her determination. When she had finished, he gave her a piercing look.

"I love your spirit," he said. Anjola's hopes soared. "I love your doggedness. People like you who live with incredible positivity, who are never overcome by futility always succeed in the end; it's only a matter of time," he said proudly.

Anjola gazed at him for some moments, soaking in his pronouncement before asking him what he would like her to buy for him from Ilorin. She wouldn't stay longer than a day or two in the first instance. He gave a feeble laugh, rugged and soft and phlegmy, but a laugh nonetheless.

"A loaf of Maraba bread," he said softly. Vitality leaped from Anjola's' eyes. It was time to speak with her mother. Athena was still sleeping. Smiling, Anjola announced in a melodious voice that she was travelling to Ilorin that morning and would return the following day or the day after. Her mother expressed her feelings by a prolonged silence.

"Don't worry, Mother, everything will be fine," she cajoled. "I can't possibly give up just like that. I mean, it wouldn't make sense at all," she pursued.

It was now her mother's turn to pace back and forth.

"Sit down, Mother, calm yourself and listen to me," Anjola said quietly, lowering her eyes. Her mother sat down on the edge of the bed. A gecko emerged from seemingly nowhere and ran across the room, then stopped briefly and ran off. It seemed as if it was looking for something. Mother and daughter laughed simultaneously but made no comment.

"It's necessary for me to think, act, learn, stumble and get up again, Mother. And I need your goodwill, your prayers and support, not fear." She paused before asking her to ignore her fears and concentrate on victory. Her mother gave a little laugh, and as she did, dimples formed in her cheeks. It turned out to be easier to convince her mother than her father.

She took bath while waiting for Athena to awake. She didn't want to disturb her sleep. Poor Athena, she had gone through so much. Anjola understood Athena as an extension of herself; she loved her because she was hers, she was defenceless and they needed each other, especially during this period of anguish. At just eight years old, she was maturing fast, growing into a friend and companion. Anjola had seen that about her daughter. A part of her wanted to celebrate not just her daughter's physical but mental, intellectual, psychological, and emotional growth, but there was also another part that tended to sympathise with the little girl. This part saw her as a child of unhappy circumstance, forced to grow beyond her years, her rightful chronological age.

By the time she returned to the room, Athena was awake. Anjola was fierce with love for her. She rocked her, pressing her cheeks to the top of her head.

"Good morning, Mum," Athena said with a smile.

"Good morning, sweetheart.

"You've bathed, are you going somewhere?"

"Yes, darling, Mum wants to go to Ilorin. I won't be long, I promise. I'll be back tomorrow or next, maximum. Do you want to come with me or you'd stay with Grandma?"

"Don't worry, Mum, I'll stay with Grandma. When's Daddy coming?"

"I can't say for sure but I trust he'll come soon." She took Athena's face in her hands and looked more closely at her.

"You are such a sweet little girl. Are you sure you'll be okay staying with Grandma? Although, I'm going to Ilorin to do lots of things, I'm sure we can manage if you'll like to come with me."

"Don't worry, Mum, I'll be fine. Besides, I love Grandma."

"That's my girl!" She lay back with Athena on the bed and held her in her arms. They kept talking in low tones for some time. She was reinvigorated by the innocence of her daughter's support.

"I've got to get going," she finally said. Athena remained unperturbed and met her mother's gaze with a bold smile. Everything is ready. Anjola muttered silently. She dressed up and left the house with great clarity of mind.

CHAPTER 31

She didn't bother to go to Uncle Gboyega's house. She was aware that neither her uncle nor his wife would be excited to see her. It was just as well. She didn't want any negative energy around her at her second attempt to find a path in her home state. Her plan was to go in search of her old friend, Kike Tomori, although they hadn't corresponded since her relocation to Kaduna. Anjola knew that Kike was still in the civil service and still unmarried. Kike also knew that Anjola hadn't succeeded in finding a job and was married to Ify. She had met Ify in Ilorin during the early period of their relationship when Anjola brought Ify to meet her parents. It was unlikely that Kike would turn down her request to stay with her. Kike was kind-hearted, dependable and caring. She hailed a taxi.

She found Kike in her office and they easily reconnected. Age had obviously touched her friend but then it was the same with everyone. She, too, must have been touched by the vicissitudes of life. Kike now had wrinkles at the corners of her eyes and mouth, and there was a tinge of dryness about her, harsh and bleak. However, there was still a desirable beauty in her clear skin in spite of the thickness at the top of her nose. Anjola observed that the changes were not only physical. Kike had changed a great deal in the way she spoke, but her mischievousness still poured out of her, something bold, spontaneous and provocative that was revealed in her defiant posture.

"Yawo ibo, omo yanmirin nko?" she hailed, teasingly enquiring after Athena.

"Na you know," Anjola shot back jocularly.

"Ibo thing strong well well o, see as my friend now look totally Ibotic."

It was pointless trying to tackle Kike at throwing jibes. She was no match for her and she knew it.

"Oya come, 'Yawo Nna, let's go to the canteen so that you can eat akpu," Kike said, laughing loudly.

"You win," Anjola replied, giving Kike a languid hand that she didn't withdraw immediately. Fufu was available as Kike had bragged but Anjola opted for eba and vegetable. As they ate, Anjola began to organise her thoughts. Kike had been in the civil service for several years and had obviously risen through the ranks - notwithstanding the fact that she didn't have a degree. Anjola had no doubt that she would know someone who would most likely know someone who would be helpful in the ultimate quest to meet a notable political personality. Kike was vivacious, boisterous and socially mobile. She had always been clear about the kind of life she wanted. She was by no means an insipid creature who bowed submissively to fate. Anjola's mind drifted to her father's warning. The thought threatened to blight her mood. It wasn't as if she didn't understand his perspective; it was just that she also recognised the generational difference between them. The situation couldn't be as hopeless as he made it seem. A flicker of a smile appeared on her lips as she reassured herself yet again that her sojourn would not be in vain.

They returned to the comfort of Kike's office which, thankfully, she had to herself. Without preamble, she sought her friend's help. Kike's immediate reaction was to give Anjola a sly look and then mutter something she couldn't decipher. Perhaps Kike didn't quite understand what she was trying to say. This was not the Kike she knew from their teen days. That Kike was not taciturn; she was confident, chatty, bold, highly opinionated and somewhat tactless. She now seemed to be a different person.

Something seemed to have made her lose her optimism and certainty. Maybe Anjola needed to explain more.

"I know you would think the time would be too short if I had proposed to take part in the 1999 elections. I mean, we have barely less than a year to the elections but with hard work and committed service on my part throughout the next five years, surely I can brave the odds in 2003," Anjola pursued, hoping she sounded convincing enough this time. Again, Kike murmured vaguely as if she were thinking out loud. Anjola peered into her friend's eyes and was baffled by what she now recognised as shock.

"It's impossible," Kike finally whispered.

Anjola's heart sank, as if drowning beneath the waves. She was looking at her friend but with her eyes unfocused. She suddenly seemed to be miles away, as if staring into the past. But was she going to give up just like that? Had she really done the best she could in the circumstances? No. She made a firm resolution to try harder. Getting Kike to agree to work with her would be the chance of a lifetime. She wasn't going to let it slip through her fingers. In spite of the fact that Kike was turning out to be a major hurdle, she would brace up to the challenge. Anyone who knew Kike in her younger days would have been shocked by her current demeanour. It was the same Kike who found her a boyfriend to help her counter her post-NYSC frustration back in the days. It was true that her relationship with Deinde Komolafe hadn't blossomed into marriage but it was a significant part of their shared history. Now she observed that apart from being shorter, Kike now dressed more soberly. Did this connote other, underlying changes? As Anjola contemplated all this, she also noticed that she looked pale, with dark circles under her eyes and an embittered expression on her face. There was a deathly silence between them now as Anjola racked her brains for better ideas that could sway her friend.

"Does what I told you make you angry?" Anjola asked. Kike didn't respond. "You're the only person I could have told it to," she continued. "You're the only true friend I have here. But maybe I'm being unreasonable and childish." Then she asked Kike to advise her. Eventually, Kike spoke:

"No, no, you're not being unreasonable. It's more complicated. Well, I know you have a strong personality, Anjola, which I must be courageous enough to let you know is a somewhat repellent characteristic in a woman. I think you have a strong character though and you should stand firm, so, maybe we could try," she concluded in a low tone.

Anjola was intrigued by her response; and, as if on cue, they rose to their feet simultaneously and hugged. Then they sat down again, wordlessly. Another silence followed but this time it was a silence like that of rest after toil. Fatigue threatened to overtake them. It was also just minutes to four o' clock, the official closing hour. Anjola was anxious to ask her when and how they would start but she knew better than to overstretch her luck. What was important was that they were on the same page. Her political journey had begun, she thought with a secret smile as they exited the Kwara State Chamber of Commerce and Industry Complex.

CHAPTER 32

Kike turned over Anjola's proposition is her mind all the way to her apartment at Tanke. Why would Anjola want to dabble in the murky waters of politics? Desperation, unbridled ambition, boredom, what? She found it almost inconceivable and the more she thought about it, the more difficult it was for her to understand. What came to her mind when Anjola first broached the subject was that her friend was insane. Apart from the fact that observable political trends would easily place her chances of success at near-zero, she couldn't fathom why a good-natured, homely and decent person like Anjola would want to venture into politics. But as she spoke, Kike couldn't deny the passion she saw. That was why she gave her consent. Anjola had committed herself to her aspiration. Besides, since when did it become a crime for a citizen to aspire to serve their country, especially given her evident zeal? As was often the case, aspirations pursued with daring were more often than not successful. She would ask Anjola more pressing questions nonetheless, but that would be later in the evening.

"What exactly do you want to do?" Kike asked as soon as dinner was over.

"At a personal level, I want to be useful, active, productive, and alive but translated into political terms, I wish to participate in the process of developing my community and building my country; I want to represent the people of Ifelodun in the House of Representatives. My father has been educating me on the political dynamics of Nigeria - and Kwara State in particular. Specifically, he told me that the people of Ifelodun would have little if any role to play in the emergence of their representative. He said I need a political godfather from Ilorin to buy into my ambition; that I wouldn't stand a chance unless and until I received the endorsement of this highly revered personality. He also told me that once the man accepts me, I have automatically earned the qualification to hold office. The Baba determines who gets what in the political equation. I came to you because you've been around for a while, having been in the civil service all these years I'm convinced that even if you don't know the Baba, or are not close to him, you're likely to know someone who knows someone who knows him." Anjola spoke with certainty, convinced of what she was saying.

"You are on a mission to find a political godfather," Kike said. Anjola smiled faintly, a little embarrassed.

"You've made one significant point, which is that I don't know the Baba," Kike continued. "My knowledge of him doesn't extend beyond seeing him on television. But you've also made an intelligent guess, which is that I'm likely to know someone who knows him closely. Yes, I do know someone like that."

"I knew I could count on you," Anjola said with something resembling triumph.

"Let me add quickly that your father told you the absolute truth about our brand of politics here," Kike said and burst into a laugh, covering her mouth with her hand.

"I knew my father couldn't be wrong," Anjola said, laughing, along with her.

"Tomorrow morning, I'll take you to a top government official. This man is a civil servant but everyone knows he's also a politician. Much more than that, you would think he's in Baba's employ judging by his strong loyalty toward him. He's certainly his acolyte; he can walk you straight into Baba's sitting room and it will then be left to you to convince Baba to accept you as a political god-daughter. If Baba does so, I would be the first person to congratulate you because it would mean that you have already become a legislator. He determines who wins the primaries and, of course, with his political machinery, he chooses the eventual winner," she said with a faint smile which looked like a grimace.

Although she hadn't said anything new, her startling bluntness left Anjola somewhat disconcerted. The lift of her eyebrows showed that she was neither happy nor comfortable with what Kike had described but said nothing. Silence separated them for the rest of the evening.

In bed, Anjola read for a long time but sleep didn't come. She rose with the first glow of dawn. They soon set out in search of the man who would serve as the link. His name was Majekodunmi Dada. He was Director of Administration in the State Ministry of Tourism.

When they arrived at the long, high-ceilinged office, they immediately became aware of what appeared to be an ongoing pandemonium. Some people were shaking with laughter. Others, especially women, frequently struck one palm against the other. All eyes were fixed on a lady who was talking. Anjola figured her to be either in her late twenties or early thirties. She had an attractive shape, a slim waist and she was dressed with great simplicity.

"He has no right to issue me a query and I have said it over and over again that I'm not going to respond to it. For heaven's sake, for how long are we going to continue this way? When we don't resist, we are encouraging them to continue to treat us as slaves. I'm saying we deserve better treatment," she said.

"But he's your boss and you can't take that from him," a woman interjected.

"My honest advice is that you should answer the query and keep your job, abi na today?" another threw in.

"I have no response to his query; Majekodunmi Dada can do his worst," the lady added, raising her right arm to the ceiling to demonstrate her earnestness.

Anjola shot Kike a quizzical look at the mention of Majekodunmi Dada's name. Kike's face clouded in confusion.

"Have you thought of the implications of your action?" a man asked.

"Yes, I have thought of it and I'm prepared for the worst, I'm sick and tired." She quivered with indignation and her voice broke. The confusion on the faces of Anjola and Kike deepened.

"Pardon my intrusion, sister, but what's going on around here?" Anjola asked.

"Well, you're obviously not a member of staff of this ministry; otherwise, you wouldn't be asking me. But I might as well tell you since the whole world already knows what's going on. My name is Moji Akinrinade. I work here, as you can guess. This is the administrative section of the ministry and our boss, Mr. Majekodunmi Dada, is the head of administration for the entire ministry. I'm supposedly his girlfriend, and when I describe myself as his girlfriend, I'm not particularly proud of it because he's a married man." She said the last part reluctantly, almost in a whisper.

"But you've been proud of it up until this morning," a short, thin man cut in aggressively.

"That's what you think but that I've been tolerating Dada doesn't mean I have been enjoying anything," Moji snapped irritably. "Dada's wife and children are not in Ilorin but he's married nonetheless. So, it's a relationship that can't lead anywhere since I know he's not going to marry me. But his marital status is not the only reason why I said I'm not proud of addressing myself as his girlfriend. The other reason is that I'm just one of several other girls he keeps, even within this ministry. We all know ourselves and everyone knows that any girl he wishes to date must agree to his proposition because of his position. If he wants to sleep with you and you say no, he can find a way to make you lose your job. The sack letter would offer a justification that would seem perfect but everyone in the know would know it was false. For more than two years now, I have been tolerating him, attending to his sexual needs. That's why people like Mr Dele Bello can assume that I was having a ball." She paused and glanced briefly in the thin man's direction. She scratched her hair and resumed.

"As I said, I'm not the only one. We all know ourselves. Any day Dada wants you, he tells you to come over to his house after work and you do as directed, knowing you are going to pass the night. He invites the one he wants when he wants her. None of us, including me, has dared to say no. Yesterday, he sent for me while we were still in the office. I knew it meant it was my turn. After work, I went home to pack for the night and thereafter proceeded to his house at GRA. You see, he has this very annoying way of treating me and I guess he treats the other girls the same." She paused, as if trying to think through how much she should divulge. The thin man, whom Anjola now knew was Mr. Bello, laughed scornfully. Moji shot him a malevolent look, sighed vexedly and resumed talking.

"He never lets me into his sitting room because he often has visitors and he doesn't want them to know what's going on. As a rule, therefore, you know that when you arrive, you must not enter through the front door but the kitchen, where you will meet his cook who will then escort you to his bedroom. So, when I arrived last night, I was unlucky because the cook wasn't around and I knew the rule. What that meant was that I had to wait outside for his cook to return. I stood for hours on end before I eventually gained access. All this time, Dada was in the house. I was exhausted by then but I was there for a purpose, on a duty of sort. The overall effect was that I didn't get much sleep. I was just about falling asleep when he woke me up and told me to get ready for the office. I pleaded with him to give me a little more time. It wasn't as if he was going to give me a free ride to the office anyway. To my consternation, he threatened that if he got to the office before me he would issue a query. I was stupefied. I'd always known he was mean-spirited but he had no justification whatsoever to treat me that way." Moji's voice had been raised in anger as she proceeded.

"I looked at him straight in the eye and told him he wouldn't go that far; that he had no moral grounds to do so. I reminded him that if he hadn't invited me over, if I had spent the night in my own bed, I wouldn't have had any reason to be late to work. Besides, he had been sleeping with me for more than two years and I'd never reported late to work the morning after. He left the house without another word and I thought the matter was settled but can you imagine? I got to the office at a quarter-to-nine and a query was waiting on my desk. I tore the envelop open, read the so-called query over and over again, tore it into pieces, walked straight into his office, and threw the pieces of paper right into his adulterous face. Some of my colleagues who are concerned that I risk being sacked went to beg him to forgive me. He told his secretary to produce another copy and that's what they are trying to persuade me to answer but I won't. I have tolerated his excesses for this long because I was stupid and because I thought I was helpless. I felt I had no choice for as long as I wanted to keep my job. But I have had enough of his shenanigans. My involvement with him has prevented me from having the clarity of mind to consider propositions from other men. Psychologically and emotionally, I've been tied to the unbridled sexual demands of a boss out of fear of losing my means of livelihood. But when he threatened me this morning, I came to the painful realisation that I stand to lose on all counts. Even if I continue to sleep with him and obey all his commands, he's bound to get tired of me one day. Given the depth of his meanness, it certainly wouldn't be difficult for him to sack me. That means I would lose the job I have been struggling so hard to keep and it would be a mere addition to the loss of my pride and dignity. I've disgraced myself enough. It's time to call Dada's bluff. Let the worst happen. Those who have been pleading with him to reissue the query know he has no right to do what he's doing but no one can say so to his face."

She stopped abruptly. Her breathing was laboured. Kike suggested they leave immediately and return the next morning. Anjola nodded her assent.

CHAPTER 33

Majekodunmi Dada had a large, heavy head. He had a severe, critical look and wore spectacles. Anjola observed that Kike felt uncomfortable in his presence.

"May we sit down, sir?" she asked courteously. He gestured to a chair. "This is my friend, Anjola," she said deferentially.

As she spoke, Dada picked up a pen, opened a large book and began writing. Silence stretched among them for a while as Dada kept writing. Kike found her voice after a while and said: "She wants to join politics; she wishes to meet with Baba, and I told her you are the only person who can facilitate it."

She fell silent again and stared at her feet. Anjola sat hunched and silent. Dada paused, pen in hand and muttered: "Wonderful. We need some new blood in Kwara politics." He spoke with detached simplicity but with a mocking glance that left Anjola not knowing if he was joking. Kike pushed back a stray hair from her brow and began to twist her fingers.

"Well, you are in luck because I was just going to see Baba to deliver a message. We may as well go together," he concluded. Kike nodded and patted Anjola's arm. Outside, they made their way to Dada's car; Kike took the front passenger seat while Anjola settled in the back directly behind her. Anjola's temples throbbed as they drove to Baba's house in silence.

As they entered the compound, Kike asked if Dada had any suggestions about how Anjola could broach the subject.

"She can make her presentation anyway she chooses," he said with a shrug. The compound had a neat, white framed two-storey house. Baba's room was on the second floor. It was spacious, with two large windows that ensured good ventilation. On the walls were many photographs of Baba with different people in a variety of places. He himself was slim, light-skinned and bespectacled. He was dressed in a sky–blue agbada and sokoto with elaborate embroidery. Two men stood behind him.

Dada saluted him with a broad smile; Kike and Anjola genuflected simultaneously. Baba ignored their greetings, as if he hadn't seen them, and extended a reluctant hand to Dada. Dada told Baba how he had carried out all his assignments; that he had seen the managing director, chief executive officer of Starlight Bank and had delivered the message about promoting Momodu Kolawole, Baba's nephew. Baba merely looked at Dada as he spoke. Anjola felt a wave of nausea. Suddenly, Baba began to speak but what he had to say had nothing to do with the message Dada had just delivered - or about Anjola and her friend. He said he constantly made trips to London, Paris, Amsterdam and New York for just two or three days and for reasons he wouldn't make clear. Mere delusions of grandeur, Anjola thought, feeling her heart shrink.

Kike indicated that they should both kneel. Anjola complied. As they did so, Kike murmured something unintelligible. For the first time since their arrival, Baba honoured them with a glance. Without speaking, he indicated for Dada to explain their mission. He told Baba that Kike was his subordinate in the civil service and that she had brought her friend to him to deliver a message. Baba turned to them. With her last scrap of willpower, Anjola explained her willingness to offer her services to her people. She told him she had a degree in English and could teach children as well as adults as part of a community development service. She said she was willing to work for the National Equity Party in any other capacity they might find her suitable.

"I believe strongly that I can be useful, Baba, and I would be glad if you would permit me to show my commitment."

She wanted to go on to explain how much she needed his endorsement but Baba removed his glasses, lifted his lined face and glared at her. Anjola hunched her shoulders, her chilly gaze on Baba's face.

"You are not making sense so get to the point." Baba said impatiently. It was the most difficult situation Anjola had ever found herself in. She was overcome by vertigo. Finally, after shuffling through a thousand possibilities about the best way to earn Baba's compassion and discarding all of them, she met his gaze and told him she could envision herself as a legislator and that she had come to respectfully seek his fatherly blessings. She told him how strongly she felt about the contribution she could make to the law-making process of the emerging democratic nation; how people of her generation could bring fresh perspectives on lingering national problems; how it had become a global trend to consider women's views as useful; and how her experience in life had prepared her for her envisioned role as a legislator in the country of her birth.

Anjola had to pause when two men entered the room and set a tray of food before Baba. One was tall and heavily boned, like a giant. The other was short and bald with a moustache. Baba didn't seem to be in a hurry to eat. Eventually, he washed his hands and gestured for the men to leave. One of the plates was pounded yam; the other was okra with intestines and fish. Silence descended on the room. He had hardly swallowed the first morsel when consternation spread over his face. He ordered Dada to summon "Ambali" to his presence. Dada leapt to his feet and returned shortly with the giant-like man in tow. Baba confronted him immediately over the soup, that it had too much salt. The giant's eyes clouded and he stuttered as he tried to apologise.

"Enough sir-ing!" Baba bawled with a threatening gesture. The room was filled with tension as Baba hurled insults at him. As the man was trying to plead for forgiveness, Baba washed his hand in the bowl and then poured the soup into the dirty water. Anjola was wondering why he thought he had to do that when, like a scene from a distasteful movie, Baba took the bowl and emptied the contents over the giant's head. Anjola squawked in horror and turned to Kike, who was staring at the scene. Baba turned his attention back to Anjola.

"Sisi, you said you want to join politics, even contest and win an election to the Federal House of Representatives," he said and laughed mirthlessly. Anjola ignored the sarcasm and proceeded to make her point.

"From the time I reached the age of reason, sir, I have dreamed of how I could serve my country. It would be a great honour for me, a dream come true, to represent the people of Ifelodun, to be among those who make the laws that benefit them, help them and project their needs and achievements to the rest of the country and the world."

Baba looked at her very gravely and said nothing for some time. Finally he murmured, full of scorn:

"Tell me sincerely, do you consider yourself a model of victory?"

Anjola nodded.

"You are a bloody idiot!" he said heatedly.

Anjola's mouth fell open. Baba continued:

"You know what? If you really want to perpetrate some piece of idiocy, to convince people you are truly an idiot, you ought to find a more creative way of doing so. Ha! Egbin. Tani baba re nile yi? Who is your father in this town, you little rat? Who the hell is your father in this town? Who and what gave you the audacity to see yourself as a political material?"

She recoiled in terror as he continued to hurl insults at her. Dada, who had hitherto been sitting quietly, sprang to his feet and began pleading with Baba to forgive her.

"It's you who are responsible for the insult I'm receiving from this obviously untrained girl," Baba said sternly.

"I'm sorry, Baba, forgive me, Baba," Dada said, concealing

a gloating smile. Then, suddenly, Baba began to shake with laughter. Anjola felt such a hatred for the two men that she wanted to pick up the nearest heavy object and throw it at them. When Baba had finished laughing, he cleared his throat. All eyes were turned on him.

"Sisi, what you are asking for is not possible. You are too small and far too insignificant to have the kind of dream you claimed you've had," he declared, taking off and putting on his glasses with the air of a teacher. Anjola was overwhelmed with futility. All these years she had been struggling to prove her ability to make a useful contribution to society, to be given a chance to demonstrate her humanity, only to end up as helpless as she was now. She took strong exception to Baba's labelling of her as "too small and insignificant," especially when the declaration was made only on account of her father not having a recognisable name in society. This was supposed to be her state, her home, but with the likes of Baba and Dada in charge, it was pointless to entertain hopes of ever communicating with the people. She thought of the countless concessions, difficulties, defeats and sacrifices she had suffered in order to reach the place she could be counted worthy to make a useful contribution to her community. But in spite of all her efforts, her experience continued to convince her that life was a battlefield. She felt paralysed, as if her arms and legs were glued to the chair. Gesturing to Kike with a wave of the hand, she muttered: "I must get out of here at once."

CHAPTER 34

Once outside, Kike suggested they wait for Dada to finish with Baba and then take them back to his office, where Kike had left her car. Anjola would not hear of it. Kike would find time to see him after Anjola must have left Ilorin. Kike understood her state of mind. They haled a taxi. Anjola closed her eyes and remembered the sunrises of her childhood up to the time she finished her degree thirteen years earlier. The vision tugged at her; memories of her undergraduate days were particularly strong. How was she to know that her life would become so drab and empty? She remembered how her existence did a summersault immediately after her graduation. Her mind momentarily drifted to Baba and she felt as if a sudden ulcer had opened in the pit of her stomach. A horrifying scream rang out. Kike grasped her hand and, interlacing Anjola's fingers with hers, asked if she wanted something to drink. Kike could feel her friend's pain and it broke her heart to know how helpless she was. Anjola's mind continued to wander. She remembered the early days of her job search after completing the youth service corps programme. That was the beginning of real life for her, the life that separated illusion from reality.

The taxi pulled up at the premises of the tourism ministry. They walked wordlessly to Kike's car, got in and drove off. They were now driving through Murtala Mohamed Way. Anjola managed to snap out of her reverie. As they approached Challenge junction, Kike began to say something about how unreliable government jobs could be in spite of the widely-held impression of security. She said it was a fallacy to believe that anyone who worked for government was secure.

"There is nothing like job security," Kike said with conviction. Anjola smiled faintly. "Besides, the job will end eventually when the worker attains the compulsory age of retirement, even for most jobs. We all must grow old and retire."

"You're right, retirement is compulsory," Anjola said, frowning. She wondered whether Kike's statement was aimed at lessening the sting of the day's unpleasant experience.

"Oh," I forgot!" Kike blurted out suddenly and made a sudden U-turn. That was it. She had hardly negotiated the turn when two Federal Road Safety Corps officials jumped in front of them.

"Wrong U-turn!" one of them shouted. The other opened a passenger door at the back and eased himself in. He ordered Kike to move forward, directing her to a particular spot where he told her to park. Kike did as she was told as she continued to apologise.

"Ignorance is no excuse in law," he said. Anjola sighed as they all came down. Kike was still trying to plead but their captor was far from impressed. He said he had instructions from his superior to take the car to their office, where Kike would pay the relevant fine. He also warned her that her car would begin to incur demurrage charges for each day it remained there. His harshness enraged Anjola and she cried vehemently: "No!"

"You're wasting your time, women, give me the car key and know that from this moment until you pay full government charges for the traffic offence you've committed, you cease to have the right to drive. The charge is only twenty-five thousand naira in the first instance, and you won't have to pay more if you can offset the amount immediately."

Irritated, Anjola muttered, "For heaven's sake," and then burst into tears, her nerves thoroughly ravaged. Kike looked confused. Suddenly, from seemingly nowhere, Dada appeared in their midst. The countenance of the FRSC official metamorphosed dramatically as Dada warmly shook hands with him.

"I sighted these young women from across the road as I was driving. They left me not quite long ago, so, I said let me park and come over to find out what's going on," Dada said; then, turning to Kike, asked her what traffic offence she had committed. Kike was about to say something but the FRSC man interrupted her with a wave of his hand. They chatted for a while and then, with a sanctimonious look, he began to enquire after Dada's well-being and that of his family. Finally, he told him deferentially that he didn't know Kike was related to him.

"You are free to go, madam," he said, bowing slightly, and then resumed his seemingly endless salutation of Dada. "Well done, sir, take care, sir, greet the family, sir, safe ride, sir, God bless you, sir," he went on and on and as Kike and Anjola left. Anjola wanted Kike to drive her straight to Offa Garage Motor Park from where she would take a bus back to Ifelodun but Kike insisted she had to stay another night - to calm down, as she put it.

"Calm down to do what, to what end?" Anjola demanded but Kike was adamant. She didn't like the state Anjola was in and didn't think returning to the village immediately would do her any good. She wanted her friend to spend another night with her so that they could think of a way forward. "Two heads are better than one," she said. Anjola reluctantly agreed.

At lunch time, Kike again took Anjola to their staff canteen. Kike tried to lighten her mood but in vain. Anjola was desolate. At close of work, Kike said she received a message from her mother requesting that she pass through her parents' house on her way from work. There was an urgent family matter to discuss. Anjola nodded. It would be nice to see her friend's mother again, although her memory of her was not exactly a pleasant one. She remembered her as a coldly distant woman with a permanent scowl on her face.

"I didn't have the chance to complete what I was trying to say before our encounter with the FRSC men," Kike said, interrupting Anjola's introspection.

"I'm now a counsellor," she said before Anjola could respond. "I offer counselling services."

Anjola found it funny; she tried to imagine her friend as a counsellor.

"Maybe I could be your client," Anjola said and laughed.

"No, no," Kike cried vehemently. "You can't be my client. What you can do is help me get clients."

"What sort of services do you render?" Anjola asked again.

"I offer counselling services to HIV/AIDs patients, people suffering from cancer, sickle cell anaemia. It's a novel service, the first of its kind in the country. People who are plagued by illness need to be encouraged."

Kike was still talking when they arrived at her parents' house and Anjola was saved from pondering the imponderables. Kike sauntered gaily in. Neither her mum nor dad was home yet. She said her father wouldn't return until much later in the evening and that her mother must be on her way, especially as she was aware that Kike would be visiting. Only the housemaid was on hand to receive them. Kike asked if there was soup in the house and she said no.

"What's in the house for dinner?" Kike persisted.

"We're making soup and stew tomorrow, Ma. Madam told me before leaving home this morning that I should prepare beans for dinner."

"Okay, is there plantain?"

"No.

"You mean you guys planned to eat just beans?"

"No, ma, not just beans, beans and gari."

Kike hissed. "What's the difference? Anyway, go ahead and prepare the beans. Be sure to cook enough to accommodate my friend, okay?"

The maid nodded vigorously, genuflected and disappeared.

Kike was determined to engage Anjola in chit-chat that would bring her out of her melancholia. It wasn't long before her efforts began to pay off. They chatted on a variety of people they had both known, including Deinde Komolafe and his unkindness. Their conversation veered into Kike's marital status. She said the best decision she had made in her life was not to allow her failure to attract a suitor to bother her.

"I live my life and don't preoccupy myself with what people think, say or feel about my being unmarried. Is it possible for me to propose marriage to me and then go on to wed myself? The answer is clearly no. Who was it that said a problem without a solution should be without regard?" she asked rhetorically. "Wo, ore, mi ole wa ku, I cannot come and die ojare," she added with a throaty laugh. Kike was categorical about the way she handled the highs and lows of her life. Anjola marvelled at her friend's strength. Surely, she had a lot to learn from her.

Kike rose from her seat. She searched through a pile of CDs and inserted one into the player. Moments later, King Sunny Ade's voice boomed from the loud speakers. Kike began to dance. She danced with a delicious rhythm and good deal of grace, smiling and softly singing the words to the song, raising her arms and moving her waist and shoulders so that her entire body shook. It was impossible not to be infected with Kike's gaiety. Anjola was about to join her when the housemaid brought their food. Anjola's mood had moderated considerably and she realised she was famished.

"You can't change," Anjola teased. They were midway through their meal when Kike's mother arrived. Anjola rose to greet her. Smiling broadly, and feeling genuinely pleased to see her again after so long, she dropped her spoon in the plate of beans and bent double, muttering:

"Ah Mummy, welcome ma, it's so good to see you after such a long time. How have you been, ma? How's work and everything, ma?" Notwithstanding Anjola's knowledge of the woman, she had hoped she would be received with more warmth than was her custom. She was wrong. Rather, the older woman interrupted her endearments with an impatient gesture. Even then, neither Anjola nor Kike could have anticipated what happened next. Murmuring incomprensibly, Kike's mother pounced on Anjola's plate and disappeared with it. Both women were horrified. Anjola wished she would die. She glanced in her friend's direction but Kike was too stunned to speak. Anjola sighed resignedly, pushed herself up from her seat and began to pace the room.

"I'm sorry to have caused you such distress," Kike finally said. Then, she, too, rose from her seat and placed her hand on Anjola's shoulder in a comforting gesture.

"Come, let me take you home," she said softly.

"Take me home?" Anjola echoed. "Where is home?" She fixed Kike with a long, hard stare. Anjola stepped away from her, reached for her hand bag and quietly left without a backward glance.

CHAPTER 35

It was late when Anjola walked out of Kike's parents' home. Kike's younger brother, Tunji, was just driving in and immediately sensed that something was wrong. He stuck his head out of the car and turned inquisitively in her direction. She waved and proceeded half-running, half-walking into the next street, whispering unintelligibly to herself. Overcome with confusion, she wandered in the side streets to give herself time to decide on her next course of action. She was sliding into a depression. What exactly had she done wrong? She recalled the circumstances leading to her journey back home. Her brother-in-law had accused her of being a layabout and preferring a life of indolence and relying solely on her husband for her every need. Ify had suggested she ignore his brother's ranting but she had felt challenged. She was determined to prove not only to Uncle Cajethan but also to herself and the world that she was not averse to hard work. She was convinced that coming back home to Kwara State would open up new vistas. This was her state, the place she called her home. Home was supposed to be a cheerful place where you ought to be able to relax and feel welcome, but she had had a feeling of tension since her arrival.

She was crushed by a sense of oppression; she felt like an orphan in her own state of birth. But how was she going to face the world from now on? What was she going to do next? Who would believe her that home was not what she thought it was?

311

Again, she had made presumptions about home and had realised how utterly wrong she was. The time had come for her to be brave and end the misery that her life had become. All her effort had been in vain. She paced back and forth in the adjourning street to Kike's parents. For over thirty minutes, her resolve to end her life grew more and more until it became irresistible. Despairing but defiant, she decided to go to Asa Dam and throw herself into the water.

With an aching heart, she set forth on a journey of no return, walking toward Ibrahim Taiwo Road, from where she would pick a taxi to Asa Dam Road. Her heart raced as if she had just run a marathon but she was determined to carry out her plan. The road was muddy so she couldn't walk as fast as she wanted. She heard a car behind her. She had full knowledge of what had happened and what she wanted; she wanted to commit suicide by drowning, not through being hit by an automobile. She stood aside to let the vehicle pass. The road was muddier at the side.

"Would you like a ride?" the driver asked. Anjola smiled feebly.

"I don't mind walking," she said without looking at him. The car slowed to a stop. She didn't know if he was afraid to splash her or if he was really stopping. She suddenly realised it looked like Kolade Durotoye's car but she was broken beyond what anyone could ever fix and resumed her walk. The occupant called after her:

"Anjola, isn't it you?"

She stopped. Kolade came out of the car. She turned and saw him, smiling and looking up in her face.

"You look a little tired, Anjola," he said. He touched her arm. "Is something wrong? Have you been ill?"

She hid her face. He stepped around to look at her more closely. He, too, looked uneasy, nervous. She wondered what he was going through.

"I'm just tired," she said. She didn't want to meet his eyes.

Her heart had begun to pound heavily again. Kolade pressed his hand against her forehead, a light, casual gesture that medical doctors did so often to their patients. Anjola felt worse than a patient.

"I can drive you to wherever you're going," he said and waited for her to acquiesce. It took a moment or two. Then he pushed her gently toward the car – not a real push, just a nudge.

"You look awfully tired," he said. She said nothing. She got into the car and let her head droop on her chest.

"Which direction are you heading?"

"No direction," she said simply.

"Well, that makes two of us. Why don't we go for a drink, then?"

She was mute.

"That way, you get to confirm that I've quit alcohol," he said in his characteristic jocular manner. That brought a smile to her face. They drove to a drinking joint off Unity Road and ordered two bottles of malt.

"I'm so glad I saw you, Anjola," Kolade quipped. "I had a strange experience that forced me out of the house." He appeared fearful. She wondered what could have frightened him.

"Earlier today, a woman was rushed in by her relatives. She had been on admission at the general hospital but apparently she wasn't responding to treatment and her relatives thought to try a private hospital. But too much had gone wrong and she was in bad shape. My examination revealed that she was unlikely to survive."

He stopped speaking abruptly. Anjola felt tense. She had never seen him look so melancholy. Silence descended on them for a long moment. Eventually, Kolade resumed.

"Yes, the medical examination revealed that although her injury would have been treatable with adequate and timely medical attention, her condition had been left to deteriorate and infection had crawled in, creating complications. I knew the probability of her survival was almost zero but I wasn't supposed to say or do anything that could aggravate her fear or that of her relatives. So, I got to work immediately, doing the best I could. But I was struck by the woman's powerful will to live. She began to pray for her own survival and, as she did so, she also begged me not to allow her to die, telling me she had young children. She said she wanted to live for their sake. I intensified my efforts, although as a doctor, I knew it was futile. But I was encouraged by her determination. She wouldn't stop praying and begging for her life. To cut a long story short, she passed away. I invited her relatives and broke the sad news to them."

Anjola began to cry but Kolade was undeterred.

"Then I went home. Let me also say that, personally, I don't believe in ghosts. I went straight to the bathroom to have a shower. I was preparing to go to the dining table for a late lunch when, suddenly, the dead woman appeared by my window."

Anjola gasped in terror. Kolade acted as if he hadn't noticed.

"She was standing outside my window, dressed in the same attire with which she was brought to the clinic. I am not given to fear by nature. First, I thought I had suffered a fit of delusion but there she was, looking at me with sadness in her eyes. I challenged her, asking her what she was doing. She responded by asking me why I allowed her to die in spite of her pleas. She said she explained to me that her children were young and she couldn't trust anyone to look after them in her absence. I told her it wasn't my fault, that I tried the best I could and that it was a pity I couldn't save her life. Then, I told her to go back to where she came from, that she had no right to torment me because I didn't cause her death. She didn't leave immediately; she stood there for a while, looking despondent. After what seemed like a long time, she turned back and walked away."

"Look, Anjola, I saluted my courage at confronting the ghost, but I became somewhat panicky after its disappearance. I've heard countless stories about ghosts and I have never believed a single one of them but experiencing it first-hand is a different ball game. I lost my appetite; I lost my composure and my peace. I just wanted to be out of the house, to drive without a destination in mind. You can imagine how glad I was when I saw you except for the troubled look in your eyes," he said, frowning.

She forced a smile, murmuring, "I'm okay."

Kolade's frown deepened. "You don't look yourself. What's the matter?" Before she could answer, he said: "Look, I got to know that Deinde didn't help you and I'm so sorry. It's very unkind of him, I must say."

"How did you get to know?"

"He told me himself and I gave him a piece of my mind."

"Did he also tell you why he didn't want to help me?"

"No, he didn't, or, more appropriately, I didn't give him a chance to. There's no justification in the world for what he did. But I also blamed myself for the humiliation you suffered in his hands. You didn't want to go to him, I put you to it; you would rather not beg but I thought you were being arrogant. I shouldn't have pushed you the way I did," he said regretfully.

"It's okay, Kolade, you wanted to help," she said candidly.

"I respect you more that you'll ever know," he said and Anjola detected earnestness in his voice. "Each time I think about all you've been through, I say to myself, Anjola has a firm hold on life. I may be laughing when I'm saying it at times but I mean it. You do have a firm hold on life. I like people who, whatever it is, they stand by, and even if they are inexperienced, they keep pushing."

Anjola looked at Kolade and her heart swelled with gratitude. What an irony of fate, she thought, as her mind drifted to the ghost. Here was a woman who wanted to live and her reason for wanting to do so was perhaps the most basic, most banal, yet, it was the most profound. Her reason for loving life didn't consist in the many mansions she had built or the enormous amount of money she had stashed away and wanted to enjoy. She wanted to live because she had children who depended on her. She didn't even consider how her children might reward her afterwards. She just wanted to live for them. Anjola realised how much Kolade's story had helped to restore her belief in life and living. She no longer wanted to commit suicide. Unlike the ghost, however, she simply wanted to renew her belief in life; she wanted to renew her faith in the order of things. She resolved never again to be overcome by the horrors of disappointment and disillusionment. Yes, she wanted to live.

"May I order another bottle of malt, please?"

"I'm so glad you're talking," he said, relaxation spreading over his face; then added, "I see you're in a sort of inspired mood. You're a steadfast woman, Anjola."

She smiled contentedly, enjoying every bit of the encomium being showered on her. Then, with an enthusiasm that verged on euphoria, she raised the glass to her lips. She would triumph eventually. She resolved that it was better to concentrate on life itself than whatever it brought. Notwithstanding her myriad disappointments, she wanted to go on living, even if it was against all logic. Besides, the ghost also had an important point. Anjola loved some people. She loved her mother, she loved her father, she loved her husband and she loved her adorable daughter. She loved them with her inside, with her belly. Now, she had a greater longing for life. She thought everyone must love life more than anything else in the world; everyone must love life more than the meaning of life.

CHAPTER 36

She told Kolade to take her to Kike's house so she could check if she had returned; otherwise, they might have to continue to hang out to buy time for Kike's eventual return. It turned out that they were in luck on their first visit. Anjola bid Kolade goodbye after thanking him profusely for 'saving her life' but without giving details. It was clear that Kolade was just as pleased as Anjola. He wanted to unburden his heart and apologise for the humiliation he imagined he caused her through Deinde. Kike opened the front door at the first press of the bell and flew into Anjola's embrace.

"Where have you been? I've been so worried about you," she said breathlessly.

"I know, I'm sorry," was all Anjola could manage. She didn't want to say anything that would remind her of the events of the last two days. She knew it would do her no good; it would only dim her spirits. Her immediate plan was to write a letter to her husband and post it in the morning before going to the motor park to take a bus back to Ifelodun. Kike saw how much Anjola's mood had calmed and was pleased to let things be.

My darling husband
This must come to you as a surprise given the way I assured you I would do my best to ensure that I get myself gainfully engaged in my home state so as to put wagging tongues in check. Well, I'm

sorry to announce that things didn't go as I expected. I apologise also for leaving Kaduna and more for leaving you all alone. I have since discovered that the idea that I was coming home to solve my problems, both real and imagined was a grand illusion. Honey, I have realised, thankfully early enough, that the notion of escaping from a particular environment and fleeing home where solutions to all problems supposedly subsist is an exercise in delusion. I have learned my lessons, sweetheart, and have been reproaching myself, day and night, since Athena and I arrived here. Why didn't I have the courage to tell Uncle Cajethan to concentrate on his own marriage and leave us to manage our affairs? You were forthright and brave, darling, when you told your brother that he had no right to send me home. Where is my home? All I want now is to be with you, sweet one. Ify, please, come quickly to take Athena and I back to Kaduna, so that together, we shall find our home, my king. We are over here in Ifelodun, waiting for you. Come as quickly as possible.

Your wife,
Anjola.

By the time Anjola finished, Kike had gone to bed. Anjola was pleased. She had spent the last two nights without sleeping a wink. Tonight was different. In the morning, as Kike prepared for the day's work, Anjola got ready to leave. Kike offered to drive her to the post office from where Anjola assured her she would easily take a bus to Offa Garage Motor Park to board an Ifelodun-bound bus. At the post office, Anjola parted her lips to thank Kike but no words came. Trying again, she could only mouth her gratitude. They hugged.

As soon as she arrived in Ifelodun, she announced merrily to her parents that Ify would come soon to take her and Athena back to Kaduna. Her mother couldn't contain her relief.

"You've made the best decision, Anjola. Together, you and your husband will find a way forward."

"You're right, Mother, I just wanted to try. It turned out that Father was right," Anjola said.

"It was good you tried," her father observed; "that's why you have been able to come up with an informed decision. You have been guided by your experience and I'm really happy for you and your husband. How soon is he coming?"

"I can't tell, Father, but I know my husband well enough to say that he'll leave whatever he is doing and come as soon as he receives my letter, which I dispatched today through the express mail service."

"You must be famished," Mama said, adding; "there's amala and ewedu."

Athena had heard the news about her father's impending visit and their planned return to Kaduna. She grinned from ear to ear. Anjola ate her meal with relish, had a bath, changed her clothes and went to sit in the front of the house. She welcomed the gentle breeze, letting it caress her tenderly. She was soon joined by Athena who wanted to know all that happened during her visit to Ilorin.

"Let's talk about you going back to school," she said, smiling.

*   *   *   *

Ify held Anjola's letter in his hands; he trembled from head to toe as if he was suffering from fever and his teeth were chattering. He read it slowly, spelling it out so as not to miss a single syllable. When he had finished, his whole body ached with the desire to hold her in his arms. He couldn't remember ever going through the kind of pain he had been through since Anjola and Athena left. He had grown pale and distracted, moving about like a zombie. He tried the best he could to convince Anjola to ignore his brother's ranting but, with her bullet proof obstinacy, his effort was bound to fail. What he had on his mind now was far from trading blame. He was overjoyed that his wife wanted to return. It was one thing to make a mistake, another to admit it. Anjola was a complete woman; she was strong and weak; she was the kind of woman no man wanted to lose. She was honest, forthright, dutiful, loving, caring and responsible. After he had calmed down, he checked the time and realised he could still make it to the bank. He withdrew what he was sure was sufficient enough to execute his journey. Then he went back home to keep the money safely in his travelling bag. He packed a few personal items and then went to have a haircut. He wanted to look good for his family and in-laws.

CHAPTER 37

By the time Ify arrived in Ifelodun, Anjola and Athena had their bags packed. Anjola's father had also ensured that a room was cleaned for his son-in-law. Pa Adeniyi's household bustled with excitement; Mama Wuraola was a beacon of joy. She went to the market and bought a large quantity of dry fish, two live chickens and freshly made yam flour. She said she could always get ewedu and other vegetables when Ify arrived, but she bought six big tubers of yam, four measures of rice, and two measures of beans. Athena and Anjola couldn't contain their joy; there was a clamour of voices in the household as everybody had something to say.

Finally, Ify arrived to a tumultuous welcome. He prostrated to his parents-in-law, surprising Pa Adeniyi, who had wanted to hug him. Pa Adeniyi quickly seized him nonetheless and held him in a tight embrace. When they had disengaged, his mother-in-law, who was grinning from ear to ear, held out her hand for a warm handshake. Ify took her hand shyly and hugged her with the other arm. Athena was next. He lifted her above his head and brought her face to his for a warm, fatherly kiss, whispering, "Ala bekee: This-one-will-take-me-all-over-the-world." Then he regarded her briefly.

"You've grown even within these few weeks. Thank you, Mama, for taking care of Athena," he said, smiling. Anjola waited patiently for her turn, her face bright as she stood for him to embrace her. He enveloped her in a full embrace and she couldn't stop her eyes filling with tears of joy and relief. He kissed her cheeks and then brushed her lips with his.

"I love you very much," he stammered.

"Come on in," she said, grasping his arm and leading him to the room that had been specially prepared for him. Mr and Mrs. Adeniyi had retreated to their rooms.

"This may not be a good thing to say but l love having my family send for me, and then waiting for me at the end of the day," Ify said, winking and hitting his chest. Then he drew her closer and gave her a deep, prolonged kiss.

"You know I don't mean it like that," he said, chuckling.

"You do and you know it," Anjola teased.

"Any man would be overjoyed to have you as a wife and would be over the moon to have you wait for him," he said. "And you are as beautiful as ever in spite of the trauma." She blushed, amazed as always by his frank adoration. She hadn't given any thought to her appearance and wore no makeup. She was dressed in jeans and a T-shirt. She was slimmer than before and her eyes were rather tired but no one in the world would have thought she was past thirty. She looked fresh and beautiful.

"Well, I'm glad you think so," she said, then ran a finger down his cheek. He unpacked his travelling bag to bring out the crayfish and ground wheat he had bought for his mother-in-law and the patterned bed sheet for his father-in-law. There were other assorted items including beverages, milk, honey and multivitamins. He bought chocolates and candy for Anjola and Athena.

After a meal of pounded yam and dried fish, Ify, Anjola and Athena took turns to take their bath. Ify changed into another shirt and trouser. Anjola wore a skirt and a light, transparent blouse that revealed the top of her breasts. They walked out of the house.

"I know a nice place to talk," she said, holding his arm and leading him toward the local primary school about five hundred metres from the house. As they walked, they heard footsteps, as if someone was coming up behind them. They turned instinctively and saw Athena. They waited for her. When she reached them, Ify held out his hand, muttering: "Cute girl." They walked to the school's football field and sat on the grass. Athena went off to play on her own. She had never been as playful as she was now, casting occasional glances at her parents as they talked.

Anjola told him in detail everything that had happened. He listened intently, occasionally asking her to repeat some of her statements. He frowned and sank into thought afterwards.

"Are you frowning because of Baba?" she asked,

"I'm frowning because of everything but I want us to banish all negative thoughts," he said, and went on speaking to her very quietly, looking into her eyes and occasionally kissing her hand.

"Let's leave the past where it belongs, Anjola; let's forge ahead courageously. It's good you've come to Kwara and have seen the way things are. It's a different thing if someone else was trying to discourage you from coming. And I love the tone of your letter. It was firm, decisive and carried no self-adulation, no false hopes, no primordial, unrealistic, sentiments. I feel blessed that my wife does not cling to illusions. We've had our challenges, we may have more as we go on in life, but it's important we agree to confront and surmount them, at least the ones we can. The ones we can't we simply accept them as they are."

"Ify, you have some wrinkles under your lids." She pressed his arms and her eyes were filled with mischief.

"What have you been doing to make your life so tense?"

He sat looking at her, not answering, and she passed her hand over his hair in her usual affectionate gesture, half-loving, half-maternal.

"You have so many gray hairs now. I gave you some, didn't I?" she asked with a laugh as she brought her face forward and gave him a bird's rapid peck on the lips.

"Have you made any progress in your job search?" she asked.

"I didn't want to be in a hurry to announce this but, now that you've asked, Julius Berger invited me for an interview. I can't tell what the final outcome will be," he said reluctantly.

"What about Uncle Cajethan? Has he visited since Athena and I left?"

"He came, ostensibly to ask for money. He appeared surprised and somewhat remorseful that you and Athena were not in the house. I told him I didn't have money; that you had gone home to look for a job, and that I was hoping you'd start sending me money," he said and burst into a long, throaty laugh.

"When are we leaving for Kaduna?" she asked.

"Let the laughter bursting inside me calm down so that I can think clearly," he said and permitted himself another round of laughter. Anjola and Athena joined him.

"Yes, Mrs Jeremiah, when do you suggest we leave?"

"I think you can take tomorrow to have a little rest and we may leave the day after." "Yes, madam," Athena said, and Anjola gave her a playful spank.

"What's your view about our continued membership of the Zelachi Development Union? I'm asking because, unless you have a contrary opinion, I suggest we pull out quietly for now. I think it's important we try to organise our lives. If we feel inclined to renew our membership after we have found our feet, we could do so. These are my thoughts and I said I would share them with you and ask for yours. We need to harmonise our perspectives and take a decision," he said seriously.

"My husband is talking tough." Anjola teased. "But seriously, I think you're right, especially as I can't figure out yet what to do in terms of getting meaningfully engaged," she said in a sort of menacing tone. A shadow veiled her eyes and her voice thickened as though she were speaking to herself. Ify quieted her with a hand placed on her shoulder.

"I've been thinking about that, too," he said, with that smile that puffed up his cheeks and made him look like a clown.

"You've thought about something? You believe I can become

productive in some meaningful way?" she asked anxiously.

He nodded, observing her with his affectionate, full-moon smile.

"Tell me about it because I have run out of ideas."

"You're too self-critical," he said.

"Again, you're right," she admitted, feeling her cheeks flush.

"I have a plan but I think we should wait until we get back to Kaduna before we discuss it in detail. We are worth more than we give ourselves credit for. Together, we can at least think, act, fail, and get up again and again."

As he spoke, her face ran through an assortment of expressions, roughly corresponding to a baffled how, what and when. Then her eyebrows rose briefly to spring apart with adoration before sinking back down to a confused understanding.

"Now I see my wife is beginning to come round."

"Truth is that you're super brilliant but don't let your head swell."

"I know, and I also know that I'm fabulously handsome. That's why you married me."

"Well, that's only part of the reason, not the whole truth but I've since discovered that you're not as handsome as I thought. You know what I think now?"

He shook his head.

"I strongly suspect you jujunised me," she said, smiling sweetly at him.

"Oh, but of course I've since become a fetishist because of you. Thanks for being so pretty and intelligent," he said. She didn't smile but the gleam of past times flashed in her eyes. He rummaged around in his trouser pocket and pulled out a nylon bag.

"Have one of these," he said. The bag was full of sweets. She started fiddling with it.

"It's cough sweets, they'll warm you up," he said. She took one and put it into her mouth. She pushed the bag toward Athena, who seized it in both hands. They had been there more than two hours and it was growing dark. They walked home shortly afterwards in companionable silence.

After dinner, he asked her if she had missed him.

"Well, let me think about..." He didn't let her finish before he threw himself at her and with all the weight of his body pushed her onto the bed. She defended herself a little at first but soon stopped. She kissed and embraced him, helping him to take off her clothes. Her body embraced his as she entwined her legs with his, her lips pressing against his, her tongue struggling with his. Her hands dug into his back and neck and she begged him to take her. And when he did, he found her body as well formed as he remembered it.

CHAPTER 38

Ify, Anjola and Athena Jeremiah were back in Kaduna. For no apparent reason, the first thing Anjola did as soon as they entered the house was walk slowly into their bedroom. She was awestruck by the beautiful new bedspread. Her eyes settled on the note in the middle of the bed. She didn't need to pick it up to read it: MY FRIEND OF A LIFETIME, WELCOME BACK. She read it over and over again, then, returned to the sitting room and stood peering at her husband, trying to decide her next line of action. The sun was shining through the door, casting strands of light on her. He smiled sweetly at her, held her by the arm and asked:

"Isn't it a beautiful day?"

"Yes, love, it is," she replied, and her lips folded into an angelic smile. After what seemed like a long moment, she turned to him again inquisitively and he folded her in his arms.

"You are a very beautiful woman," he murmured, pulling her tighter and giving her a long kiss. He felt desire, emotion, tenderness and he kissed her at length. He was mad with happiness that he had his family back. Then he pulled away gently from her, straightened his shoulders, flashed his trademark smile and gently led her to the bedroom, where they stood wordlessly for a long moment looking into each other's eyes. Suddenly, he embraced her with so much strength that she groaned and twisted shouting. "You are crushing me." After they finished making love, he pressed his ear to her navel and listened to the deep sounds of her body.

The next morning, Anjola awoke with an aching head and sore bones. She spent a long time under the shower. Ify had left the house to resume his job as a commercial motorcyclist while Anjola and Athena went to the Central Market to buy a new school uniform and other items Athena needed. When Ify returned later in the evening, he explained his plan.

"You wanted to offer a teaching service to the people of Kwara free of charge," he recalled. She nodded. "What we need to do now is to apply the same principle to the people of Magaji Ngeri. Together, we are going to work to ensure that you have a chance to serve the people here in the same capacity. Eventually, they may accept you; and Magaji Ngeri may become your home. We won't ask them to pull their children out of school and you're not establishing a school. But you'll go from house to house, telling parents you have a tutorial class where their children and wards can learn more about the English language, and where you will be assisting students in some of their homework. You will remind them that English is an important subject in all examinations at various levels, and it is important that their children and wards acquire proficiency in it. You will tell them that you have a university degree in English; you believe you are very knowledgeable about the language and you wish to use your knowledge to render public service. You will tell them that you have another tutorial class for adults. You are going to continue to emphasise that you wish to offer this service free of charge. Once you start doing this, you will have a sense of being productive but, more importantly, you will have the satisfaction of being useful, which I'm aware has been your major interest."

He stopped talking and regarded her. She said nothing at first; she seemed to be weighing her response. After a long silence, she asked:

"Mr Ify Joshua Jeremiah, you really think this will work?"

"I'm positive," he said. "Look, I'm aware that this step won't solve the whole problem since it won't bring you any income but let it start and progress, its outcome will point to the next direction for us."

"You're still harping on it?

"Yes, madam," he said, smiling.

He explained that the first task was to identify and reach out to the youth of the area, whom he said were the most critical factor because they could sensitise parents and convince them to allow their children attend the planned tutorial classes. What was most important, he insisted, was to identify a single individual with integrity among them, someone who was honest, dependable and who would introduce Anjola to some parents. If they could identify such an individual and succeed in making him believe in their interest, the task would not be too difficult to accomplish.

"You know, I've always been in awe of your ability to put things together," she said with sincerity.

A few days later, he returned home and announced that he had found someone he thought he could trust to help provide the link.

"His name is Abdullahi Mohammed," he said, his eyes sparkling "But everyone calls him Abdul.

"I'm going to trust you completely with this," she said.

"Our conversation was so agreeable that I have invited him to come and have dinner with us tomorrow so that he can meet you."

Abdul came the following evening. He couldn't have been more than thirty years old. He was chubby and short and appeared good-hearted, friendly, jovial and talkative. He had a big smile which inflated his plump cheeks even more, displaying a magnificent set of teeth. After dinner, the three of them talked for a long time. Abdul urged Anjola to tell him her life from A – Z. He wanted to know everything and insisted that she describe in detail what kind of life she had led. Anjola was fascinated by him and had a great time talking to him. He could argue for hours with great intellectual substance. He had a thirty year-old body but a fifteen year-old spirit. She told him that her life in general had been fairly sober although sometimes she did things that made it hard for her to recognise herself. On the whole, she said, she discovered that she had absorbed the moral framework that her mother taught her consequent upon which she had lived the life of a recluse, not knowing anybody, not knowing people that mattered, and not having money. She made the last statement quietly, as if lamenting a lack in her personality. She paused to allow Abdul to soak her words. After a moment of silence, she resumed talking.

"In spite of my inadequacies, however, I believe I can be of help to your people. I have had a long-standing ambition to serve people with my integrity. I have had the dream to transform people's lives positively; this dream is from my heart and it has refused to wane," she told Abdul, speaking calmly.

Within weeks, Ify and Anjola's relationship with Abdul turned into something more than friendship in spite of the differences in age, language and background. Anjola and Ify felt as if he were their brother, their buddy, an angel come down from heaven. Abdul was an excellent person. He agreed to assist them but pointed out that it was necessary to inform the district head so that Anjola's effort would not amount to an illegality. He asked to be given time, promising to ensure that Anjola had a chance to interact with him.

One day, he came to the house and told Ify and Anjola that he was arranging a meeting for her and her husband to meet with some parents who said they wanted to meet her before making up their minds. Ify was excited, Anjola had all kinds of doubts but there was no going back. Her major concern was language. It was true she had taken lessons in Hausa during the early months of her arrival in Kaduna years ago. It was also true that she had improved significantly but her knowledge of the language was not sufficient. Ify spoke Hausa flawlessly but then he wasn't the one the parents wanted to speak with. She decided to tell Ify her fears.

"It's pointless trying to communicate with people in a language other than the one they use," she said, and began to pace back and forth between the balcony and the sitting room.

"I've thought about it and my position is this: we have acquired a new language, which is English, so you'll speak English."

She forced a smile but she was still clearly preoccupied.

"Did you have to speak Hausa to Abdul?" he queried.

"Speaking to Abdul is not the same as talking to people who have a common language," she said, now pacing around the sitting room, looking high and low.

"Banish your fear, Anjola. Abdul went to school and so did most of the people you are going to meet. They value education enough to have put their children and wards in school. I've discussed it with Abdul and he knows you're going to speak English. If you say something that he thinks the people don't understand, he'll be your dragoman. Just be yourself and let your past mistakes rejuvenate you," he said reassuringly.

The day of the meeting arrived. Ify and Anjola presented themselves at the address Abdul had given them. Ify wore a light brown pant trousers under a white shirt. Anjola wore a skirt and blouse. The neck of her blouse didn't show any cleavage. Abdul was already at the venue. Astonished by the assemblage of about twenty people, comprising men and women, Anjola marvelled at how Abdul was able to convince them to meet her. Her hands were perspiring and it was hard for her to breathe.

"Be at your ease," Ify whispered. Abdul cleared his throat and a hush descended in the expansive sitting room. He began to speak in English and a wave of relief flooded through Anjola.

"Good afternoon, our royal father and distinguished parents of Magaji Ngeri. I present to you Mrs Anjola Jeremiah, who will interact with you and you'll decide whether or not she deserves your trust enough to allow your children attend free tutorial classes in the English language. Anjola is a wife and mother. She's truly an excellent woman. She's a font of wisdom for all. She's from a respectable family in Kwara State but has lived in Kaduna for a long time."

He paused. There were involuntary sounds of mirth. With Ify beside her, Anjola smiled broadly and met their combined gaze in a calm, friendly and unembarrassed way. She was undoubtedly a woman of character but also charmingly feminine. Her features were as open as her simple elegance. She radiated intelligence, wisdom, courage, determination and more. Curiously, many of the parents present felt they could connect with her in some elemental way. Some of them imagined that they had seen her before but when, where or how they couldn't say. Ify was the next to be introduced as Abdul gestured in his direction.

"Ify is Anjola's husband. He is a civil engineer. In addition, he's an expert in a great number of matters, including surviving and other things of a practical and useful nature. He's an exceptional husband and a great father worthy of emulation. He and Anjola have been married for many years. His attachment to married life grows stronger by the day. Together, they have an adorable daughter," he said and paused again.

It appeared the introduction was over. It was followed by silence. Then the district head introduced himself as Alhaji Farouk Usman and proceeded to introduce the parents present one after another. When he had finished, he hesitated for a moment before asking:

"Can we trust her? Can we judge her by her heart?"

Anjola wanted to say something but Abdul indicated that the time hadn't come for her to speak and proceeded to answer the question.

"Anjola is clear-headed. She's one woman we can trust to take good care of our children."

Anjola smiled.

"Are you sure?"

"Absolutely, sir, she's genuine and sincere. We can trust her. But I don't want to be a moralising bore. Anjola will speak to you presently."

They all laughed, Anjola along with them.

"Why don't you tell us more about her before she speaks?" a woman whom the district head had earlier introduced as Hajia Salamotu Akawu asked.

"Yes, we want to hear more about her from you first," another insisted.

"Certainly," Abdul said, ready to address their remarks.

"Anjola is thirty-four years old. She graduated in English from the University of Ilorin just before she turned twenty-one. She was an excellent teacher during her NYSC, better by far than most people of her age. She has great ambition in the arts which she hopes to realise one day. She looks at life from a serious angle but she's very pleasant company. Anjola is ready to speak to you, my eminent parents," he said and fell silent.

All eyes turned in Anjola's direction. She smiled in greeting and began to speak:

"Today is a milestone in my life. I may not have much to say to you at the moment but very soon we'll find answers to many of the questions that you are asking in your heart. The good news today is that we are all experienced parents and have our senses to discern and make the right decisions. So ours is an extraordinary and exciting story. A voice commanded me to do some extraordinary thing – something to bewilder those who do not believe in our capacity to pull together and make true progress by trusting one another. I believe we all can do something extraordinary – whatever, whoever we are. It is our doing nothing that has crushed us. So we have to strive to do something extraordinary no matter how small it may seem. This is a moment of civilisation. We must all congratulate ourselves. We must salute this splendid moment – so that we can say tribalism, ethnicity, and religious bigotry have been completely routed! That nepotism has been demolished. There should be no divisive tendencies from now on."

Ify gazed at his wife in wonderment. There was a moment's

silence before she resumed.

"I don't want to be alone to celebrate this unstoppable turn in our national history's tide," she said with sobriety. "Distinguished parents of our children, I'm not asking you to remunerate me or reward me with cash or material things; all I'm asking is that you permit me to share the little knowledge I've acquired in using the English language, which is our official language of communication. Dear parents, I don't want to be alone when a new dawn whispers in my ear that our collective will for true emancipation will make the impossible come true. Many decades ago, Nigerians were forced into a bloody war largely because of the absence of trust."

There was absolute silence in the room now. When she resumed, she spoke with some difficulty because of her emotions.

"As much as I'm passionate about helping to improve your children's knowledge in the English language, the same way I've also been trying to learn the Hausa language, I must let you know that I have my integrity which would not allow my desire to be a do-or-die affair. If you are persuaded that I can add value to your children's and wards' lives, send them to my tutorial class."

The district head kept his eyes fixed on her throughout, nodding intermittently. When she had finished, he cleared his throat.

"Today is indeed a milestone, not only in your life, Mrs Jeremiah, but in the history of Magaji Ngeri as well. You have impressed me a great deal and I have no doubt that you have done the same with everyone present here. I'm fully in support of your project. To demonstrate my approval, I will provide the logistics toward making your work successful. Yes, Magaji Ngeri will provide a classroom in case you don't have enough space in your house. The district will further assist with transport and you will decide whether you want it monetised or that a driver picks and drops you each time you have to teach. That's not all. I have close to ten children in my household and I hereby release them all to take part in your tutorial classes from this moment."

The district head's response was greeted with spontaneous applause. Anjola got up as good as new after thanking him and the parents profusely. A date was fixed for the start of her classes and nearly all the parents also came forward to say that she deserved their support and that they believed that her intervention would help their children tremendously. Abdul and Ify grinned from ear to ear as the three of them left the house together.

Back at home in the evening, Anjola leaned against the rail of the balcony and gazed at the peaceful sunset. By the time the night drew in, she was still standing there. The sky was completely clear and studded with thousands of stars. A star twinkled like a serene smile; she averted her eyes, smiling shyly. When she looked again, she saw a smiling face. She began to feel as if she had set a new world record.